Conditional Love

Cathy Bramley

CORGI BOOKS

TRANSWORLD PUBLISHERS
Penguin Random House, One Embassy Gardens,
8 Viaduct Gardens, London SW11 7BW
www.penguin.co.uk

Transworld is part of the Penguin Random House group of companies
whose addresses can be found at global.penguinrandomhouse.com

Penguin
Random House
UK

First published in Great Britain as an ebook in 2014 by Transworld Digital,
an imprint of Transworld Publishers
This edition first published in 2015 by Corgi Books,
an imprint of Transworld Publishers
Corgi edition reissued 2022

A CIP catalogue record for this book
is available from the British Library.

ISBN 9780552171564

Typeset in 11½/13½pt Garamond by Kestrel Data, Exeter, Devon.
Printed and bound in Great Britain by Clays Ltd, Elcograf S.p.A.

The authorized representative in the EEA is Penguin Random House Ireland,
Morrison Chambers, 32 Nassau Street, Dublin D02 YH68.

Penguin Random House is committed to a sustainable future for
our business, our readers and our planet. This book is made
from Forest Stewardship Council® certified paper.

www.penguin.co.uk

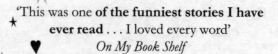

'This was one **of the funniest stories I have ever read** . . . I loved every word'
On My Book Shelf

'I loved every single character! Full of **warmth and belonging**'
Jera's Jamboree

'I adored this **gem of a book** . . . *Ivy Lane* has **everything I love about a novel** – wonderful characters, a gorgeous setting and twists ready to be unveiled at any opportunity'
Reviewed the Book

'This is a **perfect book** to take with you to your garden on a sunny summer day'
Dreaming With Open Eyes Reviews

'I loved it! Cathy Bramley is the most effortless of storytellers, she has a total knack of drawing you in. **I could read her books every day, forever**'
Donna's Room for Reading

'A **sweet, lovely story** that will leave you wanting more'
Laura's Little Book Blog

'**Captivating** . . . A wonderful quick read!'
The Love of a Good Book

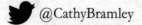
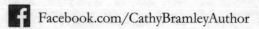

For Tony, Phoebe and Isabel xxx

Chapter 1

I woke up on the floor, wedged between the bed and bed-side table. My hip bone was bruised, my skin was mottled with cold and I had pins and needles in my arm. Painted across my face was the smug smile of a woman who hadn't got much sleep the night before. Getting up was a priority; I was freezing and I really didn't want Marc to wake up and find me down here.

It took a full thirty seconds of grunting, shuffling, in-elegant flailing of limbs and a carpet burn to my right buttock to wriggle free. Not a pretty sight.

I sighed with pleasure at the slumbering, golden-haired Adonis taking up the entire width of the mattress. He looked so peaceful. He was certainly a deep sleeper; he hadn't even woken up when he'd pushed me out of the bed.

Silently, I opened the drawer, took out the card I'd lovingly made for him with my own fair hands and slid it under the pillow. Then I slipped back under the duvet and perched on the edge, savouring the heat from his perfectly honed body. I propped myself up on my elbow and gazed at him.

It was Valentine's Day and I had a boyfriend.

I couldn't help grinning.

Last year – and the year before that, come to think of it – I had been single and I'd had to hibernate for a full twenty-four hours until the dreaded day was history and I could stop feeling marginalized by society. In fact, since Jeremy a few years ago – I shuddered at the memory of my controlling ex-boyfriend – I hadn't let anyone get close. But Marc was different.

He and I had been together for nine months and last night was the first time that he had stayed over. I'd invited him to before now but he had a stall on Sneinton market and usually had to get up for work really early and said he didn't want to wake me. But last night he'd said he didn't have to be there until nine, so he might as well stay. How romantic – to choose Valentine's Day as the first time to wake up next to me!

Right, let's get the party started.

I coughed lightly but there was no response, not a flicker of his golden eyelashes.

I coughed more sharply and this time he stirred and stretched, threatening my precarious position on the edge of the bed, and I grabbed hold of his arm.

Oh, those biceps!

'Morning, princess.' He yawned and gave me an almighty slap on the bottom.

I knew this was his idea of being affectionate but it was hardly the most romantic wake-up call. I replied with my own delicate yawn, and smiled in what I hoped was a 'Sleeping Beauty awakened by a True Love's Kiss' type manner.

He picked up his watch, swore under his breath and swung his legs over the side of the bed.

I flopped onto my back and pulled the duvet up,

enjoying the extra room in the bed. Also enjoying the view of muscles rippling across chest as he pulled his jeans up over firm thighs. What a man!

Oh no, I was a bit slow on the uptake there, he was getting dressed! That wasn't first on my agenda of love.

Marc looked down at me, his face suddenly serious. Oh my giddy aunt! He was working up to something.

He cleared his throat. 'Sophie, we need to talk.'

He sat back down on the bed and reached for my hand. Darting eyes, heavy breathing, serious face . . . If I didn't know better, I'd have thought he was going to propose. Hold on a mo – it *was* Valentine's Day, what if . . . ?

'Wait!' I yelled, making Marc flinch.

If he was going to propose, I didn't want to be lying on my back like an invalid. I pushed myself up to a semi-sitting position and rested my arms on top of the duvet.

Oops! Never flatten your arms against your body. It adds at least thirty per cent to the surface area of each limb. I read it in *Heat* magazine in a feature on how to look good in photos.

I raised my arms off the duvet and smiled brightly.

Marc frowned. Poor love; this sort of thing must be so nerve-racking. Shame really, in this day and age all the stress shouldn't be loaded onto the man. Still, the woman usually ends up organizing the wedding, so it sort of evens itself out in the long run.

'Sorry! You were saying?' I nodded at him encouragingly.

Marc exhaled and gazed at me with his baby-blue eyes. That was the look of love. Right there.

'There's no easy way to say this, princess, but . . .'

What the fudge?

I gasped, but the nerves-induced accumulation of saliva

in my throat created a strangled sort of gurgle. My spit went down the wrong hole and I started to choke. Not attractive, nor in the least bit timely.

Marc, determined to finish now he was on a roll, carried on slashing my newly minted dreams of married bliss into ribbons, while simultaneously slapping me on the back. Hard.

By the time I had found the wherewithal to hold my hands up, beseeching him to stop, he had all but finished his 'Dear Sophie' monologue.

The message had been clear, but what had he actually said? Straining to hear over my own ear-splitting wheezing, I had only caught one or two words. I must have misheard; I thought he used words like 'different things', 'boring', 'freedom' and 'nice'.

He backed away from my single bed, from me and from our relationship towards the bedroom door, holding onto my fingers until the last possible second. It was quite a poignant moment: if I hadn't been puce and completely hoarse, I might have said something profound. But other than to wail 'Why? Why?' at him, words completely failed me. So I stayed silent, doomed to for ever hold my peace.

He winked and was gone.

Happy chuffin' Valentine's Day.

'Zombie-like' was the best way to describe my mood at work over the following ten hours. At my desk in the advertising department for *The Herald*, Nottingham's daily newspaper, I barely registered the banter of my colleagues or my overflowing in-tray. My hands simulated typing on my keyboard, but in reality I was simply going through the motions and I avoided the phone all day.

The bus ride home, normally quite an ordeal, was comparatively therapeutic. At least I didn't have to talk to anyone.

It was shaping up to be the worst Valentine's Day of my entire life. What was I saying – 'shaping up'? How could it possibly get any worse? By the time my flatmates had rallied round me this morning, Jess making soothing noises and placing a mug of sweet tea in front of me and Emma threatening to cut off Marc's balls and feed them to the squirrels, I had already pronounced the day an unprecedented disaster.

I was determined not to cry again. And that was no mean feat seeing as the evening commuter bus I was on appeared to be packed almost entirely with smooching couples and women with huge bouquets of flowers, cruelly serving to ram home my new single status.

Facebook! I was going to have to update my relationship status to 'single'. But not today; I couldn't face the humiliation of declaring myself single on the international day of love.

I shook my head, still struggling to comprehend what had happened this morning. I'd been convinced that today was the day that Marc would reveal his true feelings for me. Well he'd certainly done that. Be careful what you wish for, as the saying goes.

All my Valentine's Day dreams were in tatters. I thought of the little nest egg that I'd been building up for years, waiting for the right time, the right person to settle down with. I'd begun to think that Marc could be that person. Not that we'd ever discussed a joint future, although he did once ask to dip into my savings to get a new business off the ground and we were both in our early thirties, I'd

11

assumed it would just happen one day; it was only a matter of time.

With a sigh, I shifted the dream of having my own home to the back burner, along with my other abandoned dreams; the property market was no place for single, first-time buyers at the moment – far too risky!

At my bus stop, a group of people – in twos, obviously – jostled against me as I tried to disembark. I was barely clear of the last step when the bus trundled off through a puddle, sending a spray of black slush up the back of my tights.

Marvellous.

How could snow – so white, so pure, so beautiful – turn so vile in only a few hours? It was clearly a metaphor for a love gone sour. I huffed up the steps towards home, feeling forlorn and uncomfortably wet.

The Victorian house we lived in had long ago been split into flats. I let myself in and flicked through the mail on the communal post shelf. No scented envelopes, huge bouquets of flowers or small square boxes with 'To Sophie Stone – love of my life' on them, then? No? Thought as much.

Tears welled up in my eyes and I brushed them away. Actually, why shouldn't I have a good cry? I was sad, might be properly sad for weeks, come to think of it. I loved Marc, he was so big and strong and unpredictable. Emma would say that this was a reason *not* to love him but he was exciting and I was going to miss having that excitement in my life.

For a moment, I considered sliding down the wall to the floor and succumbing to my sorrow. But it looked draughty and very public, far better to get home and let my lovely flatmates cheer me up.

I began the ascent to flat four, sniffing the air hopefully on the off-chance of catching any tantalizing aromas even though it was my turn to cook. Nothing. I waggled the key in the lock and pushed my way into the tiny hall.

'Oh, babes, are you OK? I've been worried about you all day.' Jess threw her arms round me, crushing me to her bosom.

'I'm fine.' I swallowed hard, lying through my teeth, and pulled back to examine my plumptious flatmate.

Jess narrowed her eyes. 'Sure?'

I nodded. 'Why are you wearing a toga?'

'It's not a toga, it's a chiton,' she replied, releasing me to perform a twirl in front of the hall mirror. 'I'm doing Ancient Greeks with Year Five.'

Despite my crushing melancholy, I managed a smile. Jess was a born teacher and always threw herself whole-heartedly into every topic. And even in an old sheet she looked fabulous.

'Ah, of course it is, I can tell now.' I grinned. 'You look great, Jess.'

'Thanks, babes!'

Right, food. I left her measuring the circumference of her head with a piece of string and made my way into our uninspiring kitchen.

The fridge revealed nothing much except a pack of Marc's chicken breasts. I always liked to keep high-protein food in for him in case he popped in for a snack after the gym. They were slightly grey and slimy and was I imagining it, or did they have a stain of abandonment about them? I sighed loudly and dropped them in the bin.

There was nothing else for it; it would have to be 'three-tin surprise'. Not my favourite; in fact, no one was fond of it. I had gleaned all my culinary talents from my mother; it hadn't taken long. She was to cooking what Heston Blumenthal was to hairstyling: a total stranger. This particular concoction was like playing Russian roulette with your taste buds and suited my mood perfectly.

'Come to Auntie Em!'

I turned to see Emma holding her arms out. With her overalls, stripy T-shirt and long red plaits she looked like an over-sized Pippi Longstocking.

I dived into her arms, buried my face in her neck and felt tears prick at my eyes for the umpteenth time.

'How are you doing, kiddo?' she murmured.

'Oh Emma, I'm just . . . I can't . . . you know.'

'Yeah, I know,' said Emma, soothingly.

I knew her tongue would be bitten to shreds with the effort of not blurting out, 'I told you so.'

She had never been a huge fan of Marc and I was grateful that she hadn't started another character assassination tonight; I didn't have the energy.

Emma had been my best friend since college. She had been doing an art foundation course and I was studying A-levels.

She had been taller, louder and brasher than me at sixteen. I had been hovering timidly on the edge of college life until she plucked me out of the shadows and tucked me under her wing. I had stayed there ever since.

Now she was a self-employed silversmith with a studio in a trendy part of Nottingham. The stuff she designed ranged from contemporary fruit bowls through to intricate one-off pieces of jewellery. Ironically, the only jewellery she wore was a shell she'd found in Cornwall while surfing, threaded onto a piece of leather.

'I forgot.' Jess bounded into the room, her auburn bob now adorned with a headdress made from bay leaves stuck to a bra strap. 'A letter came for you.' She placed an envelope reverently on the kitchen table. 'It looks important.'

I abandoned the quest for tins immediately, my heart beating furiously as I grabbed the envelope. Perhaps all was not lost, perhaps . . .

'It's from a firm of solicitors,' said Emma, reading the franking label over my shoulder.

My heart sank and then immediately leapt up to somewhere just below my throat.

Solicitors?

Why did I automatically feel guilty even though, as far as I could remember, I had done absolutely nothing wrong? It was the same when I passed through the 'Nothing to Declare' channel at the airport; I would blush, let out a high-pitched giggle and start making jokes about the two thousand cigarettes in my bag. I don't even smoke.

'Hey! You don't think Marc has done something dodgy, do you, and implicated you in it?' said Jess, wide-eyed.

Emma gave her a sharp look. 'Of course not, it's probably something nice. Go on, open it!'

'Yes,' I said, trying to think positive, 'it could be um . . .'

Emma nudged Jess and winked. 'I know. It's a restraining order from Gary Barlow's people!'

Jess giggled and they linked arms, started swaying and launched into the chorus of 'A Million Love Songs'.

Despite my nerves, I couldn't help smiling. The two girls were more than flatmates; they were sisters, Jess being the elder by two years. I loved them both dearly and they treated me like a third sister, which in practice meant that they both mothered me and teased me mercilessly.

I prodded Emma in the ribs. 'Hey, leave me alone. I haven't written to him for ages.'

We shared a smile and I turned my attention back to the letter in my hands.

'Oh my Lordy,' I continued. 'Listen to this: "Dear Miss Stone, Whelan and Partners have been appointed . . . blah, blah, blah . . . writing to inform you that you are a beneficiary in the last will and testament of Mrs Jane Kennedy. Please contact this office at your earliest convenience. Yours, blah, blah, blah . . ."'

I plopped down into a chair, dropping the letter onto the table. The sisters picked it up and looked at it.

'Bloody hell, Sophie!'

'A mystery benefactor!' squealed Jess. 'How exciting!'

'Well, whoever she is, I think this calls for wine.' Emma darted to the fridge and poured three large glasses while I reread the solicitor's letter.

Jess sat down next to me at the kitchen table and patted my hand. 'There you go, you see. The day might have started badly, but this letter,' she tapped it with a sharp pink nail, 'might be the beginning of a whole new adventure.'

'Exactly,' said Emma, holding up her glass. 'Cheers!'

Just then Jess's stomach gave an almighty rumble. 'Ooh, excuse me! Who's cooking dinner?'

I didn't reply. I was still staring at that letter. *More to the point*, my brain cried out, *who's Jane Kennedy?*

Chapter 2

The lift doors at *The Herald* clunked apart and I scanned the second floor, which housed my department. Excellent. I was the first person to arrive; I could faff around at my desk and make a personal call undisturbed for a few minutes.

I pressed the button marked 'tea' as I passed the drinks machine and it churned out a cup of scalding grey sludge. Wincing from the heat, I scurried over to my desk. While the computer was starting up, I checked my phone. Again. Still nothing from Marc.

My heart literally ached from missing him so much. Texting him had always been part of my morning routine. I was still staring at the screen, willing a message to appear, when a sharp voice cut into my wistful thoughts.

'Huh! Glad to see at least someone is at their desk.'

Donna Parker, head of *The Herald*'s advertising department, strode across the office, her trademark platinum hair lighting up the dim room.

'I hope you'll be more focused today,' continued Donna, pausing briefly at my desk. 'You were a complete waste of space yesterday.'

I swallowed nervously. Harsh but true. To be honest,

I was surprised that she had noticed any difference. Let's face it, I was never especially enthusiastic.

I started to shuffle a pile of papers on my desk and laughed gaily. 'Oh yes, Donna, I'm completely on top of everything. I've been here ages already.'

Donna raised a perfectly arched eyebrow and bore her skeletal frame onwards to her office.

I watched her go and let out a sigh of relief. On top of the new neat pile of papers was the envelope from Whelan & Partners, reminding me why I was in early: I needed some time off urgently. Receiving that letter was one of the most curious things that had ever happened to me. It had kept me awake for most of last night and I was desperate to get to the bottom of this Jane Kennedy mystery.

I contemplated my approach; Donna never really approved of people taking any time off, no matter how important the excuse was, and judging by her mood this morning, my request wasn't likely to go down well at all.

Coffee. That would soften the blow. I scuttled back to the drinks machine and this time selected the brown sludge labelled 'Cappuccino'.

Donna was in her late fifties and rumour had it that she had clawed her way up from secretary in a time when the newspaper industry was almost exclusively male, lunch was two pints in the Nag's Head and you couldn't see from one side of the room to the other through the smoky fug. It would be fair to say that relations between Donna and us, her long-suffering team, didn't always run smoothly. Part-time administrator Maureen referred to her as Cruella de Vil. Graphic designer Jason said she was an acid-tongued, bullying witch who did nothing except wine and dine advertising clients over long lunches. I wasn't quite so disparaging, although I did see their point. There was a touch of *The Devil Wears Prada* about her, but I did admire her steely glare – I could never keep it up like she did, day after day.

Knocking and poking my head round the office door failed to draw a response so I coughed and stepped inside, desperate to deposit the hot cappuccino as quickly as possible.

'Coffee?' I placed the scorching-hot liquid on the desk in front of her.

Still no response.

'Donna, there's been a death in the, er . . .'

The boss stared at me unblinking. Where was the death exactly? Family? Family friend? Friend's family? I wished I'd rehearsed this properly; I was floundering already.

I tried again.

'Someone close to me has died and I'll need some time off this week to sort out the will and everything.'

It wasn't strictly the truth, but I could hardly say I needed time off to see to the affairs of a complete stranger, could I?

'Oh no!' muttered Donna, pinching her lips together.

'Thank you, it has come as a complete shock,' I began. That bit was certainly true.

'The restaurant supplement is due to go to print on Friday, we've still got five slots to fill and the main sponsor is quibbling about his space allocation. This is terrible timing, Sophie, terrible . . . If it's absolutely unavoidable,' she added sourly, 'keep it brief and you'll have to make up the time.'

She fixed me with her beady eyes and flicked her head, indicating that our impromptu meeting was over. I escaped from her office gratefully, punching the air as soon I was out of sight. Success! Even if it did mean working late for the rest of the week. I dropped into my chair and reached for the solicitor's letter.

Five minutes later I had booked an appointment with Mr Whelan of Whelan & Partners for the following day. I sat back and breathed a sigh of relief; only another twenty-four hours and all would be revealed . . .

The following afternoon a smiley female receptionist ushered me through to a small office.

'Mr Whelan will be with you shortly,' she whispered in hallowed tones, as though I'd been granted an audience with the Pope. She pointed to a chair, swivelled round on her court shoes and left.

I smiled in thanks at the back of the woman's head.

My nerves were jangling and I pressed my lips together to prevent myself from whistling tunelessly. I dropped my handbag on the floor and clasped my hands together. The desk in front of me was large and old-fashioned with an inset leather blotter and one of those brass reading lamps with a green glass shade. Haphazard piles of manila folders obscured most of its surface. Behind the desk was a run of bookcases stuffed to the gunnels with lever-arch files. Whoever Mrs Jane Kennedy was, she had certainly picked a very untidy solicitor.

In the centre of the desk lay an open file. I shuffled forward to the edge of my seat and managed to read my own name at the top of the page. I inched closer still, squinting to read more.

'Thomas Whelan. Good day.'

The deep voice made me jump so much that I panicked,

slid off the chair and down onto one knee, Thus greeting the tall, thin man with dark hair, glasses and a bushy beard in some sort of weird marriage proposal stance.

His lips twitched and he gave his beard a scratch.

'Oh! Sophie Stone.' I jumped up, took his hand and pulled up the collar of my coat to hide my glowing cheeks.

'Ah yes,' he said, settling himself at his desk. He glanced at the file that I'd had been trying to read. 'You've come about your aunt's will.'

I processed this new information, hitherto unaware I had an aunt. Alive or dead.

'My aunt?'

Mr Whelan blinked furiously, referred back to the manila file and adjusted his glasses.

'My apologies, Miss Stone, your great-aunt.'

Well, that was that, then. She had to be one of my father's relations. There were definitely no great-aunts on Mum's side. There was no one at all on her side. I sighed. I suppose I'd been hoping that this wouldn't have anything to do with him. Still, I'd better be absolutely sure.

I cleared my throat. 'Could you . . . would you mind just running through the family tree for me?'

'Of course.' Mr Whelan pushed back his chair and stood up abruptly. 'But first, have you brought your passport?'

I jumped to my feet. 'Why? Where are we going?' I had been told on the phone to bring my passport when I arranged the appointment and the request had been troubling me ever since.

'Only to the photocopier,' he said, chuckling. 'I need to verify that you are who you say you are before we continue with the reading of the will.'

Thank heavens for that! I had had visions of having to

jump on a plane at a moment's notice for some reason or other.

Identity checks complete, we resumed our positions either side of the desk. The solicitor took off his wristwatch, set it to one side and then, elbows on the desk, clasped his hands together and made a steeple with his forefingers, resting his long nose on the tip.

'This office holds the last will and testament of Mrs Jane Kennedy. She was Terence Stone's maternal aunt. Your great-aunt.'

I stared at him, mesmerized by the end of his nose, which was protruding over his fingers.

Terence Stone. My father. My mouth instantly went dry.

I should stop him from going any further. There was no point in hearing what he had to say. My father had been absent for all of my thirty-two years. Mum and I had managed perfectly well without his or his family's help, thank you very much. And anyway, why would the old dear leave anything to me? It didn't make sense, we'd never even met.

'Long and tedious documents, wills.'

My eyes must have glazed over for a moment. I shook myself and Mr Whelan's eyes twinkled at me.

'There's been a misunderstanding,' I said, scooping up my bag and getting to my feet. 'My mother is estranged from her ex-husband. I've never met Jane Kennedy; in fact, I've never met my father.'

'I'm aware of all that,' he said, not unkindly. 'However, it falls to me to ensure that you are fully informed as to your inheritance. Please sit.' He flapped a hand at the empty chair. 'Would you like me to read the whole thing or cut to the chase?'

I blinked my green eyes at him. Was he allowed to say things like that? I sat back down obediently.

'The main bits, please.'

'Righto.' Mr Whelan extracted a document and a small sealed envelope from the file. He pushed his glasses up his nose and cleared his throat. I held my breath.

'Your Great-aunt Jane has bequeathed the bulk of her estate to you. You, Miss Stone, are the main beneficiary of her will. She has left you a bungalow in Woodby and a lump sum of money. We haven't finalized the amount yet but I can tell you that it runs to the thousands.'

Woodby? That was a village in the sticks somewhere north of Nottingham. *A bungalow and some money.* I repeated the words in my head. That was a house and some actual money-in-the-bank type dosh.

My chest had been getting tighter and tighter with lack of oxygen and now I was all panicky. *Breathe, Sophie; in, out, in, out.*

A house. My great-aunt had given me a house. *Of my own.* And that meant a home. How long had I been dreaming of my own home? Only all my life, that was how long.

Mr Whelan's lips were moving. He was still speaking and I hadn't been listening. 'Eighty-nine . . . in her sleep . . . neighbour.' He was telling me about Great-aunt Jane, who had seen fit to leave me all her stuff, and I wasn't even paying attention.

I flushed a deeper shade of scarlet and focused on Mr Whelan's words, my shoulders bowed with shame. There was so much to take in. I was full of questions, but my brain was like a tangled ball of wool and I couldn't find the start.

Mr Whelan was holding an envelope out to me. I took it automatically.

'As I say, there is a condition to the inheritance, but I think it would be better if you read Mrs Kennedy's letter yourself. I'll leave you in private for a moment. Can I get you some coffee?'

Condition? I blinked at him. 'Tea, please, two sugars.'

What sort of condition? I wasn't sure I could take any more surprises. Life was so much gentler without them. My heart rate was already registering at least a seven on the Richter scale.

'Actually, make it three!' I called to the solicitor's retreating lanky form.

The envelope was cream with a flowery border. My name was written on the front in blue ink, the handwriting loopy and old-fashioned. I stared at it for what felt like hours. This was the first letter I had ever had from my father's side of the family. The first *thing* ever.

The magnitude of what I held in my hands made my body tremble. This was more complicated than a straightforward inheritance from a distant relative. Opening this envelope would mean discovering a whole chapter of my own history. I wasn't at all sure I was prepared for that.

And how was I going to tell my mother? Mum referred to her ex-husband and his family as the dark side, and had done so since the day I was born. This would open old wounds for her and I knew instinctively that any involvement with my father's side of the family would really, really upset her.

I turned the envelope over in my hands. But now I was here I should at least read it, where was the harm in that?

I slid a finger along the flap to open the envelope and removed the single sheet of cream and flowery paper.

Dear Sophie,

The fact you are reading this means that I have finally shuffled off this mortal coil. I have had a long and mostly happy life. My only sadness is that I was not blessed with children and had very little family to speak of.

The chances are you won't remember the time we met. You were with your mother in Market Square in Nottingham. You would have been about five. You took my breath away with your dark curls and pretty green eyes . . .

I bit my lip thoughtfully. Actually, now I came to think about it, it rang a bell. Mum and I had bumped into an old lady in Nottingham once. She kept touching my hair for some reason and stroking my face and she gave me a five-pound note, which I spent on furniture for my beloved doll's house. The lady had asked my mum questions until Mum had got fed up and stormed off; I remembered having to run to keep up. We had moved house shortly after that. I looked back down at the letter.

It was a terrible business when your parents split up. They were very young and it was so sad that your parents couldn't forgive each other . . .

I frowned at this. Forgive each other? This great-aunt of mine made it sound as if there was fault on both sides. I made a mental note not to mention that to my mother.

It wasn't my place to interfere back then, but now I'm gone, I can be called a meddling old fool without fear of reprisal.

I want you to have my bungalow and what's left of my savings. But there's one condition. You must agree to meet your father. Just once, that's all I ask. I hope you can forgive and indulge an old lady's last wishes.

Your Great-aunt Jane

Meet my father. Just once. I shook my head vigorously. Impossible. No way. Great-aunt Jane had no idea what she was asking.

I let the letter fall to my lap.

It was no use. As amazing an opportunity as this was, Great-aunt Jane's proviso meant that this was a Pandora's box that I wasn't prepared to open. My father had turned his back on us thirty-two years ago, he would probably be as unenthusiastic about being reunited with his daughter as I was, not to mention the impact it would have on Mum.

I stood up to put the letter back on the desk. The room spun unpleasantly and my legs were trembling.

Why? I wondered. Why did she want me to meet my father? Wouldn't it be simpler to let sleeping dads lie?

Chapter 3

I had placed the set of keys that Mr Whelan had given me on my dressing table. They were like one of those creepy paintings where the eyes seem to follow you. Every time I glanced their way it was as though they were waving to me and on the first Saturday morning in March, two weeks after I first heard the name Jane Kennedy, I caved in.

It was still only eight o'clock when I tapped on Emma's bedroom door with a cup of tea.

'Don't suppose you fancy a trip to the countryside, do you?' I whispered, setting the tea down on her bedside cupboard.

She opened one eye and grinned. 'Thought you'd never ask.'

By ten o'clock we were ready to go. Jess was the only one of us with a car, but she was away for the weekend with another teacher and I had borrowed a company car from *The Herald* as I had a meeting on Monday morning.

'This takes me back,' I said as I unlocked the driver's door, 'going to look at houses together. Do you remember?'

Emma climbed in, holding the scrap of paper on which I'd scribbled down the directions to the bungalow. 'Blimey, yeah! Every weekend you used to drag me round show homes, clutching your little sketchpad.'

My obsession when I was about twenty had been interior design. I was forever visiting houses, usually with Emma in tow, and then I'd spend hours sketching out my ideas and poring over copies of glossy homes magazines. This was the first time I'd done anything like it for years and despite my reservations, I couldn't help feeling a little bit excited.

I started up the engine and laughed. 'Well, Jane Kennedy was in her late eighties, so I can't promise you a show home today.'

Woodby was one of those little villages far enough away from the centre of Nottingham to be able to claim it was in the countryside, but close enough for even the most committed townie to cope with open spaces without getting panic attacks and soon we were out of the city and winding our way along country lanes surrounded by fields.

I was concentrating hard with the effort of negotiating all the bends, but focusing on my driving was a relief. Ever since I'd made the decision to come and look at the bungalow, my brain and my stomach had been in turmoil.

I had never had any contact with my father or his family. Today, however indirectly, I would be entering into his world. It was a massive milestone and on top of that, for some silly reason it felt like I was being disloyal to Mum.

'So,' said Emma, breaking into my thoughts, 'tell me what you know about this great-aunt of yours.'

'Um.' I racked my brains to remember what Mr Whelan had told me. 'Well, she was nearly ninety, widowed, and still lived on her own. Apparently she was fiercely independent.'

'Sounds as tough as old boots. How did she die?'

'Peacefully, in her sleep. Her neighbour found her. They

used to phone each other every morning to make sure they'd both made it through the night.'

We exchanged smiles.

'I know,' I continued, 'sweet, isn't it?'

As we came into Woodby, my heart lifted at its prettiness: red-brick cottages, a village green, a pub and an old-fashioned telephone box. The grass verges were lined with daffodils, like a miniature welcoming committee all blowing their tiny yellow trumpets.

'Next on the left should be Lilac Lane,' Emma informed me, tapping the map with her finger.

I turned left. Lilac Lane was on the far side of the village. It was a short, narrow, unmade road with bungalows on one side and trees and bushes on the other, behind which I could just make out a ditch with the trickle of a stream running through it.

There were no odd numbers, only evens, so number eight was the fourth house along. I pulled onto the drive and turned off the engine. Blood was pumping so hard round my body that I had a whooshing noise in my ears.

We got out and stared at my inheritance.

The bungalow was unlikely to win any prizes for Britain's prettiest home. It had two bay windows with Georgian-style panes flanking a central front door, beneath which was an untidy concrete slab serving as a step, with thistles peering through the cracks. The walls were covered in some sort of render and painted the colour of clay. The overall effect was one of a grey, melancholy face: 'Nobody loves me,' the house seemed to be saying. If Eeyore lived in a house, I thought to myself, as I locked the car, this would be it.

I took the bungalow keys out of my bag and my stomach flipped.

'I feel sick,' I mumbled.

'It's not that bad and I'm sure it's got potential,' said Emma brightly, turning her back on the bungalow. 'And look at the views; it's in a lovely spot.'

'It's not that,' I said weakly. 'It's hard to explain, but it feels like I'm stepping into the past. This is a part of my family history that I've never known. But at the same time it could change my future, too. I'm not sure I'm ready for that.'

Emma wrapped an arm round me and hugged me. 'No one's forcing you to do anything. It's your decision. Now come on,' she shivered, 'open up. It's freezing out here.'

I swallowed. *My decision.* I was hopeless at making decisions.

I selected a key from the bunch and slid it into the lock, half hoping that it wouldn't turn so I could get back into the car and carry on with my safe, uneventful life, but the door opened smoothly.

We stepped into the dark hallway in silence. It was cold and there was a smell of damp in the air. Emma turned on the light and I pushed open one of the doors and found myself in the living room.

There were three high-backed armchairs grouped in a semicircle in front of a gas fire and a chunky television in the corner. A single framed photograph sat on the mantelpiece and two watercolours of country scenes adorned the walls. It was old-fashioned and not to my taste, but very homely.

I was in my great-aunt's living room.

My legs turned to jelly and I sank into one of the chairs and groaned.

'OK?' Emma asked.

'Oh God, Em, I feel so guilty. This old lady was family. And she died.'

'Yeah, but you didn't even know her,' reasoned Emma. She walked over to the tiled fireplace and picked up the framed photograph.

'Even so.' I sighed. 'Until now all I've thought about is what the inheritance means to me, whether I was going to accept it or not; deciding if I could possibly agree to meeting my dad. I haven't stopped to think about *her* life.'

Emma came and perched on the arm of my chair and showed me the black-and-white photograph. 'This must be her.'

A young bride smiled out at me, in her white below-the-knee lace dress, arm in arm with her dashing young husband in his dark double-breasted suit.

'They look so happy,' I said. 'And she's so pretty.'

'Hmm,' Emma agreed. 'You should keep that picture.'

I nodded. So far I had been focusing on the fact that Jane Kennedy had foisted some pretty tricky decisions on me. What I should have worked out was that her home was the most precious thing she had and for some reason she had entrusted it to me. On Monday, I would find out where she was buried and take some flowers. I was ashamed that I hadn't thought to do so already.

'Come on,' said Emma, pulling me out of the chair. 'Let's go and look at the rest of it.'

A second door off the hallway revealed a double bed covered with a rose-pink bedspread. A heavy, old-fashioned dressing table held hairbrushes, a collection of glass bottles and a china vase containing a silk rose. A faint aroma of perfume hung in the air.

'That's got to be Great-aunt Jane's room,' I whispered. 'I think we'll leave it untouched for now.'

'OK,' Emma replied. 'Why are you whispering?'

I swallowed a lump in my throat and shrugged. 'I know I'm allowed to be here, it just feels a bit intrusive.'

She rolled her eyes and opened another door. This room was at the back of the bungalow and contained a single bed and a tall thin wardrobe.

We both went in and looked round.

'I wonder if my father ever stayed here.'

'Possibly,' Emma said, opening the wardrobe to reveal neat piles of towels and bed linen, 'especially as they didn't have children of their own.'

She wandered out of the room and I sat on the bed, trying to imagine Terry Stone as a little boy. He would be in his fifties now, I guessed. There had been some photos of him lying around when I was little. But now I couldn't even picture what he looked like. I used to probe my mum for information: where did he live? Did he have another family now? Why didn't he love us? But Mum had claimed ignorance and I gave up asking in the end.

When I was about thirteen, I went through a phase of really hating him. For about six months, all my teenage angst was aimed at my absent parent. I used to plot how I would track him down and force him to face up to his responsibilities. My mum had been so relieved when *Take That* had arrived on the scene to distract me. Then, of course, I was filled with hormones of a different kind and just angst-ridden.

'Come and look at this,' yelled Emma.

I stood up and went to find her, closing the bedroom door behind me.

She was in a tiny galley kitchen, demonstrating how difficult it was to move about.

'I can't even open the oven without squashing my bum on the cupboards behind me!' she marvelled. 'I wonder how your great-aunt managed!'

'Perhaps she was very skinny,' I suggested, thinking back to her wedding picture.

'Or perhaps cooking skills run in the family and she never bothered,' Emma said, with a cheeky smile.

Run in the family. I shivered. I'd never even considered that we might share family traits.

'Oh, look at this!' She held up a hand-knitted tea cosy. 'How cute! She was a tea drinker, like you.'

'It's a real home, isn't it?' I sighed, feeling close to tears. Just what I'd always wanted.

'It is,' said Emma, tweaking a corner of wallpaper that had come unstuck. 'Although I think it must have damp. This paper is coming away in my hands. You'd have to have that looked at.'

'Don't pull it, Em. I don't want the solicitor to think we've damaged anything. I already feel like a trespasser.'

'Well, you mustn't,' she said, peering out of the window. 'This house is yours now. If you want it, that is?'

I joined her and glanced at the back garden. The plot was on a slope so that the back was higher than the front. The kitchen looked out onto a small patio with a moss-covered bench taking pride of place and beyond was a patch of lawn with a few shrubs round the edge of it.

'Of course I *want* it,' I said, turning to look at her.

Emma raised her eyebrows.

'OK, it's not the cute cottage of my dreams,' I added, 'but

as you said, it's got potential. It's just the condition in the will that's putting me off.'

Emma rolled her eyes at me teasingly. 'Sophie, what's the big deal? Just meet the man, take the money and move on. Simple. Right, I'm going to find the loo.'

I bit my tongue and breathed in as she manoeuvred past me in the narrow kitchen and disappeared in search of the bathroom. Emma made it sound so easy. It was anything *but* simple. She and Jess had had a normal childhood, with normal parents and a normal family home. It was a million miles away from my upbringing with a single parent and a succession of bedsits.

Why did my father exit my life so completely? I wondered. What sort of man walks out on a pregnant wife and then never bothers to get in touch?

I made my way back into the living room and picked up the wedding photograph again.

The toilet flushed and, seconds later, Emma walked into the room.

'I think I've seen enough,' I said. 'Shall we go home?'

Emma nodded. I placed the photograph back on the mantelpiece for now, giving my great-aunt one last look. What had she been thinking, putting that condition in her will? She must have had her reasons, but I wished she was here to give me a clue.

Chapter 4

Later that night, I unearthed an old sketchpad from the bottom of my wardrobe and joined Emma on the sofa. She had a giant bag of Maltesers in one hand and the TV remote in the other.

'We should go out tonight,' she said, flicking idly through the channels. 'It's ages since we've been anywhere.'

Floppy, comfy and drained from the excursion to Woodby, I ignored her. She didn't want to go out really; she only said it because she felt she should. Because, like me, Emma was thirty-two and single. She worked on her own in a little studio bashing away at precious metals all day and never met eligible men unless she made an effort.

'Stop,' I said, pointing at the TV. 'Go back, that was *Grand Designs*!'

I loved that show, where people overcame all sorts of unexpected challenges in order to create their dream home while watched by a presenter, quick to swoop on their mistakes and bad decisions.

'It's Saturday night,' she persisted. 'Come on, it's only seven o'clock. Let's crack open a bottle, put on some music and get dressed up. We could be in town for eight.'

I grimaced. 'Not tonight, I don't think I'm ready to put myself back on the market yet.'

Marc hadn't called once since we'd split up and as the days rolled by, it looked increasingly unlikely that he would. However, my ego was still bruised and I didn't feel up to socializing with the opposite sex in some busy bar or club. Besides, I fancied doing a bit of sketching.

Emma huffed and puffed for a bit, then said, 'Can I be blunt?'

I raised an eyebrow; Emma was never knowingly backward in coming forward. 'Go on.'

'When was the last time you went out?'

'Marc and I went out all the time!' I protested.

'I mean *out* out. Not last orders at the bar when he finally turned up after being God knows where all night.'

'It wasn't like that,' I said weakly. 'We just both liked our freedom, you don't have to be joined at the hip when you go out with someone, you know.'

Emma stared at me knowingly. '*He* had all the freedom. You just put your life on hold for him and now you've got it back. Enjoy it, that's all I'm saying.'

I saw myself through her eyes for a moment. It did sound a bit pathetic, but at the time it had seemed the right thing to do. Perhaps that's why Marc thought I was boring, whereas I thought I was being accommodating and flexible. I'd just been determined not to fall into the same trap as I'd done with my other ex, Jeremy, who had insisted on knowing exactly where I was at all times and preferably wanted me with him at all times too.

I sighed heavily; it seemed as if I could never get it right where men were concerned.

'You're gorgeous, Soph,' said Emma. 'And you can do a

million times better than waiting in for a booty call from Marc. You should be paraded round and shown off.'

'Oh, stop it,' I said, helping myself to a handful of Maltesers. 'You're making me sound like a prize racehorse.'

'You need to get back in the saddle . . .'

'So now I'm the jockey! Anyway, I'm not waiting for a booty call.'

Emma stared at me. 'If he phoned you up now and asked you out, what would you say?'

'I'd say no,' I replied smartly, although not entirely truthfully. 'Because I'm busy.'

I pinched the TV remote from her, turned the volume up several notches and then picked up my sketchpad.

'That's the first sensible thing I've heard you say about Marc,' she chuckled.

'Maybe I've turned over a new leaf,' I said, turning to a new page in my pad.

'I'll drink to that,' she said, getting to her feet. 'Glass of rosé?'

'Absolutely.'

Emma disappeared into the kitchen, while I applied myself to my sketch.

'That takes me back, seeing you draw.' She sighed, setting a glass on the floor at my feet.

I knew why she was sighing; she was thinking back to our teenage years, when our heads were full of dreams and plans, when we were still young and optimistic about life.

'Cheers,' I said, taking a sip of wine.

'At college, you used to have a sketchpad permanently glued to your hand, didn't you?'

I nodded fondly. 'And remember that giant pinboard

I had on my bedroom wall with swatches and torn-out pictures from magazines?'

'When did all that stop?' Emma eased her feet out of her Converses and wriggled her toes.

'What do you mean?'

'Back then you had dreams. You were going to go to London, remember?'

'Course I remember,' I said primly. But I'd put all those dreams behind me, along with my sketchpad, years ago.

'You were going to work on the glossy home mags, doing interiors styling for photo shoots. The job at *The Herald* was only ever a stop gap, you said, the first rung on the media ladder.'

The hairs on the back of my neck prepared themselves for a good bristle. My face felt hot and my lips were doing a passable impression of a cat's bum.

'Yeah, a stop gap until I had a reality check and found out how steep the ladder was.' I bent low over my pad and avoid her eyes.

Getting a job in classified advertising at *The Herald* when I left college had seemed like a dream start. It was media, after all, and my optimistic young self had assumed that if I worked hard, it would only be a matter of time before promotion to the editorial department followed. I planned to make my name styling glamorous homes, then swan off to London, after attracting the attention of a leading homes magazine or a national newspaper.

Unsurprisingly, the road to the big city had not been paved with gold. Once at *The Herald*, I had researched interior styling jobs in London and found to my horror that they were a) generally unpaid to begin with and b) looking for graduates. Neither category was one I had the means to fit into.

While Emma was at university, jealous of my monthly payslips and my place in the world of work, I was stuck in an office, selling second-hand bikes and unwanted baby rabbits, and managing my own finances, envious of her bohemian, carefree lifestyle, which was paid for by the Bank of Mum and Dad. My mum, by contrast, had packed a case as soon as I turned eighteen and emigrated to Spain to pursue a singing career in a club, covering everything from Abba to Olivia Newton-John.

Emma harrumphed and cocked an eyebrow at me. 'Until you met Jeremy, more like.'

I giggled. 'I can laugh about it now, but at the time it was a bit of a nightmare.'

Jeremy was a recruitment consultant who advertised regularly with *The Herald*. He was ten years older than me and the first father figure I'd ever known. I was flattered by his attention at first, and revelled in being cosseted and treated like a china doll. Without even realizing it, he gradually took complete control and convinced me that my life was in Nottingham and that I should keep my feet firmly on the ground instead of chasing the stars.

'At least you got rid of him in the end before moving in with him.'

Emma tucked her feet underneath her and stared at me. 'But you used to be so creative and full of ideas. Now you're always telling me that you're bored with work.' She flicked a stern look my way and slurped at her wine.

'Dreams are all well and good, but they don't pay the rent, do they?' I muttered darkly.

Promotion at *The Herald* had beckoned eventually, but

rather than to the sexy editorial department on the top floor, I had moved to display advertising.

Anyway, although Emma knew nothing about it, I had in fact had a chance to move to London but circumstances had got in the way and I'd had to pull out. I squeezed my eyes shut to block out the memories. It was all a long time ago. No point mooning about what might have been. Emma was right; my creative juices had well and truly dried up years ago.

'But you still love this sort of thing, don't you?' she went on, waving the remote at the TV.

'I adore all property shows, especially this one,' I confirmed, happy to change the subject.

I glanced up in time to see this week's *Grand Designs'* cliffhanger as a crane swung a huge steel beam through the glass frontage of the poor victim's new home. The presenter said something smug to camera and the show cut to the ads.

'Oops, poor things.' I grimaced. 'There, finished.'

I held my pad up to her. It was a plan of the bungalow, drawn from memory. I'd included as much detail as I could remember: the layout, doorways, the windows and even the fireplace.

Emma shook her head incredulously, scooting up next to me to take a closer look. 'That's amazing. You should do something with that talent. What's the sketch for, anyway?'

I shrugged, secretly pleased with Emma's praise but not really sure how to put my sentiments into words. Stepping into a world in which my father co-existed had shaken me to my core. I was going over and over that little house in my brain.

'I'm not sure, Em,' I said finally. 'I just thought if I could get a plan of the house down on paper, neat and orderly, my thoughts might follow suit.'

'Hey!' said Emma, twisting round to face me. 'Why don't you apply to go on that TV show, *Grand Designs*, and do something with the bungalow? Then we can all be on telly!'

'No thanks.' I shuddered. 'I want a home of my own, not five minutes of fame. Although a bit of expert advice wouldn't go amiss.'

'A home of your own, eh?' Emma folded her arms and pretended to look affronted. 'Fed up with me then, are we?'

'No,' I cried, throwing my arms round her neck. 'I love living with you two, you're like family. Anyway, if I did it up a bit, brought it into the twenty-first century, perhaps we could all move into it?'

'Mmm, maybe,' said Emma vaguely, topping up our glasses.

I sipped at my wine and stared at my drawing. I didn't blame her for not wanting to commit to anything just yet; our little flat was handy for her studio and for Jess's school and, besides, all this was theoretical at the moment, depending on whether I accepted Great-aunt Jane's condition to inheriting her estate.

And renovating the bungalow for the three of us to live in wouldn't be as easy as it sounded, either; the house had damp, only two bedrooms and the electrics and plumbing had looked ancient. It wouldn't simply be a case of a bit of cosmetic design; the bungalow at Lilac Lane would require a complete re-think. Not unlike my attitude to meeting my father, I realized. And that *definitely* wasn't as easy as it sounded.

Chapter 5

Two weeks later I was still in possession of the keys to the bungalow. In fact, I had started taking them everywhere with me and now as I sat at my desk at *The Herald* tucking into a prawn mayonnaise sandwich during my lunch hour, I reached into my handbag for a tissue and my fingers brushed against them. My stomach lurched; I had given myself until today or possibly tomorrow at a push to make a decision on accepting or declining Great-aunt Jane's estate and the pros and cons associated with it were still doing battle with each other in my poor aching brain.

'Mr Whelan is on annual leave at the moment,' his receptionist had informed me when I called to arrange the return of the keys. 'There's no rush, he says you can hold on to them.'

Which meant I still had access to the bungalow and the bungalow still had access to my every waking moment. And there were lots of them; undisturbed sleep was eluding me at the moment.

The receptionist had also told me where Great-aunt Jane was buried.

And so last weekend I had trudged round the cemetery until I found her newly dug grave, and had placed a bouquet of roses amongst the other floral tributes. I tidied up all the flowers, picked out the dead ones and rearranged them neatly. Great-aunt Jane had obviously been popular; there must have been eight bouquets and wreaths around her plot, although they were well past their best. I was glad she had had loved ones to mourn her.

I gazed at the grave. The mound of earth still looked fresh. I checked over my shoulder to see whether there was anyone in earshot, but I was totally alone.

I cleared my throat. 'Hello, Great-aunt Jane.'

How weird was this?

'Um. I just wanted to say thank you, you know, for thinking of me in your will. Except for the condition you set. That's a bit tricky for me to get my head round still, but,' I continued brightly, 'in a way the timing is perfect because I've just split up with my boyfriend and this has taken my mind off it . . .'

What was I saying? Thanks for dying, you've made my broken heart easier to deal with?

'What I mean is,' I stuttered, 'that it's given me a lot to think about. I hope you don't mind, but I'm not one to rush into decisions . . .'

And now Mr Whelan was back from his holiday and was due to phone me any moment. I finished my sandwich, wiped my fingers and put my phone on my desk. Right on cue at one o'clock, the phone, set to silent mode, buzzed in my hand.

I swallowed and answered the call with a wobbly, 'Hello, Sophie speaking?'

'Miss Stone? Mr Whelan, your great-aunt's solicitor.' Mr Whelan's voice boomed at me.

'Hi,' I said, moving the phone away from my ear to turn

43

the volume down. 'How are you? Did you have a nice holiday?'

'Pardon? Oh, yes, thank you,' he replied, sounding surprised. 'I'm calling to take further instruction in the matter of the will.'

Bam. Straight down to business. Just like that.

I sat up straighter in my chair and flailed around in my mind for some words.

'Please. Call me Sophie.'

'If you insist.'

'Thank you for calling, Mr Whelan, I've been to the bungalow and I've done a lot of thinking about my great-aunt's estate, especially the peculiar condition in the will, and I just wondered, is it legal to ask me to meet my father?'

OK, I was clutching at straws, but it was worth a shot.

'Perfectly legal, Sophie, I assure you,' Mr Whelan chuckled. 'Although I do realize that it's a big ask.'

I felt a little lump form in my throat. It was a big ask, but at the same time I had to admit that, the more I thought about it, I was a teensy bit curious to meet the man who hadn't wanted me in his life. It was my mum's reaction that was holding me back the most. I'd seen TV shows where people who were adopted as children sought out their birth parents and sometimes the adoptive parents got upset. It was how I knew my mum was going to feel – betrayed.

'Right, of course it is,' I said hastily. 'How long have I got to make up my mind?'

There was a pause. He was probably wondering what on earth I'd been doing for the last few weeks. I could ask myself the same question.

'There's no immediate rush, I suppose,' the solicitor

44

replied. I could hear a smile in his voice. 'Although I was planning on retiring at sixty-five.'

I joined in half-heartedly with the joke, but as I could never tell men's ages, I didn't fully commit. He could be forty-six or sixty-four. Plus he had a beard, which made it even more difficult to guess.

'I'm still debating what to do,' I admitted. 'My best friend says I should just take . . .' My voice faded away. It was probably not a wise move to repeat Emma's advice verbatim as it included several swear words. 'She says I should go for it but I don't think my mother will be overly keen to let her ex-husband back into our lives. I haven't dared tell her so far. She wouldn't want me have anything to do with him.'

As soon as the words were out of my mouth, I cringed. I sounded twelve not thirty-two.

Donna stalked past, glaring at me. I clamped my phone between my shoulder and ear and pretended to type.

'Do you always do as you're told?' He sounded amused.

'No, no of course not,' I laughed breezily.

Yes. Now I thought about it, I don't think I've disobeyed anyone for years.

'My granddad used to have a saying: "If in doubt, do nowt." Wise words, I'd say, at least for the moment,' the solicitor suggested. 'But at some point you'll have to make up your mind. This is about your future. Nobody else can make the decision for you.'

Hmm, I considered the saying. What about a person who was permanently in doubt? Were they consigned to do nowt for the rest of their lives? I had a feeling that me and Granddad would have got along just fine.

'By the way, I've finalized Mrs Kennedy's finances. After

fees and so on, there will be approximately twenty-five thousand pounds in her account. That would come to you as well as the bungalow.'

The phone slid out from under my ear and clattered onto the keyboard. Twenty-five thousand pounds! That was far more than I'd expected!

'Are you there, Miss Stone?'

My mouth had gone dry and I slurped some water out of a bottle. I would have a house, money to do it up and if I added my own little nest egg to it . . . All of a sudden I had options. If I accepted the inheritance. Obviously.

'What would happen if I don't accept my great-aunt's condition?' My voice was little more than a croak.

'Then the estate reverts to next of kin. Your father,' said Mr Whelan simply.

And Great-aunt hadn't wanted that. She'd wanted me to have it.

I took a deep breath. 'Twenty-four hours and you'll have my decision,' I informed him. 'I promise.'

When I arrived back at the flat that evening I could hear Jess and Emma bickering in the living room. I stuck my head round the door and grinned at the pair of them sitting like bookends at either end of the sofa.

'Hey, you two, would anyone like tea?'

Note – I did not ask what they were arguing about as I had no intention of taking sides. I was used to their little tiffs and it was only ever light-hearted. Apparently, it was what sisters did. I wouldn't know. The newspaper had run a feature last year on family dynamics. Having a sibling supposedly made children tougher and prepared them for dealing with conflict when they grew up. Which kind of made sense; I was an only child and avoided conflict like the plague.

'I only asked her for a lift to Manchester on Saturday!' huffed Emma, ignoring my question. 'Because there's a train strike.'

'It was your choice to give up learning to drive. You must face the consequences and not rely on the goodwill of others.' Jess was on the sofa, flipping through a magazine, smiling serenely.

'It's all right for you, *Daddy's Girl*. He took you out for lessons. He made me pay for my own.' Emma leapt up and hopped around the living room, fizzing with indignation.

'He did take you out for lessons until you said you couldn't bear having him in the car because it was like *Driving Miss Daisy*,' retorted Jess.

'You *so* are his favourite,' Emma tutted. 'He even helped you buy the flippin' car!'

'You're the chosen one.' Jess raised an eyebrow. 'Look at that lump sum you had towards setting up your studio!'

'Fine,' Emma scowled, 'I'll ask Dad, he won't mind helping out a member of his own *family*.'

I stared at them both, shaking my head. I couldn't help feeling envious; they had no idea how lucky they were. Despite their petty squabbles, both of them knew that their dad loved them, that he had taken care of them since the day they were born. Whenever they needed him, he dashed over like a middle-aged knight in his trusty Volvo. My dad hadn't even hung around to see me arrive into the world. He had deprived me of growing up as part of a family. I might even have had a sister of my own.

And suddenly my decision was made.

I'm doing it. I'm going to meet my dad.

A light bulb switched on in my brain. Not one of those energy-saving bulbs, which take thirty seconds to light up, by which time you've left the room. This was a bright halogen spotlight, illuminating my thoughts with a piercing beam.

My decision was made. I was going to accept Great-aunt Jane's challenge. Not simply so that I could prevent my father from inheriting her estate, but to show him what he had been missing all these years. And to tell him exactly what I thought of his behaviour.

A shiver of apprehension surged up from the base of my spine and I shuddered.

'What's up, Sophie?' asked Emma, noticing me properly for the first time. 'You look very serious.'

'Tea?' I asked again.

I made us all a drink, brought the tray into the living room and sat down in the armchair before blurting out my news. I told them about the savings I would inherit and the fact that the estate would revert to my father if I refused it.

'Good for you, Sophie,' said Emma, cradling her mug in her hands. 'I'm proud of you; I know you hate stepping outside your comfort zone.'

'I'm terrified,' I admitted. Even thinking about it gave me goose pimples. 'But I can't get away from the fact that this is what the old lady wanted me to do.' Of course she could have been a sandwich short of a picnic, for all I knew.

'It's like a fairy tale,' said Jess dreamily. She blew on her tea. 'You'll be rich, babes.'

I shook my head. 'I'll probably leave it in the bank to begin with until I have a plan. It's the bungalow I'm not sure about.'

'Can you see yourself living there, out in the sticks?' Emma asked dubiously.

I shrugged. 'Not as it is, no, but I've drawn up an idea for an extension and maybe I could use the money to do it up.'

Emma blew on her hot tea and giggled. 'May I just remind you that your idea of DIY is painting your own nails, Sophie Stone.'

'True.' I grinned. 'Remember the pictures?'

We all laughed. When we'd first moved in I'd tried to hang two pictures in my bedroom with a hammer and nails and had succeeded in removing huge chunks of the plaster from the walls. The pictures had both fallen down in the night and frightened the life out of us all and Mr Piper, Emma and Jess's dad, had come to the rescue once again and re-plastered the walls.

'Don't worry, I'll be using professionals,' I reassured them. 'In fact, I need a second opinion on the place, just as soon as I've given the solicitor my decision.'

'I'm not sure I could live in Woodby,' sighed Jess. 'It's too far from school, for one thing.'

Emma nodded. 'And it's full of sheep and mud.'

I smiled ruefully; at least that was something they agreed on this evening.

'Right, my turn to cook,' Jess declared, bouncing to her feet. 'Chicken casserole all right with everyone?'

Emma and I nodded appreciatively and watched her go. She was easily the best cook out of the three of us.

'Maybe, if you did decide to move to Woodby, this is something you need to do on your own,' said Emma softly.

I gulped. I'd never lived on my own and really didn't have any inclination to do so. 'One step at a time, eh, Emma?

Anyway, there's something else I need to do on my own first,' I said, pushing myself up out of my chair. 'Have you finished your tea?'

I collected the mugs and stood them in the sink. I opened the fridge and took out a bottle of Pinot Grigio. There were times in life when tea just wouldn't cut it and this was one of them.

It was seven o'clock, eight o'clock in Spain. I hadn't quite worked out what to say to her yet, but there was no getting away from it: it was time to tell my mother.

Mum answered the Skype call on my second attempt. As usual I was struck by her bright blue eyes and delicate features. Her blonde hair was wrapped up in a towel, turban-style, and her petite frame was draped in a kimono. I had overtaken her in height and weight when I was a teenager and always felt like a moose beside her. Tonight she was sitting on her little balcony, brimming with energy, and even though it was only springtime, she was already tanned and looked far healthier than me.

'Sophie? Is that you, I can't see your lovely face, my darling!' She frowned and leaned in close to her laptop. 'Is your webcam on?'

'Yes and I can see you,' I replied. Actually, it might not be a bad thing if she couldn't see me, it might make this conversation a whole lot easier. 'Never mind. The Internet must be playing up.'

'Smack it one!' she suggested. 'That sometimes works.'

Mum had a very crude understanding of technology and most of her solutions involved giving it a bash. I rolled my eyes but did it anyway. Amazingly the screen flickered into life.

'Ha! I'm a genius.' She grinned. 'So. What have you got to tell me?'

I should have made some notes. My mind had gone blank and I couldn't think how to introduce the subject of the will.

'Me? Oh, you know, same old,' I laughed awkwardly.

'Heard anything from that ex-boyfriend of yours?' Her eyes narrowed.

I shook my head. 'Not a sausage.'

I'd emailed her with a round-up of my news and mentioned that Marc had dumped me on Valentine's Day. She'd liked him when she'd met him at Christmas. Now he was public enemy number one. She'd even hinted in her emailed reply that she knew someone on the Costa Blanca who could 'sort him out'. I was assuming she was joking.

'Well, don't you dare call him, Sophie love,' she huffed, wagging a finger at the screen. 'If there's one thing I've learned about men, it's never to show any sign of weakness. If they mess up, they're out. No second chances or they'll walk all over you.'

I made a vague noise. That was indeed Mum's policy. Hence she'd only ever had a series of short relationships since my father. No one, it seemed, could live up to her high standards of unfaltering perfection.

'Are you working tonight?' I asked.

'Exciting news!' Mum wriggled in her seat and beamed at me. 'Paulo has asked me to do some Madonna numbers tonight. Solo! What do you think, your old mum doing Madonna?'

I laughed and clapped my hands. 'Well done, you!'

Other people's mums had jobs like school secretary or supermarket cashier. But not my mum. She was a colourful character and was happiest on the stage. I sometimes wished I'd inherited even ten per cent of her confidence.

'Thanks, love,' she continued. 'People are fed up with Abba these days. To be honest, if I never have to sing "Mamma Mia" again, it'll be too bloody soon. Meryl Streep's got a lot to flippin' answer for.'

I giggled as an image popped into my head of my mother prancing round the stage in a pink corset with cone-shaped boobs. She was in her early fifties; most women her age had swapped stilettos for sensible shoes but not her. I was suddenly struck by a brainwave.

'I'd love to see you perform as Madonna. Maybe I'll come over to visit you this summer.'

Mum clapped her hands together under her chin. 'Would you? Ooh, I'd love you to come. But I thought you were saving?'

I flushed. She did have a point. I had a habit of pleading poverty and only visited once a year and wild horses wouldn't drag her away from Spain for long. Forty-eight hours at Christmas was her limit. She claimed England gave her Seasonal Affective Disorder twelve months of the year. All of which meant that we didn't see each other often enough.

'Funny thing, actually.' Was it me or had my voice gone up an octave? I cleared my throat nervously. 'Do you remember a Mrs Jane Kennedy?'

Mum's face changed from happy to haunted. 'Who?' Her eyes darted left and right and she clamped her jaw together.

I sighed to myself; she was a terrible liar.

'Jane Kennedy. My great-aunt,' I said softly.

'Oh, her,' she grunted, folding her arms. 'What has she been saying?'

'Nothing!' I squeaked. 'At least, not for a few months. She died in February.'

'How do you know? What's it got to do with you? What's been going on?'

Poor Mum, her face had gone an angry shade of red and huge blotches were appearing on her neck and spreading down to her cleavage.

'Her solicitor contacted me. Apparently I'm the sole heir to her estate!' I kept my tone bright and breezy.

Mum's eyes widened to impossibly huge blue globes and she muttered something under her breath that I couldn't quite catch but I thought I heard the words 'meddling cow'.

She shuffled closer to the screen. 'Sophie, don't you have anything to do with it. Don't even answer their letters. I mean it,' she said ominously.

Awkward. Too late for that. I cringed, watching Mum's eyes blink furiously.

'Don't get yourself upset, Mum. Remember your solo later.'

'Nosey old bag. Wouldn't leave us alone. Wanted pictures of you and all sorts. We had to move house at one point just to get away from her.'

I was confused. Much as I wanted to side with my mum, I couldn't reconcile the Jane she was describing with the happy young bride in that wedding photograph.

'It was good of her to remember me in her will,' I said weakly.

'You can't do this to me, Sophie. It would kill me,' she pleaded. 'You and me, we've got each other, you don't want to get involved with that lot. This will be the thin end of the wedge. Next thing you know, Terry will be back on the scene.'

I held my breath. She only ever called him Terry. Not 'your father'. She said that he hadn't earned the right to be called that. I exhaled slowly, as if I was blowing out a candle.

Stay calm, Sophie.

If only she knew how close to the mark she was.

Mum twisted her laptop round and I shared the view from her balcony. I could just make out the deep blue of the swimming pool mirroring the glimmer of ocean in the distance, the dusky sky tinged with orange from the setting sun. The laptop turned and Mum's face filled the screen again.

'Forget all about it, Sophie, and come out here for a few days. It's so beautiful in spring. I wish you could smell the evening air – orange blossom and jasmine – my little piece of heaven. What do you say?' She stared at my image on the screen, nibbling at her lip. 'Please, Sophie.'

Right, I was going to tell her. Well, I was going to tell her half of it. Her reaction had been far more explosive than I'd expected and I didn't want to upset her unnecessarily.

'Mum, I've decided to accept the inheritance.' *And meet my father*, I added to myself.

Her face fell, her shoulders sagged and she shut her eyes for one, two, three seconds. Then they sprang back open full of tears.

'Well, thank you very much for ruining my night!' she said in a wobbly voice. 'And to think I brought you up to be an independent woman. Think about it, Sophie: if you accept you'll never have the satisfaction of having paid your own way in life.'

The breath caught in my throat.

'Mum, that's unfair!' I gasped.

She'd hopped off to Spain as soon as I was legally an adult; I hadn't had much choice to be anything other than independent!

She sat up tall in her seat, shoulders back and lips primly pressed together. 'What happened to that glittering career you used to dream about? Where's your sense of adventure? You've been festering at that newspaper for years. Anyone with any backbone would turn down handouts from Terry Stone's family after the way he treated us.'

My mum's face suddenly loomed large, filling the screen. 'You've let me down, Sophie.'

Then it went black; she'd cut me off.

Blimey! My heart was thumping against my ribcage with guilt. Poor Mum. Thank goodness I hadn't mentioned meeting her ex-husband.

I sat on my bed and waited for her to call back in case it had been an accident.

Was Great-aunt Jane a meddling old fool? And if so, what exactly was she meddling *in*? The sooner I got in touch with Mr Whelan to accept the challenge – I mean, the inheritance – the sooner I'd find out what all this was about.

Chapter 6

Next morning the bus into the city was packed and it was impossible to hold a private conversation. I was sure the man behind me with the lumpy briefcase on his knee was nudging the corner of it into my bottom on purpose and there was a studenty type opposite shoving huge sweat patches my way as he held onto the overhead rail.

'When I inherit that money, the first thing I'm going to do is buy a car,' I grumbled, raising my voice to reach Emma, who was standing three passengers away. 'Anything has got to be an improvement on *this* journey.'

'Oh, I don't know,' Emma called back, grabbing onto a pole as the bus veered round a corner. 'A coach ride to Derbyshire with sixty kids maybe?'

Emma was wedged between two teenaged girls who were shouting to each other to avoid having to remove their earphones.

'True,' I replied; 'rather Jess than me.'

Jess had volunteered to lead the Year Five three-night outward bound trip next week and professed to be really excited about it.

'Weirdo.' Emma grinned, rolling her eyes. 'Mind you,

I'm sure the chance to meet the fit instructors has got something to do with it.'

I laughed and looked out of the window.

Jess was a sucker for an action hero. Add a uniform into the mix and she lost all use of her legs. Deep down, Emma was just as romantic as her sister and was secretly searching for someone to sweep her off her feet too. Unfortunately, it was usually Jess who inspired such devotion; Emma's abrupt manner had a habit of making men run for the hills although I was quite envious of her ability to get straight to the point.

Only two more stops until Emma got off. The skies were grey and menacing clouds looked ready to explode.

'How did your mum take the news about the will?' Emma asked.

I grimaced. 'Worse than expected, she cut me off in the end.'

Emma pulled a face. 'Oh dear. Well done for facing up to her. That's the hard part over. What did she say about your dad?'

I sighed. 'I didn't tell her that bit. I figured she doesn't need to know. I'll just make sure she never finds out, it'll be less painful that way. You should have seen her face, Emma; she looked so hurt when I mentioned the will.'

She frowned. 'Hmm, I don't blame you, but I hope that little white lie doesn't come back to haunt you.'

'What do you mean?' I asked.

'Well, what if your dad wants to keep in touch? What if he meets you and doesn't want to let you out of his life again?'

I shook my head firmly. 'He's had thirty-two years to do that. Surely if he was so keen to have me around he wouldn't have waited this long. Besides, Mr Whelan told me he lives in the States.'

'Wow! Well, I hope you're right about your mum,' Emma arched an eyebrow. 'But families are funny things. See you later.'

Well, mine certainly is, I thought wryly as I watched Emma press through the crowd to the exit.

The bus decanted her and several other commuters out into the morning rain and I shuffled further up the bus into an empty seat, turned the radio on my phone on and put my earbuds in to catch the morning news.

'Yes, there's a housing deficit, and yes, we need more houses at affordable prices,' said a male voice, 'but the Government needs to accept that giving planning approval for all these social housing projects is like putting a sticking plaster on a broken leg.'

Normally, the words 'crisis' and 'Government' were enough to have me changing radio stations, but my new preoccupation with houses meant that I was quite interested, so I sat back in my seat and listened.

'Nottingham is very fortunate to have some amazing architecture,' the man continued. 'That's one of the reasons I moved here in the first place. But now our architectural heritage is being sacrificed for the sake of short-term solutions. These tiny new houses may be cheap but they are poorly designed.'

He had a smooth voice, youngish, professional, and he sounded clever. But what struck me most was his passion. I'd never given our 'architectural heritage' a moment's thought, but for some reason, I now felt rather protective about it.

'They won't stand the test of time like our Victorian

terraces, which have been providing accommodation for over a hundred years. In ten years' time—'

'Thank you, Nick Cromwell,' interrupted the radio presenter. 'Can I turn to you, Councillor Malcolm Shaw from the city's Housing Department? How do you respond to claims that these new houses are not fit for purpose?'

There was an exasperated sigh and a second, deeper voice joined the debate. 'Our housing policy is clear: to provide clean, modern accommodation for the people of this city,' droned the councillor. I could almost see him thumping the desk for emphasis like a politician. 'To allow our residents to get a foothold on the property ladder in a difficult market.'

Was it just me, or had he ignored the question? I frowned at the radio.

'You're not answering the question, Mr Shaw,' interrupted the nice man.

Mr Shaw gave a derisory laugh. 'I'm sure Mr Cromwell is well intentioned if not well informed but—'

'Excuse me?' Mr Cromwell was becoming more passionate by the second.

Yeah, fighting talk, I thought with a smirk.

The housing councillor continued, ignoring his adversary. 'But not everyone can afford the luxury of an architect-designed home.'

'Wrong,' said Nick Cromwell forcefully. 'Architecture should be for everyone, not just the wealthy.'

These words were spat through gritted teeth and I gave the man a mental round of applause.

'Our budget cuts don't allow—' began Mr Shaw.

'With a bit of *thought*, Nottingham's older properties can be adapted to suit modern living and preserve our heritage at a fraction of the cost of new builds,' argued Mr Cromwell.

'Er, that's all we have time for,' interjected the presenter. 'My thanks to architect Nick Cromwell and Councillor Malcolm Shaw.'

Architect Nick Cromwell. How fortuitous.

I was a strong believer in fate. Things happened for a reason in my book. Which is why I scrawled the name *Nick Cromwell* on an old bus ticket before I forgot it. He sounded exactly the kind of man to give me some expert advice about Great-aunt Jane's bungalow.

The morning dragged by at work. Not that I wasn't busy; I had plenty to do. But I was counting down the minutes until my lunch hour when I would be able to call Mr Whelan and confirm that I would be accepting Great-aunt Jane's conditions. Eek! I got goose pimples every time I thought about it. And if I had any time left over, I would even call the architect and make an appointment to show him the bungalow to see if he had any bright ideas to improve it. But until twelve thirty I was supposed to be creating promotional ideas for a travel agent's May bank holiday advertising campaign and I was finding it hard to concentrate.

The problem was that I'd been doing this job too long; I'd created the strapline for this campaign for them last year and the year before that and there were only so many puns you could make with their company name, Great Escapes.

My life had been rumbling along for aeons at the same unhurried, unexciting pace and now – ever since Marc had dumped me, in fact, after mentioning something about being boring, I seem to recall – it had gathered speed like an express train and everything was changing.

Everything except work, I realized, forcing myself to focus on my computer screen again.

Mum's words had stung last night. 'Festering' at the newspaper was a bit harsh in my opinion – there's nothing wrong with a bit of job security – but I had to admit there was a grain of truth in what she'd said; my career needed a boost.

Maybe I should try to be a bit more assertive at work, use my initiative, demonstrate to Donna that amongst her team I was the one to watch, the one to rise to challenges.

I peered over the top of my screen and checked what my colleagues were up to. Jason was watching YouTube and Maureen was knitting under the desk, her wool tucked out of sight in her shopping bag. I stifled a giggle; the competition wasn't particularly stiff. All I needed was an opportunity to shine.

A strangled scream from Donna's office interrupted my flow. She appeared to be yanking all the cables out of her laptop.

'She's finally flipped,' hissed Maureen. 'One of you will have to go and help her.'

Jason curled his top lip and glared at her so I jumped to my feet.

'I'll go,' I said, ignoring their surprised looks.

'Walk tall. This is the "new you". Show Donna that you mean business,' I muttered to myself.

I knocked on her door and poked my head in.

'Everything OK?'

The boss had her head on the desk. Her laptop was hanging by a solitary cable, suspended over the waste-paper basket.

She lifted her head up. 'Can you do Facebook?'

I nodded. I was of the Facebook generation, addicted to updating my status on an hourly basis. If I ever suffered amnesia, I would be able to reacquaint myself instantly with my entire life by checking my page.

'Twitter?'

Once again I nodded. This second nod wasn't strictly true, but in the spirit of my new 'can-do' attitude, I decided to wing it. How hard could it be? Donna let out a long whistling breath through her nose.

She pointed at a chair. 'Sit.'

I sat, apprehension starting to build in my stomach.

'I need you in the boardroom with me at noon.'

Wow. I hadn't expected that. Me. In the boardroom. At noon.

'Er, great!' I grappled for the right words, wanting to sound keen and calm but feeling anything but.

On the other hand, *Seek and ye shall find*. Or *ask and ye shall receive*. Whichever the correct proverb was, I had been looking for a leg up the ladder and appeared to have stumbled over one.

'The board has asked me,' Donna sat back, folded her arms and cleared her throat, 'I mean us, to give a presentation on social media to help them decide what *The Herald*'s stance should be. Should we be Twittering and Facebooking, that sort of thing.' She waved her hand around vaguely.

I had lots of questions but all I could think was, *Presentation, me, boardroom, noon*.

'But . . . but . . . why us in advertising, not editorial?' I stuttered.

'They don't want it to be news-led. They want promotions, vouchers, competitions, that sort of thing.'

The digital clock on her wall changed to 11 a.m.

I gasped. 'We've only got an hour. They can't possibly expect us to produce a report in that time!'

My heart was beating double time at the thought of it. Donna looked down at her desk.

'Well, we'll just have to make the best of it. Just rustle up a few handouts, nothing too detailed. Most of them won't even know how to use the Internet, I'm sure. I'll introduce you and let you do the rest.'

'Me? You want me to do the whole presentation?'

Donna pursed her lips. 'Is that a problem?'

I faltered; it was hardly ideal – my first time in the board-room and I had almost no time to prepare. On the other hand, it might just give me the chance to shine that I'd been looking for.

'Not at all,' I chuckled with false jollity. 'I would just have liked more notice to make sure I do a good job.'

'You've got fifty-five minutes to do a good job, so,' she did that irritating head flick at the door, 'get on with it.'

Striding back to my desk, heart pounding, I was a little bit dazed. I had less than an hour to produce something that under normal circumstances would take all day.

Maureen placed a cup of tea at my elbow and I gave her a tight smile of thanks. I took a deep breath and opened up a new document on my computer.

Sophie Stone, Social Media Advisor to the board. I could do that.

Chapter 7

Fifty-nine minutes later, I stood next to Donna outside the boardroom on the dizzy heights of the top floor, waiting for the signal to enter. The USB stick I was clutching felt slippery against my sweaty palm.

Donna was eyeing me as if she doubted I could pull this off. To be honest, I wasn't sure myself. Her eyes travelled downwards to my dress and high heels. Her bosom rose as she inhaled deeply and looked away. I glanced down, smoothing my free hand over my stomach as I sucked it in.

I tugged my dress down, wondering if it was too short. I considered asking Donna but Wendy, the Managing Director's PA, poked her head out of the door.

'We're ready for you, ladies!' she trilled.

I managed a nervous smile. Donna led the way into the room and stopped in her tracks, her face turning pale before my eyes.

'The Chairman's here,' she hissed at Wendy.

'Yes,' she winked, 'aren't you the lucky ones!'

My mouth went dry. Other than at the Christmas party, I'd never even been in the same room as him.

Wendy distributed my handouts to six men seated round a super-shiny mahogany table and we made our way to where a laptop was connected to a projector screen. I fumbled to find the right hole for my USB stick. My hands were shaking and I was starting to feel a bit light-headed.

Donna grabbed my arm.

'You'd better not mess this up,' she hissed, 'or both our careers are on the line!'

Gee, thanks for the pep talk, Boss.

I looked round at my audience. Average age I guessed to be around fifty-five and not a smiling face amongst them. With the exception of Wendy, hairstyles ranged from receding to bald. The Chairman, stern and bespectacled, sat at the head of the table, with the Managing Director on one side and Wendy on the other.

Donna kicked us off. 'I'd like to introduce Sophie Stone, my advertising executive, who is going to give you an overview of social media and the role it can play in business, illustrated with case studies.'

Case studies? My insides flip over. Donna hadn't said anything about *case studies*. My eyes darted to the closed door. I contemplated making a run for it and leaving Donna to sort out her own mess. My boss had tiny beads of sweat forming on her top lip.

Sophie Stone to the rescue, then.

I took a deep breath, peeled my tongue from the roof of my mouth and began. And once I'd started, I was fine . . .

'So you see,' I declared, fifteen minutes later, 'using social media in a targeted and strategic way can result in an open and instant dialogue with our readers in a way that our print newspaper can't achieve. It would also allow our sponsors and advertisers to get direct feedback from their campaigns and promotions.'

The presentation was going well. The board seemed genuinely interested and the questions they asked had all been straightforward. Donna had even stopped sweating.

'I'd now like to open up Facebook and Twitter so we can look at how other businesses are using it.'

I clicked onto Facebook and sent up a silent prayer that none of my friends had posted anything salacious recently.

'Let's look at some case studies.' I flicked my eyes over to Donna accusingly. Time to improvise.

'Would anybody like to suggest someone to look for on Facebook?' I looked around the room, hoping for some audience participation.

'You can have a look at my Facebook page if you like,' said the Human Resources Director, cramming a chocolate digestive into his mouth and brushing the crumbs off his moustache.

'Er.' I shot Donna a second glance. So much for the board not knowing their Explorer from their elbows. Donna, very unhelpfully, gave a little shrug.

'I was thinking more of a company, a brand or a celebrity?'

'*The Times*!' called out one of the men I didn't know. The board members sat up taller and leaned forward to watch as I located the right Facebook page.

It was a piece of cake. I explained how the national newspaper drop-fed snippets of news to its readers and used its Facebook page to sell online subscriptions. Murmurs and nods ran round the table like a corporate Mexican wave.

'What about our local competitors? Are they on it?' asked the Chairman. *The Chairman* had asked me a question.

Knock his socks off, Sophie. Blow him away with your superior knowledge!

Bumbags. I didn't know the answer. The old, un-motivated Sophie couldn't be bothered to check up on competitors. The new Sophie could kick her. Hard.

Think, think, he's waiting.

I could feel my face heating up as I typed in the name of a newspaper from a small town about half an hour away. Oh, thank goodness! It was there. Bit embarrassing, though. They were much smaller than us and by the look of it had been on Facebook for a while. I searched for something negative to say about their efforts.

'This one is not quite in our league,' I said conspiratorially, receiving one or two nods of approval, 'but it is fairly local.'

The last post by the newspaper was ten days old and there were comments from readers – some of them not particularly nice – which had not been answered. Bingo!

'Oh dear. Once a business enters into the fray of social media, it's vital to maintain that commitment or customers will lose interest.' I wagged a finger to hammer home my passion for the topic.

Totally confident in my pitch now, I began to walk from one side of the projector screen to the other, smiling and making eye contact with each member of the audience.

'Here is a classic example of how not to do it. They started well, posting new information and pictures every couple of days, responding to readers' comments, etc. But now it looks like the novelty's worn off. They've made a complete dog's . . .'

The Managing Director inserted his little finger up his nose. He began to root about, head on one side, oblivious to my stare.

'A complete dog's . . .' I repeated, transfixed and thrown off my train of thought.

He pulled his finger out of his nose and examined his quarry with the look of a man who had hit the jackpot and, thankfully, wiped his finger on his handkerchief.

What was I trying to say? My mind had gone completely blank.

'Dog's . . .' I tried again, racking my brains for the end of the phrase. Something beginning with *b*. Come on, concentrate.

Donna gave a huff of exasperation behind me.

'Bollocks!' I yelled.

All the eyes in the room stared at me. Several jaws dropped. Donna gasped.

Mortified didn't begin to cover it. My legs had turned to mush and my face was on fire.

The tense silence was broken by the Chairman, who looked at me over the top of his half-moon reading glasses.

'I think the word you were looking for, young lady,' he said imperiously, 'is breakfast.'

'That's the one,' I squeaked.

'How could you?' snapped Donna two minutes later as we made our way back down to our own floor in the lift.

I looked sadly at the button for the top floor. I would never need to press it again.

'You've let me and the entire department down.'

As soon as the lift doors opened, Donna was off. I skulked behind her.

'You were so busy showing off, wiggling your backside about and grinning like the village idiot, that you lost concentration.'

It was the bogey man's fault, not mine. The dirty pig. Now my chances of promotion were non-existent. Ironic really, I'd made a complete dog's breakfast of it.

'Apart from that, though, I thought it went quite well, don't you?' I ventured, trying to salvage something from the wreckage that was my career. Donna glared and slammed her office door.

At lunchtime I was still too glum to make any personal phone calls. Speaking to the solicitor and the architect would have to wait until I felt less miserable. I treated myself to a calorie-laden sandwich with extra mayo and sat down at my desk to eat in miserable silence. I was just easing half of the sandwich out of its wrapper when Donna's door opened briefly.

'Sophie! In here!'

I sighed. She'd already torn me to shreds over the whole fiasco, couldn't we all forget about it now?

I trotted over to her office obediently and stuck my head into the lion's cage but to my surprise Donna's teeth were bared in what I knew to be her version of a smile.

'The board was very impressed with our presentation.'

Our presentation?

'Apart from the dog's breakfast element, of course. And they would like us to handle a special project to set up social media for the newspaper. Run by you.'

'Seriously?' I bounced on the spot and Donna frowned.

'The MD wants to see a six-month action plan, an idea of any extra budget, and,' she paused, 'it goes without saying that *nothing* goes live without my approval.'

'Understood. Absolutely. Thanks, Donna.' I hovered at the door. 'Um.'

She stared back icily.

'Do I get a pay rise?'

'No.'

'Can we change my job title to Social Media Strategist?'

'No.'

'Right. Fine. No problem.' I grinned, flapping a hand.

I skipped back to my desk, with a celebratory air punch. Small details like public recognition and extra pay weren't as important as the fact that only this morning I had planned to boost my career and it was beginning to happen already.

Tomorrow, I would call Mr Whelan and officially accept the terms of the will, and I would call that architect and get the ball rolling on the bungalow. And after that my glittering future awaits!

Chapter 8

Five hours later I gave a cursory glance at the post on the communal shelf and ran up the stairs to the flat. I couldn't wait to tell Jess and Emma about my day. The house rule was that we vowed to celebrate everything, every triumph, every bit of good news, no matter how small. We kept a supply of cheap bubbly in stock for any such occasion. Promotion to (unofficial) Social Media Strategist definitely called for at least one bottle, if not two.

I stuck my key in the lock and opened the door. My ears picked up the signals like two little satellite dishes: movement in the living room; giggling women; the chink of glasses. My heart squeezed with love for my girls: they must have already seen my Facebook update and they were waiting for me to come home.

'Is that you, Soph?' yelled Emma.

'Yes,' I cried, dumping my bag in the hall. I burst into the living room to see Jess reclining on the sofa, glass in hand and Emma easing the cork out of a second bottle. *Second?*

'Hey!' I beamed. 'Started without me, eh?'

'Yes, sorry, Soph, we're just so excited. Here,' said Emma, 'have a drink. We've both had a brilliant day.' She thrust a full glass in my hand.

'Oh! Me too,' I squeaked, only slightly disappointed that the bubbly hadn't been wheeled out solely in my honour.

'Excellent.' Emma grinned, perching on the window sill. 'A triple celebration! Go on, Jess, you first.'

Jess's cheeks were flushed, and her eyes were shining. 'We had a school inspection today and my teaching was judged as outstanding! I can't believe it, babes. You can't get better than that. Mind you, I thought I'd blown it when I dissected a bull's eye and two of the kids were sick.'

'Congratulations! Very well deserved.' I sat down on the sofa and squeezed her tight. She was a brilliant teacher, everyone loved her. An asset to any school, our Jess. Little tears of pride pricked at my eyes.

'But even more exciting than that,' Jess continued, pulling away, 'I've got a date with a policeman!' She squealed and drummed her feet on the floor and told me how a drop-dead-gorgeous officer had come to school that afternoon to arrest a mother who wouldn't release a teacher from a strangle-hold. Fortunately, the school inspectors had already left by then. The policeman had called back later for her number. Still in uniform.

'Tell Sophie his name,' snorted Emma.

Jess giggled. 'Spike, well, that's his nickname anyway. And Emma's got good news. Tell her, Em.'

'Well.' Emma flicked her plait back over her shoulders. 'I had a call from the Lord Mayor's office today.' She paused for effect and I obliged with a gasp. 'I've been commissioned to make a commemorative silver platter to go in the Council House!'

I leapt from my seat and flung my arms round her and we rocked from side to side as I hugged her tight. Emma's business had been struggling for a while. This was just what she needed and I was so happy for her.

Jess topped up our glasses. 'And what's your news?'

I sipped my Cava, enjoyed the sensation of the bubbles bursting in my throat and sat down in the armchair.

'I realized that I've been, er,' – I opted not to use my mum's expression of 'festering' – 'coasting along at work and that it was about time I did something about it. I've been doing my job so long I can do it blindfolded and I need more of a challenge.'

I grinned sheepishly at Emma who cocked an eyebrow in a told-you-so gesture.

'So today I said "bollocks" in the boardroom and I've been promoted, well, sort of!' I held my glass aloft. 'Cheers!'

Emma and Jess snorted with a mix of laughter and disbelief as I explained about my new role of creating social media profiles for the newspaper and my faux pas in the boardroom and we were laughing so hard that we didn't hear the door buzzer until whoever was downstairs decided to lean on the button continuously.

'I'll go,' said Jess, wiping tears of mirth from her cheeks.

I listened as she pressed the intercom button in the hall.

'Who is it?' she shouted.

'It's Marc. Is Sophie in?'

Emma and I gasped and stared at each other. Marc? It was well over a month since he'd dumped me and I hadn't heard a word from him in all that time. My stomach fluttered nervously. What could he possibly want? What if he wanted me? And if so, did I want him . . . ? I started to breathe heavily.

'Er . . . hold on a minute,' Jess yelled, 'I'll just check.'

'Calm down,' said Emma kindly, taking in my panicky expression. 'You're in control, remember?'

I nodded and did my best impression of a cool, calm, confident woman.

Emma frowned. 'Do you think he's heard about your inheritance?'

I blinked at her. 'I doubt it, why?'

She shrugged. 'I wouldn't put it past him to get in touch if he had. Just a thought.'

It was an uncomfortable thought and one which rather took the wind out of my sails. Emma stood up and peered out of the window and scanned the street. 'Can't see his car,' she said, 'but there's a red sports car revving its engine and a pink sleeve hanging out of the driver's window.'

Jess reappeared back in the room, wringing her hands together. 'What shall I say?' she hissed.

I grabbed the bottle, topped up my glass and sank down into the armchair. 'Send him up.'

Emma and I listened as heavy footsteps reached our floor and Jess opened the door. We didn't have to strain our ears; it was only a tiny flat. There was no such thing as a private conversation here. We had to text each other if we wanted to keep anything a secret.

'Looking gorgeous as ever, Jess. Pink to make the boys wink, eh?' said Marc, referring to Jess's voluminous sweatshirt. She wore this to plan her PE lessons in, said it made her feel more sporty.

Jess giggled. I didn't blame her; Marc had that effect on women. I glanced at Emma. Well, most women. Emma's mouth moved from gaping to scowling and back again in rapid succession.

OK, steel yourself, I told myself. *This man broke your heart, remember? Putting aside the issue of the pink-sleeved driver for a moment, if he wants you back, he must work for it. You must not cave in as soon as you see him, repeat, you must not—*

Oh God! Jess ushered Marc into the room and my resolve went the way of a Lindor chocolate: all melty and soft-centred. So much for the steel. There was no escaping it; Marc Felton's manly presence filled the room entirely. He looked like an extra from an action movie: fit, stubbly, with a seductive twinkle in his eye.

A little moan escaped from my throat. Emma took a protective step towards me and muttered 'Tosser' under her breath.

Marc's eyes roamed over my body and he broke into a sexy grin. 'Like the dress.'

I glanced down to see that my dress had ridden up to reveal all of my thighs and almost certainly offered the rest of the room a glimpse of the gusset of my tights. Damn.

'Thanks,' I muttered, blushing to the shade of the sports car now tooting its horn outside.

I stood up too quickly and managed to slosh Cava down the front of my dress. Marc, an eye on the prize as usual, strutted forward producing a tissue from his pocket.

'Let me help with that,' he chuckled.

'Back off, Felton,' Emma snarled. 'What did you want anyway?'

Marc stepped back, held his hands up and then looked at me. 'I've got something to ask you, Sophie.'

I held my breath. If he was coming to ask forgiveness, he might feel uncomfortable doing it in front of the Piper sisters and it was on the tip of my tongue to ask them to give us a moment.

'I can't find my Nickelback CD,' he continued. 'Have you got it?'

You know that feeling when you get a helium balloon on a ribbon at McDonald's and then you walk outside and the ribbon slips out of your fingers and you watch helplessly as it floats away out of reach, until it's a tiny speck and then it disappears from sight?

Well, that.

I nodded and fled from the room. His precious CD was in my bedroom. We'd listened to it the night – the only night – he'd stayed over after he'd rejected all the music on my iPod as 'too girlie'. I collected the beloved item and considered scratching it with my nail file as I slipped it into its case.

Me? Instantly forgettable. Crappy album? He can't live without it.

I stomped back in to the room and thrust it at him.

'Here, take it and blob off.' I picked up my glass and drained it.

'Oh great! Thanks.' Marc grinned, oblivious to my annoyance, annoyingly.

The car horn beeped three times in succession outside.

'Is that for you?' asked Jess, peering out of the window.

Marc frowned. 'Possibly.'

'Yeah, who is that, by the way?' demanded Emma, refilling my glass to the brim.

Marc rubbed his nose and shrugged. 'Just a girl from work.'

Odd, I thought he worked on his own? He must have meant from the market generally. Anyway, what did I care? Oh, who was I kidding? I was desperate to know who she was.

'Well, don't keep her waiting,' I said airily. 'Besides, we need to get back to our celebrating.'

I made a show of lifting my glass in a toast, before taking another sip. I was beginning to feel a bit light-headed. Alcohol was zipping willy-nilly around my bloodstream on an empty stomach.

'That's right.' Emma nodded, raising her own glass. 'To Sophie and her promotion and her new single life of fun, fun, fun!'

'Yay!' Jess skipped forward to clink our glasses, elbowing Marc out of the way. 'And to her inheritance! Cheers!'

'Jess!' hissed Emma.

The car horn sounded again. This time one long continuous honk.

'On your way,' Emma said, gesturing towards the door.

'Inheritance?' Marc deliberately ignored Emma and locked his eyes on me. He ran his tongue over his lips.

I nodded, my heart thundered and my lungs were fighting for breath. He hadn't looked at me like that for ages and as much as I tried to conjure up my anger again, my hormones were getting in the way.

The pink-sleeved one started sounding her car horn to a beat not dissimilar to 'Nelly the Elephant'.

Marc growled, took his phone out of his pocket and punched some numbers. The assault on our collective eardrums ceased. He turned away and murmured into the phone, 'Sorry, prin—' His eyes flicked to me. Too late, I'd heard it. He had a new princess. Fine. Whatever.

Emma flashed me an I-told-you-so grimace.

'Sorry, mate, I'll just be a minute,' he continued. 'How about you nip up to the garage and get me a can of Coke?'

In a seamless manoeuvre, he ended the call and pulled

me down on the sofa next to him. Emma, steam virtually whistling out of her ears, glared at us all in turn, especially Jess, and squeezed herself next to me on the two-seater sofa.

We all heard the sound of a revving engine, followed by a screech of tyres and the retreating roar of a sports car.

'An inheritance?' Marc prompted.

'Sophie . . .' Emma warned in a low voice.

I flashed her a look that told her I was totally in control of this conversation and gave Marc a condensed version of the whole Great-aunt Jane situation. He was captivated, Emma was tutting furiously and Jess was oohing, aahing and sniffing like she did during the royal wedding.

Marc narrowed his eyes. 'How much are we talking, savings-wise?'

I gave a weak shrug. 'Too soon to say,' I lied. Not as daft as I look, me.

'And to qualify, I mean – thingy – inherit, all you have to do is agree to meet your dad?'

'All!' squawked Emma. '*All!* You've no idea what a big deal this is.'

'Absolutely,' agreed Jess. 'The repercussions of upsetting the status quo vis-à-vis Sophie's entire family dynamic are not to be underestimated.'

I stared at her. What was she on about?

'I hope you said yes. It's a no-brainer!' cried Marc, throwing his hands in the air. 'Just meet the man and take the money.'

Emma twisted her mouth angrily and bit her cheek. This was almost word for word what she had said and I knew how much she would hate sharing an opinion with Marc.

I stood up with as much dignity as I could muster. Not

easy, seeing as I was wedged in snugly between Emma and Marc and the sofa cushions were as supportive as custard.

'It's all very exciting,' I said, scanning the room for the bottle, hoping for another top-up. 'In fact, in the last month, ever since you dumped me, my life has been a complete roller-coaster of events and in the morning, I'll be calling the solicitor to accept.'

'Good for you.' Marc nodded. And was I imagining it or was there a spark of respect in his eye?

For once in my life, where Marc was concerned, I had the upper hand. It was thrilling. It was a landmark moment in our relationship. It was just a shame it had to come after he had apparently found himself another princess. Nevertheless, I was going to milk it for all it was worth.

'Marc, please leave now,' I said, pointing to the door.

'But my lift's just gone,' he protested.

'You heard the lady.' Emma suddenly went all Mafia, hoicked fifteen stone of muscle off the sofa and bundled my ex-boyfriend towards the hall.

Marc tried to make eye contact with me over the top of Emma's red mane. He made the shape of a phone with his thumb and little finger. 'Call me if you need any help, yeah? Princess?'

I smiled vaguely. 'Of course,' I said as I watched Emma push him out through the doorway.

I sank down onto the sofa, delighted with the way I had handled myself. I had a curious feeling that a new, more confident Sophie Stone had just arrived.

Chapter 9

Three weeks had gone by since the day of the Big Decision. I was now officially going to inherit Jane Kennedy's estate. And after a particularly grim day at work, I was driving back to the bungalow to meet Nick Cromwell, the architect. I'd wasted no time in phoning him and had arranged to see at him at soon as he could fit me into his schedule. Unfortunately, his earliest free slot had not been until mid April. But that was fine; I'd had plenty to keep me occupied. Mr Whelan was on the case with regards to Great-aunt Jane's will and I had launched myself into my new social media project with a vengeance. There wasn't a thing I didn't know about hashtags, promoted posts and viral videos these days.

Nick Cromwell had sounded very business-like on the phone and had listened politely, saying merely 'hmm' and 'I see' when I'd tied myself in knots trying to explain why I might, but might not need an architect. Then I started telling him what a massive fan of *Grand Designs* and all the other TV property shows I was and he'd interrupted me, suggesting we meet up at the bungalow to discuss it 'on site'.

'Hurry up,' I muttered, gripping the steering wheel and

chewing a bit of loose skin on my lip until it tore off painfully.

'Ouch!'

A quick look in the visor mirror confirmed it: I'd cut my lip. Great, now I was going to turn up late *and* looking like I'd been in a fight.

I hadn't been in a fight, although I'd felt close to thumping the client who I'd just had a long meeting with. Frannie Cooper was the owner of a hair salon chain called Fringe Benefits and I dreaded meetings with her. She changed her mind like the wind and today she'd rejected all the ads that I had shown her for the next campaign, despite them being exactly what she had asked for.

Then I'd had to stop to buy some cartons of juice. Frannie hadn't offered me as much as a glass of water as usual and I was gasping for a drink. And now I was running late and to make matters worse, it was raining. My curls turned into candyfloss when it rained.

Spring had well and truly sprung since my first visit to Woodby. Despite the drizzle, the countryside was lovely; the fields were full of scampering lambs and the sight of the undulating landscape lifted my spirits. *This could be my daily commute*, I thought happily.

I began to feel a bit fluttery as I approached the village; I was twenty minutes late and the architect would probably be at the bungalow already. My sketchbook lay on the passenger seat next to me. Not that I was planning on showing Nick Cromwell what I'd drawn, I simply wanted to check I'd got my proportions right. Since that Saturday night, I'd done a few more scribbles – just a few ideas, like putting an extension on the back and making it all open-plan. Nothing I could show a professional. But I was

81

surprised at how much I'd enjoyed sketching again, after all this time.

There was already a grey hatchback on the drive taking up all the room. It looked like a very sensible car, not the sort of thing Marc would go for. He didn't look at anything without spoilers and twin exhaust pipes and preferably a souped-up engine.

I tried to blot Marc out of my thoughts and concentrated on parking the car at the bottom of the drive without causing an obstruction for the neighbours. The architect was already out of his car, sheltering from the rain under the porch. His face was hidden by the hood of his waterproof jacket, also grey. He looked big and bulky.

My stomach churned nervously and it suddenly dawned on me that I'd agreed to meet a total stranger in a deserted house and I hadn't told anyone else about it. Talk about 'stranger danger'; Jess would be horrified. Oh well, no time to send emergency texts now, I couldn't bear to leave the poor man (or axe murderer) in the rain any longer.

Stuffing all my things into my bag, I grabbed my umbrella and made a dash for the house.

A brown and white dog on the driver's seat watched me as I gingerly tiptoed past the architect's car, trying to avoid getting my shoes wet in the puddles.

'Hello, I'm Sophie Stone,' I called. 'Pleased to meet you.'

I finally reached the porch and shook his outstretched hand, simultaneously lowering my brolly.

'Nick Cromwell, likewise,' said the architect, looking down to see rivulets of water dripping from the tip of my umbrella onto his shoes.

'Eek, sorry,' I yelped, whipping the umbrella up, only for it to jab into his leg. I dropped it hurriedly onto the step and attempted a confident smile. 'And sorry to keep you waiting, too. Clients, eh?'

'Indeed,' he said, his lips twitching into a smile.

I felt my face grow hot. I was referring to *my* client, who had made me late. My fault for not explaining, but he obviously thought I meant me being *his* client, which made me feel even more embarrassed.

He lowered his hood and I took a proper look at him. He had grey eyes behind slim trendy glasses, thick dark eyebrows and thick dark tufty hair. He wasn't at all like an axe murderer.

'Will your dog be all right in the car?' I hated awkward silences and had a tendency to fill them with mindless small talk. Of course the dog would be all right, it wasn't as if it was scorching hot or anything.

Nick looked over at his car and grinned. 'Oh, yes, he loves sleeping in the car. Loves sleeping full stop, actually.'

'I've never had a dog, or any pet, come to that,' I said. I'd never had the time or the space before. A dog would love it here, though.

I turned to unlock the front door. Last time it had opened smoothly, but today the key stuck in the lock. I set my bag down and twisted with both hands. My cheeks were pink and I could feel a prickle of heat under my armpits.

'I find dogs easier to get on with than people,' he said, watching me struggle with the lock. 'Would you like me to try?'

'No, I'm fine,' I grunted. 'Why's that then?'

'You know where you are with a dog. He's completely loyal, always in a good mood and loves me unconditionally.'

I laughed. 'He sounds better than my ex-boyfriend.'

'There you go, then.' Nick grinned. 'Are you sure I can't help you with that?'

I shook my head, gave the door a hard shove and it opened. A pile of junk mail had been wedged underneath it. I picked up the letters and surreptitiously laid a hand on my face. As I thought: I was steaming hot and probably purple with exertion.

We both edged into the hallway and I waited while he took off his shoes and coat and then I showed him into the living room.

Nick Cromwell wasn't as bulky as I'd first thought, I noted, as he hung his coat neatly over the back of a chair; it had been all jacket. He removed a notepad and a pencil from his rucksack and turned his phone onto silent and I supressed a smile at the precision of his movements.

'OK,' he said finally, 'I'm ready.'

'Can I offer you a drink?' I asked automatically, before remembering where I was.

Please say no.

'Yes, please.'

We both slurped away through straws at our cartons of blackcurrant juice, perched on the high-backed armchairs, teetering on the precipice of an awkward silence and for want of something to do, I pulled my sketchpad out of my bag and laid it on the coffee table between us.

Now we were here, I felt shy. This was a man who obviously saw himself as a champion of architectural heritage, passionate about preserving our old buildings for future generations. And I'd brought him to view a dreary, characterless 1930s bungalow. *Sorry, Great-aunt Jane, no offence.*

'So,' we both said at the same time, and then shared a polite laugh.

'You first,' I said.

'OK. So what are we talking about here, a replacement scheme?' Nick asked.

'Um?' I pulled a face, not sure what he meant. Windows maybe or carpets . . .

He took another sip from his straw and stretched a leg forward to deposit his carton on the table.

'A replacement scheme means demolishing this place and replacing it with something new, rather than, say, extending it,' he explained.

I watched in horror as the purple juice siphoned itself out of the carton and all over the cover of my sketchpad. I was only just starting to process his last statement when he lurched forward, cursing his clumsiness, and ripped the cover off the pad.

We both looked at the sketch he'd revealed in the coverless pad. It was entitled 'Bungalow Extension'.

I squeaked and grabbed the pad from him.

Nick groaned. 'Sophie – can I call you Sophie?'

I nodded.

'I apologize. I assumed that's what you wanted and with you mentioning *Grand Designs* on the phone the other day . . .' He shrugged awkwardly. He laid the wet paper on the hearth, straightened the straw to stop it dribbling and rubbed a hand over his face.

'Oh God, I'm making it worse,' he muttered.

'No, it's fine, really,' I blurted, placing the pad face down on the carpet. 'Ignore the drawing. I have no idea what I'm going to do with it. If anything. I'm open to suggestions, an extension, replacement, anything could happen at this stage.'

Nick stared at me for a moment as if checking I was telling the truth and then picked up his notepad.

'Music to my ears,' he said, writing the date neatly in the top corner of a clean page. 'Because sometimes it's cheaper and easier to knock down and start from scratch, than to attempt to shoehorn lots of new requirements into an existing bungalow.'

'I thought you were all for renovation and preservation,' I said, remembering his radio interview.

'When buildings are worth preserving, yes.'

What a cheek; I knew my first impression of the bungalow hadn't been exactly glowing, but even so.

'What I mean is,' he stammered, catching the look on my face, 'properties built in the nineteen thirties like this were often poor quality with no damp-proofing and no insulation.'

'I see,' I said briskly, insulted on Great-aunt Jane's behalf.

Nick swallowed and laughed nervously. 'I don't know what's come over me today, I'm not normally so clumsy or so terrible at expressing myself.'

'Good to know.' I smiled, taking pity on him.

He smiled back. 'Right. Well, I took the liberty of walking round the back before you arrived. Not that you kept me waiting long,' he added. 'And the good news is that the bungalow has never been altered since it was first built.'

'That's good news?' I frowned.

'Absolutely.' Nick pushed his glasses up with his index finger. 'It adds to the potential.'

My heart began to race. 'You think it has potential, then?'

'Definitely.' Nick nodded. 'You've got all sorts of options. Either you can extend as you've already drawn up . . .'

I flapped a hand at him. 'Please, forget you ever saw those.'

His lips twitched. 'OK. Or you could opt for the replacement scheme that I mentioned, or you could just apply for planning permission to build and sell the bungalow with the planning permission in place. It would be worth a lot more money then.'

'Wow! I'd never thought of any of that.' I grinned at him. 'Do you think we'd get permission for all those ideas in this village?'

Nick bunched his eyebrows up in thought. 'Planners are difficult to predict but I think we could make a strong case for the advantages of replacing the bungalow with a modern cottage.'

'That sounds lovely.' I sighed. A modern cottage. My own little house designed to my tastes, for my life. Somewhere to call home . . .

I sat up straight and coughed. No use in getting carried away. I needed to be practical about these things and, anyway, I wasn't sure how much any of this would cost.

'I'm a bit busy at the moment, so it might take me a few weeks but I could do a feasibility study for you, if you like?' Nick offered.

I nodded. 'Sounds great.' Whatever a feasibility study was.

'How long have you owned the property, Sophie?'

I felt my cheeks redden. 'I don't yet.'

Nick's eyebrows shot up.

'It's complicated,' I hesitated. Nick blinked at me, waiting for an answer. 'I've been left it in my great-aunt's will. She died recently.'

Nick's solemn grey eyes roamed the room and he nodded gently. 'I'm sorry to hear that.'

I smiled at him. 'Thank you.' I was just about to say that I hadn't known her when he reached across and touched my arm.

'You must have meant a lot to her.'

Oh, if only he knew. 'Really, why do you think that?' I asked.

'A home is the most precious gift you can give to someone,' he said with a soft laugh, 'well, except . . .' His voice faded away and he shifted awkwardly in his seat.

'Except?'

He cleared his throat and ruffled his hair. 'I was going to say except your heart,' he said shyly. 'Before I realized that it wasn't a very professional thing to say.'

We stared at each other and my heart squeezed for him. That was one of the sweetest things I'd ever heard. 'Maybe not professional,' I smiled, 'but absolutely true.'

A faint blush crept over Nick's face and he bent down over his bag.

'Do you mind if I take a couple of photographs?' he asked, producing an impressive-looking camera.

'Um, no, I suppose not.' My stomach flipped; I probably looked a complete mess and I quite possibly still had blood on my lip.

Nick fiddled with the lens cap and checked the settings. While he was distracted, I smoothed my hair down, straightened my coat and tried to remember the tips in *Heat* magazine. I think I was supposed to turn to the side, and then look back over my shoulder, tilting my chin up.

I sat up tall and plastered on a big smile. 'Ready.'

Nick stood up and blinked at me. 'Oh, not of you. Sorry, I meant pictures of the plot, the garden and the lane. For reference.'

I blushed furiously. 'Right, yes, of course. Thank goodness for that! Very professional camera!'

'It's a hobby of mine.'

'Really? What do you take pictures of?'

'Dogs mainly.'

'Really? Oh. How . . . unusual.' I coughed. 'Right, I'll show you out into the garden.'

I led Nick through the kitchen and out into the back garden. The rain had stopped, but the little patio was wet and slippery.

'I'll wait inside if you don't mind?' I said, mindful of my impractical shoes.

He was bent over his camera and didn't look up. 'Of course. Won't be long.'

Fifteen minutes later I was in the kitchen unearthing a drawer full of old receipts when Nick tapped on the kitchen window making me jump.

'I'm done,' he called.

'OK,' I replied, pressing a hand to my heart. 'I'll come out.'

I went outside to say goodbye. His dog was with him, on a lead. It was a rather stout beagle with a very waggly tail.

'I hope you don't mind the dog getting out,' said Nick, 'he needed to stretch his legs before we go home.'

'Not at all. Hello.' I held my hand out to stroke the dog. 'What's his name?'

The dog sniffed my hand and immediately jumped up, leaving two muddy paw prints on my coat.

'Norman, get down!' cried Nick, tugging at the dog.

'Hello, Norman,' I giggled.

'I'm so sorry, he gets excited around women,' said Nick,

looking a bit pink. He opened the car door and the dog bounded in.

'I take back what I said earlier,' I said, rubbing at my coat as Nick climbed into the car, 'he's actually a lot like my ex-boyfriend.'

Chapter 10

Jason, *The Herald*'s graphic designer, looked up from his computer screen and rocked his chair back until it was balanced on two legs.

'You got another meeting with the board?' he grunted, staring at my outfit.

I sighed inwardly at his attitude. We used to be mates but since I'd been given this new project, he had barely spoken to me. And when he did speak, it was usually to make snide remarks.

Jason was convinced that the social media project was rightly his; according to him he spent his whole life online and was adamant that he would have done a better job than me. I didn't like to point out that recording every aspect of his life via Instagram was not what the newspaper meant by a fully integrated digital communications strategy.

In truth, I'd begun to wish that he *had* been given the project instead of me. My initial enthusiasm had worn off; I'd had to write countless social media policies, I was in and out of meetings constantly, Donna was breathing down my neck every five minutes and, to cap it all, I hadn't been given a pay rise or promotion for the privilege.

'What makes you say that?' I sighed, flicking a quick glance over my new blazer, dress and knee-length leather boots.

I had booked the afternoon off work to go and see the architect who had phoned to say that he had completed his feasibility study on the Lilac Lane bungalow and inviting me to go and see his portfolio. The portfolio bit sounded like a cheesy chat-up line to me and I'd sniggered at first but apparently he'd been deadly serious. Anyway, I hadn't been conscious of making a specific effort with my clothes but I probably did look smart.

'You always look a bit more, you know,' Jason waved his hand around his face and chest, 'when you've got a board meeting.' He made apostrophes with his fingers around the word board. Very childish.

'I look a bit more what?' I jammed my hands on my hips.

Jason dropped his chair back onto four legs and squinted at his screen. 'Tarty,' he smirked.

I gasped and reached for my compact mirror but my mobile rang before I had chance to inspect my face.

'Tut tut. Taking personal calls. What would the board say about that?' Jason added slyly.

It was Mr Whelan. My pulse started to race.

'It's not personal, it's business,' I said haughtily if not entirely truthfully.

Grabbing the phone, I disappeared to a quiet corner of the department and sat down in a comfy swivel seat as far away from Jason as I could get.

My Whelan had been quiet for the past few weeks, although he assured me that he was 'setting the wheels in motion'. One of his first jobs was to arrange a meeting with my father in order for the will to progress. I knew he had contacted him and we were waiting for Terry Stone to confirm when he would be arriving in the country.

Consequently, I turned into a gibbering wreck whenever the solicitor's number flashed up on my phone. Even the thought of talking about the impending meeting with my father was enough to send my blood pressure skywards. I knew that at some point Mr Whelan would be ringing with news of the time and place and this call could be it.

'Bad news, I'm afraid. Mr Stone can't make it to the UK until August,' said Mr Whelan.

August was ages away! A lump in my throat throbbed and I wilted in my chair. Did I really have to have this hanging over me like a storm cloud for months?

'He's trying to get out of it, isn't he?' I said, my heart hardening by the second.

As far as I was concerned, it was fine for me to dread meeting Terry Stone, but unforgivable if he were to try to do the same. I was an abandoned child, after all.

'I don't think so.' The solicitor was being cagey. I knew him well enough by now. Certainly better than I was ever going to know my own father, by the look of things.

'He has absolutely no idea what this delay means to me.' I frowned down the phone.

Honestly, the nerve of the man! My father, not Mr Whelan. Meet him and move on. That had been my plan. Ha! That's what happens when you plan. It backfires.

I wasn't sure I could maintain my web of deceit with my mum that long. This was only going to work if I could get the meeting over with quickly. And, I realized with a sinking sensation, I was due to visit her in Spain in August. How was I going to fit that in now?

I swivelled my chair from side to side, pushing off from

the wall and grimacing at the black marks I'd made on the white paint.

'I don't think it can be avoided in this instance.'

'Why not? Why can't he put himself out?'

'I'm not at liberty to say, Miss Stone, but I believe something has come up. A personal matter.'

'Oh, well, if it's a *personal* matter, that's fine then. We wouldn't want his daughter, who he's never even met, to stand in the way of a personal matter,' I muttered through gritted teeth.

I added 'inconsiderate' and 'selfish' to the list of insults I was intending to hurl at him when he eventually deigned to get off his unreliable backside and cross the Atlantic.

'I'll just pencil it in my diary then, shall I, in case something else comes up?' I could hear the sarcasm in my voice. A prickle of shame slithered its way down my back. Poor Mr Whelan, it wasn't his fault.

'There's nothing stopping you emailing him yourself,' the solicitor suggested. 'I could put you in touch directly, if you wish?'

'No, no. No rush,' I said hastily.

'But I thought—'

'Thanks, but no thanks.'

Despite my protestations, I did feel a pathetic sense of relief at the delay. And I certainly didn't want any extra-curricular communications. No, I preferred to keep Terry Stone at arm's length – Mr Whelan's very long arm.

On the other end of the phone, the solicitor was being uncharacteristically quiet. I put my rant on hold.

'Is there something else?' I asked.

'It's rather awkward, really. Until the conditions of your

great-aunt's will have been met, I'm afraid I can't release the funds or sign over her property to you.'

Oh. That was a nuisance. Now that I'd finally been jolted out of my terminal apathy, I had a list of things I wanted to do: buy a car, replace most of my clothing, do something with the bungalow . . . all this would have to wait. And I had an appointment with Nick this afternoon too.

If I wasn't careful, when I eventually did have some serious money, it would disappear as fast as a Solero ice cream on a hot day. Perhaps some advice wouldn't go amiss?

'Mr Whelan,' I sighed, 'could you recommend a good financial advisor?'

'Do you have a pen handy? I'll give you Max Fitzgerald's email address.'

I scribbled down the information, said goodbye to Mr Whelan and emailed the financial advisor immediately. *And to think I used to be a serial procrastinator*, I mused happily . . .

Chapter 11

I left the office as planned at two o'clock and jumped on a bus, which took me out of the city centre, into the suburbs and dropped me in an unfamiliar, quiet residential area with nothing like an architect's studio in sight.

I checked the piece of paper that I'd scribbled Nick's address down on.

Yep. Definitely in the right place. Perhaps he worked from home?

It was a pleasant, if slightly dull, crescent-shaped road lined with pairs of post-war, semi-detached houses. I walked straight ahead, scanning the buildings to check for house numbers.

The address he had given me led to a house with a racing-green front door. The front garden had a neat lawn and I recognized his grey car parked on the gravel driveway.

I had no idea about his marital status, I realized. He could be married with five children, for all I knew. Or he could still live at home with his parents. Or alone. A shiver of apprehension ran through me.

There were two door bells. One had a small label on it marked *Cromwell Associates*, which looked promising, so I pressed it and stood back, peering through the bay window for signs of other possible inhabitants but slim Venetian blinds blocked my view. I thought I heard the dog barking in the garden, but no one answered the door. I pressed the bell again, this time taking several paces back to check the upstairs windows for movement.

A wooden gate opened at the side of the drive and Nick appeared with his dog.

'You found us, then?' He laughed awkwardly. 'Obviously. Stupid thing to say, sorry.'

'Yes.' I nodded equally superfluously. 'I did.'

We stared at each other until he waved his arm. 'Come in, come in!'

The garden was large, square and mainly grass. No signs of old people, or wives or any kids. Just several chewed tennis balls on the lawn. There was a patio at the back of the house and slabs continued in a path to the bottom of the garden. All very ordinary-looking, except for an ultra-modern wooden and glass cabin at the end of the path.

'It's a while since I've been led up the garden path,' I said with a laugh as I followed behind him towards the cabin.

He turned and stared at me in alarm.

'You're in perfectly safe hands, I assure you,' he said sincerely. 'I never mix business with pleasure. I'm very strict about that.'

'Well, that's a relief,' I said, raising an eyebrow and trying not to sound too offended.

That told me.

It was a perfectly acceptable policy to have, I acknowledged, but there was no need to be quite so blatantly disinterested. A teeny bit of flattery wouldn't have gone amiss, even if it was only in a being-nice-to-a-client way.

Nick blinked and I thought for a moment that he was

going to say something else but the dog got in there first and started licking my hand.

'Get down, Norman!' said Nick. 'He's a bit of an attention seeker, I'm afraid.'

'I don't mind.' I bent down and held out my hand to the dog, which he sniffed and then promptly rolled over on his back.

'Shame I don't have this effect on the other men in my life,' I giggled.

Nick eyed me quizzically and we both looked down at Norman who was casually displaying his doggy tackle. I felt my face heat up.

'Um, his name suits him,' I said, in an attempt to navigate the conversation to safer waters.

'Thanks, I named him after Norman Foster.'

'Oh?' I must have looked blank.

'The British architect? You know – he designed the Gherkin in London.'

'Ah yes,' I said, '*that* Norman Foster.'

If I ever went on *Who Wants to Be a Millionaire*, Nick was going to be on my phone-a-friend list.

He held the door open for me and I went in.

Bookshelves covered one entire wall, holding trade journals, thick folders and neat piles of brick and roof tile samples. The opposite side contained a scarily tidy white and chrome desk on which sat the biggest computer screen. A matching round table took up the centre of the room, with a state-of-the -art coffee machine squeezed in near the door.

I loved it. It was nicer than our flat.

'It's a bit like the Tardis in here!' I said, taking a seat. The dog settled himself across my feet. 'Very smart. In fact, it's the nicest office I've ever been in.'

Nick smiled and a dimple appeared in his left cheek. 'Thank you. I particularly like the short commute.' He picked up two small white mugs from a tray. 'Coffee?'

I wasn't keen on posh coffee; it was always too strong and made your breath smell. But I couldn't see any tea-making facilities and didn't want to be any trouble.

'Yes, please.'

He switched on the machine and handed me a document to read while he made the drinks.

'My report. As I thought, there are no obvious obstacles to planning permission on your bungalow. Extension or complete replacement. Perfectly feasible. The site is ripe for development. Up to you.'

My budget, I thought. *That's a potential obstacle.* But I had a hastily organized meeting with Max Fitzgerald, the financial advisor, later on, which should give me some idea of what was achievable with my small fortune.

I flicked through the report obediently while the coffee machine hissed and steamed and Nick fiddled about with sugar and milk.

'Nick, this is brilliant. I love all the pictures you've put in. Thank you so much,' I exclaimed.

The report was far more detailed than I'd expected and the sight of the little bungalow – my little bungalow – made my heart jolt with unexpected affection.

'You're welcome,' he said, placing a mug of coffee in front of me. It was covered in thick frothy milk and topped with cocoa powder. It smelt divine. 'There's no rush, of course, take it away and read it thoroughly and if you've got any questions, I'm only at the end of the phone. Or you could visit again?'

We exchanged smiles and my heart gave a second jolt.

Nick was quite a sweetie really, obviously not great with women, or perhaps people in general, but he had such an endearing shyness that made me feel almost protective towards him.

'Right,' said Nick, breaking the moment. 'Time to bore you rigid with this.'

He fetched a large black folder from the bookcase and laid it on the table. It took up most of the space and I edged my mug closer towards me for safety.

'If you do decide to go ahead with any building work in Lilac Lane, it might help to see some of my work. Perhaps it would give you an idea of the possibilities.'

'Ah yes, your portfolio.' I twinkled my eyes at him, picked up my cup, blew on the froth and sipped it delicately. See, I could be grown up: no sniggering at all this time.

Nick opened the folder and I edged my chair towards him so that I could see more clearly. I sneaked a quick look at him while he talked me through some of his previous projects. The folder contained a mixture of architect's drawings and before and after photographs. I detected a note of pride in his voice and his face became animated as he pointed out the details of his designs.

I had a sudden vision of him as a solemn-faced little boy sitting at his mum's kitchen table, trying to draw the perfect skyscraper, completely absorbed in his make-believe world.

A bit like me and my doll's house.

'It's amazing what can be done,' he was saying, pointing to a photograph of a house with a massive extension, 'even with the most unpromising properties.'

I coughed.

'Not that . . . I mean, yours isn't. Yours is very promising.' Nick gave his glasses a quick polish. 'More coffee?'

I shook my head. It was delicious but still very hot and I'd hardly touched it.

'Oh,' I gasped, pointing to a country cottage with a huge glass extension on the back. 'Tell me about that one.'

'Ah! Now, that's in Woodby too, funnily enough.' Nick smiled proudly, tapping the photograph. 'Belongs to Mr and Mrs Lafleur. One of my favourite projects. We salvaged a rundown cottage and brought it into the twenty-first century. Do you like it?'

He ran a hand through his hair while I stared at the pictures.

It was absolutely gorgeous. If he could do that with an old cottage, imagine what he could do for me – I mean my bungalow. Nick had amazing talent, truly amazing. I still had a variety of hurdles to overcome yet, sorting out my finances and – gulp – meeting my father, but despite all of that, I had a feeling that he was the right man for the job.

And until this precise moment, I hadn't known what the job was. But now I did.

Nick cleared his throat, waiting for my response.

'Oh,' I stammered. 'Yes please.'

Nick raised a worried eyebrow. 'I don't think it's for sale, I'm afraid.'

'But that mix of old and new . . . I love it. Last time you mentioned a lovely modern cottage to replace the bungalow?' I said. 'Do you think you could design one for me?'

I blinked furiously. It appeared I had just engaged an architect. That was a surprise, not to mention a bit spontaneous. I wasn't especially known for my spontaneity when it came to decision-making.

Nick stared at me, his dark grey eyes looking slightly

startled. 'Are you sure? Don't you want to go and read the report in greater detail? Make a plan or something?'

I pulled a face. 'Gosh! I don't plan.' I grimaced, making air apostrophes round the word plan? 'I'm more of a "seat of the pants" sort of girl.'

Nick nodded, although his expression was one of confusion. I bet he was a planner. I bet he had a diary with everyone's birthday in it and recorded the number of miles to the gallon he'd done every time he put petrol in his car.

'Right,' said Nick, 'well, in that case I'd be delighted to design a replacement scheme for you, Sophie.'

He extended a hand very formally, which I took. And shook. It was dry and warm, his nails were clean and short, long fine fingers. Nothing like Marc's, which were quite sausagey with bitten nails. Nick coughed. I blushed and released his hand.

'First I'll need a brief, can you send me one?'

'A brief?' I suppressed a snort. Not briefs. *Grow up, Sophie.*

'An idea of style,' he said, waving a hand at his portfolio. 'Sketches, pictures, written description. However you like. It's fairly straightforward, even for, er . . .' He flicked a glance at me.

An idiot? I bit my lip.

'. . . a novice.'

'Absolutely!' I grinned. I'd been designing my perfect home in my imagination since I was a little girl. I didn't need asking twice!

'I need to see some idea of your preferences,' he said. 'Oh, and the Grand Designs Live show is on at the exhibition centre in a couple of weeks' time. That would give you lots of ideas. I've got a spare ticket if you would like to go?'

The coffee scorched my throat as I swallowed a huge mouthful. I gave a yelp and panted to cool my throat.

'Sophie?'

Now he thinks I'm panting at him.

'Burnt my throat,' I croaked.

'Would you like a ticket?'

I chewed my lip.

Him and me. A whole day together. Was this his idea of a date? What would we talk about? I wasn't sure if I was flattered or freaked out. But I loved *Grand Designs*, I'd never been to the live show and it would be useful, plus I would have my own personal expert on hand to give me advice. I could always find some excuse to wander off on my own if we ran out of things to say to each other.

'Oh, so we could go together? Um, great idea. Thank you.'

'Er, ah, no,' stuttered Nick. 'Not together. I'll be working. Giving a talk, actually. I need to get there very early so . . . er . . .'

'Of course,' I trilled, hoping my cheeks didn't betray my embarrassment. 'I might see you there. Or not.'

Oh cheeseballs! It wasn't a date, then. Now I was disappointed. Not because I fancied him. But who doesn't like being asked out? Served me right for jumping to conclusions.

He strode over to his desk and began rummaging in the drawers.

'Here we go. Found it. Oh, I've got several. You could take a friend, perhaps? Girls, um, women, er, ladies love shopping, don't they?' he said, shoving a handful of tickets at me.

Oh yes, shopping, baking cakes, sewing a fine seam . . .

103

He must have spotted my expression and pushed his glasses further up his nose with a forefinger. 'That came out wrong.'

'Not at all. Good idea, we'll have a girls' day out. Thank you. Good grief, is that the time? I'd better be off to my next meeting,' I said, pushing myself up from the table before either of us had chance to say the wrong thing again.

'Right,' said Nick, rocking back on his heels. 'Keep in touch.'

We shook hands again and this time I made sure not to cling onto his fingers too long and he waved me off from the gate.

'Bye!' I called. 'I'll be back with my briefs, I mean brief, just as soon as I can.'

As I walked away, I checked back over my shoulder to see if he was still watching me. He was. My architect . . . I had employed an architect. I exhaled deeply and my stomach performed a tiny somersault; I had the feeling that I'd just made one of the most important decisions of my life.

Chapter 12

By six thirty I was in a small office sitting on the visitor's side of a pale wooden desk. The financial advisor bounced back in a leather chair with the nervous energy of someone who does not like to sit still for long. I had just been asked where I currently kept my savings and I had a feeling that my answer hadn't gone down well.

'In the post office?' Max Fitzgerald repeated incredulously.

I nodded again, this time less confidently.

What exactly was wrong with keeping your savings in the post office anyway? The way I saw it, it was the only bank where all the staff looked poor. You didn't see the postman swanning round in a Bentley flashing his Rolex watch as he dipped his hand in and out of his big sack. Jess had gone out with a postman once, mainly because of his uniform. He turned out to be a bit dull, but had incredible calf muscles.

I was also feeling a bit wrong-footed because I had been expecting Max Fitzgerald to be a fusty old man with tufty ear hair and a black ledger that sent clouds of dust into the air when he snapped it shut. Instead, Max*ine* was an impeccably coiffed thirty-something, with a sharp suit, sharp tongue and a sharp retractable pencil which, following my revelation, was hovering over her notepad.

'You can trust the post office,' I said darkly.

I remember trooping down to the post office to open my first savings account when I was eleven. I had proudly handed over my red plastic moneybox filled with coins. The adults flashed indulgent smiles at me and my mum as I signed my name in the box for the first time. By the time the cashier had finished counting out all the change, however, a red-faced queue of impatient pensioners had built up and Mum had hustled me out. Despite that slightly fraught experience, I had been a dedicated saver ever since, squirrelling away ten per cent of my earnings every month since I was eighteen.

'Sophie, you have built up considerable savings. The funds should be working for you in ISAs, or high-interest savings accounts, or fixed-rate bonds, not just sitting there. Unless this money is for a particular short-term purpose?'

I shook my head. 'My long-term goal has always been to own my own home.'

'And?' Max blinked furiously. 'What's stopping you?'

Keep saving. Make sure you're secure. You never know what the future's going to bring. This was my mantra and I'd been chanting it for so long, I didn't even think about it any more.

'If I buy a house, I won't have any money left and I won't feel secure.'

My mum had a 'live for the moment' attitude to savings, i.e. she didn't have any. And this had led to some extremely insecure moments in my childhood, moments that I had no desire to relive.

Max sighed and a shadow of irritation crossed her face. 'You are sitting on savings of twenty thousand pounds. I could easily have secured you a mortgage by now. Have you never done any financial planning? Have you thought about the future?'

I shuffled in my hard-backed, unbouncy chair.

How could I put into words that until this last month I hadn't wanted to think about the future? My life hadn't really moved on in the last ten years. And that was down to me, I accepted that. I had been jogging on the spot and going nowhere. Now that I gave it some proper thought, I felt a bit of a wuss.

Well, not any more. I cleared my throat. I was going to grasp my future and any new opportunity that came my way and live life on the edge.

'Do you think I could get a mortgage for this?' I withdrew Nick's feasibility report from my handbag and told her about my dream to create my own home.

Max flicked through her notes, tapped on her calculator, scribbled some figures down on her pad and then beamed at me.

'Well,' she began, turning her notes around so I could read them, 'based on your salary, I think you could borrow as much as this.'

My eyes took in the row of noughts on the page and my mouth went dry. The amount Max was suggesting was a small fortune.

'That should just about cover it,' I stuttered.

What a day, I mused on my way out of Max's office. I'd spoken to a solicitor, an architect and a financial advisor all in one day. I felt very pleased with myself and what's more the beginnings of an action plan were starting to form in my rusty brain. *An action plan*. I liked the sound of that. And the first action would be to write a design brief for my lovely modern cottage and send it to Nick. I bought the equivalent of my own body weight in glossy homes magazines, jumped on a bus and went home.

There was no one in at the flat. Fantastico! Some privacy. I could get part one of the plan under way immediately.

I sat down at our tiny kitchen table and began flicking through my new magazines. Thirty seconds later I heard a key in the lock and in waltzed Jess, humming 'A Spoonful of Sugar'. She flung down her bags in the hall and joined me in the kitchen.

'Hiya,' she said, dropping a magazine next to mine on the table. It was entitled *Tomorrow's Leaders Today*.

'Hey.' I smothered a smile; my magazines looked a lot more fun.

Jess had been chosen to become the new deputy head teacher from September. While this was wonderful and much deserved, she had turned into a bit of a career bore and was taking her promotion ultra-seriously.

'Planning, preparation and perseverance,' she informed us on a regular basis. 'That's what it takes to get ahead.'

'I thought it was: "If you want to get ahead, get a hat",' I'd dared to reply on one occasion, at which Emma had hooted with laughter. Jess had simply shaken her head sadly at the two of us.

Privately, we couldn't wait for her relationship with the policeman to move to *the next level*, so we'd get a break. She was due to go all moony and floaty any day soon.

'How did the meeting with the architect go?' she asked, putting the kettle on.

'Brilliant.' I took a deep breath. 'I've asked him to design me a new house.'

Jess broke off from making tea to give me a hug. 'How exciting, Soph!'

I swallowed. 'It is, isn't it?'

My eyes flicked up to the kitchen ceiling. There was a yellow patch where the roof had leaked and the landlord hadn't got round to repainting it. Two of the cupboard doors didn't close properly and one of the rings on the hob didn't work. It was no wonder that I didn't like cooking.

Despite its shortcomings, this flat had been my sanctuary, cocooning me from the outside world for years. We all still lived like students and part of me (the biggest, cowardliest part) wanted to stay exactly as we were. That wasn't possible, though. At least not for me; Great-aunt Jane's will would change everything. Life as I knew it was running out and it made my heart thump every time I thought about it.

Jess set a mug of tea down in front of me and gazed at me intently, concern etched into her well-meaning face. 'You're doing great, Sophie,' she said kindly, patting my hand.

I grinned at her gratefully. 'Thanks, Jess. I don't fancy cooking, do you? Shall we have Chinese tonight?'

She nodded and I leapt up from the table to retrieve the menu.

The remains of a Chinese banquet littered the living-room floor. Tinfoil dishes barely touched, piles of congealing spare ribs and a mountain of prawn crackers pointed greasy fingers at our excessive over-ordering.

'Who's having the last sweet and sour prawn ball?' I said, holding it precariously between my chopsticks.

'Over here,' said Emma, holding up her plate.

Jess groaned. 'No more for me. I've got Stuffed-a-litis,' she said from her position flat out on the floor.

We all giggled and I sighed with contentment. We'd had a massive discussion about my inheritance and meeting my dad in August and the architect business and they'd both agreed I was doing the right thing. I didn't know what I would do without Emma's dogged loyalty and Jess's gentle support.

The entry buzzer sounded. Jess squeaked and sat up instantly. 'That'll be Spike. He finished work at nine. He said he'd come straight round. In his uniform!'

'I hope we won't be seeing his truncheon,' sniggered Emma.

'They use a collapsible baton these days,' said Jess primly. She pushed herself up from the carpet, checked her face in the mirror over the mantelpiece and fluffed up her hair.

'You've had a conversation about truncheons?' I asked, cocking an eyebrow at her preening.

She giggled in response and dashed to the door as the buzzer was pressed a second time. Emma and I exchanged amused glances. We were yet to meet Jess's new hero, although it felt as if we knew him already.

'Come up,' she yelled into the intercom.

I strained my ears, grinning in anticipation of their kissy-kissy hello.

The door opened and there was a pause before Jess finally invited him in.

She came back in almost immediately, a look of confusion on her face.

'It's for you,' she said, her eyes scanning mine. I could see she was panicking, unsure if she had done the right thing. I reassured her with a smile.

Marc stood behind her. All shoulders and stubble, sexy and sultry. His face broke into a lazy grin and he held out a bunch of flowers. I cursed my body's reaction, but couldn't help it; the sight of Marc Felton in my living room sent my libido soaring skywards, diving into a fluffy white cloud and kicking her heels in the air with abandon.

Emma looked from me to him and back to me and tutted with undisguised loathing.

Be cool, Sophie. He might have just lost another CD.

I stood up, sending a shower of egg fried rice to the floor.

'I'm as stuffed as a pot-bellied pig,' I said, patting my stomach.

Very classy. Seriously, I could not be less seductive if I tried.

Jess dipped her head to stifle a laugh, Emma started to choke and the bunch of flowers in Marc's hand drooped a little.

'Flowers, how lovely!' I took them from him and sniffed. All I could smell was Marc's rather pungent deodorant, but they looked pretty.

'Which petrol station are they from, Esso or Texaco?' muttered Emma, still wheezing. 'Take them out, Sophie, I'm allergic.'

They did look as if they'd come straight off the forecourt, but he had never bought me flowers before. Ever.

I headed to the kitchen to find a vase and Marc followed close behind.

'Fancy going for a drink?' He snaked his arms round my waist, nestled his chin against my cheek and pulled my body backwards to meet his.

Hold on a minute! Flowers, drinks, dangerously close body positions. Was this a date? My mind zoomed back several hours to when I had asked myself the same question about Nick's proposition. I had been wrong then. I didn't want to end up with egg on my face. I brushed my hand over my mouth. Or rice.

The warmth of his body against mine was electrifying, his breath soft in my ear. I slowly wrapped my arms over his. The moment felt magical and I could so easily have fallen under his spell . . .

Sophie, we've spoken about this, cool and detached, remember?

I took a deep breath.

'Actually, Marc,' I whirled round to face him and eased his body away from mine, 'I've got work to do. Sorry. My architect . . .' I paused letting the words sink in and noticing, with some satisfaction, Marc's pupils dilate, 'is waiting for an important document from me. I really don't have time right now.'

A shadow passed over Marc's face before he collected himself, shrugged and gave me a peck on the cheek. 'No worries, princess, another time, yeah?'

I smiled non-committally and showed him to the door, eminently proud of myself. If – and it was a big if I took him back it would be on my terms. No turning up unexpectedly and expecting me to drop everything. He couldn't just call me 'princess', he had to treat me like one too. Then, and only then, would I let Marc Felton back into my life.

I closed the door on him and turned round to see Emma leaning on the doorframe, arms folded, a big grin plastered across her face.

'I'm liking this new Sophie.'

'Ha! Me too,' I laughed, 'me too.'

Chapter 13

The flat, Midlands landscape flashed by through the grimy window of the train. Power stations, rivers and fields blurred with motorways, houses and shops as I sipped my tea and hummed the *Grand Designs* theme tune under my breath.

It was a sunny Saturday morning in early June and I was on my way to the exhibition. Sadly, the girls' day out that I'd envisaged hadn't materialized.

Jess had made plans with Spike, her policeman. I had finally met him last weekend. He was tall and thin with the most alarming hair, which stayed spiky even under his helmet. But what had surprised me most was how quiet he was, I would almost go as far as to describe him as sullen. Apart from the physique and the uniform, I couldn't see what Jess saw in him. But she was undeniably smitten, so I couldn't help but be glad for her.

Emma was otherwise engaged, too, making a pair of matching platinum wedding rings for a couple who had seen her silver platter for the Lord Mayor. I had never seen this platter, although Emma had talked about it so much I felt like I'd designed the bloomin' thing myself. More importantly, other people were talking about it too and that had resulted in more lucrative commissions than she had ever had.

Our lives were beginning to pull in different directions. Gone were the girlie nights in together, the Saturday mornings spent sitting on the sofa chatting away in our pyjamas. Jess was spending more and more time at Spike's house and Emma was often at the studio until all hours. Perhaps this was what happens, I reflected glumly. Friends grow up and away from each other, like little moons joining somebody else's orbit.

I opened my bag and removed the tickets Nick had given me and a show guide I'd printed off the website, plus a checklist he'd sent me of things to consider in my brief. Bricks, tiles, windows, lighting, flooring . . . The list was a bit daunting, to be honest. Perhaps it was just as well I was alone; at least I would be able to explore the show at my own pace.

I flicked through the show guide to the events schedule and stopped at the eleven o'clock seminar entitled: *Let There Be Light by Nick Cromwell – illumination and other bright ideas.*

Would he want me to go and listen to him speak? Would he prefer me to *not* go and listen? What if I didn't go and he was offended? After all, he had mentioned it and he had given me free tickets. That could be construed as an invitation.

I would go and sit at the back, I decided, and if he caught my eye and looked horrified, I would sneak out.

After following the signs to the exhibition, giving my spare tickets away and queuing to enter, I was in. I only had five minutes before the start of Nick's talk and was going to have to hurry.

I glanced down at my feet. Dashing anywhere right now

might be a problem; my high heels were already killing me.

What had possessed me? I scolded myself, wincing and mincing my way along the main thoroughfare. All around me, women were bouncing along on their comfy air-filled soles, fully prepared for a day on their feet. At this rate, I would be on my knees by noon.

The lecture theatre was, naturally, right at the opposite end of the exhibition centre and by the time I arrived, there were barely any seats free. I hovered at the entrance, deciding where to sit. I did a rough count-up. There must have been over a hundred people in the audience.

I wondered how Nick was feeling. Waiting in the wings, probably, having a last-minute rehearsal. I couldn't imagine him speaking in public, in front of an audience of humans.

'Excuse me, dear.' A tiny old lady squeezed past me and eased herself into the last seat in the back row.

Now there was only one space left. Front row, obviously. I took a deep breath and tiptoed self-consciously up to the remaining seat, which was directly in front of the podium. So much for being unobtrusive and making an early exit. Never mind, I would pretend to make notes and avoid eye contact.

I joined in with the applause as a tanned compère appeared.

'Put your hands together and give a warm welcome to architect Nick Cromwell. As he says, "Let there be light".'

Nick appeared on stage, looking very professional in a smart grey suit and a purple tie. He stood at the podium and I saw his hands shake as the compère passed him the remote control for the projector. My seat was a mere two metres away from Nick's trembling trousers.

I slumped down in my seat and hoped he didn't think I was a stalker.

Nick turned to the audience and grimaced in lieu of a smile. Oh bless! I felt nervous for him.

As if he'd heard my thoughts, he looked straight at me. The controller slipped out of his hands and clattered to the floor near my feet. The projector screen came to life, flipping through image after image, racing through Nick's presentation. His mouth fell open and a look of panic crossed his face.

I jumped out of my seat and handed it up to him, giving my widest, most encouraging grin. He smiled back, mouthed his thanks and blew his cheeks out in a gesture of composure.

'Of all the elements that combine to create the ambiance of your home, light is the most magical,' he began.

And he was off. His thirty-minute speech flew by. I was enthralled. He was a different person, with his dazzling delivery, brilliant observations and expert knowledge. I felt like a proud parent.

That's my architect, I wanted to say to the lady sitting next to me, *isn't he good?*

I glanced round at the audience; they were hanging on his every word. It was obvious from his delivery how much he loved being an architect. I felt quite envious. I wished I was in a job where passion for my work spilled out so much that I inspired others like he did. What could I talk about with such intensity, such passion? I dredged the deep recesses of my brain for a few seconds, but other than being able to name all of Take That's number ones, I came up empty-handed.

'Thank you so much,' concluded a beaming Nick.

The audience was clapping, some people already on their feet, keen to move on to the next event. A couple approached Nick and he fished a business card out of his pocket. I pretended to check my phone to give me an excuse for not leaving straight away. The couple moved away and I saw my chance. I dropped my phone back into my bag and was just about to go over and invite him for coffee when a woman in a denim jacket and a flowery miniskirt pounced on him.

Oh bother, I'd have to leave now. Failure to do so would make me look like an adoring fan and it appeared he already had one of those.

I looked over at him one last time. He seemed relaxed, with his arms folded, leaning against the podium, nodding and smiling. I could only see her from behind, but I could tell from her stance that she was much younger than me. She had her hands clasped in front of her, pivoting from the knees like a child.

I turned away disappointed. Back outside in the main hall, I consulted the show guide. High heels notwithstanding, I would spend the next two hours scouring the show for ideas, stop for some lunch and then rest my weary legs in the Grand Theatre to hear what TV presenter Kevin McCloud had to say.

By lunchtime, I was exhausted but exhilarated. I plonked a tray with a mug of milky tea and an over-priced and under-filled baguette down on the table with relief. The balls of my feet throbbed as if I'd ground them into hot coals, but I didn't care. My arms were aching under the weight of the brochures I'd collected, but I barely registered the pain. I was in my element.

Thank you, thank you, Nick, for suggesting that I came!

I was buzzing with inspiration, mind-blown with the things I'd seen. My list of 'must haves' had grown as I made my way round the show. I could envisage the mood boards I would pull together to give Nick; I could imagine exactly the sort of interiors I wanted to create for my own home. I could feel myself coming alive like a new leaf unfurling in the sunshine. My creative spirit, which had been supressed for so long, was waking up and I couldn't wait to get started.

I swallowed the last mouthful of my lunch and scanned the busy cafeteria for a place to stack my tray. My gaze encountered a familiar profile – dark tufty hair, wide forehead and slim glasses. My hand flew up in an automatic wave, but Nick was too engrossed in his companion to notice me. It was the girl from the lecture theatre; I recognized her from the denim jacket and flirty body language. I saw Nick smile and I felt an unexpected spark of jealousy fizz through me as his dimple appeared.

I felt myself frown and relaxed my face back into neutral. Where had those sudden feelings sprung from? I was getting carried away, I reassured myself. It would have been nice to share my day with another person, that was all. I was bursting with enthusiasm and ideas and wanted someone, anyone, to talk to.

The girl giggled as she flicked the end of his tie up in the air. I watched as Nick smoothed it back down and realized why I felt so put out.

He'd told me most firmly that he didn't mix business with pleasure. But maybe he'd just meant where I was concerned, because he was certainly having fun now. And for some reason that made me feel a little bit sad.

Chapter 14

The next morning I woke up as soon as the sunlight began to filter through a chink in the curtains. I rubbed the sleep from my eyes and sat up. My face broke into a smile as I remembered my plans for the day and I jumped out of bed and drew back the curtains. The turquoise sky was completely unbroken by cloud. It was a perfect English summer's day and the weather forecast had promised sunshine all day. I planned to take a rug outside and spend the whole day in the communal garden finishing off the design brief for Nick.

But first, I'd make some tea and call Mum.

Mug in hand, I padded back to bed, fired up my laptop and dialled her number.

Mum had grudgingly resumed contact on Skype, although she couldn't resist peppering her conversation with little digs about my decision to accept Great-aunt Jane's inheritance. I was determined to persevere; she was bound to defrost eventually. I would just have to convince her that my accepting the will wouldn't affect our relationship one bit.

This morning, Mum was wearing a tropical-print sarong, huge sunglasses and her hair was pinned up in a neat ballerina-style bun. She sucked in her cheeks and sipped at a glass of water.

'I suppose you'll be off somewhere exotic this August? Spain not good enough for you now, I should imagine, with your money,' she sniffed, launching straight into her favourite topic.

'Course not,' I soothed, biting my tongue as the lies tripped off it. 'I'm very busy at work so it might be September this year, before I can make it. When the weather has cooled a little bit.'

And your ex-husband is safely back on the other side of the pond, I added silently.

'You had your inheritance yet?' she added. 'Taking a long time, isn't it? That family was always slow to put their hands in their pockets.'

I shook my head, refusing to rise to the bait.

'I'm surprised the old lady didn't leave her estate to my father,' I ventured. Over the years, I had learned that I had to pick my moments to ask her anything about him. 'What sort of man was he, Mum?'

She rolled her eyes and her shoulders sagged. 'For goodness' sake, Sophie. Why all the questions?'

One question, I thought, *just one and why won't you answer it*? I closed my eyes, counted to three and changed the subject, although the topic was just as controversial.

'I've asked an architect to do some work for me in Lilac Lane, Mum.'

She pulled an appalled face. 'You're never going to live there? Just sell it! I don't understand why you would want to be tied down. What do you want to saddle yourself with a house for, and *there* of all places?'

I saw her shake her head and it took me right back to my

childhood. She could never understand my love of home-making.

'What happened to my doll's house, Mum, can you remember?' I said suddenly.

I had spent hours lost in a make-believe world inside those tiny rooms. It had been my favourite ever toy.

Mum scratched her nose. 'No idea.'

Now *she* was the one being economical with the truth. I could distinctly remember her handing it over to a man at the door in exchange for a handful of notes. I had cried for days.

'You're too old for make-believe now, Sophie,' Mum had scolded at the time.

I slurped my tea and considered tackling her about her big fat lie.

'Lost in the move, I expect,' she sighed now, pretending to inspect her nails as if the whole topic was too boring to bother with.

Which move? For her, our succession of flats and bedsits had never been important, just somewhere to leave her stuff. We had moved countless times while I was growing up. I knew now that occasionally we had had to move when she couldn't pay the rent.

I shuddered. I never wanted to live like that again.

The flat I shared with the Piper sisters was as close as I'd ever come to putting down any roots and that was what I longed to do. Build a home where my friends would gravitate to at weekends, at Christmas, barbeques in the summer and movies and popcorn on dark nights.

'Look, Sophie,' Mum moved closer to her computer screen and pushed her sunglasses up onto her head, 'why not forget all this architect nonsense and move over here?

We could use your money to buy a little bar and rent a villa.'

Good grief, much as I loved her, I couldn't think of anything worse. I shook my head and attempted to keep my voice level. 'It's a lovely idea. But I'm a homebird, Mum. Spain isn't for me.'

Mum dropped her sunglasses down, but I could still see the displeasure in her pinched lips. 'Where's your sense of adventure, girl? Sometimes I wonder whose daughter you are.'

You and me both, I reflected sadly as I ended the call. I wasn't at all like Mum, which was why I was so intrigued to know what sort of man Terry Stone was. My heart pounded suddenly: only eight weeks to go and I would be able to find out for myself.

By midday, I had arranged myself, a pile of magazines, sheets of card, scissors, glue and pens on a picnic blanket outside.

I leaned back on my heels happily. This was utter bliss. All those years of drawing fantasy houses with spiral staircases and four-poster beds, walk-in wardrobes and bath tubs the size of swimming pools, and finally I had the chance to do it for real.

I plucked a magazine off the top of the pile and flicked through it. The blingtastic tasteless pad of a lottery millionaire filled the first ten pages. I dropped it back down with a grin and picked up my sketchpad instead.

You could keep your palatial mansions; I wasn't interested in plush and fancy, or trendy and minimalist. I wanted my home to be a haven, like coming in from the cold to a big warm hug.

I selected a pencil, chewed the end and stared at the

blank page. Nick would design the building; all I had to do was to supply the detail, the feel, the heart of the home. All of a sudden, I felt awkward. I was only an enthusiastic amateur compared to him. What if my silly scribblings weren't good enough?

I took a deep breath. *Come on, Sophie, you used to love doing this. He's not the only one with passion. Have some confidence.*

I began to draw, slowly at first, letting my hand move across the page as if it had a mind of its own. A smile spread across my face – this felt good. I felt free and more alive than I had done in years. As my excitement bubbled, the ideas came faster and faster, filling page after page.

Big, folding glass doors opening out onto the garden, perfect for summer parties. A real log fire with a rustic fireplace. A kitchen big enough to actually cook in. Yep, I might even learn how to cook. A squishy sofa under the window where I could snuggle up and read. An en suite bathroom with a walk-in shower.

An hour later I had nearly finished the whole brief, all I had to do was stick in a few pictures from magazines to give an idea of materials and colours and I was done. I flicked through my drawings and stopped at the page showing the master bedroom. I'd sketched a king-sized bed in the middle of the room. I sighed and pulled up a tuft of grass, letting the cool green blades fall through my fingers.

Moving out of the flat meant leaving Emma and Jess behind. I'd accepted that. Despite my pleadings, they were adamant that they didn't want to move to Woodby. But the prospect of living on my own for the first time gave me butterflies.

What was the point of having a lovely home if I had no

one to share it with? Who would keep me company in that big bed?

Marc?

'No, I am an independent, intelligent woman,' I muttered to myself. *Besides, I don't need a man to be happy*, I thought as I finished off the design brief for my dream home. I was doing pretty well by myself these days.

Chapter 15

July had arrived, hot and sultry, and with it the best day ever. Well, I thought so, although I could tell without even looking at her that Emma was scowling.

'I think you're barmy. Bonkers. In need of serious help, in fact,' she said. 'He will be after your money, Sophie, I just know it.'

She was lying on my bed watching me get ready. The window was open to let in some precious fresh air and a delicious aroma of barbecue wafted in. I hadn't eaten because I was saving myself and the smell made my stomach rumble.

I ignored Emma and studied my reflection. Was green eyeliner too much with green eyes? I stood back from the mirror and blinked. No, I decided, brushing on some mascara. My eyes looked massive. And shining with happiness.

'I know you're just looking out for me. But can't you just be happy instead?' I pleaded. 'And have a little faith in me, hmm?'

Emma harrumphed and huffed, but I refused to let her spoil my good mood.

Today was going to go down in the History of Me as a particularly excellent day for three stonking reasons.

Number one: an email from the Managing Director this morning informed me that I was doing a marvellous job with *The Herald's* social media. Feedback from our advertisers was very encouraging, reader engagement was positive and so far I had far exceeded my targets for Facebook likes and Twitter followers.

This had made me smile. But nowhere near as much as my second reason. Nick Cromwell had also emailed me today. I'd read it so often that I knew it off by heart:

Sophie, received your brief today. I am very impressed! You have real talent. This is by far the best brief I have ever had for a project. Are you sure you haven't done this before?! I know exactly the sort of style you are looking for and I am very much looking forward to working on your project with you.
Nick

The architect approved of my efforts! He had even used exclamation marks! My face had glowed with pride for the rest of the afternoon.

I was still basking in his glorious words when the third reason for my jubilation had occurred: Marc had called, asking me out on a date.

Me. Marc. A date.

When he'd phoned I'd had no intention of going out with him. None whatsoever. But he'd rung to let me know that he'd finally left his job at the market and had started up his own business.

'I bought my first car from an auction, a couple of weeks ago. Just one,' he'd said humbly. 'I thought I'd start small and build it up. That way I don't need to borrow any capital.

Anyway, I've done the car up: new wheels, a paint job and twin exhaust and it's ready for re-sale. I wondered if you fancied going for a spin and maybe stopping at a pub, you know, no strings . . .'

I was so pleased and proud of him and if that wasn't proof that he wasn't interested in my money, then I didn't know what was.

'Oh Marc, well done you!' I'd cried. 'I'd love to come for a drive.'

Emma propped herself up on her elbows and kicked her legs in the air.

'If it was anyone else, I'd be ecstatic,' she grumbled. 'That architect, for example. You're always waffling on about him.' She paused waiting for a reaction from me. She didn't get one. 'But Marc?' she huffed. 'I thought we'd got rid of him.'

'This time I'm doing it differently, if he messes me about I'll be showing him the door,' I reassured her. Instead of showing him what a doormat I was, like I had done in the past. The past being the operative word. I was a new woman these days.

'And don't worry, I'll be taking it slow,' I added. 'No jumping back into bed with him at the first opportunity.'

I blushed, glad that she hadn't seen me slip into my best undies or I'd never have got away with that comment.

'Glad to hear it,' she said, jumping up and giving me a hug. 'You're just getting your life together again, Soph. I don't want the Incredible Hulk buggering it up for you.'

'He won't. I promise,' I said blithely.

I gave myself a final check in the mirror. In my summer dress and sandals with my dark curly hair loose around my shoulders, I felt very feminine. Marc would approve.

I picked up a cardigan, kissed Emma goodbye and ran downstairs.

Marc was waiting for me at the roadside, leaning out of the window of an electric-blue sports car.

'Get in then!' he called to me impatiently as a car tooted at him for double parking.

'Sorry, I was just giving you a twirl,' I grinned at him. 'Do you like my dress?'

'Very nice,' he said, glancing into his rear-view mirror and revving away. 'Let's go for a drive into the countryside and stop at a pub for a drink.'

'Great!' I pressed a hand against my grumbling tummy. Silly me for assuming 'date' meant 'dinner'.

'What do you think of the car?' he said with a grin.

'Great,' I said again. 'Very . . . sporty.'

Marc's car was extremely noisy, making conversation difficult so I contented myself with sneaking a peak at his handsome profile instead. We were soon on the ring road and then the dual carriageway and finally we left the suburbs behind.

'Hey, we're not far from Woodby,' I shouted above the throb of the engine, as we sped along winding country lanes.

'Yeah?' Marc flashed me one of his knee-trembling smiles and a minute later we pulled up outside a quaint little pub.

As we walked up to the bar, Marc took hold of my hand. I saw our reflection in the mirrored panel behind the counter. We looked like a couple. Perhaps we were a couple? My heart began to pummel my chest at the speed of the William Tell Overture and my cheeks flushed. I squeezed his hand back and gave him my best twinkly smile.

'What can I get you?' he said.

A lie-down in a darkened room, preferably with you? I remembered belatedly my promise to Emma to take it slow and let go of his hand.

'White wine, please,' I replied.

A barmaid, almost wearing a black vest top, pouted her shiny pink lips at Marc as she took his order. She flicked her hair over her shoulder and managed to look down her nose at me at the same time. I placed a hand nonchalantly on Marc's arm but he hitched his shoulder up as if I was tickling him and I saw her smirk.

'And one for yourself.' He winked at her.

'Shall we go outside?' I said brightly as Marc handed me my wine.

The pub had a large patio festooned with hanging baskets and planters stuffed with bright summery flowers. Marc steered us over to the only free picnic bench, took a long drink from his pint and gave an appreciative sigh.

'This is nice, isn't it?'

The table wobbled every time one of us moved and I clutched the edge of it and tried to relax. 'Yes, lovely.'

It was nice: summer's evening, country pub, handsome, attentive man at my side. Maybe I was just out of practice with the whole romantic date thing, but my insides were churning with nerves.

Were we getting back together? I needed to know where I stood, but was too scared to ask. Hardly a good advertisement for women's lib, was I? If a relationship takes two, surely I had some say in the matter?

Go on then, say something!

Yes, yes, I will. When I've finished this drink.

I cast my eye around the patio in search of something

to talk about. In front of us was a couple with a sleeping toddler in a pushchair. The mum, roughly my age, had her blonde hair swept up into a perfect bun. Lucky thing, I couldn't even manage a pony tail without it going all lumpy. She was wearing white linen trousers, a black vest top and flip-flops. On me that sort of outfit would look scruffy, but she looked elegant and sexy.

Her man obviously thought so too; he pulled her towards him and gave her a long and sexy kiss. Wow! I averted my eyes. I was a bit prudish about snogging in public. This couple certainly weren't, though. Their little boy woke up and started to whimper. They both smiled and rolled their eyes at the interruption.

'So what's new on the property front, then?' asked Marc, dragging his eyes away from a table of raucous women in the corner. 'How's it going with the architect?'

'Good! He's designing me a brand-new house.'

Marc's eyes widened. 'Really?'

I nodded.

'I'm impressed.' He squeezed my shoulder and I tried not to wince. He didn't know his own strength sometimes. 'My little mouse! Property developing, eh?'

He gave me a noisy kiss on the cheek.

OK, so *mouse* wasn't the most promising of endearments. And *my* mouse – did I want to be his? The jury was still out on that one, I decided.

'Well, I wouldn't call it that,' I laughed modestly.

'Big place, is it? Plenty of potential?' His eyes were totally locked on mine. And I had to admit – it felt wonderful.

'We could go and look at it if you like?' I took a sip of wine. 'It's only about ten minutes from here.'

'Really? What a coincidence! Great idea.' He drained

his pint and pulled me up from the bench.

'Now? Oh. OK.'

I took a huge gulp of wine as Marc grabbed my hand and pulled me across the patio. Help! I couldn't swallow and trot at the same time in these shoes. I had a face like a pufferfish as I passed the elegant mother. She smiled. I smiled back and squirted a jet of warm wine at her child's pushchair. I shot her a look of panicky apology but she was too busy mopping up to notice, an expression of disgust on her face.

I was right; we were only ten minutes from Woodby. But it was half an hour before we pulled into Lilac Lane. My sense of direction wasn't that great and Marc's car, for all its fancy accessories, didn't have SatNav.

Marc hadn't spoken to me for the last twenty minutes. When I'd tried to hold his hand that was on the gear stick, he had moved it to tweak the volume on the stereo and I was sensing an atmosphere. In my defence, I hadn't been planning on coming to Woodby, or else I'd have brought a map with me. And the keys to the bungalow, I realized belatedly.

'This is it,' I said with relief, pointing to the driveway of number eight.

I realized with a pang of guilt that I hadn't been here since showing the architect round back in the spring. But strictly speaking, it wasn't my property yet and I wasn't totally sure I should be here now.

The little bungalow looked a lot more inviting now it was summer. The bay windows seemed less prison-like, the grass was neat and the side border was brimming with purple and white flowers. Even the thorny branches looked friendlier now that they were green and leafy. I wondered if Mr Whelan had employed a gardener.

This will be my garden next summer, I thought happily. And seeing as I couldn't tell a dandelion from a dahlia, that gardener might have a permanent job.

Marc looked a lot more cheerful too now we were finally here. He stood in the front garden, hands on hips, shaking his head. He turned in a slow circle until he was facing me.

'Wow, princess! I like it.'

A chorus of angels gathered round my head singing 'Hallelujah'. I was his princess again!

I took his hand shyly and pulled him towards the side gate. 'Come on, I'll show you the back.'

We sat on the mossy bench in the back garden and chatted. He shook his head and tutted when I told him that my father had delayed everything by not arriving until next month.

'He sounds like a right character.'

'I'm dreading it, to be honest,' I admitted. I hardly dared think about it. August was fast approaching and I felt sick with fear.

'Would you like me to be there?' asked Marc, thumping his fist into his palm. 'If he gives you a hard time or anything, I'll sort him out!'

He couldn't have said a more perfect thing if he'd tried. He was the first person to offer to come with me and I felt tears prick at my eyes. It was such a thoughtful thing to say. On the other hand, turning up with a boyfriend with fists like breeze blocks might not be the wisest move.

'Thanks,' I said diplomatically, 'but this is something I need to do alone.'

Marc nodded solemnly and sighed. 'You are lucky, you know. What I wouldn't give for a leg-up like this. You're sitting on a gold mine here!'

I stared at him and felt my heart squeeze with affection. He seemed different somehow, more caring, and he certainly had a little more respect for me these days.

'I know I'm fortunate,' I said softly, 'but I think gold mine might be overdoing it. And all I want is a little house, nothing fancy.'

A shadow passed across his face.

I bit my lip. That had come out all wrong. It sounded selfish and greedy, as if the house was just for me, when really I'd be delighted to share it with someone. Here I was, sitting pretty, when he was still living at home with his mum, struggling to get his own business off the ground. My heart went out to him. It didn't seem fair that he couldn't chase his dream like I was chasing mine.

The combined voices of Jess and Emma warned me to stop and think, but I batted them away and took a deep breath.

'I could loan you some money to kickstart your car business. I know you said you're going to start small but . . .'

His eyes lit up and he beamed. 'Do you mean it?'

I nodded and then he cupped my face in his hands and kissed me with such force that I felt like I was going to lose my tonsils.

'Lovely offer,' he said a few minutes later when we both came up for air. 'But I want to do this by myself. It's a matter of honour, you know?'

'I understand.'

I was brimming with pride for him as I nestled against his chest. Oh, happy days! He wanted me, not my money.

Emma was wrong. He wanted me! I stroked the back of his head and pulled his lips close to mine again.

'Would you like to stay over tonight?' I asked.

'What the hell do you think you're doing?' hissed Emma several hours later when she found me in the kitchen in the early hours of the morning.

'Shush!' I hissed back, jumping to my feet and closing the door so no one would hear us.

I was polishing off a plate of buttered toast. Going without any dinner, followed by Marc and I reacquainting ourselves with each other's bodies, had taken its toll and I was ravenous.

'It just happened. I needed an ego boost,' I explained, refusing to meet her eye.

'A wolf whistle from a builder is an ego boost. A new bloody haircut is an ego boost. Not a shag with the world's most uneligible bachelor. Is he still here?'

I nodded and she turned away in disgust to pour herself a glass of water.

'What happened to taking it slow?' She gulped at her drink and glared at me over the rim. I gulped too, somewhat guiltily. Had I said that?

'I think we're back together,' I hissed. 'So why wait?'

'You *think* you're back together?' Her jaw dropped open and she folded her arms.

All of a sudden I snapped. What right did she have to lecture me like this, all judgemental and glinty-eyed? Why couldn't she just give him a second chance like I had? She had never liked Marc, never trusted him, and had always been quick to point out his failings. The problem was that she didn't understand him the way I did. Or was there some other reason behind her disapproval? My heart began to race uncomfortably as realization dawned.

'Yes, I think we are and I tell you what else I think,' I whispered angrily. 'I think you're jealous.'

Emma reeled back from the strength of my attack. 'I'm your best friend and not the least bit jealous.'

'Then be happy for me!' I retorted.

She shook her head sadly and stomped back to bed.

'And it's *in*eligible,' I muttered glumly to the empty room.

Chapter 16

It was my birthday and August was nearly over. I had dark shadows under my eyes from lack of sleep, a face full of spots and I hadn't been able to stray too far from the loo for the past two hours.

The reason for this lapse in poise and inner calm? Not because I was one year older, although frankly, that didn't help. But because somewhere in this fair city, Terry Stone was preparing to meet his estranged child. Right now, my father was probably staring out of the window of a chintzy hotel, waiting for his full English breakfast to arrive and pondering what on earth he was letting himself in for.

'Your father arrives in the country next week,' Mr Whelan had announced portentously, when he'd phoned me with the news. 'After the bank holiday. If that suits?'

Not really, I'd huffed to myself. I could have gone to Spain to see Mum as usual and been back in time to meet him and she would have been none the wiser. As it was, she had been emailing me every few days, badgering me to sort out my flights.

Putting the Costa del Sol out of my mind for the moment, I sorted out a pair of navy shoes from the bottom of my wardrobe and chose a handbag to match. I'd treated myself to a navy dress and jacket for today's meeting. Very smart: the sort of thing you could wear to a wedding. Meeting my father felt like a very formal occasion. Like a reverse wedding, with my father waiting for me after a thirty-three-year walk down the aisle.

I popped my purse, keys and phone into my bag, being careful not to damage my nails. I'd just had a French manicure and the white tips were squared off like little spades. I'd had my hair done especially too. Gone were the curls; for a brief few hours my hair was sleek, shiny and smooth. I stood up and examined my reflection. A calm and – though I said so myself – elegant woman looked back at me. Which took me by surprise because my insides were churning like a cement mixer.

I couldn't put it off any longer. Time to meet my father.

I stepped out into the drizzle and sighed. Even though it was still August, autumn appeared to have arrived. The sky was grey and a cool breeze rushed past my bare legs, giving me goose pimples.

Shivering with cold and nerves, I made my way across the city on two buses to Mr Whelan's office.

I hammered on the solicitors firm's door, desperate to be inside in the warm and rescue my hair before it returned to its natural texture of bird's nest.

After confirming the date – my stomach had churned throughout our conversation and incidentally every moment since – Mr Whelan had asked me where I wanted to meet. I'd ummed and ahhed so long that he'd eventually taken pity on me. 'Might I suggest our meeting room?'

'Yes,' I had sighed. 'That would be perfect.'

I was five minutes early for my appointment but even so, my father had apparently beaten me to it. I followed the smiley receptionist as she swished her way down the corridor, my heart thumping faster with every step.

'Just go on in,' smiled the receptionist, leaving me at the meeting-room door. 'They're waiting for you.'

'Right.' I nodded. 'Yes. I'll just . . .' I cleared my throat and watched her walk away, while I collected my thoughts.

On the other side of this door was my father. A person I should have been close to, one half of my parents, half of me.

My mouth was dry and my throat had almost completely closed up. Just as well, I thought nervously, it would help to keep the vomit in. I placed my hands on my hot face and concentrated on my breathing.

Why hadn't I told Mum about the condition in Great-aunt Jane's will? She could have talked me out of it. Why did I agree to this? Why the bobbins didn't I bring someone with me?

I took a deep breath and drew myself up tall. I could do this. I really could . . .

My knees trembled as I gripped the cold metal door handle and pushed the door open halfway. I gulped. Sitting at the table was a tall thin man, grey-haired, with a bushy beard and an encouraging smile. Mr Whelan. I let my breath out in a high-pitched whistle and forced myself to enter the room.

Bang smack opposite my trusty solicitor, invisible from my first view of the room, was Terry Stone.

All of a sudden, my mind started whirring as if someone had put my brain on a fast spin cycle. I saw Mr Whelan stand up, make introductions, his hand outstretched, but all

I could hear was *whoosh, whoosh, whoosh*, and then he touched my arm gently and left the room.

Leaving just the two of us. United by name, divided by everything else.

Terry jumped to his feet. He stumbled towards me, tripping over two chairs in the process.

From a distance he could be anyone: average height, average build, bit of a tummy. But as he approached me, his face told the real story. Green eyes flecked with brown, short lashes like mine. His wavy hair was thick, brushed back off his face, as dark as mine although tinged with grey. I suspected that if he grew it long, it would be just as curly as mine too.

I touched my own hair automatically, and was shocked to find it so smooth and flat. My visit to the salon felt like weeks ago.

He was only inches away, staring at me. We both gave a stilted laugh, although the situation was anything but funny.

Awkward. Do we shake hands? Hug? No, definitely not hug.

I heard a noise escape from his throat. He was about to speak. I knew without doubt that his first words to me would remain in my memory banks for ever. He scrutinized my face, his brow furrowed in concentration.

'Sophie? You *could* be my daughter, I suppose.'

What the chuff?

My mouth dropped open. I screwed my face up into an angry gurn.

'That's it? That's all you can say after thirty-three years?' I gasped.

Frustration gripped hold of me and I shoved him. Two

hands to the chest. His face paled. He staggered back and landed skew-whiff on a chair, one hand clasped across his body.

'Of course I'm your daughter! What do you think this is, an identity parade?'

He turned his head to the side and mumbled something under his breath.

'What?' I swivelled towards him, hands on hips. My heart thundered against my ribs with anger. 'What did you say? Spit it out!'

'I said, you've certainly got your mother's temper.'

I blushed in spite of myself. I was aware what a terrible impression I was making but I was completely unable to control myself.

'That's no surprise, is it? I'm hardly likely to have any of your mannerisms, am I?'

I scowled and folded my arms. I seemed to have regressed to my teenage self. Even down to the spot on my chin.

Terry slid an envelope towards me across the table. 'Happy birthday, by the way.'

That shocked me. He knew it was my birthday. He had remembered. A tiny spark of hope flickered inside me; that must mean something, mustn't it? But what about last year, had he thought about me then? Or the year before that? The little spark disappeared.

'Ooh, thanks.' I did a teenage-style sarcastic shimmy, shoving the envelope unopened into my bag. 'Does that cover the last thirty-two birthdays as well?'

'Of course not.' His eyebrows furrowed and met in the middle.

My limbs felt all gangly and I wanted to escape his gaze. I threw myself down onto the seat furthest from him.

'I'd like to get to know you, find out about you, I've missed so much,' he said.

You've missed everything, I wanted to yell, but instead I rewarded him with my most withering look and waved a hand carelessly. 'Fire away.'

'Um, let's see, what do you do for a living?' he asked.

Of all the questions! I shrugged, not bothering to impress him. 'Advertising sales for *The Herald*.'

'Enjoy it?'

'Not really,' I muttered, seething with frustration.

Small talk, small talk. What about big talk? There were so many things we should have been talking about. Like had he loved my mother? How could he have abandoned her? Abandoned me, a new-born baby?

I took a sideways peek at him. He still had a hand to his chest and his face was a picture of misery.

Why bother to see me now? Why return after all these years? There must be something in it for him, I realized with a jolt. Something more than simply indulging his aunt's last wishes. I wondered if he got a pay-out from her estate too, on condition that *he* agreed to meet *me*.

'So where have you been all my life?' Privately, I was very pleased with my line. If I hadn't been so cross, I would have smiled.

His mouth twitched, only for a second, until he noticed my glare.

He sighed. 'It's a long story.'

'Then shorten it. Tea?'

Someone had left us a tray of tea, coffee and biscuits. I decided to be mother. No use waiting for him to display any parental inclinations.

'Milky, two sugars please,' he said.

That was how I took mine. I felt ridiculously possessive of my tea preference all of a sudden. I poured myself a weak cup of coffee instead. It didn't taste anywhere near as nice as the one Nick Cromwell had made me but then I didn't come here for the refreshments.

We sipped our drinks in a weighty silence for a minute or so.

Terry set his cup down and sighed, rubbing a hand over his face. He looked as rough as I felt; he was tanned, but looked far from healthy. There was a yellow pallor to his skin and the bags under his eyes looked big enough to set sail in.

He nodded. 'OK. I split up with your mother, joined the Royal Navy for ten years, met an American nurse, married her, left the navy, moved to Nevada, had a son—'

I spluttered into my tea. 'Son? I've got a brother?'

Terry nodded and chewed on his lip, his eyes shifty.

I had a brother. Half-brother.

My breathing came short and fast as I took in this new information. Why had this possibility never occurred to me before? It was inevitable, really. My father had moved on. Started a new life. No wonder he hadn't been interested in me and Mum; he'd replaced us with newer models.

Damn him. I could easily walk away from a father who hadn't wanted me, who had shown no interest in me. But a brother? Different ball game! What about a sister-in-law, nieces, nephews? My arms prickled with goose pimples. My biography was being torn up and rewritten, new pages, new chapters added.

'How old?'

'Twenty.'

Still a boy. I'd been thirteen when my brother was born.

142

'Name?'

'Brodie.'

I was interrogating him. He probably felt like he was on trial. He was – crimes against fatherhood.

Now I should like to call Terence Stone to the witness box.

His eyes were darting left and right as if he was watching a ping-pong match.

'He's here with me, as it happens.'

The hairs on the back of my neck stood up and I shivered. Here? Had I walked past him in reception?

Terry smiled briefly. 'Not *here* here. In Nottingham. I left him at the university finding his feet. He starts his engineering degree next month.'

Oh. Suddenly the fact that he couldn't meet me until August made sense. My head started to nod. To an outsider, it would have looked fairly benign. But the heat of my anger was rising rapidly from red hot to seething white.

Terry Stone hadn't travelled to the UK to see me, his only daughter. Oh, no, he'd tagged it on to a trip to settle his beloved child – the chosen one – at uni.

'Did you go to university?' he asked.

'No. I did not.' I crashed my cup back on its saucer. 'Although I'd have loved to.'

My father flinched.

'We couldn't afford for me to go to university. Like we couldn't afford the school trip to Paris, or the geography expedition to . . . wherever it was. Do you have any idea how tough it was bringing up a child on your own in those days?'

'That is a shame.' He shook his head sadly. 'Further education can open so many doors.'

Really? You think?

143

That was it. I'd heard enough and this conversation was going nowhere anyway. I blinked back my tears; there was no way I was going to cry in front of him.

I stood, pushing my chair back roughly, my face set hard.

'OK. Well, we've met. I've fulfilled my end of the bargain. Presumably, so have you.'

I tried to ignore the look of hurt on his face. That wasn't my problem. He'd got his precious Brodie to comfort him.

He stood and stepped towards me, touching my arm.

'Mr Whelan warned me that you weren't sure about meeting me,' he said, looking directly into my eyes. 'I hope it's not too late for us to get to know each other.'

I stared at him open-mouthed and brushed his hand away. A sense of outrage began to build.

'You've made no effort to see me for my whole life. Even this meeting was conveniently fitted round your son's university trip.'

Terry recoiled in horror. 'Sophie, that's not true at all.'

'I'm nothing to you. Mum was right,' I grunted, jamming my hands on my hips.

He shook his head. 'I can see why it might look that way but—'

I held a hand up and my face twisted in disgust. 'Terry, please, don't bother.'

He opened his mouth and then must have thought better of it and closed it again. A few moments of silence hung between us until he spoke again: 'How is your mother? Is she well?' His eyebrows furrowed as if he was searching for memories. 'Still singing Abba songs?'

'She's fine. Lives in Spain. And it's Madonna these days.'

My father's face softened and his eyes adopted a faraway look. 'Ever the party girl.' He smiled ruefully.

I glared at him incredulously. I bet she wasn't partying when she brought a new-born baby home to an empty house. 'You have no idea.'

All of a sudden I couldn't be bothered with this charade any more.

'Well, this has been a blast,' I said, scooping up my bag from the parquet floor. 'But all good things must come to an end.'

The smile slid off his face. He rubbed a hand over his face and shrugged helplessly.

'Sophie, don't go. Please. I've come all this way and there's so much more I need to say. To explain.'

I ignored his pleading and shook my head. 'I've heard enough.'

He grabbed my hand and I felt callouses on his palms, the warm, dry skin. My flesh and blood. The hand of a stranger. I tried to pull away but I wasn't quick enough. He placed his other hand on mine.

'I need you to know this, Sophie, I've carried you in my heart all these years,' he said gravely, before I snatched my hand back.

We stared at each other until I looked away.

'I don't believe that for one second,' I said quietly.

Terry's shoulders slumped. 'No. I can see that.'

My anger subsided and an all-encompassing sadness washed over me.

'Goodbye,' I said, lunging for the door handle.

I strode away as quickly as I could so that he didn't see the tears streaming down my face.

Chapter 17

I ran from Whelan & Partners without even signing out of the visitors' book. Outside on the busy street, I was amazed to find that nothing seemed to have changed. Shoppers laden with bags, mums with toddlers, teenagers loitering, pensioners at bus stops . . . It all looked the same.

Life was still carrying on as usual.

How could that possibly be?

My life had just changed beyond belief. I was no longer Valerie's daughter; I was Terry's daughter too. I would be able to conjure up both of their faces when I was filling in the blanks of their marriage, their break-up, my birth.

I hovered on the solicitor's doorstep to let my pulse and my breathing return to normal and wondered whether Terry Stone would run after me, beg me to hear him out.

But of course he wouldn't pursue me, he wasn't interested. He was probably already on the phone to his precious son, telling him what a narrow escape he'd had, how awful I was.

So it was over. I'd met him and I'd never, ever have to see him again. I cast my eyes heavenwards.

Are you there, Jane Kennedy? Did you see that? I did what you asked; I met my father. And what did it achieve? A big fat nothing, that's what. An absolute disaster. Happy Birthday to me.

I shivered and pulled my jacket tighter across my chest before stepping onto the pavement. The wind had stepped up its efforts, but at least the rain had stopped. A few weak-willed leaves had already fallen off their branches and joined the plastic bottles and crisp packets rolling along the gutter. I let the wind blow me along too. I could feel the cold air through my thin dress and jacket; it blew into my hair, lifting it off my shoulders. I smoothed it down, but it was futile, the curls were making a comeback.

I started to run and I kept on running. Past the bakers, past the pharmacy and past the stationers. I ran until my toes pinched and the balls of my feet burned and until the shops on the high street had disappeared.

I didn't know where I was or where I was going, but I didn't care. If I couldn't find a bus, I'd treat myself to a taxi home. I felt as if I'd sold my soul to the devil, by meeting my father, but at least now my money worries were over. My eyes were welling up with tears and I let them fall, not caring what a sight I must look.

I wiped my face and the back of my hand was streaked with black. I might sue *Cosmo*. They had specifically said that this mascara would withstand all the emotions of a busy day. Perhaps they hadn't factored in a first and only reunion with a good-for-nothing, pathetic, irresponsible, uncaring father.

My legs were tired, I felt wobbly with emotion and ready for a sit-down. There were some wide gates ahead and a signpost above them indicated that I'd come across a park. Perfect; I would sit in solitude for a while, rest my feet and compose myself before going home.

I headed up the path and kept an eye out for a sheltered seat. There was a wooden bench ahead, underneath an oak tree. My feet were killing me so I stepped onto the grass and slipped off my shoes. The sensation of the cold damp grass on my poor crushed toes was bliss.

I sat down on the bench and pulled my collar up to protect me from the dripping branches overhead. Rapid footsteps approached and I quickly hid my face under my hair. The last thing I needed was some do-gooder asking me if I was all right. I turned away as the steps got closer.

'I tell you,' I heard a familiar voice mutter, 'TV property shows have got a lot to answer for. Everyone thinks they're a bloomin' architect these days.'

'Nick?' I said as he drew level with the bench I was on.

My architect stopped in his tracks and the dog jerked up on his hind legs as the lead strained. Nick stared at me.

'Oh. Not you,' he laughed.

'No, it is me. It's just that I look a mess.' I peeled my hair back off my wet face and saw his eyes widen in surprise.

I dropped my hair back onto my face; it was entirely possible that I wasn't looking my best.

Norman recognized me, pulled at the lead and immediately began licking my bare feet.

Despite my black mood, I began to giggle. I was incredibly ticklish and Norman's tongue was very soft.

'Actually, I meant you're not a would-be architect,' said Nick, trying to rein Norman in. The dog wagged his tail merrily and carried on licking between my toes. I squealed and lifted my feet off the ground to escape his tongue. Norman barked, thinking it was a game, jumped up onto my lap and knocked me sideways, presenting his master with a bird's eye view of my gusset.

'Christ, I'm so sorry.' Nick looked mortified. He instantly dropped the lead, helped me back up to a more dignified position and gawped at my bare knees, which were now covered in muddy paw prints. Norman scampered off to sniff the oak tree.

'It's OK, I'm fine,' I said, still giggling. Nick produced a tissue and for a moment I thought he was going to spit on it and scrub my knees himself.

I took it from him, thanked him and wiped away the worst of the mud. The poor man looked so awkward, dithering around in front of me, shuffling from foot to foot. I gestured to the other end of the bench and he sank down with a sigh.

'What I meant, when you heard me talking to the dog, was that sometimes I work with clients who, after watching *Grand Designs*, or one of the other shows, think they know everything there is to know about architecture.'

I bit the inside of my cheek while I weighed up whether his comment was an insult or not. I was pretty sure I was guilty of falling into this category. And hadn't I mentioned to him that I had adored property TV shows?

Yep. Definitely an insult.

Five minutes of peace and quiet in the park to get my head together. That was all I asked. But it didn't look like I was going to get it and actually, I realized, after the morning I'd just had it was quite a relief to have company. I felt the corners of my mouth twitch.

Nick offered me a tentative smile in return, unbuttoned his jacket, clasped his hands in front of him and jiggled his leg awkwardly.

I bit back a smile; he was a handsome chap, although he didn't seem to realize it and he really had no idea how to talk to women.

'Clients like me, you mean?' I lifted an eyebrow.

'No, no.' He held his hands up in apology. 'Oh, Christ. I keep saying the wrong thing.'

I chuckled and waited, giving him the chance to say the right thing, unlikely as that seemed.

'It's just that,' he paused with a sigh, 'some people are too quick to jump on the latest bandwagon: like technology and ecosystems and fancy glass.'

He took off his glasses and rubbed them on his pale pink shirt. His movements were neat and precise as he inspected the lenses and popped them back on. I caught a whiff of aftershave as he moved, it was delicate and delicious, a mix of spice and wood. I resisted the urge to press my nose against his cheek and inhale his scent.

He flashed me a shy smile. 'I'm more old-school, I'm afraid,' he continued. 'The beauty is in the form, the shape of the building, the way people use the house and the way it uses the space. All these gimmicky details – well, they blur the beauty.'

His awkwardness had been replaced by sincerity. There was no doubt how much Nick cared about good design. Even so, I couldn't help grinning at his earnest expression.

'I thought God was in the detail?' I challenged him with a smirk.

His face lit up and for a split second I thought he was going to kiss me. I was just deciding whether that was a bad thing or not when he whooped with joy.

'Mies van der Rohe?' He threw his head back and laughed. 'He's been a huge inspiration to me! You're a fan too?'

I swallowed. No. Obviously. Never heard of him. It was just one of those sayings, wasn't it?

'Aren't we all?' I gave a non-committal laugh and shrugged my shoulders.

Nick's cup looketh liketh it runneth over and his eyes twinkled at me. 'I suppose so.'

He *was* going to kiss me. My heart thumped, which sort of indicated that regardless of what my brain thought, my body was quite happy about it. Which was very wrong of my body because I had a boyfriend. Marc. Who, I realized, I hadn't thought about for hours.

I clicked my fingers at the dog, who obligingly trotted over and sniffed my feet again. I bent down to rub his furry head and simultaneously hide my blushes.

'My feet must stink,' I remarked, which probably cured Nick of any desire to kiss me. I glanced back at him; yup, his nose had definitely wrinkled.

'Sorry about Norman's bad habits,' he chuckled. 'Sometimes when I've been for a run he'll lick me all the way up to my knees.'

Too much information.

I slipped my shoes back on and winced, regretting all that angry stomping away from the high street.

We sat in silence as Norman spotted another dog and lolloped over to say hello. It suddenly occurred to me how bizarrely my day had turned out: I was miles from home in a smart outfit, sitting in a park with my architect watching his dog sniff another's backside and the heartache of meeting my father had, if not disappeared, definitely dimmed.

'What are you doing here anyway?' I asked.

He scratched his chin. I heard the rasp of his fingers against his five o'clock shadow of stubble. What was the time? A quick look at my watch told me it was, in fact, nearly five. I really should be on my way; it would probably take me ages to get home and I was due out for a birthday dinner later.

'See that building through the trees?'

I nodded. Almost concealed from view was a rather grand old mansion house.

'That's the council's office for this area. When we apply for planning permission for your new house, that's where we'll send it. I had a meeting with the planners this afternoon.'

By the way he was clenching his jaw, I guessed it hadn't gone well. Hence the muttering when I'd first spotted him.

'What about you?' he asked, running his eyes over my ensemble for the first time. 'You're very smartly dressed for a walk in the park.'

'Me?'

Without warning a lump lodged itself in my throat. I tried to speak but no words appeared and my throat started to burn. To my horror, huge fat tears sprang out from nowhere.

Nick's face had panic written all over it as he patted his pockets. I held up the muddy tissue he'd already given me and dabbed my face with it.

'Sorry, that was my last one,' he said. He shuffled closer and patted my shoulders awkwardly while I carried on crying.

I couldn't possibly tell him about my meeting at the solicitor's; once I started, the floodgates would open and my entire family history would escape. I wasn't embarrassed exactly, but I wasn't particularly proud either.

After a few minutes the tears stopped and I began to get my jerky breathing under control. Nick was looking at me expectantly. He inched his way even closer and moved his patting to my arm.

I blinked at him, hoping that he wouldn't say anything kind in case I burst into tears again.

He waved a finger in the direction of my face. 'Um, there's mud on your cheek and a black smudge, actually smudges – plural – under your eyes.'

For once I was grateful for his inability to say the right thing. A bubble of laughter broke through my misery and I grinned at him. 'Anything else?'

He hesitated and then plunged on. 'Your neck's gone blotchy.'

My mouth gaped and he gave a helpless shrug. 'I'm not very good in these situations.'

'You don't say,' I muttered.

'But are you all right?' He peered at me through his glasses.

I nodded and dragged myself up. It was time to take my muddy, make-up-streaked, blotchy face back home. Pain shot through my feet and I yelped. My shoes had mysteriously shrunk by two whole sizes.

Nick didn't look convinced.

'It's my birthday today,' I said flatly. 'I always get a bit emotional.'

'Ah.' He nodded, brushed imaginary specks of dust off his trousers and stood up.

I rolled my eyes. Ah? What was that supposed to mean? Ah yes, at your age, it's only natural to feel depressed?

Nick was saved from further cross-examination by Norman, who reappeared and sat down between us. I wondered how often Nick's dog had rescued him from awkward social moments. Plenty, I imagined. I bent to stroke him. Nick chose to do exactly the same thing and I squealed in pain as my head collided with his cheekbone.

'Ouch,' I yelled. 'You idiot.'

Nick got the brunt of it and a vivid red mark appeared on his face. We both rubbed our wounds and stared at each other in stunned silence.

'Sophie, I'm so sorry, and on your birthday too. Are you all right?' He looked so pathetic that I instantly felt guilty.

'I'm fine. And I apologize for yelling,' I mumbled, still wincing. 'It's your dog, you get first pat.'

For some reason a line from a children's nursery rhyme popped into my head: 'We all pat the dog'.

The idea of us taking turns to pat the dog was so ridiculous that I snorted. I looked at Nick and saw his mouth twitching too.

I sniggered. His eyes, normally so serious behind his glasses, sparkled as he started to chuckle. That set off my giggling. Soon my shoulders were shaking again, only this time it wasn't with tears; I was laughing, loud, raucous, un-restrained laughter.

We both laughed until we were out of breath. My ribs were aching, but I couldn't stop. Every time I got my breathing back under control, we would catch sight of each other and off we'd go again. I hadn't laughed so much in ages.

Eventually Nick wiped the tears from his eyes, fastened Norman's lead back on and gave me a regretful smile.

'I'm so glad I bumped into you today,' he said, straight-ening up, 'even though I seem to have made you cry and bashed your head.'

'Likewise.' I smiled, realizing that I meant it. 'But I'd better go; I've got a big night out tonight.'

Nick's eyes met mine and for a moment he looked a bit deflated and then he cleared his throat. 'Of course, your birthday. By the way, the design for your house is almost complete; I'll be in touch soon.'

'Really?' I beamed. 'Yippee! Can't wait to see it.'

He smiled and then, leaning forward, placed a gentle whisper of a kiss on my cheek. 'Happy birthday, Sophie. It has been a delight as always.'

My hand flew to my blushing face and I watched my architect and his dog stride away.

As I hobbled to the entrance of the park to find a bus, it struck me that today had been the weirdest birthday of my life.

Chapter 18

The Italian restaurant I had chosen for my birthday night out was a cheese-fest in romantic Italian decor. A mural of the Leaning Tower of Pisa covered the alcove behind us, dribbling candles stuffed into Chianti bottles decorated the tables and the rumbling tones of Italian opera were just audible above the clinking and scraping of cutlery.

The romance, cheesy or otherwise, was a bit wasted on me and my fellow diners, though, because I'd turned down a night with Marc to be with Emma and Jess. Since our little late-night argument last month, Emma and I had agreed to differ about Marc and had sworn not to let him come between us. I was determined to show her that not only had he changed but I had changed too. And spending my birthday with my friends instead of him had definitely scored me a few points in that department.

Besides, I mused, as the waiter popped the cork on a bottle of prosecco, it was them I really wanted to be with tonight.

'Cheers!' I held my glass up and took a calming swig.

And relax.

My head was still in a whirl from my meeting with Terry Stone and right now a stress-free night with the girls and a bottle of bubbly was exactly what the doctor ordered.

'Ah, cheers, babes, happy birthday.' Jess clinked her glass enthusiastically against mine.

She looked like a Roman goddess tonight with rather a lot of cleavage on display, and completely blended in with our Italian backdrop. Her voluptuous appearance wasn't lost on other people either. Several of the male diners kept glancing our way and our waiter was gratifyingly attentive.

'Yeah, happy thirty-third birthday! Down the hatch!' Emma raised her glass and chucked half of its contents down her throat. She was letting her hair down in both senses of the word tonight, and a pre-Raphaelite cloud of red hair fell across her T-shirt as she reached to top all our glasses up.

I felt quite staid in my navy dress. The journey back to the flat on two buses had taken over an hour and I hadn't had the time or energy to change anything other than my shoes. My feet were now comfortably ensconced in a pair of flip-flops. It had been that or trainers; I had blisters on my blisters this evening.

I winced. 'Don't remind me how old I am!'

'Nonsense,' said Jess firmly, closing her menu and casting her eye round for our waiter. 'Women are happiest at thirty-three. I read it the other day on some website or other. Apparently, we're confident, we've lost all our insecurities and we know exactly where we're going in life.'

'It's all downhill from here then.' Emma looked up from her menu and sniggered.

'Absolutely not!' Jess took a dainty sip and smiled serenely. 'My life is getting better all the time. I've got my promotion to deputy head next term. Can't wait. And then there's Spike.' Her eyes glazed over. 'I honestly think we were made for each other.'

'Blurghhhh.' Emma grabbed one of my gift bags and pretended to vomit in it.

'Oh, shut up, you,' giggled Jess. 'Have you decided what you're having?'

I grinned at the two sisters as they exchanged light-hearted insults. It was hard not to feel jealous of Jess sometimes; she did seem very together these days. Unlike me. I felt less confident now than when I woke up this morning.

I'd made a complete mess of my meeting with my dad. Instead of giving him a piece of my mind and making him realize what he'd missed out on all these years, I'd acted like a sulky child and lost my temper.

I sighed and took another sip of my prosecco. Too late now. Besides, he hadn't exactly gathered me up into his arms, declared his fatherly love and apologized for abandoning me, had he? I shifted in my seat uncomfortably. Just as well; I'd have probably pushed him off anyway.

I thought about what Jess had said about being thirty-three. Was I happy? I certainly shouldn't be unhappy: I had a job, good friends, my health, enough money . . . lots to be happy about.

Anyway, happiness didn't mean spending all day laughing hysterically. A smile crept its way across my face as I recalled laughing until my sides ached with Nick earlier. That had been the strangest thing ever. I had seen a different side of his personality today, a side that I could relate to a lot more than his usual buttoned-up self. And what about that birthday kiss? My cheek burned where he'd kissed me and I pressed the back of my hand to my face. How unexpected was that?

'Well?' said Emma. She and Jess were beaming at me tentatively, clearly misinterpreting my smile. 'Are you going to tell us what happened?'

They had been badgering me to spill the beans on how the father–daughter reunion had gone, ever since I arrived home. So far I'd fobbed them off, saying I needed alcohol before I could talk about it. The truth was that my emotions were in turmoil and I wasn't absolutely sure that I could talk about it without bursting into tears.

Luckily the waiter chose that moment to take our order and I smiled at him gratefully.

'The sole for me please,' I said and handed the menu back.

'Lasagne and garlic bread, please,' said Jess, 'but go easy on the garlic.'

The waiter's pencil hovered uncertainly over his pad, but he dutifully made a note.

'I'm staying at Spike's tonight – don't want to knock him out with garlic breath,' she giggled.

'Is the chicken free-range?' asked Emma, narrowing her eyes.

'Yes!' The waiter nodded.

'Hmm.' Emma chewed her lip for a good thirty seconds. 'Margherita pizza.' She snapped the menu shut and handed it back without looking at him. 'Now, we want details.'

'Oh, but can't I open my presents first?' I pleaded, batting my eyelashes. 'I've been waiting all day.'

'Of course,' cried Jess, leaning forward to organize the unwrapping ceremony. 'This one first,' she said, handing me an envelope with a Spanish stamp on it.

A bullet of guilt ricocheted through me. If Mum only knew what I'd been up to today, she wouldn't have sent me anything at all. Inside the card was a voucher for a massage at the beauty salon in the hotel near her apartment.

'Oh, how lovely!' I exclaimed. 'And if that isn't a big fat hint to book my flights, I don't know what is.'

'This one next,' said Emma. She passed over a pink gift bag.

'It's from both of us,' added Jess, wriggling with excitement.

As well as two envelopes, the bag contained some tissue-wrapped Clinique moisturizer and body lotion.

'My favourites!' I cried, squirting a dot of cream onto the back of my hands. 'Thanks, girls.'

'Come on, the envelopes!' said Emma, tipping the bag upside down.

The first contained a year's subscription to *Elegant Homes* magazine. I reached across and hugged them. That had always been my favourite magazine. I'd treated myself to a copy recently to do the house brief for Nick and had fallen in love with it all over again. I was touched that they had remembered.

'And one more. I can't wait!' squealed Jess as I picked up the second envelope.

Emma grinned at me over her glass. 'You're going to love this. It was my idea.'

I frowned as I read the enclosed letter, trying to make out what it was.

'It's a taster day at the London College of Interior Design,' said Jess impatiently.

'We want to bring back the Sophie who had her head full of designs and schemes,' said Emma, jabbing me in the ribs with a breadstick. 'When you were doing that work on the bungalow, we could see how happy it made you.'

'It's only a day,' said Jess. 'But who knows, you might get the bug and take it up again.'

This had to be the kindest, most thoughtful present that I had ever had. My eyes filled up with tears and I transferred them first to Jess's face and then to Emma's as I hugged them both.

'I love it,' I managed in a croaky voice, wiping my tears away. 'You two are the best, really you are.'

Twelve years ago, a gift like this would have been my idea of heaven. Now? I wasn't so sure. Surely it was too late to pick up my dreams and run with them again?

'You big softie,' said Emma, waving the last parcel in front of my face. 'Come on, let's see what lover boy Marc got you.'

I took the hastily wrapped, rectangular parcel from her and placed it in front of me. The box was fairly light and smaller than a shoe box, but too big to be jewellery. I shook it. It didn't make a sound.

'Careful!' cried Jess. 'It could be fragile.'

Emma huffed impatiently. 'Hurry up, the food will be here in a minute and I want to hear about what happened with your dad.'

Our waiter reappeared and very slowly topped up our glasses. I caught him staring at the parcel and he quickly looked away.

There was a card taped to it. I opened it and read the message aloud.

Happy birthday, princess, I know how busy you are at work, so thought this might be useful. Love Marc xoxo

'How intriguing!' I said.

I tore off the paper to reveal the gift that the man in my life had decided was the perfect present for me and my heart sank. It was a battery-operated abdominal toner. I dropped the box back onto the table and automatically sucked in my stomach. Jess gasped. Emma swore. The waiter set the bottle down in the ice cooler and scurried away. I could swear I heard him snort.

'I'm sorry, babes.' Jess bit her bottom lip and patted my arm.

'Tosser,' said Emma.

I picked up the box again and tried to decide how I felt about my gift.

I was unfit. Marc was super fit. We had originally met at the gym and I'd stopped going months ago. It made sense that he would want any girlfriend of his to share his passion. But whichever way I looked at it, there was no denying it was a thoroughly crap present. I bet Nick Cromwell wouldn't give a woman . . .

My heart thumped.

'What's the matter, babes?' said Jess, reaching for my hand. 'You've gone all pale.'

'Nothing,' I stammered, looking down at the box. 'Results in eight weeks, it says here.'

'What – and then he'll go back out with you?' Emma looked ready to punch someone. I hoped the chef didn't mess up her pizza or there would be trouble.

'I have to say, my Spike loves me for the way I am. He wouldn't dream of criticizing my figure,' said Jess, biting her lip.

Emma's fierce huff extinguished the candle flame. 'There is nothing wrong with Sophie's stomach. Marc is totally out of order. End of.' She folded her arms and glared at me.

'It's the thought that counts,' I answered feebly. Although, on balance, I wished he hadn't thought at all.

'Bollocks,' said Emma. 'This is about him. As usual. I did warn you—'

'Spike says he loves my womanly curves,' Jess said hurriedly, her eyes darting from me to Emma. 'He says if I was thinner there wouldn't be so much to kiss, to caress and run his tongue—'

'All right! Enough.' Emma stuck her fingers in her ears. 'Let's not say another word about it.'

'Good.' I heaved a sigh of relief. A little seed of doubt was worming its way into my brain and I really didn't want to deal with it at this precise moment. Even if Emma *was* right.

'I've got you this, too. Well, I made it, actually.' Emma reached into her jeans pocket and dropped a silver chain into my hand. I looked at the necklace. On it was a locket in the shape of a house. I prised it open to find a tiny gold heart suspended inside it. It was the most exquisite thing I had ever seen.

'It's beautiful,' I breathed. Emma's eyes looked suspiciously moist. I threw my arms around her and kissed her cheek. She helped me fasten the clasp and then pulled back to look me in the eye.

'Don't lose sight of your dreams, Sophie, OK?' she murmured. 'Not for anyone. Not again.'

My stomach flipped with love for her and I nodded. 'I promise.'

The waiter approached and slipped our plates in front of us with a flourish. *'Buon appetito.'*

'So, finally,' said Emma, cutting a large wedge out of her pizza, 'tell us about your dad.'

My dad. My stomach lurched queasily. I still couldn't think about him as my dad. In fact, I didn't really want to think about him at all.

I laid my cutlery down onto my plate and abandoned my fish.

'I've got a half-brother called Brodie,' I said lightly.

'What?' squeaked Emma and Jess in unison. They couldn't have looked more shocked if I'd ripped off my dress and begun dancing on the table. I filled them in on the bones of my encounter with Terry Stone.

'Did he explain why he's never been in touch?' Emma asked.

'No,' I said, raising an eyebrow. 'He didn't explain much at, all to be honest.'

'Was he nice? Does he look like you?' Jess tore off some garlic bread and popped it into her mouth, evidently not bothered about its effect on Spike any more.

I thought about it for a moment. 'He wasn't *not* nice. He was just . . .' I shrugged, searching for the right word, 'Nothingy. And actually, yes, he did look a bit like me.'

'Did he get you anything for your birthday?' Emma wanted to know.

I shook my head. Apart from a card, which I'd left in my other handbag. 'He wished me happy birthday. That was it.'

'Does he regret his behaviour? Did he weep with guilt?' Jess asked dramatically.

I picked up my glass and took a long slurp before answering.

'I don't think he regrets a thing.' I sighed. 'I think he was simply fulfilling his end of the bargain. I wouldn't be surprised if he got some sort of financial incentive from Great-aunt Jane for meeting me. Anyway,' I picked up my

164

knife and fork again, 'I won't be seeing him again.'

Emma nearly choked on her pizza. 'But your half-brother? You've got to meet him.'

'No point.' I looked down at my plate. I'd hardly touched my food, but I wasn't hungry any more.

Jess took hold of her sister's hand. 'But, babes, having a sibling is the most special bond in the world.'

Emma nodded sincerely. 'It's true. We share the same blood. No friendship can ever compare to the ties you have to your own family.'

I gazed at her sadly. 'A brother would have been nice, but it's far too complicated. To meet him, I'd have to get back in touch with my father and then there's Mum to consider . . .'

'I don't get it,' declared Emma. 'Why is it you're prepared to give Marc umpteen chances, but your father, your own flesh and blood, who's flown thousands of miles to see you, gets the cold shoulder?'

'You don't understand,' I replied.

Jess reached out and wiped my cheek. I hadn't realized I was crying.

'My father isn't interested in me. He wasn't even convinced I was his daughter at first! We have absolutely nothing in common. Let's face it, if he'd wanted to get to know me, he could have easily tracked me down before now. After all, we've still got the same surname. I think it's for the best. Honestly.'

They squeezed my hands, dried my tears and ordered another bottle. Emma topped up my glass and Jess took the stomach toner box off the table and dropped it onto the floor.

I took a deep breath. 'I've come to another major decision, too. I'm going to tell Mum the truth about meeting him. I'll feel better if I come clean and besides, I won't be seeing him again so there's nothing for her to worry about.'

Emma peered at me anxiously and squeezed my hand. 'Good on you. Are you going to tell her when you go to visit?'

I shook my head, feeling as though a weight had already been lifted from my shoulders just by making the decision. 'I'm not sure; I'll see what happens next time I call her. Anyway, my father is not going to ruin my birthday night out.' I raised my glass again and grinned. 'To being thirty-three, the happiest year of my life! Cheers!'

Chapter 19

Two weeks after my birthday, I was still struggling to put my encounter with my father behind me and it didn't help that I hadn't managed to catch my mum at home to talk it through with her either. Meeting Terry Stone had thrown up far more questions than it had answered and although I couldn't wait for the meeting to end at the time, now I wished I'd been less hasty to get away.

Consequently, I wasn't sleeping well, couldn't concentrate at work and Marc was complaining that he didn't see enough of me any more. At least that was easily solved, I thought, as I dashed back to my desk after lunch. We'd arranged to go to the cinema tonight to see a film of my choice. A date. Planned in advance and not spur of the moment. Even Emma had been mildly impressed; especially when she found out we were going to see a new rom com together.

'That was a long lunch hour, or should I say hour and a half?' said Maureen, leaning low across her desk to stay out of Donna's eye line. 'The boss has been up and down like a jack-in-a-box waiting for you to get back.'

I shoved my shopping bags under my desk and groaned. 'Has she? Oh knickers. I lost track of time choosing a new outfit for tonight. I'm going out with my boyfriend.'

'I had to cover for you in the end,' said Maureen, knitting her eyebrows together anxiously.

There was a sarcastic tut from Jason, who seemed to relish me getting into trouble these days.

'Thanks, Maureen, I'm really grateful,' I said, still out of breath from the dash back to my desk. 'What did you tell her?'

'Dentist. Emergency filling.'

I stared at her incredulously. Now I would have to fake a numb face and dental pain for the next hour.

'Sorry,' said Maureen, pulling her cardigan tighter and folding her arms. 'You know how nervous she makes me. It was all I could think of. Anyway, you'd better get in there. Oh, and someone called Nick phoned. He asked you to call him back ASAP.'

'Nick!' My face broke into a huge smile and I reached for the phone instantly.

This was fantastic news. I hadn't heard from him since he kissed me on my birthday – I mean, since I bumped into him on my birthday – and I'd been hoping he'd call me soon. For one thing, this must mean that the design for my house is ready and for another . . . well, in a funny sort of way, I'd quite missed him.

'Your boyfriend?' Maureen smiled indulgently.

'No, no, no,' I laughed, 'he's my, er, my . . .' I hadn't told anyone at work about my inheritance from Great-aunt Jane, which made having an architect slightly difficult to explain.

'Donna's coming,' hissed Maureen, pointing over my shoulder just as Nick answered the call. 'You've had a filling remember, act numb!'

'Or dumb,' muttered Jason, 'shouldn't be too tricky.'

'Sophie! Hi!' said Nick. 'Thanks for calling back.'

He sounded all chirpy and pleased to hear from me and I found myself grinning inanely. Until Donna perched herself on the end of my desk.

'Vat's OK,' I replied, pretending to mumble through swollen lips.

'I thought you might like to know that I've got something to show you,' he said, sounding all pleased with himself.

'Gweat,' I squeaked.

Donna fixed me with an impatient stare, placed a hand on her hip and began tapping her toe on the carpet.

I looked at her and shrugged helplessly. 'Shorry, Donna, ish ve pwinters.'

Maureen's eyebrows lifted with curiosity and I shot her a silencing glare.

'Sophie?' said Nick in a confused voice, understandably so; he probably thought I was drunk. 'Are you free on Tuesday?'

I flicked through my diary. 'Er not shoesday, no. I can do dmowwow?'

Donna rolled her eyes. 'Come and see me as soon as you've finished,' she muttered and thankfully marched off to her office.

'Sophie, are you all right?' asked the poor architect.

I breathed a sigh of relief. 'Absolutely, Nick. See you tomorrow evening, OK?'

I put the phone down and prepared myself to get through a meeting with Donna whilst pretending to have a sore face. Clutching my jaw and ignoring Jason's sniggering, I hurried over to Donna's office.

If there was one thing Donna despised, it was her staff moaning about their ailments. So when she actually asked me if I was all right, I didn't have to act: my face was numb with shock.

'Yeff fankf,' I nodded, taking a seat opposite her. 'Ve dentist pold me a go home, b I fay I'm foo bibby.'

'Don't worry about talking,' said Donna, patting my hand. This was getting seriously freaky. That was a blatant display of compassion. If Donna had a motto, it would be 'spare me your problems and tell someone who cares'.

'Just nod and shake your head,' she went on.

I nodded.

'As you know, the trial period for your social media project finishes this month.'

Did it? I'd been so preoccupied lately that it must have slipped my mind. I nodded anyway.

She opened a black folder in front of her and ran her finger down the front page. Reading upside down, I could just make out statistics for Twitter and Facebook activity. I stifled a smile, before remembering I was supposed to have a numb mouth. Trust Donna, the technophobe, to have a paper copy of an Internet report.

'These results reflect very well on the department,' she said, tucking an invisible stray hair back into her shimmering chignon. I held my breath. Now she was really scaring me: that was unmistakably a compliment. I cast my mind back over the years I had worked for her. Yup, definitely a first.

'The board is very pleased and I would like to offer you a promotion.' She pushed a white envelope towards me.

A promotion, for real this time! A few months ago, this was exactly what I wanted. Only now, for some reason, I couldn't muster up much enthusiasm. I picked up the envelope and pulled one side of my mouth up in a lopsided smile, relieved that my imaginary dental work excused me from giving her an effusive response.

'There will be a modest pay rise,' she continued. 'But the important thing is that this is an area the board is willing to invest in. Play your cards right and in six months, we could consider increasing the Social Media head count. You could have your very own assistant! Digital marketing, Sophie. That's where the future is.'

As she continued to babble on about what an excellent opportunity it was, my heart plummeted. I suddenly saw my career stretching out in front of my eyes like a single-lane highway through the desert. No highs, no lows, no twisty-turny corners or hidden obstacles. Simply more of the same.

Was this it? Had I reached the pinnacle of my career? Had there, in fact, been a pinnacle, or was it one long plateau? Where was the pride, the achievement, the satisfaction? Emma, Jess and Nick all had careers they truly cared about, felt passionate about, whereas I . . .

'You know, Sophie,' said Donna, leaning forward to deliver her final blow, 'you remind me a lot of myself when I was your age.'

Noooo! The ultimate insult. I could not end up like her. I refused to still be in this department in twenty years' time, bitter and twisted and making everyone else's life a misery.

I gave a low moan.

'You poor thing,' murmured Donna.

'Fank you,' I said, bending the envelope to avoid eye contact.

'Off you go.' She flicked her head at the door to terminate our meeting. Normal service resumed. I almost sighed with relief.

Sixty minutes later, I reasoned that the effects of my anaesthetic would have worn off by now. After a gentle massage and some exaggerated facial stretches outside Donna's office window, I reverted to my usual voice when the phone on my desk rang.

'*The Herald*, Sophie Stone speaking.' Ironically, my face ached for real now, after all that pretence.

'Hello, Sophie. It's Terry Stone,' and after a moment's pause he added, 'your father.'

I froze, my hand unable to remove the phone from my ear and my jaw rigid. Calling me at work, calling me ever, in fact, had not been part of the deal. Only a couple of hours ago, I'd been thinking that I had questions to ask him, but not now, not at work in front of Jason and Maureen.

'Sophie?'

My voice came out all high-pitched. 'My father? You're sure about that, are you now? Last time, you thought I only *could* be your daughter.'

Despite my acid wit, I was as nervous as hell. My heart was pounding and I felt an instant flush to my face.

'Yes, sorry about that. I was expecting someone with curly hair,' said Terry smoothly. 'As first sentences go, it wasn't the most impressive.'

My hand reached automatically up to my curls. I'd had it straightened on the day I met him, but that didn't explain how he knew I had curls.

I shook my head irritably; I wasn't particularly interested in why he had given me such a lacklustre greeting any more, it was water under a very wide bridge. I was suddenly aware of an air of silence around me. No tapping of keyboards, no other phone calls. I swung round on my chair to see Jason and Maureen blatantly staring at me. In my fourteen years at *The Herald*, I had never taken a call from my parents.

'I'm not supposed to take personal calls, Terry. Why are you calling?'

He cleared his throat. 'When we met, I felt it didn't go very well.'

Understatement of the century. That was like saying that the England football team hadn't done as well as expected in the World Cup.

'At least that's something we agree on.' I laughed nervously.

'There was – there is – so much I want to tell you about what happened before you were born. I'm going back to the States soon and,' he hesitated as if steeling himself to continue, 'I'd really like the chance to set the record straight.'

Part of me was flattered that he wanted to see me again; I mean, I must have been a teensy bit important to him if he was prepared to put himself through another grilling. Let's face it, it had been no picnic for him either. But now more than ever I realized that I needed a chance to tell Mum the truth before I met up with him again.

I bit my lip, unsure how to put it. 'I'm sorry but I can't see you again,' I said finally. 'Not at the moment. There's something I have to do first.'

'Take my number then, Sophie, please, in case you change your mind.'

I agreed and scribbled a mobile number down on a scrap of paper.

'Although there is one thing I'd like to know now,' I said suddenly. 'Why wouldn't you come to the UK before August? If it was so important to meet me and set the record straight, why wait?'

My father let out a deep sigh and there was a long silence before he spoke.

'I lost my wife earlier this year and after that I . . .' His voice petered out.

My stomach lurched. It hadn't occurred to me for one moment that Terry had his own life, his own problems to deal with.

'I'm sorry.' The words came out in a hoarse whisper. 'I had no idea, I thought— Eek!'

A bony hand squeezed my shoulder and I nearly dropped the phone.

'Sophie, are you there?' I heard my father say.

I clamped my hand over the mouthpiece and raised my eyebrows at Donna enquiringly.

'Your injection has worn off then?' She smiled tightly at me.

'Yes. Sorry,' I stuttered, 'it's my father. I was just . . . telling him my good news.'

I fully expected her to force me to end the call – Donna hated personal phone calls almost as much as she hated illness. But to my surprise she narrowed her eyes and nodded.

'Just this once. But keep it brief,' she said.

I blinked at her, waiting for her to leave.

'Go on!' she urged, tightening her grip on my shoulder. I shrank down in my seat. I wondered momentarily whether I could suddenly reinstate my dental numbness, but abandoned the idea as the lesser of two evils. I peered up at Donna. She was definitely waiting for me to tell him my good news.

'Um, I got a promotion today,' I said in a small voice.

'Good. Er, that's great, Sophie. I'm very pleased for you,' he replied. He sounded so confused by the change of subject that I almost felt sorry for him.

This was a nightmare. Not only were Maureen and Jason

174

giving me daggers (I hadn't even told them yet), but Terry would take my announcement as a sign that I wanted to continue our conversation.

'I'd better let you get back to work but if you change your mind and think you might want to get to know me properly then—'

'Righto,' I said chirpily. I put down the phone and beamed at my boss. 'He told me to work hard and do my best.'

Donna strode away, apparently satisfied. I exhaled with relief and felt my body slump. I looked at the clock. Was it time to escape yet?

Chapter 20

It was eleven o'clock when I let Marc and myself into the flat later that night after the cinema. Jess was staying the night at Spike's and judging by the aroma of lavender and the light coming from under the bathroom door, Emma was in the bath.

'I'm starving,' said Marc, heading straight for the kitchen. 'Got any eggs?'

I hovered at the door, watching him make himself an omelette. When Marc was in there he filled the tiny room completely. Yet despite his bulky frame, he was extremely nifty in the kitchen. He claimed he had learned to cook as a matter of necessity due to having a mother who didn't bother. On that basis I should have been a cordon bleu chef.

'Perfection on a plate.' He tipped his masterpiece out, abandoned the frying pan and sauntered into the living room, with me close behind.

I was about to comment on the washing-up, but thought better of it. Why ruin the moment? We'd had a lovely time together. Unfortunately, we'd been too late to get tickets for the rom com I'd wanted to see so had ended up watching a scary movie instead. I hadn't really minded;

it had given us a good excuse to cuddle up in the dark.

Marc demolished his omelette in seconds, pounded his fist on his chest and produced a belch loud enough to wake the dead. He wiped the back of his hand across his mouth and planted a kiss on my cheek.

I smiled indulgently at him, relishing the feel of his stubble on my face if not the whiff of egg on his breath. I took the plate from his lap and slid it onto the carpet.

'This is nice, isn't it?' I snuggled up against him on the sofa and he pulled me into his arms. 'Just the two of us.'

'Mmm,' he mumbled into my hair.

I took a deep breath and then added breezily, 'We'll be able to do this more often, once the new house has been built.'

Marc cleared his throat. 'Actually, talking of that place, I met a bloke at the gym the other day. His brother-in-law is a property developer in Manchester with a new office in Nottingham. Mostly pubs and clubs, but they're looking to expand into residential. He reckons you could get three houses on that plot of yours.'

'What do I want three houses for?' I laughed and traced a finger across his chest.

'Don't laugh! I'm serious.' He frowned and shifted away.

'Sorry, Marc, but I can only just afford to build one house,' I said soothingly.

Marc sat up straight and gripped my shoulders. 'Three houses! Just think of the money! Divide the plot up, get planning permission for three houses and sell two. You'd make a killing!'

A vision of Lilac Lane with an extra two houses on it flashed into my mind. I didn't think the neighbours would be too happy. Anyway, the plot wasn't that big;

dividing it into thirds would mean no privacy and no gardens.

Marc mistook my hesitation as a good sign.

'Good idea of mine, yeah?' He winked at me and pinched my cheek. 'And don't worry about the business side of things, all the negotiating with the developers and what have you. I'll do all that. For a small fee.'

I'd managed just fine on my own so far. I wasn't sure I needed any help. Especially for a fee.

'It's a good idea,' I said diplomatically. I glanced up at him long enough to see his eyes light up. 'But it's not only about money. I wouldn't want to live there squashed next to two other houses. It would—'

'Why don't you ask the architect? See what he thinks about it? It's just a suggestion.'

'All right,' I yawned, feeling tired all of a sudden and wanting to end the conversation. 'I'm seeing him tomorrow. I'll ask him them.'

He rubbed his hands together and grinned. 'Good girl. And who cares if they're squashed? We'll have enough money to buy somewhere bigger, somewhere in town. You don't really want to be stuck out there in the sticks, do you?'

We. He said *we'll* have enough money. I wasn't especially materialistic, but we seemed to have gone from Marc earning a fee to outright sharing.

I shook my head. 'Actually, Marc, you're wrong. I really do want to live there.'

It was true. Building my own house was my number-one priority. I had something to prove now. I might not have gone to university like my half-brother, I might have given up on my dream career in interior design, but I would create the perfect home for myself. By myself.

'Whatever, princess,' he chuckled.

He wasn't listening. I sighed inwardly, too tired to argue. He moved closer until his breath whispered against my ear and sent tingles from the nape of my neck to the bottom of my spine. I melted against him as his lips brushed mine. It felt good to be back in his arms. My life had been bonkers for the last few months and just for a few minutes it felt good to lean on someone else for a change.

'Shall we go to bed?' he murmured, inclining his head towards the door.

'Yes please,' I sighed gratefully. 'You go ahead, I'll just tidy up here.'

I collected the dirty plate and glasses and dumped them in the kitchen sink. The washing-up could wait, the fifteen-stone stud muffin in my bed couldn't. I turned to leave, a smile playing on my lips.

Emma stood in the doorway, in her dressing gown, arms crossed and eyebrows furrowed. I clutched at my chest.

'Jeepers, Emma! You frightened the life out of me!'

'I heard all that about building three houses; he's muscling in on your inheritance,' she whispered. 'I knew he'd do something like this.'

'It's fine, Em,' I whispered back. 'It's all under control. Not that you should have been eavesdropping.'

'Just looking out for you,' she huffed.

I glanced towards my bedroom door to check Marc wasn't lurking within earshot.

'And I appreciate it,' I said, giving her a hug. 'I offered to lend him some money, you know. To invest in his second-hand car business. Do you know what he said?'

She shook her head warily.

'He wants to do it himself, pay his own way.' I pulled back, hoping to see her lighten up a bit.

Emma shrugged. 'Glad to hear it. I'm sorry, I want to be happy for you, but I just don't trust him.'

'It's different this time. I'm standing up for myself much more these days.'

Well, sort of. I wasn't sure Emmeline Pankhurst and friends would have been cheering from their graves at my pathetically submissive display of five minutes ago.

My bedroom door opened and Marc appeared wearing only his boxer shorts. Emma yelped with embarrassment and ducked out of sight.

'I'm waiting, princess,' he crooned seductively, waggling his eyebrows.

'See,' I winked at Emma as I passed, 'he adores me.'

'Just be careful, Sophie,' called a hushed voice from the kitchen.

A noise woke me up ludicrously early. I opened my eyes and shut them again. It wasn't time to get up yet. A smile crept across my face; Marc was still here and this time I'd managed not to roll out of bed during the night.

I pulled the duvet up around my shoulders. Shame he couldn't stay in bed a bit longer for a cuddle. I could hear him getting dressed; jangling keys, rustling papers, the soft clicking and beeping of his phone . . . his phone? I turned over and attempted to focus on his shadowy shape in the dawn light.

'Marc? What are you doing?' I rubbed my eyes and squinted at him.

He whirled round from his position at my dressing table and the folder containing all the Lilac Lane documents fell to the floor. He dropped to his knees and scooped up the paperwork.

'Whoops, clumsy of me, sorry,' he laughed.

'What are you doing with your phone?' I repeated.

'Er, you looked so gorgeous lying there asleep, I thought I'd take your picture. Say cheese!' He held his mobile up and it flashed.

'Oh God, delete it!' I groaned, my hand flying to my bedhead hair. I probably looked like one of the Muppets. 'What do you want a picture of me for?'

'Mum was asking what you looked like.'

While I was in bed? I frowned. Was it me or was that a bit weird?

'That's nice of her,' I muttered. 'Let's have a look at it, then. The least you can do is to show me how bad it is.'

'No time, princess. Gotta get to a car auction and I want to beat the traffic. See you later, yeah?' He leaned over, kissed my forehead and was gone.

I was about to drop back off to sleep again when I remembered what day it was. My eyes sprang open and I kicked my feet excitedly. I was seeing Nick today and I could not wait.

Chapter 21

I was so keen to see what Nick had done that I trotted up the path towards our appointment ten minutes early. His suburban semi was as neat and orderly as the last time I had visited; grass mown in perfect stripes and not a stone out of place in the gravel drive. It suited him down to the ground.

Now that I knew him a bit better, I would love to have a snoop around his house to see if he was as meticulous in his private life as he was on a professional level. I reckoned he was the sort of man to fold his pyjamas, polish his shoes and iron creases in his jeans. Marc, on the other hand, wouldn't know what to do with an iron, other than bicep curls. Thinking of Marc made me remember how oddly he'd acted this morning. I had a suspicion that he'd been doing his own spot of snooping in my Lilac Lane folder. I didn't buy that line about a photograph for his mum for one second. I made a mental note to keep an eye on him from now on because there was something decidedly iffy going on there.

I went through the side gate and into the garden as instructed and knocked on the cabin door. For the next hour or so I was going to have a lovely time with Nick talking architecture and put Marc Felton firmly out of my mind.

Nick's face lit up as he let me in and he had a phone tucked under his chin.

Hi, he mouthed cheerily, gesturing for me to sit. *Won't be long.*

Norman jumped up from his bed to give me an enthusiastic greeting. This time I was ready for him; I kept my handbag in front of my crotch and fed him pieces of biscuit. Eventually, I ran out of crumbs and he wagged his tail and sloped back off to his bed.

I watched Nick surreptitiously for a while, trying to suppress a smile. He must have been frustrated; his dark hair was standing up in peaks, his pens and pencils were lined up on his desk like soldiers on parade and he had polished his glasses twice since I had been here.

The phone call was dragging on. I eavesdropped at first, but he appeared to be talking to someone about the circumference of trees, which was very boring, so, feeling self-conscious, I stood up to study the framed photographs on the wall.

Most of them were of building sites, but the one that drew my eye was of a young Nick, puppy-faced and without glasses, looking stiff and resplendent in a mortar board and gown, holding a paper scroll. Next to him, with his arm around his shoulders, was an older man, with sparse grey hair and a sun-tanned complexion. Judging by the expression of pride on his face, he must have been Nick's father. That would be my half-brother in a few years' time: graduating from university, my father beaming at his side. A stab of jealousy made me frown and I tried to dismiss the mental picture.

Luckily Nick's phone call came to an end and I turned round to face him.

'Hi.' I smiled. *You kissed me last time we met.* Oh God, now my face had gone red. *Professional, Sophie, be professional.*

'I'm so sorry to keep you waiting,' said Nick, rubbing a hand over his face. 'Planning issues as usual.'

'No problem.' I flapped a hand. 'I was early anyway. Too excited to stay away any longer.'

Do we shake hands or are we now officially on kissing terms, or is that only on birthdays? I found myself wondering how long it would be until his birthday.

'Really?' His face broke into a smile.

I nodded. 'Oh yes, I'm dying to see how you interpreted my brief.'

'Ah, of course.' He cleared his throat. 'Anyway,' he said, stepping forward with his hand outstretched. 'Glad you could come at such short notice.'

I shook his hand, feeling faintly disappointed.

'I must admit I was a bit worried about you yesterday on the phone,' he continued with a frown.

'Were you?' My heart melted. He was such a sweetie.

'Mmm,' he nodded. 'You sounded a bit . . .'

Please don't say drunk.

'. . . distracted. Would you like coffee?'

'Lovely, thank you,' I said, taking a seat. *Right, Sophie, this is your chance to actually impress him. No bursting into tears, no clumsy accidents and no sounding drunk. Focus, focus, focus.*

'I've been looking forward to today too.' He blinked solemnly and placed a cup of coffee in front of me. He'd remembered how I took it: milky with two sugars. I don't think Marc would have known that. In fact, now that I thought about it, I wasn't sure Marc had ever made me a drink.

'Oh,' was all I managed to utter.

My heart was racing and I hadn't even had a sip of my coffee, so I couldn't blame it on the caffeine.

From a pile on his desk, Nick selected a folder and set it on the table. Then he picked up the two large mood boards I had created as a brief and propped them up on the floor where we could both see them.

A warm glow filled my heart as I looked at the boards. I had to admit, they were lovely.

'I've thoroughly enjoyed working on your project. And I meant what I said.' He sat down opposite me with a nervous smile. 'The brief you gave me was outstanding. You've got a real eye for layout. You're not an interior designer, are you?'

I held my cup up to my lips to hide my embarrassment. I was delighted. So far I hadn't done anything stupid and I'd impressed him.

I smiled modestly. 'It's only a hobby; well, not even that any more. It was a dream I had when I was younger. I used to spend hours designing interiors.'

'Never tempted to make a career out of it?'

'No. Throwing some ideas around for this house is the nearest I've ever come to making that dream happen,' I replied.

'What was it Thoreau said? "If you have built castles in the air, put foundations under them." Something like that, anyway.'

I cocked an amused eyebrow at him. I had no idea who Thoreau was but I liked his thinking.

'That's your job, I hope,' I said, eyeing up the folder between us.

'I'd like to think I've captured the big picture, the overall concept of what you want. But in truth, the finer details, well, I've lifted them straight from your boards.'

Enough already with the ego-stroking, I was getting all hot under the collar here. If Nick didn't open the folder soon, I would dive on it myself.

He pulled the folder in front of him and began to open it. This was it. I held my breath. After dreaming about my own home all my life, I was about to get my first glimpse.

He closed it again. My shoulders sagged.

'These are just ideas. If you don't like them, it'll simply be back to the drawing board. And please be honest.'

I nodded, willing him to get on with it.

Finally, Nick removed a large piece of paper from the folder and handed it to me. My hands trembled as I placed it on the table and a shiver of electricity crackled through me.

'I can't believe this is happening to me, you know,' I breathed. 'I'm usually such a procrastinator; I never make decisions, never grasp the nettle, never stray from my comfort zone. In fact, my . . . never mind.' I closed my mouth. I'd been about to say that Marc had even once said I was boring, but I didn't want Nick to know that.

'I find that very hard to believe.' He smiled, his eyes dancing with amusement. 'I've always found you to be full of life and completely unpredictable.'

I laughed. 'I'll take that as a compliment.'

'Are you going to look at this design, then?' he said, raising an eyebrow.

I looked at the two drawings on the sheet of paper. The top one showed the front of the house. My eyes scanned the design: the pitched roof with a chimney, the row of three windows upstairs, and a window each side of the front door below.

'I've tried to incorporate the contemporary open-plan

feel that you like with the more classic cottagey look.'

I continued to stare, drinking in the details. The design wasn't ground-breaking – in fact, it was quite conventional – but there was something pretty and feminine about it. I couldn't speak. My throat felt tight and tears weren't far away.

'I thought it would fit in with the older, more traditional houses in Woodby village.'

I glanced up at Nick to see him massage his forehead with his finger and thumb.

'OK, no problem,' said Nick curtly. 'I can see I've misinterpreted the brief. So . . .' He reached across and tried to take the drawing off me.

'It's perfect,' I whispered.

'Pardon?' He frowned.

I cleared my throat and tried again. 'It's beautiful.'

'This is you happy, then?' He smiled uncertainly.

I nodded and laughed. 'Would you prefer it if I wagged my tail?'

He let out a long breath. 'It would certainly make you easier to read.'

'Seriously, I love it.'

'What a relief!' He laughed shakily. 'Personally, I think it suits you to a tee.'

I nodded eagerly. 'In fact, it's just like the drawings I used to do when I was a little girl!'

I could tell instantly by the look on his face that I'd said the wrong thing. Maybe comparing a seven-year-old's scribble to the sketch of an experienced architect, who'd spent donkeys' years at university, wasn't such a compliment.

'What I meant was,' I continued, 'that this is exactly what I've always dreamed of.'

Nick whistled and raked a hand through his already tufty hair.

'We make a good team then, don't we?' he said quietly, not meeting my eye.

'We do,' I whispered back.

Nick took me through each of the elevations, describing the structure in great detail from the blue bricks at the bottom, which had something to do with damp, to the row of patterned brick under the roof, which was simply to make the house look pretty. He opened the folder again and withdrew drawings of the interior layout, pointing out each room in turn.

'Downstairs there's a large L-shaped space incorporating kitchen, dining and living room.'

'Very sociable.' I nodded, already imagining it.

'This small room at the front of the house could be used as a study or a little sitting room when you want some peace and quiet.'

Upstairs there were three bedrooms and a bathroom, the master bedroom having an en suite and a small, but perfectly formed, walk-in wardrobe.

I couldn't help myself. I squeaked at the walk-in wardrobe. Emma and Jess were going to be green with envy when they saw it. The flat had next to no storage space and we all had suitcases of clothes crammed under our beds. Except without me, I supposed they could use my room for all their stuff.

I was sad that they wouldn't consider moving with me; there was plenty of room for all of us and we could carry on sharing as we had done for years. But maybe it was time for me to move on, to grow up.

A tiny spark deep inside me flickered with excitement.

Even though they were only rough, these sketches held a glimpse of what my future could hold. I tuned back into Nick's words, struck once again by how animated he was when he talked about his work.

'You get a real buzz from this, don't you?' I said.

Nick looked surprised by the question and didn't answer straight away.

'I love structure. I love making the best of space,' he said eventually, replacing the sheets of paper back into the folder. 'Always have. I remember sitting at my parents' kitchen table, telling the builders that if they flipped our staircase round, there would be enough room for a play-room for me upstairs. I was eight.'

My eyes strayed to the graduation photograph on the wall.

'I guess your dad is really proud of your career?' I asked, pointing to the picture.

'Was,' Nick corrected, his voice wavering. 'He passed away four years ago. Before I started my own practice.'

'I'm so sorry,' I murmured.

'But I think he was proud of me.' He nodded fondly. 'He was a big presence in my life. I still miss him.'

'Was he an architect too?'

He shook his head and gazed at the photograph. 'He ran a garden centre in Derbyshire. But as soon as he knew I was serious about architecture, he supported me one hundred per cent. We used to go off on day trips together to look at buildings.'

'How lovely.' My mum had never really commented on my career choice, other than to criticize and my father . . .

'Anyway,' Nick cleared his throat as if he was embarrassed to have revealed personal details, 'I'm sure your parents are proud of you for undertaking a project like this on your own, aren't they?'

I blinked at him, working out how best to answer that one. The contrast between our two backgrounds could hardly have been greater. I thought back to the phone call from my father yesterday and his desire to tell his side of the story. Terry Stone knew nothing of my hopes and dreams, my friends or my life.

To my embarrassment, my bottom lip suddenly acquired a life of its own and began to wobble.

Not again! Sophie, do not cry! He was going to think I was an emotional wreck. I pinched my lips together to hold it in.

'It's not still about your birthday, is it?' he asked with a half-smile.

I shook my head and managed to lift the corners of my mouth in reply.

Nick's eyes darted round the room in every direction except mine. He patted my arm a couple of times while I attempted to regain my composure. Then his eyes alighted on the empty coffee cups and with an audible whistle of relief, he dashed over to switch the machine on again.

Nick placed a hot drink in front of me and winced as he took a sip from his own steaming cup.

'My parents don't know,' I mumbled.

'Why not?' Maybe this was wildly inappropriate, especially for a man who never mixed business with pleasure, but Nick was looking at me like he was all ears.

I shrugged my shoulders and sighed. Why not indeed?

'It's complicated,' I began.

During the time it took him to slurp his way through a frothy cappuccino, his face screwed up with concentration,

I explained how my parents had split before I was born and how I'd had to agree to meet my father before inheriting Great-aunt Jane's estate.

I sat back and waited to see his reaction.

'Mmm,' he said. 'Your dad ran off to join the Navy when you were born. Your mum is a cabaret singer in Spain. You've got a half-brother who you've never seen. Your dad wants to get to know you but you don't want to hurt your mother.'

I nodded. Summarized like that, I felt like a character out of a soap opera. If it wasn't my life we were referring to, I would almost find it funny.

A shiver ran down my spine as the truth dawned on me. I had only refused to meet up with Terry out of loyalty to Mum. If there was even a tiny chance that she wouldn't find out or if I thought for a moment that she wouldn't mind, I would have said yes. I knew it was crazy, but all of a sudden I realized I was curious, I wanted to know more about him. I wanted *him* to know about *me*.

'Well, that makes my trip to Buckingham Palace with a packed lunch look a bit tame,' said Nick, raising his eyebrows.

'Oh God! Give me tame over angst-ridden, dysfunctional and cross-continental any day of the week,' I said and sighed.

Nick chewed on his bottom lip. 'Are you absolutely sure that your mother wouldn't approve? Wouldn't she be pleased if your dad tried to redeem himself after all these years?'

I shook my head sadly. How could he possibly understand, coming from his perfect 'happy families' upbringing? Despite living a thousand miles away, I was all Mum had; my loyalties had to remain with her, it was only fair.

'I only ask because – and this is entirely none of my

business, so feel free to ignore me – if I had a chance to have my dad back in my life, even for one day, I would grab it faster than Norman eats dog treats.'

Norman pricked his ears up hopefully.

'Perhaps you should ask yourself what's really holding you back,' Nick went on earnestly. 'Your mum or your own fears?'

I gasped. His words pierced my happy mood and my face fell. 'You have no right to say that.'

Nick paled. 'I'm sorry, Sophie.'

My eyes narrowed. 'Everyone thinks they know better than me: you, Emma, my boyfriend, my mum . . . Well, I'm fed up of it. I can make up my own mind, thank you very much.'

His eyebrows shot up. 'No, that's not what I meant . . .' he stammered.

I stood up abruptly, grabbed the folder and stuffed the papers back inside.

'Are these drawings for me?' I snapped.

'Yes, this is your set,' said Nick, getting to his feet. 'Sophie, wait!'

I didn't meet his gaze. My cheeks were blazing and I could feel tears pressing at the back of my eyes. 'Thank you. I'll see myself out.'

Norman stood up and wagged his tail but I ignored him and stormed out of the cabin and out of Nick's garden.

I made it as far as the bus stop before stopping to catch my breath, Nick's words ringing in my ears. Was he right? What was really holding me back? My heart thumped as I reached into my purse and unfurled the scrap of paper on which I'd written my father's number. Was I brave enough to face my fears? And if so, what was I going to do about it?

Chapter 22

By early next morning, I was totally fed up with myself. I got barely a wink of sleep that night and lay tossing and turning until two o'clock, fiddling about with my pillows in an attempt to find a route to the Land of Nod. At one point I lay on my back with a pillow under my knees and finally on my side with one between my knees. This last position was quite comfortable, but I had gleaned it from a child-birth programme and couldn't get the image of panting women out of my head and so failed to drop off to sleep.

I flipped the duvet back irritably and checked the clock. Six a.m., seven in Spain. Too early to get up.

Perhaps Nick was right. Maybe Mum would have softened and wouldn't snap my head off if I rang her and demanded some answers? Maybe she'd think that having Terry in my life, even if she hated his guts, would be better than having no father at all?

Yeah, right, and Willy Wonka was alive and well and living in London . . .

It sounded so easy when I tried out the conversation in my head: *Hi, Mum, I've got something to tell you: I've met my father . . .*

Deep breaths, deep breaths.

Quarter past six. Was that all the time that had passed? Fifteen minutes? Still too early.

Creative, artistic, sensitive – those were the adjectives I had used to excuse my mother's emotional behaviour when I was growing up. I had quickly learned that it simply wasn't worth asking her to go into detail about why her marriage had broken down and why she thought my daddy didn't want to know me. She would fill up with tears or sulk or descend into a silence that could last several days. So all I knew was that they had married young and in haste and that all men would let you down in the end, however respectable they might appear. My dad was respectable, then, I'd always thought, at least outwardly.

Even though I sometimes had to tiptoe around her, Mum had been great fun when I was a child. My friends were in awe of her; she was far more unconventional than all their mothers; the girls were fascinated and the boys all used to blush when she met me at the school gates. She was no use when it came to helping me with my science homework, but I always had the most detailed fancy dress costumes and the best birthday parties.

But those days were gone now, I scolded myself, it was time to grow a thick skin and tackle her about my dad. I had only spent a few minutes in his company and obviously, he might have changed over the last thirty-three years, but Terry Stone didn't seem a particularly bad person.

All of a sudden, getting to the bottom of the events surrounding my parents' spilt became too pressing to ignore for a single moment longer. I wanted answers.

The time was six twenty. Emma and Jess wouldn't wake up for another hour. It was still too early to call Spain really, but it would have to do.

I pulled on my dressing gown, picked up my laptop and tiptoed softly into the kitchen so as not to wake Emma and Jess. I put the kettle on to make a cup of tea and checked my emails while I waited for it to boil.

To my surprise, there was a new message from Nick waiting for me in my inbox. My face reddened instantly as I clicked on it to open it; so much for creating a professional image yesterday. Goodness knows what the poor man must be thinking of me now. In fact, I thought gloomily, this email was probably to terminate our contract. I sat down at the kitchen table to give Nick's words my full attention.

Dear Sophie,
I am writing to express my sincere regret at my lack of tact yesterday. You are entirely correct; I had absolutely no right to comment on your private life and, if you can forgive me, I guarantee nothing like that will happen again. I will, of course, completely understand if you would rather not continue with our working relationship.
Yours sincerely
Nick

Oh. His words should have made me happy but actually, I had been quite enjoying getting to know the softer side of my architect and now I felt unexpectedly disappointed. Besides, I had a sneaky feeling that the reason I'd reacted so strongly yesterday was because there had been a hefty dose of truth in his words. I tuned back into the end of his email and my face softened into a smile.

PS I hope this isn't the case because, although I shouldn't say this, yours is currently my favourite project.

Lilac Lane was his favourite project, which had to mean that I was his favourite client, didn't it? After a celebratory air punch I closed his email, remembering belatedly my promise to Marc to ask Nick about putting more than one house on the plot. Never mind. I would email Nick back later on. But first I had a family mystery to solve.

I dialled mum's number and focused on deep breathing while I waited for her to answer.

There was a crackle on the line, followed by an echoey voice and finally she came into view.

'Goodness me, Sophie love, you're up early!' said Mum.

She was never one to be under-dressed, but even for her she looked quite startling for this time of day; she was wearing a gold sequinned boob tube, her hair was pinned up with glittery hairslides and she was sporting enormous fake eyelashes and a pair of diamanté hoop earrings.

'Sorry, Mum.' I winced. 'I couldn't wait. You look very . . . sparkly this morning; where are you off to?'

'Bed!' she laughed. 'I've just got in, been out all night!'

Just got in? Has anyone told her she's in her bloomin' fifties!

'Whoohoo! What a party!' She grinned and took a sip from what looked suspiciously like a shot of vodka.

'Salsa dancing in Torremolinos. I've danced my flippin' feet off. All I've got left is stumps. Look!' She leaned back and held a foot up to the webcam and hooted with laughter. Was that a leather miniskirt?

'Talk about raunchy! Ooh, those Latin American men know what to do with their hips.' Mum closed her eyes and shook her head. 'I'll take you when you come over. You'll love it. You could do with loosening up a bit.'

She peered at the screen. 'Actually, you look like you've

had a late night yourself. What have you been up to?'

I could do with a slurp of Mum's vodka right now. I took a gulp of my tea instead for courage.

'I went to bed early, but I didn't get much sleep.'

'Ooh!' She winked. 'Should I be hearing this?'

'I didn't get much sleep because . . . because . . .'

'What, love?' Mum frowned and shifted closer to the screen. 'Spit it out, you can tell your mum anything, Sophie.'

I could feel my pulse throbbing in my temple and I pressed a hand to it.

'Mum, there's something I didn't tell you about Jane Kennedy's will.'

Her eyes narrowed. 'What do you mean?'

I exhaled, feeling all panicky and wishing I'd never started this. *Come on, Sophie, you're a big girl now. Besides which, you deserve the truth.*

I took a deep breath. 'OK, but let me finish because it's not as bad as you think . . .'

'Go on.' She blinked her blue eyes at me and ran her tongue over her lips.

'In order to inherit her estate, I had to agree to meet my father.'

Mum flung herself back in her seat and gasped, a hand pressed to her mouth.

'It was fine,' I said hurriedly, 'honestly, nothing to it. I've done it already and I wasn't going to say anything because I didn't want you to get upset and anyway I had no intention of ever seeing him after that first time, but the thing is . . .' I paused and crossed my fingers. 'The thing is he wants to keep in touch and . . . Mum, are you all right?'

All of a sudden, my mum looked every single one of her fifty-two years. It was as if my words had sucked all the life out of her. Her shoulders had slumped, her mouth sagged and she sat motionless, staring at the screen.

I chewed on my lip. I should have waited. I should have told her face to face, I was visiting her soon anyway and then I could have put my arms round her and reassured her. Poor Mum. Too late now, I could have kicked myself.

She turned her face away and muttered, 'Well, no doubt you've heard the whole sordid story?'

Sordid? I blinked at her.

'Not at all, Mum,' I said, doing my best to maintain an even voice. 'But you were both young and these things happen, couples do split. I know you felt humiliated and—'

'No, Sophie.' Mum sat up suddenly and I saw with horror that her eyes were full of tears. 'You don't know how I felt then or how I feel now.'

My heart squeezed with love for her. Whatever my father wanted to tell me, one thing was for certain, my loyalty was, and always would be, to her.

'No one's blaming you in any of this, Mum,' I stressed. 'You've done a brilliant job of bringing me up on your own. He let us both down from the start. But there are still gaps in my childhood and I need to talk about it to understand what happened between the two of you.'

I took a deep breath. I felt so guilty for doing this to her, but for once, I was determined to get my own way.

'And I'd prefer to hear it from you rather than him.'

She drew herself up tall in her seat and threw the rest of her vodka down in one. Her voice, when she spoke, was so low, I thought at first there was interference on the line.

'All the sacrifices I made for you and this is how you repay me. All this . . . this prying, digging up dirt. Why, Sophie? It was over thirty years ago. He broke my heart then and now you've done it all over again. How could you?'

'It doesn't change anything, Mum. Even if I get to know Terry, I'll always love *you*,' I pleaded.

'If you loved me, you wouldn't go behind my back like this. No, I'm sorry, Sophie. It's him or me and it sounds like you've already made your choice.'

'But, Mum . . .'

I noticed her chin was wobbling as she clamped her lips together and shook her head. She reached towards her laptop and whispered, 'I hope you'll be very happy together.'

And the screen went black.

My heart sank. I couldn't leave it like this between us. I called her back instantly, but she didn't answer. I tried her mobile but it went to voicemail.

'Let me explain, Mum,' I said to her answerphone. 'Please pick up.'

With shaking hands, I turned the laptop off and threw the rest of my tea down the sink. I jumped and grabbed my phone as a text message came through from her: *I've cancelled your birthday massage.*

My heart pounded; what had I done?

This sudden interest in my father, was it worth damaging my relationship with Mum for? Perhaps I was dredging up ancient history that would be better off left buried in the past.

Either way, it didn't look like I would be enjoying *La Vida Loca* anytime soon.

I trudged out of the kitchen. My bedroom opened its shabby-chic arms and surrounded me like a comfort blanket.

All the sacrifices I made for you, Mum had said.

I sat down at my dressing table and contemplated the sacrifice that I had made for her, the one she had never known about.

At twenty-one, I had been utterly confident of a successful future. I'd had it all mapped out in a three-year plan. By twenty-four I would be an interior stylist for a top London magazine. The world would be my perfectly accessorized oyster.

I had set myself a goal and worked my butt off to get there. I spent hours working on my portfolio, designing schemes for rooms of all shapes, sizes and styles. From Shaker to chic, beach house to Bauhaus, rustic to romantic, I'd had more ideas than Ikea. Finally, after writing letter after letter, applying for job after job, I'd cracked it.

I wiped the tears from my cheeks and opened up the slim drawer of my dressing table. It would still be in here, I was sure of it; there was no way I would have thrown it out. My fingers scrabbled around, pushing past the bank statements, old bus passes and photographs until they found their quarry.

There it was. Underneath a decade's worth of detritus, hidden but not forgotten, a white envelope, ordinary enough, except for the franking label.

House magazine.

My heart leapt as I read it, as it had all those years ago when it had arrived in the post. I remembered squealing with joy reading the words: *We are delighted to offer you the position of Junior Stylist.*

Jess and Emma hadn't been at home for some reason and I was bursting to tell someone so I decided to ring Mum in

Spain. She would be so proud of me. My dream was coming true, I was on my way!

I cast my mind back to that night. It had been a nightmare to get hold of her. Mobile phones were really expensive in Spain at the time, so I could only ever speak to her when she was in her hotel room, and as she was such a sociable creature, that was virtually never!

I finally caught up with her late that night but I never got round to telling her my exciting news. As fate would have it, she had news of her own. The local Spanish hospital had removed a lump and she wanted to come home to start a course of treatment and convalesce. She wanted to stay with me, she explained, so that I could look after her, so she could see her old English doctor with whom she felt more comfortable and had no problems with the lingo. It would only be for six months. That wasn't too much to ask, was it? She'd be no trouble, she'd promised.

I'd sobbed with worry for her and told her that I'd love to have her to stay. She could have my bed for as long as she needed to.

Writing back to *House* magazine to tell them I wouldn't be joining the styling team after all was one of the most painful things I had ever had to do. I never told anyone about that job offer. It didn't seem fair to burden Mum with it and I didn't want Jess or Emma to pity me; I could manage that quite nicely on my own.

Later that year, once Mum had fully recovered and had gone back to Spain, I resumed my London job search, but then I met Jeremy. I fell in love and put my life on hold again and by the time I'd untangled myself from his clutches, I felt like the boat carrying my dreams had sailed and I had missed it completely.

Now, though, with Mum's accusations ringing in my ears, I couldn't help but wonder whether I'd been wrong to give up. And whether perhaps it was time to follow my heart again.

Chapter 23

Before I knew it, September had turned into October, Mum had refused to answer any of my calls and I'd had to cancel my flight to Spain. But when I peered out of the window one Saturday morning, I couldn't help but feel optimistic: it was one of those crisp and clear autumn days when you get the urge to run through piles of carefully swept-up leaves for the sheer hell of it.

However, my task for the day was much less fun. I had been putting off clearing Great-aunt Jane's bungalow for weeks. The idea of digging through a stranger's possessions was giving me the heebie-jeebies. But as I had run out of excuses, today was the day.

I pulled on my jeans, a hoodie and a pair of warm boots and went in search of willing assistants.

'Ah, sorry, babes,' said Jess, head bent over the kitchen table. She put a final stripe of varnish on her thumb nail. Her nails matched her purple leggings perfectly.

'Spike and I are calling in at Mum and Dad's later.' She beamed up at me, her face all gooey with excitement. 'It'll be the first time they've met him! I can't wait.'

I smiled back at her as I popped some bread in the toaster and did a rough calculation; she must have been going out with the policeman for about six months now. It was un-heard of for her to be so restrained about getting the stamp of approval from her parents. Normally, the poor chaps are subjected to a 'Meet the Parents' ordeal within the first few weeks. Jess must be serious about Spike to be playing it so cool.

Emma appeared with her cheeks bulging, accompanied by a strong whiff of antiseptic. She gargled loudly, spat into the kitchen sink and grimaced.

'I'm sure I'm coming down with laryngitis,' she moaned, reaching for the kettle to refill it.

'Come home with me and Spike. Mum will make you soup and a hot-water bottle,' said Jess.

I hid a smirk. I was always amused when either of them referred to their parents' house as home. Well, amused or envious. The flat was the only home I had, unless I counted the bungalow, which I didn't yet.

'No thanks,' said Emma, looking like she'd rather have all her teeth removed with pliers than play gooseberry to her sister. 'I'm helping Sophie clear the bungalow.'

'Yay; thanks, Em.'

She smiled at me and coughed delicately to reinforce how much of a sacrifice she was making.

Jess waved her nails in front of her face to dry them.

'Dad is going to love him.' She sighed. 'Spike is every parent's dream for their daughter.'

'He'll certainly send them to sleep,' snorted Emma, pouring hot water in a bowl. I took the kettle from her and made myself a mug of tea with the remains of the water. She did have a valid point; the most interesting thing about Jess's boyfriend was his name.

Jess smiled dreamily. 'We are two peas in a pod, Spike

and I. Two servants of our community: I shape the young minds of the future generation and he keeps the streets safe, putting himself in danger so that we can sleep soundly in our beds.'

'Give it a rest, Jess,' said Emma, lowering her face down over the steaming bowl and covering her head with a cloth. 'To hear you talk, you'd think he was trawling the streets of Miami instead of directing traffic in Nottingham.'

The doorbell rang. Jess pushed herself up from the table, still with her hands outstretched.

'Jealous,' she whispered to me.

'I heard that,' muttered Emma from under her towel.

An hour later, Emma and I were rattling along the country lanes towards Woodby in my new car. I had bravely dipped into my savings and bought a ten-year-old Mini from a lady who had advertised it in *The Herald*. It was a luxury to hop from the flat and straight into the car and I periodically kicked myself for not having done it sooner.

Emma wasn't taking any chances against the autumn wind. She was wrapped in a thick jacket, wore a fleecy hat with ear flaps and had a scarf wound several times around her neck.

'Marc too busy to help today, then?' Emma gave me a sideways glance.

'He said he would have helped,' I replied airily, 'but he'd promised to watch the football in the pub with his mate and didn't want to let him down.'

She curled her lip and tutted. 'But letting you down is perfectly acceptable, I take it?'

I elected not to reply; I was beginning to feel the same way myself so I changed the subject.

'I'd rather have you with me anyway, Em. But I'm surprised you didn't fancy visiting your parents with Jess.

Emma shifted in her seat. 'To be honest, Soph, I'm a bit jealous.'

'You don't fancy Spike, do you?' It was news to me if she did. She used her special brand of sarcasm when she talked about him, the one usually reserved for Marc.

'God, no!' She looked at the clock on the dashboard. 'Jess'll be there now, parading her perfect boyfriend and their perfect jobs under Mum and Dad's noses.'

Emma sighed deeply and I smiled at her sympathetically. I hadn't had much experience of sibling rivalry. Except that recently I had started imagining my father with a proud arm around his son. I shook my head to make the mental picture vanish.

'I'm sure your parents are just as proud of you as they are of her.'

Emma turned away and gazed out of the window. 'No, Dad said once that teaching was a proper career. He might as well have said that my silversmithing was a "Mickey Mouse" profession.'

I slammed the brakes on as a tractor pulled out of a farm gate in front of us. Emma yelped and gripped the door handle so hard her knuckles turned white.

'Prove him wrong, then!' I said, peering round the tractor and overtaking it as fast as the little car would allow. 'Can't you enter an award or something? There are always prizes being handed out in my industry. There must be an equivalent for jewellery? Your dad couldn't fail to be impressed, plus it would do wonders for the business.'

Emma frowned and popped a throat lozenge into her

mouth. 'That's not a bad idea. Not that I'd have a chance in hell of winning.'

'Rubbish. I can see it now,' I said, pulling onto the drive of number eight. 'Emma Piper – award-winning silver-smith.'

'Yeah, right.' Emma rolled her eyes, but I noticed her lips twitch. 'Talking about parental approval, what are you going to do about your mum?'

'Let her stew for a while,' I replied, yanking the keys out of the ignition with more force than was entirely necessary. 'I've called, emailed, left messages and so now the ball is in her court. I mean, really, I've done nothing wrong, it's my right to see my father, isn't it?'

One side of Emma's mouth lifted in a half-smile.

'What?' I demanded.

'Nothing.' She grinned. 'Good for you, that's all. It's about time you stood up to her. Don't get me wrong,' she said, catching a glimpse of my indignant face, 'I love your mum; she's the life and soul of the party. But you're always walking on eggshells around her.'

I opened my mouth to object but she cut me off.

Anyway,' she nodded towards the bungalow, 'back to the task in hand. What are we going to do with all the junk in there?'

My stomach lurched as I contemplated the ordeal ahead. Apprehensive didn't begin to cover it; the idea of sifting through a dead person's things gave me the dithers.

'No idea. Come on, let's get this over with,' I said, climbing out of the car.

Once inside, we stood in the living room in silence. The bungalow was so damp and cold that we could see our own breath. My eyes took in all the furniture, the pictures and

207

the knick-knacks. I dreaded to think about what lay in wait for us in the bedrooms. The place was full of stuff and it would take us hours to sort through everything.

Emma opened up the writing bureau. 'Blimey, look at all this lot.'

I was contemplating admitting defeat and retiring to the pub when I heard a 'Cooee' coming from the porch and an elderly lady let herself in. She was rake thin, as tall as Emma, but slightly stooped, with white hair swept up in an elegant bun.

'Audrey Davis,' she pronounced, striding forward with an outstretched hand. 'From next door.'

I shook her hand and introduced myself and Emma.

'I found Jane, you know,' said Audrey, in a stage whisper. 'It gave me quite a fright, I can tell you. Still, best way to go, in your sleep: no fuss.'

She looked at the roll of black bin bags in my hand. 'Having a clear-out? Good idea,' she continued without waiting for a reply. 'I've got the number of a house clearance company in my book. Follow me. I'll make tea and we can get cracking.' And off she marched.

Emma and I stared at each other and then, like giggling schoolgirls, we scurried after her.

Over tea and cake in Audrey's bungalow, we devised an action plan. Well, Audrey did. I wouldn't have dared argue with her even if I'd wanted to. She was the living definition of 'formidable'.

'We're off to a great start, thanks to you, Audrey,' I said, smiling at her.

'And great cake,' mumbled Emma, through a mouthful of walnut cake.

Audrey had booked the house clearance company to collect everything except Great-aunt Jane's personal items. She arranged for a charity shop to take all her clothes and books, and bed linen and towels were going to the local hospice. All Emma and I had to do was pack up photographs and paperwork, and she would take care of the rest.

Everyone should have an Audrey, I decided, dabbing my finger round my plate to collect the last few crumbs.

'Right. Onwards,' declared Audrey, striding to her front door.

Emma released the radiator reluctantly and shrugged her jacket back on. 'She's even bossier than Jess!' she whispered in awe.

Audrey offered to tackle the kitchen and, within seconds, the clatter of pots and pans filled the little bungalow.

I paused outside my great-aunt's bedroom, one hand on the door. So far I hadn't dared go in.

'It doesn't seem right going through her things,' I hissed to Emma.

'She's dead, she won't mind,' she replied with her trademark bluntness. 'Besides, you did as she asked and met your father, you've earned the right to be here.' She squeezed my arm as I pushed open the door.

The bedroom seemed warmer than the other rooms and even after all these months, there was a lingering scent of floral perfume.

I sat down on the pink bedspread and tried to slow my breathing. I wasn't one for believing in ghosts, but I did feel more of her presence in this room than the others. I shuddered; my arms were covered in goose pimples.

I did it, Great-aunt Jane. I met him, like you asked. But I'm none the wiser. What was the point? What were you hoping to achieve?

'I'll do the drawers and you do the wardrobe,' said Emma, breaking the spell and galvanizing me into action.

Emma started lumping clothes onto the bed while I looked inside the wardrobe. There was a shelf above the hanging rail. At first glance it looked empty, but I could just make out the edge of an object. I fetched the stool from underneath the dressing table. There was a shoe box right at the back and, using a coat hanger, I managed to hook it close enough to reach.

I climbed down off the stool and blew the dust off the box. The lid was broken and there was sticky tape at two of the corners where it had been mended in the past.

I took a deep breath and removed the lid. At the top was a handful of old photographs, some black-and-white and some colour. I held my breath; the pictures must have marked significant moments in her life to have been stored in this special box and I would have loved to have found a picture of my parents' wedding.

Suddenly I gasped; I'd found something.

'Look at this!' I waved a picture at Emma. 'It's my mum and dad!'

It wasn't of their wedding, but both of my parents were in the photograph. It looked as if they'd been at a party. My mum was wearing a short dress and heels, and she looked very young. She was standing next to two young men, a glass in her hand and her head thrown back in laughter. Terry, on the other hand, was a picture of abject misery. He was standing on the far edge of the group, scowling like a grumpy teenager. He had a long curly fringe covering one eye; the other eye was trained on my mum. Whatever she had found funny, he clearly didn't share the joke.

'That's him,' I said, pointing out my father to Emma.

Emma sucked her breath in. 'Looks like the writing was on the wall, even then,' said Emma. 'What else is there?' She took a handful of pictures out of the box and rifled through them.

My eye was drawn back to the box. Underneath the pictures was a pink envelope. I plucked it out and stared at it as my hands started to tremble: it was addressed to me, care of my great-aunt. My eyes flew back to the box. There was another envelope just like it, this time in white. And underneath that several more. All with my name on them.

The hairs on the back of my neck stood to attention as I slipped my finger under the flap and ripped it open.

'Oh my God. I don't believe it.' I swallowed.

'Sophie, what's up?' asked Emma, dropping the photographs back into the box.

I stared at her as my legs gave way and I sank back onto the bed. There was a huge lump in my throat and I struggled to get my words out. 'He sent me birthday cards.'

Happy sixth birthday Sophie, love Dad.

He hadn't forgotten me. I tore open the next one while Emma picked up the first.

Happy birthday Sophie, hope you have lots of fun, love Dad.

He had remembered my birthday when I was growing up. Not just my thirty-third.

Wishing you a very happy eighth birthday Sophie, love Daddy.

Terry had cared about me.

'Bloody hell,' said Emma, collecting up all the torn envelopes. 'There's a card here for every birthday from six till you were twelve.'

'She wanted me to find these,' I said, looking up at Emma through eyes brimming with tears. 'She warned me that she was meddling, in her letter. I think this was what she meant.'

These cards didn't fit with my mum's side of the story. According to her, Terry had never shown the slightest interest in his wife or daughter after they split up. These birthday wishes proved otherwise.

'Emma, I've got to find out the story behind these. This changes everything.'

She wrapped an arm round my shoulders and gave me a squeeze. 'I agree. It looks as if he was thinking about you even though you never got the cards.'

I collected the cards up and was about to put them back in the box when I heard Audrey tutting loudly.

'There doesn't seem to be much activity in here,' she said, tapping her toe as she leaned on the doorframe. 'The kitchen is all packed up!'

Her beady eye took in the box on the bed and the cards in my hand. 'Ah.'

'Do you know about these?' I asked, springing to my feet.

The old lady looked uncertain for the first time. 'Jane might have mentioned something about it . . .'

I looked down at my feet and huge tears rolled down my cheeks. 'I thought my dad had never bothered with me.'

Audrey stepped towards me and patted my shoulder. 'Jane used to say that Terry was always one for sticking his head in the sand. Anything for an easy life.'

I felt a twinge of recognition at that description; I'd stuck my head in the sand for far too long about a lot of things.

'So what happened, then? What's the story?' asked Emma, flopping down on the bed.

Audrey shook her head. 'It's not my story to tell. That's

why Jane wanted Sophie to meet him. It's up to her to decide whether she wants Terry back in her life.'

I felt my face flush. Great-aunt Jane had given my father and me the perfect opportunity to set the record straight, but we'd wasted it.

'Right, let's finish up here, Emma,' I said, plastering on a bright smile. 'The sooner it's done, the sooner we can get home.'

I picked up a bag and began filling it with clothes but inside I was in turmoil. Finding those birthday cards had totally thrown me. It didn't make sense. Why start at my sixth birthday? Why stop at my twelfth? As far as I could remember, I had never received a card from my father. Except this year. And I hadn't even opened that. All of a sudden I couldn't wait to get home to read what he had written in this year's birthday card. Perhaps then I would understand what on earth was going on.

Chapter 24

Three o'clock. I was convinced that Donna somehow tampered with the clocks in our department to slow down the hands of time. It felt like I'd been at my desk for at least eighteen hours.

My state of mind probably didn't help; I couldn't concentrate on anything. Ever since finding that stash of birthday cards, my uneasiness had been accumulating like the used teabags in our kitchen sink.

An hour ago, or maybe it was only five minutes, I couldn't really tell, *The Herald*'s Twitter account had hit fifteen thousand followers. Last week, this event would have had me tweeting my own trumpet to all and sundry. Today I could barely muster a follow-back to my new Twitter friends.

Last night was as bad; I was so preoccupied with my thoughts that when Marc phoned to ask if he could come over, I'd turned him down flat. He hadn't been very impressed, but for once I didn't care. He had also badgered me about Nick.

'Have you mentioned anything to that architect about developing the land yet?' he'd wanted to know.

I'd bristled but just stopped short of telling him to

mind his own business and let him continue.

'You should definitely put more than one house on it. It's a no-brainer. My mate says—'

'Tomorrow,' I'd promised firmly. Anything to get him off the line so that I could go back to my thoughts. 'Now, really, Marc, I've got to go.'

I'd put the phone down and pretended not to see the impressed looks that passed between Emma and Jess.

The problem was that I couldn't make sense of my father's behaviour. I'd assumed that my parents' divorce had been particularly acrimonious, hence my father disappearing without trace. But finding those birthday cards had given me a new feeling of hope. He obviously had tried to contact me. And the message in this year's card implied that the door was still open.

I'd rummaged through my wardrobe to find my navy handbag as soon as we'd come back from Lilac Lane and torn open the card Terry had given me on my birthday back in August.

Happy Birthday Sophie,
This might be the first card you've ever received from me, but I hope it won't be the last. I know you have your own life and I haven't been able to be part of it until now. I'm not going to pressure you, but if you ever need me, I'll always be there.
Best wishes
Dad

I had never had that before: a dad who was there if I needed him. It made me feel all sort of . . . wanted.

And then there were Nick's words: *If I had a chance to have my dad back in my life, even for one day, I would grab it . . .*

How would I feel if my father were to die and I'd never bothered to get to know him, never learned anything about him or his family? I'd never forgive myself, that was how I'd feel.

Right. I checked round the office to see that no one was watching me and I made a list of what I knew.

Fact one: I had millions of unanswered questions.

Fact two: there was no way Mum was going to answer them.

Fact three: Great-aunt Jane knew more than she let on in her letter and she wanted me to find out the truth for myself.

Hardly the finest piece of deduction; however, the list led me to a gut-churningly inevitable conclusion: if I really and truly wanted to get to the bottom of the situation, I was going to have to eat my words along with a large slice of humble pie, ignore the express wishes of my mother and contact my father again.

Later that evening I was sitting in the kitchen with a mug of tea staring at the mobile number that Terry had given me before he'd left England to go back to the States. I was psyching myself up to make the call when Emma arrived home lugging a heavy box.

She set it down on the kitchen table and grinned. 'You know that thing you said about entering to win an award?'

'Ooh yes? Are you doing it?' I stood up to pour her some tea from the pot.

'I am. What do you think of these?' She carefully removed three shiny objects packed in bubble wrap from the box.

It was a set of teardrop-shaped jugs, small, medium and

large, with the point of the teardrop forming the spout. The smallest was the size of an elongated tennis ball. They were made of highly polished silver, but what made them so exquisite was their copper lining.

'Oh my word!' I gasped. 'Absolutely stunning! Did you make them?'

Emma grinned. 'Yeah. You like?'

'I love!' I said, picking up the smallest and turning it round in my hands.

'Cheers, mate. It's my entry for the National Silverware Awards.' She smiled coyly and started wrapping them back up.

I was chuffed to bits that she had taken my advice. 'Your parents are going to be so proud of you for doing this,' I said.

'You inspired me, Soph.' She wrapped an arm round my shoulders and gave me a squeeze.

'Me?' I said, feeling my face grow pink.

She nodded. 'Building your own house, Sophie. Making plans, going places. I'm proud of you. Even the way you treat Marc is a million per cent better these days.'

I beamed with pride. Emma wasn't one to dole out compliments willy-nilly and I was genuinely touched. 'Thanks, Em. And on that note,' I said, picking up the piece of paper from the kitchen table, 'wish me luck. I'm off to ring my father. I've decided I need some answers. And I need them now.'

I shut myself in my bedroom and spent a good five minutes double checking that I had worked the time difference out correctly and trying to get my hands to stop trembling. I knew Terry lived in Nevada, but not a lot else. By my reckoning it would be midday there. What if he didn't answer? And even more scary, what if he did?

I flicked my eyes over the list of questions I had prepared as a prompt in case nerves got the better of me. Then, with fluttering heart and trembling hands, I dialled the number.

Instead of the long single ring tone, like I'd heard on American TV shows, it rang out as a double, just like in England, which wasn't at all what I'd expected.

'Hello?'

Weird! The voice on the other end was male, but even from that solitary word, I could tell it was too young to be my father.

'Oh, hi, I was looking for Terry Stone.'

'This is Brodie Stone, Terry's son. I'm afraid my father is no longer staying with me.'

I panicked. I dropped the phone from my ear and covered the mouthpiece with my hand. The soft American drawl was unmistakeable in a longer sentence.

OHMYGODOHMYGODOHMYGOD.

Terry must have given me Brodie's number and not his own and now I'd dialled my half-brother. I glanced at my list of questions but they were no help. I hadn't factored in this conversational twist. Now what?

Put the phone down. Put the phone down. Sophie! HANG UP NOW!

'Er . . . I'm Sophie Stone.'

There was a harsh laugh down the phone. Oh God, I should have put the phone down while I had the chance.

'Is that so?'

Hold on a minute! What was he getting all high-horsey about? *Is that so*? All snippy and snarky.

I pressed on regardless. 'Yes, and I was hoping to speak to Terry. Do you have his number, please?'

'He's my father. Of course I have his number.'

I took a deep breath. 'Then can I have it, please?' *Keep calm, Sophie. Do not rise to the bait.*

'No,' came the curt response.

'No?' My jaw fell open.

'No, you may not.'

'Why on earth not?' I demanded. 'He's my father too and what will he say when he finds out that you prevented me from talking to him?'

Brodie huffed down the phone. 'You stay away from him. Don't you think you've done enough? You and your crazy aunt?'

Technically, Great-aunt Jane was as much his as mine, I wanted to point out, but decided to let that one go.

'What have I done?' I cried indignantly.

Brodie was quiet for a moment and then replied in a low furious tone, 'He flies halfway around the world, against doctor's orders, to honour the old lady's last request and what does he get for his trouble?' Brodie paused momentarily. Long enough for me to register the doctor part.

'He was pushed around, shouted at, accused of all sorts of lies—'

'What do you mean, against doctor's orders?' I recalled the bags under the eyes, the unhealthy skin tone. I had put that down to jetlag.

'Jeez.' He whistled. 'Didn't you talk about anything but yourself when you met him?'

'We had a lot to catch up on,' I retorted, glad that Brodie couldn't see my flushing cheeks. 'What's wrong with him?'

'He had heart surgery earlier this year. Officially he wasn't supposed to fly until September, but your solicitor kept pushing him for an appointment.'

The breath caught in my throat and I closed my eyes in horror. And all this on top of losing his wife. I was a terrible person. No wonder he didn't want to pass on Terry's number.

'I brought forward my arrival date at uni, so that I could travel with him. *To keep him safe,*' Brodie continued, stressing the last part.

'I had no idea about any of this,' I stuttered.

'He didn't want you to,' he replied. 'Nor would he take any money for the flights, even though the old lady had provided for them in her will. He wanted you to have the money.'

I felt my throat burn. 'That was kind of him,' I said quietly.

'He is kind. He's a good man. For the life of me, I cannot understand why he insisted on meeting you. But he did. Because he is a kind and loving father. But you rejected him out of hand without even hearing him out.'

This was my cue to apologize and much as it stuck in my throat when Brodie was being so difficult, I knew that if this phone call was going to achieve something other than bruising my ego it had to be done. I took a deep breath.

'Brodie.' It felt odd saying my brother's name. I said it again. 'Brodie, I was hurt and confused when Terry came to see me. I realize now that I may have jumped to conclusions. I really need to speak to him. I'd like to apologize and hear what he has to say. Truly.'

There was a long silence on the line.

'He's at home recovering right now. I can't risk you setting his recuperation back again.'

'But this time I won't—'

'He'll be back for Christmas. It'll be the first year without Mom, so we thought we'd spend it here.'

My heart plummeted. I felt sorry for my little brother for the first time. Christmas was going to be really tough for them this year.

'I'm sorry for your loss, I really am. Look, I won't ask to speak to him now. It can wait. But please, would you tell Terry that I would very much like to see him at Christmas?'

Brodie sighed. 'OK. But if you step out of line again—'

'I won't. I promise,' I added hastily. 'Goodbye, Brodie.'

'Bye, Sophie.'

I collapsed on my bed in an emotional heap. How surreal was that? My first contact with my brother. I got the impression that he wasn't very enamoured with his big sister. And I still didn't have Terry's phone number. I did a quick count-up and sighed impatiently. Eight weeks until Christmas. Two whole months until I could hear my father's side of the story. Two whole months until I had to face my fears and find out the truth. But in the meantime, there was someone else I owed an apology to.

Chapter 25

It was barely light and very icy when I had left home for Nick's office. Before I set off I had had to scrape the frost off the car with my credit card, which snapped in two. Obviously. And by the time I was on my way, I'd made a promise to buy de-icer and thicker gloves at the earliest opportunity.

Nick's car was on his drive. Good, that was the first of my concerns dealt with. My visit was a spur-of-the-moment thing and I didn't have an appointment. I drove past his house looking for a space to park. It was only eight o'clock and the road was lined with cars. I squeezed my little mini in between a skip and a transit van, collected my folder of drawings and locked the car.

Not bad, I thought, looking back at the car to check out my parking skills as I crossed the road. Slightly diagonal, but then it was a tight space.

Somehow a whole month had whizzed by since I was last here. A month since I'd seen Nick. My stomach flipped as I realized I'd missed him. The last time I was here I'd stormed off in a strop and if I was honest with myself, I still felt a bit embarrassed about that, hence I'd been dragging my heels about seeing him again. But today I planned to apologize in person, put all of that childish behaviour behind me and start afresh.

My finger hovered over the two doorbells. Home or office? The blinds in his front room were closed. Perhaps it was too early to call round? I should have phoned first, but if I'd left it any later I would have been late for work.

I chewed my lip and dropped my hand down to my side. This saying sorry lark was becoming a habit; Brodie last week and Nick today. What was more worrying was my bad behaviour in the first place. I didn't know what was wrong with me; I always used to be so easygoing. These days I ended up arguing with everyone I came into contact with.

One person who wasn't getting an apology was Mum. Much as I loved her, this time I refused to play the peacemaker. All my life I had avoided asking questions about her and my father when really it was my right to know about my family background. There had been a girl at my school who had been adopted and even she had known more about her birth father than I did! Perhaps when Mum had got over the shock and had had time to get used to the idea, she would come round? Hopefully, before her annual Christmas visit.

I was still prevaricating on the doorstep and my toes were in danger of going black and dropping off from frostbite.

Come on, Sophie, just ring the bell. He'll answer, hopefully not in his pyjamas, you can hand him your amendments and apologize.

I rang the house bell. No response. I tried the office bell, but again there was no response. It was ten past eight. Knowing Nick, he would definitely have been up by now. In fact, I was sure he would be in his office. Perhaps he was on the phone and couldn't come to the door? Last time he'd told me to just let myself in, although he'd been expecting me that time . . .

I shrugged. No harm in trying.

I went in through the gate and followed the path towards the patio. Within seconds my ears picked up the strains of loud music from the house and I automatically turned and looked through the glass doors into the kitchen.

Oh my word. What was going on?

On the other side of the glass, no more than two metres from me, was a woman wrapped only in a towel. She was skipping round the kitchen like a little pixie, looking very at home and dancing with the dog. I had never seen Norman so excited. He was jumping up on his back legs and wagging his tail wildly. Between his barking, the pop music and the woman's singing, it was no wonder they hadn't heard the bell.

I felt a sudden pang of disappointment. Nick had a girl-friend. Not that he wasn't allowed one – I mean, I had a boyfriend anyway – it was just that he'd never mentioned anything. I was pleased for him. Obviously. It was a shock, that's all.

It dawned on me that I was gawping at a semi-naked woman like some sort of weird peeping Tom. I was about to drop to my knees and crawl back to the gate out of sight, when the pixie whirled round to face me.

We both screamed.

She waved rather pathetically and I turned scarlet.

Oh God.

Next time I would make an appointment. I began to sidle towards the gate when the door opened and the girl appeared clutching the top edge of her towel.

'Hey,' she said, looking gratifyingly embarrassed.

'I'm so sorry to intrude,' I blurted. Norman ran up to

me and I bent down to stroke him, hiding my beetroot-coloured face in his fur. 'Please don't bother Nick. I only came to drop some papers off for him.'

'OK,' she muttered.

I stood up, averting my eyes, and extracted an envelope from my folder.

'I've clearly come at a bad time.'

I held it out and studied her properly. Oh my God, she was only about twelve! Nick was old enough to be her father. What was he thinking? I wondered if her parents knew where she was.

'There are just a few amendments to make to his original design.'

'Oh cool, are you building a house?' she said, taking the envelope.

I nodded as she read my name on the envelope. 'Sophie Stone,' she nodded. 'Yes, he's mentioned you.'

Was it my imagination or was she smirking? My stomach fluttered; he had probably told her that I was mentally unstable, wildly erratic and suffered from terrible mood swings.

'I'm Poppi, by the way.' She held a cold little hand out to me, which I was forced to shake. 'I'm new,' she added.

Very new, I thought uncharitably.

'Anyway.' I mustered a smile and turned to go but she gripped my arm.

'Look, er, can we pretend this didn't happen?' she asked. 'It's just that Nick can be a bit of an old far . . . grump. And, you know, the whole meeting-a-client-in-a-towel thing.' She waggled her head side to side. She was standing like a little girl; knees turned in, with the toes of one foot tucked underneath the other.

I suddenly recognized her. It was the girl I'd seen chatting him up after his talk.

'Weren't you at the Grand Designs Live show?'

'Yeah. That's where we met! He was brilliant.' She sighed.

Oh God, she was a groupie! How did an architect in grey wool trousers get a groupie?

'I won't breathe a word,' I replied untruthfully. She had to be joking; I was going to tell Emma immediately. Not that it was any of my business but I was really surprised at Nick's behaviour.

'Phew, thanks,' she said, rolling her eyes comically.

I ruffled Norman's fur and said goodbye.

'He likes you,' she called as I reached the gate.

I blinked at her, blood pounding in my ears. What did she mean?

Back out on the road, I barely registered the traffic jam, the line of drivers tooting their horns at a tow truck that was blocking the street or the cluster of men in hard hats standing round my car. I paid scant attention to the round of slow applause I got when I unlocked my car, finally allowing the truck to hook up to the skip.

Poppi had been referring to Norman, hadn't she?

During a lull at the office later that morning, I drafted Nick a quick email. I was proud of myself; I'd managed to avoid any reference to scantily clad nymphs in his kitchen, just a simple message about the amendments I'd made.

I hit the send button and my phone rang about ten seconds later.

'Amendments?' Nick sounded insulted.

'You said feel free to make any changes!' I couldn't help but laugh. Besides, for some stupid reason, I felt a warm sensation in the pit of my stomach at the sound of his voice.

There was a pause on the line and then he chuckled. 'Did I say that? I didn't mean it.'

'Don't worry,' I grinned, 'there's nothing to bruise your ego. A couple of additions to an almost perfect house.'

I had added big bi-fold doors in the living room to give me the perfect view of the garden. I'd also included a small utility room, not that I had a single appliance to my name at the moment. And finally a shoe cupboard, because I did have plenty of those.

'That's all right, then. Well, of course, any changes would be fine. Your prerogative. Obviously.' He cleared his throat. 'And I understand you met Poppi earlier?'

'I did.' *None of your business, Sophie; hold your tongue.*

'My new intern. She only started on Monday and I've already lost my place in the hierarchy of my own company,' he said wryly.

Intern? Dressed in a towel first thing in the morning. I swallowed. 'Right.'

'She is a bit full-on,' he continued blithely. 'But to her credit she stepped into the breach admirably.'

'Right.' *I bet she did*, I thought, practically chewing my tongue indignantly. 'Great.'

'I should be back from Derbyshire this evening, depending on the trains.'

'Derbyshire?'

'Yes. Didn't Poppi explain?'

'No,' I laughed, 'so you weren't in when I called round?'

Nick groaned. 'No, I wasn't and the fact that you're laughing, well, I dread to think . . . Anyway. My mum called to say she'd broken her ankle so I came over for the night to help out. Poppi offered to stay late to feed Norman and arrive early this morning to walk him. Very good of her, considering how far away she lives.'

'Right.' I pressed my lips together to stop myself from giggling.

It looked to me as if Poppi the intern had somehow neglected to go home in between. No wonder she didn't want me to mention it to Nick.

'Sophie, are you OK?'

'Me? Never better!' And strangely relieved to know that Poppi the intern simply was the intern.

'Excellent. Well, I look forward to seeing your notes when I get home. And if you've got any more questions, fire away.'

'There is one thing,' I said, remembering my promise to Marc.

'Go on.'

'The plot at Lilac Lane is quite a decent size, isn't it?'

'Certainly big enough for your needs, yes.'

I couldn't help squirming. Deep down, I already knew what Nick would say and I didn't want him to think badly of me. Still, a promise is a promise.

'Do you think it's possible to fit another house on it? Or two?'

There was a sharp intake of breath down the line.

'If you're asking if I'll try to shoehorn another house on the land, then no,' said Nick firmly.

I winced at his choice of words.

'Not one and certainly not two. Another architect? Maybe. A property developer? Certainly. But not me. If that's what you want then—'

Now he would think I was greedy. Blast Marc and his grand schemes.

'No! Me? No! It was just something someone said months ago. Forget it.'

Nick sighed. 'Glad to hear it, because over-developing is completely against my principles.'

'Oh, mine too.'

Marc would just have to accept it: Lilac Lane would be a home and not an opportunity for a quick buck. I was with Nick on this one.

Chapter 26

By November, the bungalow had been completely cleared and on my first free Saturday I took a drive over to Woodby with a bunch of flowers to say thank you to Audrey. I had seriously fallen on my feet inheriting her as my neighbour in Lilac Lane; she had organized everything for me at the bungalow and I couldn't have done it without her.

Mind you, I had picked the worst possible day to visit. Winter had set in, the roads were icy and the fog, which had been nothing more than light mist in town, hung over the fields like heavy smoke. I had had to pull over to turn on my fog lights, which had required consulting the manual, and I could barely make out the car in front of me.

The weather conditions had forced me to slow right down, which was a good thing because if I hadn't been travelling at the speed of a three-legged tortoise, I would have missed Nick at the side of the road altogether.

He was circling the 'Welcome to Woodby' sign with a camera, snapping it from all angles with the dedication of a Japanese tourist.

I stopped the car at the kerb, wound the window down and gave him a big smiley wave.

'Hello, Nick!' I called.

He turn towards me and raised a hand. 'Sophie! Hello there!'

I waited until he approached my open window and chuckled. 'What on earth are you doing? Let me guess, you've run out of dogs to photograph and you've started on village signs?'

'Um . . .' Nick blinked his grey eyes at me and looked momentarily confused. I realized belatedly that although I seemed to be able to recall every detail of all our conversations, he had probably forgotten the first time we met and the whole misunderstanding about the photographs.

I waved a hand dismissively. 'Never mind,' I said airily, feeling my face heat up. 'What brings you out here on a cold day?'

'I'm taking photographs for your planning application,' he said, turning the camera screen towards me and leaning in through the window. 'Look, I've already taken some of Lilac Lane and the church.'

I peered at a grey image of the Woodby sign surrounded by swirling fog on the digital display.

'Oh, very atmospheric,' I said, unsure whether I really wanted the design for my lovely modern cottage to be accompanied by Gothic images of the brooding November gloom.

Nick shifted from foot to foot. He looked frozen. Or nervous. Hard to tell. He pushed his glasses up. 'I'm glad I bumped into you. I was planning on warming myself up with a coffee at the pub when I'd finished. Would you care to join me?'

Out of the blue a memory of the kiss he gave me on my birthday resurfaced and I suddenly found the buttons on my coat really fascinating.

'It's not your birthday, is it?' I asked, trying to keep my voice level.

Nick scratched his chin and thought for a moment. 'If I say it is, will you come?' He grinned.

'I'll come anyway,' I said, twinkling my eyes at him. Was he flirting with me? More to the point, was I flirting with him? Oh heavens. Time to go.

I put the car into gear and Nick took the hint and extracted himself from the window.

'Great,' he beamed.

'See you in half an hour?'

We said goodbye and I continued on my way, feeling unaccountably chirpy all of a sudden.

I turned the car into Lilac Lane and spotted a smart black car parked on the lane between Audrey's bungalow and mine. Which meant she had visitors. My heart sank. I had been looking forward to catching up with my favourite octogenarian. Never mind; I would just have to drop off the flowers and go in search of Nick.

I parked on Audrey's drive and before I'd even had chance to knock, she opened her front door.

'Oh, they're lovely,' she cried, taking the bunch of lilies from me. 'You shouldn't have.'

'Yes I should,' I argued, reaching up to kiss her powdery cheek. 'You're the best neighbour ever.'

'Come in, come in,' she said, pulling me in out of the cold.

'I won't stay, if you're busy,' I said, peering past her for any sign of guests.

'Not at all! You can be the first to try my orange shortbread.'

I was only too happy to get out of the cold. She led me

through the kitchen and filled a vase with water.

'Help yourself,' she said, indicating a batch of biscuits on a wire rack. They smelt divine. There was a distinct possibility that I would get fat living next to Audrey.

I watched with envy as she confidently snipped at least a third off the stem of the lilies and plunged them deftly into a vase. I was always nervous of cutting off too much and consequently my arrangements ended up lolling around in the vase looking spindly and too pathetic to hold their heads up.

'Now tell me,' she said, as I selected a still-warm piece of shortbread, 'who's that hunky chappie poking round your bungalow?'

My eyebrows shot up. Nick must have been here earlier. Why was I going red? It wasn't as if I fancied him. Nick was lovely but such a gentleman. Not that there was anything wrong with being a gentleman, I was just used to men that were a bit more . . . I don't know . . . rude. Did I mean rude? Well, more like Marc anyway. Only last week, he had said the skin on my bottom was so soft it was like sinking his hands into feather pillows. I couldn't imagine Nick ever saying anything like that. Although why would he? He was my architect; he had no right to be thinking about my bottom. Or touching it.

Now my ears had turned scarlet too.

Audrey, whose beady eyes had been watching my every move, smirked. I adopted an innocent expression and pretended not to notice, taking a big bite of biscuit to hide my embarrassment. It was crumbly and buttery and very difficult to swallow.

'Tall and slim, dark hair?' I said gruffly, trying to remove a layer of shortbread from the roof of my mouth. 'That's

233

my architect. He was probably taking photographs for his report.'

Audrey poured us both a cup of tea and frowned. 'No, no, not him. Nick was here earlier. Sat where you're sitting. Although you're right, he is lovely too. He always pops in to say hello when he visits.'

'I didn't say he was lovely.' I shifted awkwardly on my seat. *Visits*? Plural? Just how often was that?

'No, this one was much more stocky. One of those testosterone-fuelled young men. Head to toe in sportswear. Quite a twinkle in his eye when he said hello. Called me "darling", the cheeky beggar.' Audrey raised an outraged eyebrow.

'I did wonder who he was, swaggering round Jane's – sorry, dear – *your* bungalow, like he owned the place. But obviously, he's here to meet you.'

'That's Marc.' I choked as tea hit the back of my throat and went down the wrong way. My pulse was racing as fast as my thoughts. That had to be Marc. But why was *he* here? Without me?

'They arrived in that black car parked outside. Still there presumably,' said Audrey, pausing to blow on her tea. 'The other man is very smartly dressed. Although I only saw the back of his head as the pair of them went in through the front door.'

They? And more to the point how did Marc get hold of a key? I had never given him a key to the bungalow. Why would I? It would be knocked down before too long anyway. I kept the bunch of keys on my dressing table and as far as I could remember they were still there. Mind you, now I came to think about it, there was a week when I couldn't find them, but then they had turned up again, so I had thought no more about it.

Why was *he* showing someone round *my* house without my knowledge?

Audrey banged me on the back firmly until I stopped spluttering and I gave her a reassuring smile.

'Marc's my boyfriend. He's helping me with the property side of things. Anyway, he'll be waiting for me so I'd better go.'

She eyed me shrewdly. 'Hmm.'

Hmm indeed, I thought, as I stepped back out into the fog and waved goodbye to Audrey. I hadn't spoken to Marc for several days. In fact, since the conversation about Lilac Lane he hadn't been in touch at all. Marc had been excessively annoyed when I had reported back after speaking to Nick as promised.

'He's having you on,' Marc had said harshly. 'Pulling the wool over your eyes.'

'No, he's not,' I had replied calmly. 'Quite the opposite. The bigger the build, the bigger Nick's fees would be. If he wanted to make more money, he would jump at the chance of cramming more houses onto the plot.'

Marc had huffed crossly. 'It's not cramming, it's . . . oh, never mind.' He'd muttered something about never trusting a woman with business, but before I could quiz him on what he meant, he'd had rung off. And that was the last I had heard from him.

Now it looked suspiciously like he was up to something behind my back. But what?

The fog was still dense and I picked my way carefully towards the front door of my bungalow. The fog inside my head was just as murky; I couldn't shake my confusion. If Marc really had my best interests at heart, why was he sneaking around behind my back?

I trusted him, didn't I? Didn't I?

My heart was beating like the clappers as I knocked hard on the door. Ironically, I hadn't brought my own key with me. My whole body tensed and I held my breath as I heard the thud of footsteps echoing through the empty bungalow towards me.

Don't jump to conclusions. There might be a totally plausible explanation.

Yeah right. There was no excuse for Marc being here without me and I felt nauseous thinking about it.

The door that I usually struggled with flew open. A look of surprise illuminated Marc's face in the semi-darkness. This was rapidly followed by a flash of anger, before his normal charming smile reappeared. He held his arms out to me and cocked his head to one side.

'Busted,' he said, grinning sheepishly. 'This was meant to be a surprise.'

'What are you doing in my house?' I stepped past him, ducking out of reach as he tried to kiss me.

Standing in the living room, tapping away at his mobile phone, was an older man in a sharp dark suit. He strode across the small room and pumped my hand as Marc hurriedly made the introductions.

'This is Phil Strong,' he said, rubbing his head in rough circular motions. I had never seen him so edgy. 'Remember? The property developer I told you about.'

'Vaguely,' I said. 'Pleased to meet you.'

'I was just saying to Marc—' began the property developer.

I turned my back on him and shoved my hands in my pockets so Marc couldn't see them shaking.

'And do you remember what I told *you*?' I said fiercely, stepping closer to him.

'Er, do you think you could give us a minute, mate?' said Marc. He rolled his eyes at Phil as if to say, *Women*.

If I thought he would even register the pain through the thick wall of muscle, I would punch him.

'I'll be in the car,' said Phil, winking at Marc.

'Look, I was doing this for us, princess, for *you*,' he said as soon as Phil was out of earshot. He moved towards me and tilted my chin to within kissing distance.

'Sneaking behind my back?' I stepped away and brushed him off. My heart was pounding. A few hours ago, I would have gone weak at the knees at the slightest sign of his affection. Now it felt like the kiss of Judas.

He held his hands up in defence. 'I know how scared you are of taking risks. That's why I thought I'd get an expert in, to go through the options. It's not as if I was making any decisions without telling you.'

'Without telling me? They aren't your decisions to make. Full stop,' I gasped and folded my arms.

Marc reached out to stroke my cheek and I flinched. 'But you and me, Soph, we're good together.'

I shook my head. 'You're here, in my house, without my permission. Presumably by having a key cut, also without my permission.'

Marc smiled indulgently and ploughed on, ignoring my mounting fury.

'There's so much more you can do with this place.' He grabbed hold of the tops of my arms, his eyes shining. 'That architect of yours is small-minded, he's got no vision.'

I bristled at that. How dare he criticize Nick's talents? Nick had more passion and creativity, not to mention a far more accurate moral compass, than Marc could ever dream of.

'Phil reckons we could . . . you can easily double, if not treble, your money!'

'But it's not what I want,' I said, shaking my head incredulously. Hadn't he listened to a word I had been saying?

'Think about it, princess,' he said, giving me his special twinkle, the one that normally made me lunge for him and drag him off to the nearest soft surface. 'With a few quid behind us, we can buy somewhere much bigger. Away from this place in the back of beyond.'

If I didn't know better, I'd almost say he sounded desperate.

I backed away from him and perched on the ledge in the bay window. I hid my eyes behind my hands and sighed as a wave of sadness threatened to drown me. Would he ever care what I wanted? Would he ever stop to put me first?

I knew the answer to that.

If I gave in to him now I would have to resign myself to a future with Marc calling the shots and me trotting behind in his wake, grateful for the occasional crumb of attention.

And maybe once upon a time that would have been enough.

But I had changed in the last few months and had started to face my challenges head on. This time last year, I wouldn't have dreamed of doing half the things I'd done this year. I was out of my comfort zone most of the time. But despite that I was happier now than I had been for years. I didn't need a man to make my life complete. I was quite capable of facing my future alone. A future I was determined to build on my own terms.

I looked across to the empty mantelpiece; Great-aunt Jane's wedding photograph had gone but I could still picture her smiling face.

I'd got her to thank for my new-found confidence and I was pretty sure that if she could see me now she would be proud of what I was about to do.

I watched Marc leaning against the wall, arms folded. There was no getting away from it; he was gorgeous, but that didn't mean he was gorgeous on the inside. Far from it. And I deserved better. He stared at me from under dark eyebrows as if he knew bad news was coming his way.

'You don't get it, do you?' I said, shaking my head sadly. 'I'm not interested in making a fortune. I want a house. *One* house. This place on Lilac Lane belonged to my family. Now it belongs to me. And Woodby is not the back of beyond. It's home.'

'What about me?' He kicked his trainer up behind him, scuffing the wallpaper and gave me his little-boy grin. 'We're a team, aren't we?'

But the grin didn't work. A tingle ran down my spine as I realized he'd lost his power over me.

I shook my head. 'No, Marc, not any more.'

Marc was no longer my boyfriend. It only took a few minutes to end that chapter of my life. I shooed him out of the house, made him hand over the key and ended our relationship in no uncertain terms. I had done the right thing. Definitely. I told myself this repeatedly on the journey back to the flat. The last time Marc and I had split up I had been crushed under the weight of my own misery.

This time I felt surprisingly light and liberated. Well, I would be as soon as I'd stopped trembling. From now on I would be doing things my way. And that abdominal toner was going straight in the bin.

It was only when I saw the flash of a speed camera as a car streaked across a red light that I remembered another camera snapping away in Woodby.

'Nick!' I yelled. I stamped on the brakes causing the car behind me to swerve round me and toot its horn.

I'd stood him up. How could I have forgotten all about Nick? My stomach twisted with remorse imagining him sitting in the pub on his own, staring into a cold cup of coffee. Poor thing! I checked the clock on the dashboard. It was far too late to go back; he would have given up on me by now. Or be cursing the day he ever met me. I would text him as soon as I got in and apologize.

Was it only a couple of hours ago that I'd dismissed Nick as being too gentlemanly? My chest heaved with a deep sigh. Right now some time in his company would have been exactly what I needed . . .

I tutted at myself sharply. *One thing at a time, Sophie.* I'd still got family stuff to sort out, a house to build and my career to focus on. A love life would have to wait for a while. Love life? *Love life?* I laughed at myself and turned on the radio; Nick *so* wasn't my type. Was he?

Chapter 27

Decorations are my favourite thing about Christmas, they make everywhere look magical. Even our tired old flat could be transformed with a bit of sparkle: the tinsel, the fairy lights, the holly and, of course, the tree. Over the years I had gradually brought the official start to the Christmas season forward until now, in our flat at least, it started on December the first with our annual trip to the garden centre to pick out a tree. Which was today. And this year I was determined to make the flat look even more special because in three weeks' time . . . drum roll please . . . my father was coming to visit.

Despite his blatant animosity on the phone, Brodie had evidently passed on the message to Terry that I wanted to speak to him. And last week I'd had an email from him. My dad would be in England for two weeks over the Christmas holidays and he'd said it would make his Christmas if I wanted to spend some time with him.

I'd emailed him straight back and said that I'd like that and had suggested he come over the day after his flight arrived in. And the date had been set. Now all I had to do was get the flat ready for Christmas and somehow hope that I could smooth things over with my mum, who *still* wasn't speaking to me, before he arrived.

Emma and I were almost ready to leave on our Christmas tree mission.

'Bushy but not too fat,' Jess piped up from her position on the sofa. She had declared herself too tired to come with us, but apparently not too tired to issue precise instructions. 'Make sure there are no bald patches and not so tall that we can't reach up to put the angel on top.'

'So *you* can't, you mean, shorty,' said Emma, flicking her pony tail over her shoulder. She stood in the corner of the living room where the tree was destined to go and stretched her arm up to estimate the height of the ceiling.

'Sure you won't come with us?' I asked, slipping on my warmest boots.

Jess undid the top button on her denim miniskirt and sighed with relief. 'I'd love to but I've got thirty-four school reports to finish off and then I need to make animal masks: three camels, two sheep and one donkey. And I'm shattered already.'

She did look pale.

'You OK?' I asked.

'Yeah, it's a busy time of year at school with the nativity, carol concert and all the children's parties. But I'm really looking forward to Christmas. It's going to be the best ever. For all of us.' She gave me a warm smile.

'I hope so,' I said, pulling a nervous face. 'I'm going to buy my dad a Christmas present. Never done that before; I'll need some tips from you two.'

'I love Christmas shopping,' Jess sighed and then gave me a secretive smile. 'Hey, I think I know what Spike has bought me.'

'Really? Tell me more!' I sat down on the sofa next to her, ignoring Emma's impatient eye-rolling and watch-tapping.

She nodded. 'Something I've been dreaming of all my life.'

Emma smirked from the doorway. 'Not the Sylvanian Families windmill?'

Jess's lips twitched but she tutted and turned back to me. 'We arranged to meet in town on Saturday. I arrived early and saw him coming out of the jeweller's. He wasn't carrying any bags!'

I looked blankly at her. 'I don't get it.'

'Whatever he bought must have been really tiny. Like a ring!' She beamed. 'I think he's going to propose!' She squealed and drummed her feet on the floor.

I hugged her and caught Emma's unimpressed face over Jess's shoulder.

'I hope your dream comes true, then.' I kissed her and stood up to leave.

'And I've got the perfect present for him,' she continued, her eyes shining happily.

'Let me guess. A personality?' said Emma, hopping out of the way as Jess waved the TV remote ominously in her direction.

In truth, neither of us had warmed to Spike. He seemed so nondescript compared to Jess's colourful character. I kept my feelings to myself. I was possibly the least qualified person to comment on whether he was suitable or not after staying loyal to Marc for so long. Unfortunately, Emma had no such qualms.

'You're just jealous, Emma,' said Jess primly. 'Anyway, my lips are sealed. But he's going to love his present from me.'

'Jealous?' snorted Emma. 'I've got my own dreams coming true. Check this out.'

She took a piece of paper from her jeans pocket, unfolded it and handed to me. It was a letter from the National Silverware Awards.

'Yay! You've been shortlisted for a prize!' I exclaimed. 'Well done you!'

Emma was grinning so widely, I could see her tonsils. I hugged her until she groaned in pain.

'Ah, well done, babes,' said Jess, staring at the letter. 'I had no idea you were so talented!'

Emma rolled her eyes.

'Of course she's talented.' I gave Jess a warning look. 'We'll have loads to celebrate this Christmas, so we should get going, all the best trees will have gone,' I said, dragging Emma into the hall before she had chance to reply. We made it as far as the front door when the doorbell rang.

I gripped Emma's arm. 'If it's Marc, I'm not in.'

She nodded, rolling up her sleeves. 'OK. I'll go downstairs and open the main door. Then if it is him, I'll get rid of him with pleasure.'

'Thanks,' I replied, shutting the door behind her and pressing my ear to it.

I hadn't heard a thing from Marc since I'd dumped him and I was quite keen to keep it that way. I wasn't surprised; his ego would be too bruised to attempt to win me back. However, I thought, as I strained to hear who our visitor was, there was no harm in being cautious.

A couple of minutes later, two sets of footsteps made their way back up the staircase.

'Not at all!' I heard Emma cry, an octave higher than usual. 'She'll be pleased to see you.'

I breathed a sigh of relief. Not Marc then.

'We've heard so much about you,' she continued.

My pulse was thumping in my ears as I strained to tune into a second, much lower voice. It couldn't be my father, could it? He wasn't due into the country until the twentieth of December.

Before I had a chance to speculate any further, I was forced to jump out of the way as an overexcited Emma flung the door back on its hinges and sprang into the hall.

'It's Mr Cromwell,' she said, nudging me and waggling her eyebrows with all the subtlety of a pantomime dame. Sure enough, Nick followed closely behind her, clutching his briefcase in front of him like a shield.

'Oh, call me Nick, please,' said my architect, who looked, if it were possible, even more uncomfortable than me.

After standing him up over his offer of a cup of coffee, I'd sent him a brief text of apology and hadn't seen him since. And now I felt embarrassed and pleased to see him all at the same time.

He stood in our tiny hallway, all wrapped up in a thick coat, packed between Emma and the front door like a woolly sardine, and grinned at me.

'Hi,' I said. I was still wearing my coat and suddenly started to overheat.

'Hello, Sophie, sorry to barge in unannounced, but I was passing and I wanted to . . . Oh. Are you on your way out?'

'No, no, not at all! We've just got back in, I'm Emma, by the way,' boomed Emma, narrowing her eyes at me. 'Come on, Sophie, what are you waiting for? Get your coat off! And you, Nick.'

The space was so confined that with all three of us

removing our outer layers at the same time, it was like a vertical version of Twister. Nick and I were both glowing from the exertion as I showed him into the living room.

'Ooh,' said Jess, looking from him to me and back again. 'Ooh.'

I introduced everyone properly and ushered Nick into the armchair.

'Sophie?' called Emma from the kitchen. 'Would you help me with the drinks?'

'Make yourself at home.' I sent Nick an apologetic look and did as I was told.

'You crafty bugger!' hissed Emma, pouncing on me as soon as I walked in. 'When you said architect, I imagined a crusty old git with baggy trousers, one tuft of hair and those glasses you balance on the end of your nose.'

'They're called pince-nez,' whispered Jess, materializing suddenly and making us both jump. 'He's divine. So masculine, so sexy, so—'

'So not my type,' I said, hiding my face in the fridge on the pretence of fetching the milk.

'Do you think he's here to ask you out?' said Jess, squeezing my wrist.

I rubbed at the white marks she had made on my skin and shook my head. 'He'd never do that. He never mixes business with pleasure.'

'Ha! You've talked about it then,' said Emma with a snigger.

'Perhaps he can't deny his feelings for you any longer.' Jess sighed, clutching a hand to her bosom.

'For God's sake, you two!' I snorted and started to go back to the living room. The poor man would be really uncomfortable in there; it was so obvious we were talking about him. How many women did it take to make a cup of instant coffee, for heaven's sake?

'You fancy him,' declared Emma. 'That's why you haven't talked about him.'

'Shush,' I said, raising my hands. 'He'll hear you. And no, I don't.' I turned away before she spotted my crimson face. Too late.

'Well, get back in there, see what he wants!' she smirked.

I lowered myself onto the sofa and smiled. He was resting one ankle on the opposite knee and jiggling it up and down. He didn't look like he had made much headway with making himself at home.

'Nick, can I just apologize again? I'm so sorry that I didn't make it to the pub in Woodby last month for that coffee. Something unpleasant came up.' I fiddled with the buttons on my cardigan.

Nick frowned. 'Sorry to hear that, anything I can help with? Was it to do with the bungalow?'

'Yes. No.' I waved my hands around. 'Well no, not any more. It's dealt with now so . . . thanks anyway.'

He looked a bit confused and I debated whether to elaborate, but then Emma and Jess came in with drinks served in our best mugs and the moment was gone. Jess perched daintily on the sofa next to me, all traces of her earlier tiredness apparently banished, while Emma handed him his coffee.

'Thanks.' He nodded at Emma before turning his attention back to me. 'Forgive the imposition, but I need your help.'

'You need *my* help?' I repeated doubtfully, feeling flattered nonetheless.

Emma mouthed *Posh* at Jess silently. I glared at them

both surreptitiously, signalling for them to make themselves scarce. Jess pretended not to notice and Emma gave me a look that said, *No chance.*

Nick took a sheaf of papers out of his briefcase and handed me a photograph of a dilapidated single-storey farm building.

'Some new clients have asked me to design a scheme to convert an old cowshed into a home.'

I peered at the picture. The brick was a lovely honeyed yellow, contrasting beautifully with the warm red roof tiles. With a bit of imagination, it would make a very attractive home, but at the moment it was little more than a shell.

Nick raked a hand through his hair and frowned. 'I'm convinced the layout I've come up with is the right one, but the clients can't envisage the finished article.'

He handed me a drawing, which I unfolded on my knee.

'It looks great,' I said with a frown. 'But I don't see how I can help?'

'He wants you to go round there and tell them not to be so dim,' said Emma unhelpfully.

Nick laughed and then, catching Emma's eye, turned it into a cough. 'This is a big ask, so feel free to say no, and it's really not a problem if you're not keen—'

'Whatever it is, I'm sure she'd love to help,' said Jess sincerely.

The blush I had just managed to banish came back with a vengeance. I slurped my tea and tried not to drip on the paper.

'It needs to be brought to life,' said Nick, polishing his glasses on the front of his shirt. 'It's not enough for them to see the house as a flat plan. They need to be shown the possibilities, how they could use the space. That's where your talents come in.'

'Is it?' I said, trying to ignore Emma and Jess, who were nudging each other like proud aunties.

Nick sat forward in his chair and stared at me. A little tuft at the front of his hair was sticking up. It was all I could do not to lean over and smooth it down.

'When I was in my office pondering my next move, I spotted the boards you made for your own house.'

A warm glow spread through me as I remembered how much I had enjoyed creating them.

'One room. That's all it would take,' he said. 'I thought maybe the living room? If they could see how it would look full of furniture, colours, fabrics, textures, all the detail that you so expertly poured into your brief, then I'm sure they would get it.'

An interiors scheme. For a real house. Designed by me.

I was so touched that he would even consider asking me that for a moment, I couldn't speak.

'Would you pay her?' asked Emma, narrowing her eyes.

'Of course!' said Nick, running a finger round his collar. 'What do you think? If you haven't got time, just say.' He was staring at me again.

'No, no, I'm not too busy,' I said, finally finding my voice.

'I'd need it before Christmas.'

'I'd be honoured,' I replied earnestly.

Nick beamed. And there it was. The little dimple in his left cheek.

'Thank you,' he sighed. 'Your spark of creativity is exactly what the project needs.'

'Thank *you*,' I mumbled before catching Emma's poorly disguised amusement.

After a brief discussion of the clients' tastes – primary colours not pastel, leather not chintz, Pollock not Picasso – I showed Nick to the door.

'Could you meet on the twenty-third, do you think?' He opened up a small diary and took out an even smaller pencil.

I hesitated. That gave me three weeks to do the work. Which should be plenty as long as I came up with some good ideas.

'I can meet you in town,' said Nick hopefully. 'Besides, I still owe you that coffee you promised to have with me.'

'It's a date,' I said, smiling, instantly regretting my choice of words.

I heard giggling coming from the living room. The girls had their ears pressed to the door, I just knew it.

'Oh, nearly forgot.' He held out a set of drawings and the photograph of the farm building. 'You'll need these.'

Our fingers touched as I took them from him and I felt the heat from his skin. The hair at the nape of my neck tingled and my face flushed.

Was it my imagination or did his fingers hold onto the drawings for just a second too long?

Chapter 29

Four days until Christmas Day. The flat was looking its twinkliest best; fairy lights hung around the fireplace. The tree, which was bushy and not too tall, was laden with baubles; the hall was festooned with garlands of holly; and optimistic bunches of mistletoe hung from every light fitting. I'd even managed to find some 'Christmas-scented' candles, which were burning merrily on the mantelpiece.

I plumped up the cushions and tucked the TV remote out of sight. There was an empty crisp packet in the waste-paper bin and I bent to scoop it out. Emma watched me from her position at the living-room window with muted mirth. 'For goodness' sake, Sophie, will you sit down? You're making me dizzy.'

'Sorry, I'm just, you know, petrified. What if it goes wrong again like last time?'

I dropped onto the sofa with a sigh and checked my watch. Five minutes to go until my father was due to arrive. A wave of panic propelled me up again. I went to join Emma at the window and scanned the street below.

'Last time was totally different. This time he's coming at your invitation,' she said, squeezing my arm.

'True.' I sighed.

I'd invited my dad to come to the flat because I'd thought I would feel more confident on home turf, but as the date had got closer, I had become more and more nervous about it. Right now, I was terrified. As much as I wanted to finally set the record straight, I had the feeling that neither of my parents would come out of the story well, and after all these years, was it really worth all the heartache?

Jess waltzed in wearing a loose-fitting chiffon tunic, dotted with sequins, and matching tights. 'What do you think?' She gave us a twirl. 'Is it suitable for being proposed to?'

She was totally convinced that Spike would be saying 'Merry Christmas' with an engagement ring. I wouldn't like to be in his shoes if he didn't deliver.

'You look lovely,' I reassured her. 'Do I look all right?'

I was wearing a wool dress and woolly tights; my new winter outfit.

Jess gave me a tight squeeze. 'Gorgeous. But your dad will love you whatever you wear. I'm so sorry I can't stay. But with Spike working over Christmas, today's our only chance to exchange presents.'

Actually, Spike did have Christmas Day off but he would be spending it with his mother. Jess had been devastated to learn that she was not invited.

The door buzzer sounded and my stomach dropped to somewhere below my knees. I smoothed down my dress and tried not to panic.

'OK. Remember the plan. Jess, you let him in and offer him a drink. I'll be waiting by the Christmas tree. Emma, you don't leave my side unless I give you the code word. Which is?' I pointed at her.

'Patricide.'

'Emma!' I jammed my hands on my hips.

'Mince pie. The minute you say "mince pie", I'll leave you on your own.'

'Correct,' I said, diving under the tree to turn on the fairy lights.

Buzzzzz.

'Go, go, go!' I flapped my hands at them both and clambered to my feet.

But as soon as I heard Jess open the door, curiosity got the better of me.

Oh, sod it.

I shrugged my shoulders at Emma and raced into the hallway, abandoning my plan.

I got there just as Jess stepped aside to let him in. My dad. Here, in my flat, all bundled up in a thick coat and holding a plastic bag. His eyes found mine and a nervous smile lit up his face. He looked a lot healthier this time: his face was tanned and although there was a lattice of fine lines across his forehead, the dark circles under his eyes were gone.

I took a step forward and Terry did the same. I held my arms out.

The look of sheer pleasure mixed with apprehension on his face did weird things to my insides. My hands were clammy and my heart was beating wildly. He stepped into my arms and we hugged. Our first hug. Tears sprang to my eyes and my throat felt tight.

'Hello,' I whispered hoarsely. 'Thank you for coming.'

He pulled back and took my hands. 'Thank you,' he said. 'For inviting me and for giving us a second chance. It's wonderful to be here,' he murmured, gazing directly into my eyes.

He had worker's hands. Rough compared to Nick's. I

realized that I had no idea what Terry had done for a living since leaving the Navy. So far, all conversation had focused on the events *circa* 1980: the year I was born.

'Oh, hello!' said Jess. I looked over Terry's shoulder and followed her gaze.

A tall young man with a mop of wavy dark hair filled the doorway. He wore a thick orange hoodie and jeans.

'I thought I should bring Brodie along too. I hope you don't mind?' said Terry, raising his eyebrows and looking anxiously from his son to me. 'I should have asked your permission, I suppose.'

'Not at all,' I said, doing my best to sound like I meant it. 'You're both very welcome.'

So this was the guy who'd chewed me up and spat me out over the phone. I swallowed. I hadn't bargained on Brodie tagging along too. From the look on his sulky face, he didn't seem particularly happy to be here either.

'Brodie, this is your sister Sophie.'

'Half-sister,' Brodie and I said together.

We stared at each other, him looking me up and down from under his floppy fringe, hands on hips.

Jess clapped her hands.

'Drinks?' she said, and merrily took orders in the cramped hallway. Milky tea for Terry, beer for Brodie and a glass of wine for me. Large. She bustled off to the kitchen.

'I was chuffed to bits when Brodie said you'd called,' said Terry.

Brodie leaned back against the wall and huffed.

'Daft of me to give you his number instead of my own, but I thought you might ring while I was still in the UK,' Terry added.

I shrugged awkwardly. 'I didn't give you a chance to

explain anything, or tell me about yourself last time we met. I'm sorry about that and I'm sorry about your wife and your heart surgery . . .' I swallowed a lump in my throat.

'Don't blame yourself,' he said. 'Anyway, we're here now. Oh. This is for you. For Christmas. In case I don't see you again. I mean before Christmas.'

He took out a rectangular box, beautifully wrapped and tied with Bloomingdale's ribbon. I took it from him and pressed a swift kiss to his cheek.

'Thank you.' I smiled. 'I'll put it under the Christmas tree.'

'And these are for now. We can't get decent ones in the States.' He handed me a box of Marks & Spencer's mince pies.

As I helped Terry out of his coat, he touched my hair.

'Your curls.' He shook his head softly. 'Just like Aunt Jane said. Just like mine.' He paused. 'And Brodie's.'

Brodie glowered at me as I ushered them both into the living room in front of me and I sighed with frustration. I considered telling him to make himself scarce and leave us alone for an hour. But no sooner had Brodie stepped into the living room, he reappeared with a smile on his face before I'd even had a chance to follow.

'Who's the hot redhead?' he hissed.

'Emma, my flatmate,' I replied, unable to keep the amusement out of my voice.

'Is she single?' he said, blinking his green eyes at me hopefully.

'Yes and thirty-three. Same age as me.'

He shook his head and gave a low whistle.

I pushed Brodie ahead of me just as Jess came in with the drinks.

Emma introduced herself as Terry lowered himself onto the sofa and I sat next to him. I was so close that I could smell his scent. It was a Christmassy blend of wood and cinnamon and I found myself tempted to bury my nose in his neck for a good sniff. Brodie perched on the end of the sofa next to his dad and gazed adoringly at Emma, who grinned back at him from the armchair.

'Sorry not to join the party,' said Jess jauntily, looking anything but. She handed Terry his tea and Brodie his beer. 'I'm meeting my boyfriend for a very special dinner.'

She waved from the doorway and scooped up her bag. 'Wish me luck.'

Emma and I exchanged glances. 'Good luck!' we called.

And then she was gone.

We sipped at our drinks in silence for a few moments.

'So,' I said, unable to stand the tension any longer. 'Terry, tell me how you met my mother.'

He took a slurp of his tea. 'I don't know how much you know, so I'll start at the beginning.'

I nodded some encouragement. He leaned forward, elbows on his knees.

'We met at a club. Someone's birthday, I think. She wasn't a guest, she was singing.' He smiled and his eyes softened. 'Your mother was the most beautiful creature I had ever seen. I was star-struck, there's no other way to describe it. She was so full of energy and life, a free spirit, I suppose.'

I smiled. 'That's her to a tee.'

Terry flicked a brief glance at me and I heard Brodie huff.

'She was the complete opposite to me. I'd finished my apprenticeship as a tiler. I was earning good money. All I wanted to do was settle down, buy a house, start a family.'

'Go on,' I said. So far he sounded like perfect husband and father material.

'Most of Valerie's friends had gone to uni or were still at school. She liked the fact that I was a bit older and had a steady job. I couldn't believe my luck when she agreed to marry me. We had only been together six months.'

Terry set his mug down, reached into his wallet and took out some photographs.

'I thought you might be interested in these,' he said.

He passed me a picture of him and my mother on their wedding day. Tears pricked at the back of my eyes.

'You look so young,' I exclaimed. *And so happy*, I thought, looking at the two of them together.

Terry was handsome in a dark suit and sapphire-blue tie. But it was my mum who I couldn't take my eyes off. Even from this old photograph I could see her blue eyes sparkling. She looked radiant in her long, puff-sleeved wedding dress. She was holding hands with her new husband and laughing. I wiped away a tear. I didn't think I'd ever seen her that happy in my whole life. I passed it across to Emma.

'This was a few months later,' said Terry quietly, handing me a second picture. I took it from him and was shocked by the different story it told. It looked as if there was a celebration going on in the background, but the couple definitely weren't in the party spirit. Terry had his arm around Mum, but her body language was telling him that he wasn't wanted. She had her arms folded and shoulder turned away.

'Wasn't it around then—' began Brodie.

'Quiet, son,' said Terry sharply. 'Let me tell the story in my own time.'

Father and son glared at each other and Emma and I exchanged worried glances.

'Mince pie, anyone?' I said, reaching for the box in an attempt to lighten the mood.

Emma leapt up out of her seat. 'Brodie, fancy nipping out to the pub? I'll buy you another beer.'

'Cool,' said Brodie nonchalantly. He followed Emma out of the room and punched the air behind her back.

'How do you feel about younger men?' I heard him ask as they left the flat.

'Cheeky!' snorted Emma.

'Sorry about Brodie,' said Terry. 'This is tough on him. He'll come round.'

'It's fine, don't worry,' I answered. 'You're right, it's just as hard on him as it is on me.'

In truth, my offer of a mince pie was a genuine one, I'd forgotten about the code word. But Emma and Brodie had seemed keen to get away and actually, now that we were getting to the crucial part of the story, I was glad it was just the two of us.

'Tell me more about this photograph,' I said, changing the subject.

He linked his hands and began twirling his wedding ring round and round with his opposite hand. Then one knee started twitching. Whatever he wanted to say, it was clearly difficult to put into words.

'This second one was taken on the Valentine's Day after we got married.' He pressed his lips together into a thin line. 'We were at a party. Your mother loved parties, I was happier at home, really, just being together.'

'She doesn't look that happy to me,' I said.

He shook his head unhappily. 'We had just found out she

259

was pregnant. With you. And . . . well, we'd had an argument. We argued a lot at the time.'

I squeezed my eyes shut briefly, feeling sick all of a sudden.

Terry laid a hand on my knee. 'Finding out your mother was having a baby was the happiest day of my life. Even better than our wedding day. I felt like the luckiest man in the world.'

I studied his face: the penetrating green eyes, thick eyebrows showing the first signs of grey, dense dark hair. Already he was becoming more familiar to me. His eyes glazed as he looked at the photograph in my hand.

He sounded sincere; he looked as if he meant those words.

'Why, Terry? If you were so happy, how could you have walked away?'

He stared at me for what felt like an eternity. The tension was building in me like a balloon filled with too much air. Something was going to burst any second, I could feel it.

Breathe, Sophie, breathe.

'When I met you on your birthday, I could tell from your, um, attitude, that perhaps you hadn't heard the full story.'

My whole body was trembling. So there was more to it. As much as I wanted – needed – to hear what Terry had to say, I was scared. All at once, it felt as if my whole life had been leading up to this moment.

'Go on.' My voice was so shaky, I hardly recognized it.

Terry exhaled as if psyching himself up. I held my breath. 'Your mother—'

Buzzzzz.

We both jumped. A very persistent person was leaning on our entry bell.

I leapt up, shooting my father a look of apology as I ran to the door.

'Probably Emma, forgotten something.' I released the outer door without checking who it was.

I waited in the hallway expecting her to bound up the stairs with her long legs. Instead, there was a slow shuffle, a thump and a grunt. Intrigued, I poked my head out over the stairwell. It couldn't be? I blinked several times to make sure my eyes weren't playing tricks on me.

'Mum?'

I raced down the steps and took Mum's heavy suitcase from her.

'I wasn't expecting you,' I said, trying not to sound panicky.

She paused, out of breath, and gave me an injured look. 'Well, if it's not convenient?'

'It's a nice surprise, obviously,' I added.

The shock of seeing her on my doorstep had taken my breath away, but the change in her appearance gave me even more of a jolt.

My mum was always immaculately turned out. But not today. Today, she had bags under her eyes that wouldn't pass the Ryanair baggage allowance, her hair was flat at the front and all bird's nesty at the back, and instead of tanned and healthy she looked tired and old.

I led her inside, put the case down in the hall and hugged her. A wave of relief washed over me; after not hearing from her for so long I was so glad that she was OK. I held her away from me and scanned her face. Her chin had a distinctly unhappy wobble to it.

'Mum?'

She collapsed against me and her petite frame started to shake.

'Forgive me, Sophie,' she sobbed. 'I'm a terrible mother, I know that, but you're all I have.'

'Oh, Mum, there's nothing to forgive. Nothing at all.' I stroked her hair gently. I don't think I'd ever seen her so upset.

'When you called to say that you'd met up with Terry, my world fell apart. I've barely been able to sleep, I've been so upset.' She took a tissue from the pocket of her thin coat and dabbed her eyes. Her mascara made black streaks down her cheeks.

My heart melted for her and I felt so guilty for putting her through all this pain.

'Gosh, I had no idea, I wish you'd told me how you felt,' I said. 'I only wanted to know more about him, about why you never kept in touch after you split up.'

'I thought I'd lost you,' she whispered into my neck. 'And I was too proud, too ashamed . . .' Her voice broke off as she started to cry in earnest.

I shook my head in sorrow. She had nothing to be ashamed about. Loads of my friends at school had parents who had got divorced. She shivered and I peeled her coat off and hung it up. No wonder she was cold. She was wearing a skimpy jumper, a thin camisole and skinny jeans. Fine for a Spanish winter, but not warm enough for England. I put an arm round her shoulders.

'Come on,' I murmured, pulling her close. 'Let's warm you up in front of the fire. You look frozen.'

'Thanks, Sophie, love,' she sniffed and allowed me to lead her into the living room.

'Bloody hell!' cried Mum as she walked in ahead of me.

Her knees gave way and I tried to grab her but she slipped through my arms and landed in a heap on the floor.

'Hello, Valerie,' said Terry, getting to his feet to help her up.

'Oh, yes,' I gulped. 'I forgot to mention that Terry's here.'

Terry's face was ashen and I guessed it was as much of a shock for him as it was her. Between us we managed to lay her on the sofa. I covered her with a blanket and waited for her to open her eyes.

My heart was pounding, my dress was tight and I was feeling a bit breathless. But despite the shock of having both my parents in the same room for the first time in my life, I was actually quite excited. This was the best chance I'd ever have of hearing both sides of the story.

'What's he doing here?' croaked Mum, opening her eyes.

'I came to see Sophie,' said Terry curtly. 'But I'll go.'

'No way,' I said, shaking my head. 'You're staying.'

I had had enough of taking the soft option, avoiding conflict and doing anything for an easier ride. My father had disappeared before, presumably when times got tough, and before Mum had made her dramatic entrance I had been on the cusp of finding out why.

Terry sighed and began to pace up and down our small living room, raking a hand through his hair.

Mum groaned. She sat up gingerly and winced. 'Have you got anything to drink? And not tea.'

'Sure.' I darted off to the kitchen to pour her a tumbler of Baileys.

I settled back on the sofa near Mum's feet and handed her a glass. 'Now then, both of you, I've got some questions that need answering.'

Terry turned to face his ex-wife, legs apart, arms folded,

his face set like granite. 'Actually, I've got a question for you, Valerie.' He took a deep breath. 'Why did you lie to me and tell me Sophie wasn't my baby?'

I gasped and a cold shiver ran along the length of my spine.

Chapter 30

Terry crouched down in front of me and took my hands in his.

'Sophie, I never would have left you if I'd known. I'd never have let you grow up not knowing who I was. Even if your mother and I had divorced, I'd still have been there for you.'

My heart was beating double time as I stared at her, willing her to deny she had ever said such a thing.

'Mum, is it true?'

To my horror, she nodded weakly and her face crumpled as a fresh batch of tears coursed down her cheeks.

'It was after that row we had about the party.' She sniffed. 'Getting married was so exciting. But *being* married . . .' She shuddered. 'All you wanted to do was stay at home, tinker with your DIY and watch TV. I wanted parties, fun, excitement. I was so angry with you. I felt trapped. And I still thought I could be the next Whitney Houston.' She laughed, which turned into a sob and her nose started to run.

'Mum?' I gasped. 'I can't believe what I'm hearing.' I handed her a tissue on autopilot and took one for myself.

Terry stood up, pinched the bridge of his nose and closed

his eyes. I couldn't read his expression. It might have been pain or fury. Possibly both.

'Angry?' he said simply. 'You stole our baby from me because you were angry? To win a stupid argument?' He shook his head and stared at her.

He was incredibly controlled. I would have been lunging at her and wringing her neck by now.

'What do you mean?' I stuttered, swiping at my tears with shaking hands.

He shook his head. 'Your mum was suffering terribly with sickness. I said I wouldn't take her to some party or other and it escalated into another argument.'

I swallowed. 'And then what?'

Terry stared at mum but she wouldn't meet his eye. 'And then she said she was going to the party and it was none of my business because the baby wasn't mine anyway.'

'That was a wicked thing to say, Mum,' I said, my eyes boring into her's. 'Because I was, wasn't I?'

'Yes, love,' whispered Mum.

Blood pounded in my ears as the three of us sat in silence.

Finally, Terry spoke. 'I didn't find that out until Aunt Jane saw you and realized I had to be your dad. The likeness between us was too much of a coincidence.' He smiled at me briefly, before turning his attention back to Mum.

'You lied.' His eyes pierced hers so forcefully that she dropped her gaze to her hands. 'You deprived me of the chance to be a father to Sophie. That is unforgivable.'

'You were pretty quick to believe that it was true, though, weren't you? I might have been a bit of a flirt, but nothing more. I would never have cheated on you, Terry. It was just a game, I was young . . . '

'A game?' He dropped heavily into the armchair, covering his face with his hands. 'When you forced me move out of our home, I lost everything. You broke my heart.'

Mum fumbled up her sleeve for another tissue and blew her nose loudly.

'I was wrong, I admit it. I was selfish. And after a while I regretted it. I came looking for you in your local pub, just before the baby was due. I was going to tell you the truth and ask you to give us another chance. I saw you across the bar, getting friendly with a barmaid. I thought you'd moved on, didn't need me any more. As I watched you, I realized that I was relieved that you'd found someone to make you happy. I would never have been a good wife to you and having a baby together would have only made things worse.'

Terry narrowed his eyes, as if trying to cast his mind back all those years. 'I can't even think who that barmaid might have been, but she would only have been a shoulder to cry on. There was no one else for me until I met my second wife.'

I had been listening to this incredible exchange as if it was a scene in a TV soap opera. Suddenly, the impact of her selfish actions hit me and I snapped.

'What about me, Mum? Because, actually, you did have a baby together, remember? Didn't I deserve a father? And why let me believe that it was *him* who abandoned *you*!'

Mum chewed on her lip. The lipstick had worn off long ago, just a shadow of colour remained where it had bled into the fine wrinkles round her mouth. She reached out to touch me but I snatched my arm away.

'I'm so sorry, Sophie, I've been a terrible mother. All the

time you were growing up, I dreaded your father getting in touch; I knew how badly I'd behaved. When Jane challenged me about Terry being your father I panicked; I was terrified of losing you.'

I shook my head. Everything I had just heard contradicted what I thought I knew about my parents' divorce, about my own start in life. It was so much to take in. And if it hadn't been for Great-aunt Jane I'd never have known.

'I haven't lost you, have I? We had fun, didn't we?' she pleaded. 'We made a good team?'

I stayed silent and let my mind wander back through the years of my childhood.

Having fun had always been high on her agenda. The day Gary Barlow made an appearance at Virgin Records sprang to mind. I was in the middle of my GCSEs, but she wrote me a note excusing me from school so I could join the crowds and get his autograph. *Live for the moment*, she had told me. But I had needed more than fun; I'd wanted a family and a proper home. She had denied me both of those.

'No,' I sighed, 'you haven't lost me. But I want to be able to have a relationship with both of my parents.'

I flicked a sideways glance at Terry and we shared a smile.

'In future I'll be the one to decide what's right for me. If I want to stay in touch with my father, I will. There's room in my life for both of you.'

She nodded. 'Of course. And I'm sorry. Terry . . .' She sighed. 'You were a good man.' She laughed sadly. 'I never met anyone as good as you again.'

I looked down at her. Her eyes were drooping and her skin was so pale it was almost translucent. Despite being furious with her, I could see she was in no fit state to take much more.

'Why don't you get some sleep in my bed?' I suggested. 'We can talk again later.'

Terry put the kettle on while I helped Mum into my room.

Five minutes later, it was just the two of us again, him on the sofa, me in the chair. This time we both had tea – milky with two sugars. We sipped our drinks in silence. I didn't know what to say. Terry had definitely been dealt a raw deal by my mum but his aunt had bumped into us when I had been about five years old and he hadn't exactly fallen over himself to make contact, had he?

Terry seemed like such a supportive parent to Brodie, a real father figure. Having someone like that in my life when I was growing up would have made a massive difference. Why hadn't he fought for me?

As if reading my mind, Terry groaned and looked me squarely in the eye.

'We've made a right mess of things, me and your mother. I can't lay all the blame at her feet. I'm sorry for how all this has affected you, love.'

'Why didn't you come and challenge Mum as soon as you found out the truth?'

Terry massaged his forehead and groaned.

'Dad,' I said, sitting next to him and patting his arm awkwardly. 'Talk to me.'

He looked up at me and smiled. 'You called me Dad.'

'Oh yeah, I did, didn't I?' I grinned back.

In that moment, he had somehow become Dad. Not my father. Dad. A warm glow filled my heart as he took my hand and squeezed it. It felt quite nice to have a dad.

'I realize this will sound feeble, but here goes. When Aunt Jane wrote to me to say she'd seen Valerie with a pretty curly-haired, green-eyed little girl, I'd already been in the Navy for five years. I had a bit of a nomadic lifestyle and it was easy to stay away. I told myself that by sending you a birthday card, I was at least making some effort. Aunt Jane tried to make contact with your mother, but she couldn't track her down. I kept sending the cards on the off-chance.'

I nodded. 'I found the birthday cards in her bedroom unopened, she'd kept them all these years.'

'My aunt was always badgering me to come back to England and find you, but too much time had gone by. And besides,' he flicked me a sideways glance and sighed, 'I've always been a bit of a bugger for taking the easy way out. I told myself that if it was meant to be, we would be reunited at some point in the future.'

'One thing I've learned this year,' I replied, 'is that you have to go out and make your future, not sit around waiting for it to find you.'

He turned and met my gaze, his expression etched with decades of regret. 'I know that now. And although it's of no consolation to you, I vowed when Brodie was born that I would do better the second time around. To my eternal shame, once he was born, I stopped sending the cards. I figured I might just be making things worse.'

A pang of sadness struck at my heart. So he had just pushed me to the back of his mind. Filed under 'daughter: whereabouts unknown'. But with a new wife and a new baby, was it really so difficult to understand?

A thought struck me suddenly. 'You haven't told me anything about your second wife?'

He laughed shakily. 'I think today has been emotional

enough without telling you about Maggie. Next time, perhaps. There will be a next time, I hope?'

Where do lumps in the throat come from? One minute you're absolutely fine and then without a word of warning, a lump the size of a tennis ball materializes in your throat and you can't speak, swallow or breathe.

I nodded.

Then, on impulse, I put my arms round him and hugged him tight. Dad instantly returned my hug.

'I'd like that,' I whispered, my eyes full of tears. 'Although I'm not sure Brodie will be so keen.'

'I'll let you into a secret,' he said, his eyes twinkling. 'He's been boasting about having an English half-sister all his life to his friends.'

'Really?' I grinned.

Dad nodded. 'He's just feeling a bit overwhelmed and unnecessarily over-protective.' His hand moved involuntarily to his chest, a gesture which wasn't lost on me.

'Anyway,' he said, standing up reluctantly, 'I've taken up enough of your time. You've got your mum to look after. I'd better round up Brodie and pour him into my hire car.'

We walked out into the hallway and I unhooked his coat from the peg. I was in the middle of giving him directions to the local pub, when we heard a disturbance coming from the stairwell. A noise like an injured animal was coming from the floor below.

Terry looked at me and frowned. At first I shrugged but Emma's voice wafted up to us.

'You grab her arm,' she grunted.

'Jeez, her bag weighs a ton!' That was Brodie.

I flung open the door and gasped as the two of them fell into the flat, lugging Jess between them.

'Jess, what on earth's happened to you?' I cried.

Jess's face was pink and puffy and her mascara had slid down onto her cheeks.

'Come on, lovey,' said Emma gently. So gently, in fact, that I did a double take. 'Let's get you onto the sofa.' She wrapped an arm round her sister's waist and Jess allowed herself to be led into the living room.

That sofa was seeing some action today.

Jess collapsed into its saggy cushions gratefully, her body still shaking with juddering sobs.

'Poxy sodding earrings,' I managed to decipher between her gulping. 'With the birthstone for May.'

'Is that what Spike bought you for Christmas, earrings?' I asked, catching Emma's eye. We both pulled a face. Earrings were definitely not on Jess's Christmas list.

'Yes.' Jess sniffed, flinging an arm over her face.

'But your birthday's in March,' said Emma, perching on the edge of the sofa to remove Jess's shoes. This observation produced a fresh set of wails.

Jess nodded. 'And they're naff. Not half as nice as the ones you make, Em.'

Emma couldn't resist a prim smile. Compliments from her sister were as rare as hens' teeth.

Dad and Brodie lurked by the doorway. Brodie looked like he was enjoying the drama a little too much. Dad's eyes were darting all over the place and he shifted from foot to foot uncomfortably. I could tell he wanted to make a hasty exit, but I was too worried about Jess to talk to him for the moment.

I knelt on the floor beside her. 'It's still early days with Spike,' I said. 'Perhaps he doesn't feel ready for the sort of commitment you were hoping for.'

Jess wiped her nose with the back of her hand and I handed her my last tissue.

'He's dumped me,' she sobbed.

'For not liking his crappy earrings?' cried Emma. 'The tosser!'

'No,' she said, shaking her head vigorously. 'You don't understand. He dumped me when I gave him his present. And I thought he would love it.'

She pressed the tissue to her face and cried loudly.

Emma and I exchanged worried glances. Jess had resolutely refused to tell us what she had got Spike for Christmas, which in itself had rung alarm bells; she was the world's worst secret-keeper.

'Well, go on then,' Emma urged, obviously running out of patience. 'Tell us what it is!'

'Pass me my bag,' whimpered Jess, pushing herself up to a sitting position.

Brodie stepped forward, dragging Jess's voluminous handbag across the carpet. I knew why it was so heavy: she had packed her toiletries just in case they had decided to book into a hotel to celebrate their engagement.

She fished a flat rectangular package out of her bag, still in its torn Christmas wrapping paper. It didn't look particularly impressive; perhaps he had dumped her out of disappointment, having expected something bigger?

Emma took the paper off to reveal a small picture frame. We both stared at it. Brodie squeezed in beside me and looked over my shoulder and a heavy silence settled on the room.

After ten seconds of nobody saying a word, Brodie sighed.

'Will someone please explain what we're supposed to be

looking at,' he said, pushing his curly fringe out of his eyes. 'It's just a fuzzy picture to me.'

All the clues had been there, I just hadn't added them up: the tiredness, cutting back on alcohol and even – though I hadn't wanted to mention it – a slight increase in girth.

I took a deep breath and reached out to squeeze Jess's trembling hand. 'It's a baby scan picture, Brodie. Jess is pregnant.'

Chapter 31

I collected my cappuccino from the counter in Starbucks and looked round the busy café for a seat.

There was one free stool in the window next to a couple of teenagers who were alternating between snogging and feeding each other hot chocolate from a long spoon. I squeezed myself into the tiny space and tried not to stare. I would have to keep my eyes open for a spare table; there was no way Nick would be able to fit in here next to me.

I turned my back on the teenagers and stared at the festive scene out of the window. On the opposite side of the street was a collection of Christmas stalls; hot chestnuts, holly wreaths and cheerful wrapping paper. The street was jam-packed with people laden with shopping bags, but despite the crowds and the icy weather, there was a tingle of Christmas excitement in the air.

This Christmas was certainly going to be memorable for the Stone family, I thought as I took my coat off. I hadn't seen Dad again, but we'd spoken on the phone.

I kicked my bags under my stool, out of the path of a passing waitress. I'd had to dash out and buy presents for them all. Not that I minded; I loved Christmas shopping.

Choosing something for a new father and a new brother had been a bit tricky; I'd plumped for a hoodie for Brodie and a golf jumper for Dad and guessed their sizes.

We had decided that it was probably best to celebrate Christmas Day apart, so he and Brodie were spending the day at his hotel and Mum and I were having a quiet day at home. And then Mum, Dad and I would be together on New Year's Eve while Brodie was out partying.

Mum was very subdued at the moment. My feelings towards her varied with my mood. She had acted unbelievably selfishly. I recognized now that she had always been a bit selfish; doing exactly as she wanted with scant regard for other people. Maybe she had been right not to try to get back together with my dad? I certainly couldn't see them as a happily married couple. However, forgiving her for depriving Dad and me of having any sort of relationship would take a little while. But for now I was happy to call a Christmas truce.

Emma, who hadn't left Jess's side for two days, was taking her back to their parents' for a week. Spike hadn't been in touch at all and I had a feeling that we had heard the last from him. Jess was adamant that she was keeping the baby and now Emma and I had got over the initial shock, we were super-excited about being aunties and agreed that Jess would make a great mum.

I took a sip of my scalding coffee. I'd been getting into coffee recently; it was OK if there was enough sugar in it and it wasn't too strong. This was nice. Not as good as Nick's, obviously . . .

Sophie Stone, I chided myself. I'd done it again. For some reason my mind had been gravitating towards Nick far too often just recently: *Nick would say that, Nick wouldn't do this, that stranger reminds me of Nick* . . . I had no idea why, it wasn't as if he had ever shown any interest in me.

Although, I mused, he did think I had a talent for interior design.

I slid my sketchpad out of my bag. My nerves jangled as I flicked through the pages. I'd finished my ideas for his barn conversion, but with the whole family conflab thing going on, plus Jess's pregnancy, I hadn't had a chance to mount the designs properly on boards. I would go through them with Nick now as planned and then ask for an extra day to finish off. I hoped he wouldn't be annoyed, I hoped he liked my work, I hoped he was impressed.

I scanned the pages, reminding myself of the design. I'd planned an exciting and social space rather than a cosy haven. I loved it, but would the clients? Would Nick? I chewed my lip for a second as my stomach fluttered. I'd done my absolute best, Nick couldn't ask more than that, besides, it was too late now.

The clock in Market Square chimed noon. He would be here any minute. My heart jolted in anticipation of seeing him . . . of presenting my work to him, I corrected myself. No other reason.

A couple walking by, wrapped in each other's arms, caught my eye. They paused in front of the window to kiss and I averted my eyes. The man had cropped blonde hair, the same colour as Marc's. I wondered what he was doing now. In all probability he would have found someone new already. Unlike me. I didn't miss him, though, although I did miss having a special someone. It was harder being single at Christmas somehow; I felt awkward walking into parties on my own.

I blew a hole in the froth of my cappuccino and took a tentative slurp.

Last year had been mine and Marc's first and only Christmas together. He'd come round on Boxing Day and met my mum, charmed her with a box of chocolates and presented me with a posh Mont Blanc pen. Only after he had gone did we notice that the chocolates were out of date and the pen read 'Mond Blanc' – a fake he'd picked up at the market where he'd worked, presumably.

No, I decided, giving my shoulders a little shake, I didn't miss Marc one bit.

'Hello,' said a familiar voice.

I looked up, startled to see Nick smiling at me.

'Hi!' I replied. Should I stand, or stay where I was? Shake hands or kiss? *The Dutch have it so easy*, I thought randomly, they just go straight for three kisses and everyone knows where they stand . . .

He pointed to my face.

'You've got froth on your lip,' he said. 'You look like Santa.'

'Oh that,' I laughed gaily, 'I always do that at Christmas.'

Great. I grabbed a napkin and wiped my mouth feeling flustered. Just as well I didn't opt for the kissy greeting.

He was doing a pretty good Santa impression himself: all bundled up in a red ski jacket, several carrier bags in each hand. He even had a red nose. Lovely eyes, too. Although I wasn't sure Santa had grey eyes that crinkled when he smiled, that lit up when he was excited or clouded over when he was embarrassed.

'Can I get you another?' he was saying.

I shook my head. 'No thanks, this one is still at boiling point.'

The teenagers, having long ago finished their drink, were now being moved on by the manager and I dragged one of the newly vacated stools over for Nick, who returned with an icy frappuccino.

'I know it's weird having a cold drink on a winter's day,' he said, in answer to my amused expression, 'but I've spent an hour in a toy department in this jacket. I thought I was going to pass out.'

He peeled off his jacket, hung it over the back of his stool and breathed a sigh of relief.

'Christmas shopping?' I asked.

He winced as he took a sip of his drink, leaned forward and whispered. 'Yes. I love shopping for my nephews. It's a great excuse to play with all the toys. There was a remote-control helicopter to try out which caught my eye and I was tempted to buy one for myself.'

I watched him line up three packets of sugar on the table and empty them, one at a time, into the glass.

He seemed so different from the solemn, serious man I'd met back in March. Then, he had barely been able to string a sentence together. Now he was quite chatty, playful almost. Perhaps he was excited about Christmas, or maybe, he was just more relaxed around me these days.

'Your planning application is almost ready to go,' said Nick, breaking into my thoughts. His face had returned to its usual serious expression. Shame.

'We'll wait until the New Year to submit it. Otherwise it will get lost in all the holiday post.'

I nodded. In truth, I'd almost forgotten about it! Bizarre, given how long I'd been dreaming about having the security of my own home. Maybe meeting my dad and finally knowing the real story had something to do with it. Maybe I felt more secure of my place in the world. I certainly felt happier knowing that Dad didn't wilfully abandon me.

Nick was staring at me. I wiped my mouth again automatically.

'Are you OK?' he said, laying a hand gently on mine. 'Only you've barely spoken. That's quite out of character for you.'

Hadn't I? I stared at his hand, his skin against mine. My pulse began to race and I swallowed hard. He was touching me and I felt his warmth infusing my body. It was this whole not having a special someone thing, I realized. The first bit of male attention and I start reading more into it than I should be.

I looked at his hand again. It was a concerned hand that was all.

I had no idea where my next words came from.

'Jess is pregnant!' I blurted out. 'My flatmate.'

Nick raised his eyebrows. 'Ah. The teacher or the silversmith?'

He had remembered! I was touched.

'The teacher. And her policeman boyfriend has left her because of it.'

His body stiffened and a shadow passed across his face. He released my hand, shook his head and stared into the middle distance.

'I don't understand that. What sort of person wouldn't want to see their own child grow up?'

'A total idiot in this case.' I sighed. 'Fortunately, Jess has got us. And she's got really supportive parents, so I think she'll be better off without him.'

Nick groaned. 'Oh, Sophie, I'm so sorry, how insensitive

of me. I'd forgotten that your father did the same to you, please forgive me.'

He touched my hand again and my heart soared.

'Funny story, actually; I followed your advice and contacted my dad.'

I don't know why I chose the word 'funny' to describe the lies and subterfuge my mother had employed for over thirty years, but heyho.

Nick listened to my news completely engrossed, sipping at his drink every now and then. By the end of it he was the one sporting a creamy moustache. I was close enough to reach out and rub my thumb over his top lip. My mouth dried at the thought. I chickened out, handed him a napkin and pointed at his lips.

'So you were right, it is a good feeling having my dad in my life. And I'm sorry I over-reacted when you suggested it,' I said with a self-conscious shrug.

Nick rolled his eyes and smiled. 'Phew! Thank goodness for that. I was livid with myself for interfering at the time. And so will you keep in touch with your father?'

'Absolutely. He says he'll be coming over to England regularly while Brodie is at uni and he's even invited me to the States when I'm ready.'

Nick nodded. He scrunched up the torn sugar packets and poked them into the top of his empty glass.

'I'm not surprised. If I had a beautiful daughter like you, I would definitely want her in my life,' he mumbled.

My breath caught in my throat. *Beautiful.* I swallowed hard. That was one of the loveliest things anyone had ever said to me.

'That's a lovely thing to say, Nick.' I looked at him over the rim of my cup. 'Although I must say I'm surprised.

Didn't you say that you never mix business with pleasure? Aren't you breaking your own rule?'

My voice had gone up an octave. I coughed to bring it back down.

'Did I say that?' Nick winced.

'Yes.'

'You must have thought I was a complete idiot.'

'No. I just thought you didn't fancy me.'

I didn't know where to look. I couldn't believe I just said that. My flaming cheeks couldn't believe it either. I decided to brazen it out.

'Just joking!' I laughed to prove it. 'I thought you were very professional and I appreciated it. Still do. Obviously.'

Eek! Got away with that one.

Nick wiped away the condensation from the window and sighed.

'The thing is . . .' he began.

I held my breath. Despite me filling him in on all the ins and outs and ups and downs of my complicated life, I still knew next to nothing about his. And I wanted to, I realized. I wanted to get to know Nick Cromwell better.

'Before I set up my own practice, I worked in Manchester for a large firm.'

I nodded. I knew that already, I had searched him on Google before I'd first contacted him.

'It was all going well, I bought an apartment, got a promotion and then I had an affair with a client. She moved in with me even though we had to keep it secret from our employers. We were together for a year. I'd hoped . . . Well, anyway, it ended badly. It was a bit of a mess, actually, and nearly ruined my career.' He exhaled deeply and ruffled a hand through his hair and my heart went out to him. Only

Nick could succeed in summing up what was obviously a painful period of his life in one short speech.

'I'm sorry to hear that, Nick,' I said softly, covering my hand with his.

'I couldn't risk that happening again, so I made a pact with myself that clients were strictly off-limits from then on.'

We looked at each other but his eyes hinted at a deep-rooted sadness. Whatever had happened between him and the woman from Manchester, he was still getting over it.

I scrabbled around to think of something to get the earlier light-hearted mood back. I reached for my sketch-book.

'And now in an unexpected client role reversal, I present to you, drum roll please, my contemporary cowshed!'

It worked. For a happy few minutes we flicked through the pages, me explaining my scribbles and him asking pertinent questions. Nick was back. His love of architecture and design seemed to be strong enough to lift him from the gloom of failed relationships.

And he loved my design. Hurrah!

'I knew asking for your help was the right thing to do,' he said, with a proud smile. My smile was pretty proud too; I should have acted more modestly but I was having a hard time keeping the corners of my mouth down.

'Now if I can just take this . . .' He picked up my pad and began to put it into one of his bags.

'No!' I squeaked. 'It's not finished. I need to mount the pages properly first, arrange them on boards. I just ran out of time.'

Nick chuckled. 'No need. This is fine as it is. I'll just scan in the pages I need and let you have the book back.

Besides, I promised I'd get them to the client to look at over Christmas.'

'All right, if you're sure.' It looked like I didn't have much choice in the matter. At least it saved me a job, I supposed. And I was very busy. I glanced at my watch.

'Have you got time for another?' said Nick, peering into my empty cup. 'I still haven't managed to buy you a drink yet!'

'Well,' I hesitated. I was famished. If I didn't eat soon my stomach would be grumbling like a grumpy bear. I couldn't very well ask him to buy me lunch as well, could I?

'No problem, I understand,' said Nick, jumping to his feet before I had chance to answer. 'I'm very busy too. Busy, busy. Must press on, in fact. I expect you've got a hectic few days coming up too?'

My heart sank. I had been looking forward to another half an hour or so of his company, but it appeared he had other ideas.

'Just a quiet one for me this year,' I said bravely.

Mum would probably wake up around ten on Christmas Day, we would sit in bed with a cup of tea and exchange gifts, which would take all of five minutes and then we would watch telly and outdo each other in who can do the most damage in the kitchen. Maybe not too hectic.

Nick and I both started to pull on our coats. Starbucks had filled up even more since I had arrived and there was hardly room to swing a scarf let alone a cat. As I struggled to do up my top button with my elbows pressed to my sides, we found ourselves nose to chin.

I laughed awkwardly, but he looked down at me seriously.

'I regret saying what I said,' he mumbled.

'Do you?' I blinked at him, a bit confused. 'Which bit?

Christmas being busy or offering to buy me a drink. Or . . .' I gulped at the thought. 'Don't you really like my design for the cowshed?'

Nick fumbled with the zip on his jacket. Was he blushing or was it just reflection off his red fabric? 'About not dating clients.'

Stomach, I'd like you to meet some butterflies . . .

'Oh,' was the best I could manage.

He looked at the floor. 'I don't suppose . . . no, forget it . . . it doesn't matter.'

'No, go on!' I smiled at him encouragingly. 'Please.'

He took a deep breath. 'Well, I was supposed to be going skiing with a friend over New Year, but he has torn his Achilles tendon and has had to cry off.'

I felt my mouth go dry. Please don't ask me to take his place. I've seen *Bridget Jones*. I've seen the damage mini-breaks can do to a relationship. And I can't ski. I'd be even worse than Bridget.

'So Poppi, my intern, has asked me to go to her party.'

I sighed with relief; a party I could manage. 'That's a shame. About the skiing, I mean.'

He nodded. 'Very disappointing. But anyway, I wondered if you fancied coming to the party with me. It will probably be full of students swigging Vodka Redbulls and dancing to music I've never heard of, but I thought in the absence of anything better to do . . .'

His voice petered out when he saw my face. A face that told him that he wasn't doing a good job of selling it.

'I thought . . .' he stuttered, trying a different tack. 'I thought I'd enjoy it a lot more if you came.'

'Thank you.' I gazed up into his eyes with a shy smile. 'That's such a sweet thing to say.'

'Plus the fact that if you did come, you'd help me increase the average age by about ten years.'

I gasped. 'I'm not that old, you know. I can still dance without a walking stick, for goodness' sake!'

Nick's face sagged. 'That came out all wrong.'

I couldn't help laughing. I was surprised he had ever managed to have a girlfriend if that was his best chat-up line. And I knew by now that there was sometimes a gap between what he said and what he meant to say.

'It's OK,' I said.

He smiled back at me, gratefully. 'What I mean is, that you're funny and talented and interesting and . . .' he paused to catch his breath, 'beautiful and I can't think of a person I would rather see the New Year in with than you.'

'Wow,' I mumbled, inadequately. 'That the best offer I've had all day. Does Poppi know you're inviting me?'

'Oh yes,' he said blithely. 'It was her idea.'

He grinned at me sheepishly.

It was her idea. Great. I felt a twinge of disappointment at that, but then an even bigger one when I realized that I couldn't make it.

'I would love to come,' I said, pulling the corners of my mouth down into a genuinely sad smile, 'but unfortunately I'm already busy that night.'

Nick adjusted his glasses. 'No problem. Silly of me to have suggested it. Of course you would have already sorted out your New Year's Eve plans by now.'

My heart sank at his expression. Should I tell him that it would be the first and quite possibly the last time that I would ever spend New Year with both of my parents? That I would much rather be with Nick, laughing at each other's jokes and making fun of the students who would no doubt drink far too much. And then at midnight . . . I shook my head, trying to rid it of images of the two of us locked in each other's arms while a circle of inebriated teenagers sang 'Auld Lang Syne' around us.

I'd missed my chance. Anything I said now would seem like I was making excuses.

'I'm sorry,' I said weakly. 'Another time perhaps?'

He bent down to collect his shopping bags.

'Sure,' he said with a curt smile. 'Like the coffee.'

I cringed and tried to think of something to say to redeem the situation but my mind had gone blank.

'Goodbye then,' he said.

As I pushed in my stool, he attempted to shake my hand and somehow our carrier bags managed to get tangled together.

'Sorry about this,' said Nick, frowning.

I bit back a giggle as I turned in towards him to try to free my hand. Our right arms were pressed together and my shoulder nudged against his chest. A tingle of excitement ran through me as I felt the muscles in his chest flex. He was surprisingly firm and much more natural than Marc's pumped-up physique. I tried tugging my hand free, but the handle of a particularly tough bag cut into my wrist painfully.

'Let's drop the bags,' I suggested, after several seconds of grunting and pulling unsuccessfully.

The bags fell to the floor. Nick stooped to pick them up and handed mine back to me. My fingers closed over his. I smiled up at him in thanks and held onto his hand for an extra beat.

Our eyes met and we smiled at each other.

Oh, stuff it, it's Christmas! Kissing your architect is

definitely allowed at Christmas, I'm sure I read it some-where . . .

I reached up on tiptoe, closed my eyes and pressed a soft kiss to his lips. My stomach trembled and it took all my self-control not to weave my fingers into his hair and make the kiss go on and on . . .

'Merry Christmas, Nick,' I murmured opening my eyes and staring straight into his.

'Merry Christmas,' he replied hoarsely.

I dropped my gaze from his and turned into the melee of the café. I made it as far as the door before the tell-tale blush on my face betrayed me as not being as brave as I looked.

I risked peeking over my shoulder for one last look at him. Nick's fingers were resting lightly on his lips, but his feet hadn't moved an inch. My heart sang as he smiled and waved goodbye and I waved back and joined the crowds on the street, the taste of his lips still on mine – nutmeg and cinnamon and sugar – the perfect Christmas kiss.

Chapter 32

The Microsoft symbol appeared on my screen again, bouncing from one corner to another as my computer got bored of waiting for me and went for a lie-down. I sighed and wiggled the mouse to wake it back up.

January was always a bit flat at *The Herald*, with clients pleading poverty after Christmas. Just as well; concentrating on anything except Nick was proving to be difficult. My brain was like a scratched record. I had replayed the last part of our meeting (yes, hard to believe, but it had been a bona fide meeting) more times than I cared to remember. I relived the moment he invited me to the party, right through until I kissed him, analysing his every word, his every look and cringing at my every response.

It was obvious that I had blown my chance with him. He asked me out and I turned him down. He wasn't likely to ask me again, he wouldn't want to risk the rejection. Then, just to confuse the poor man, I had to go and kiss him! Talk about mixed messages. No wonder he hadn't been in touch since.

I prodded the screen on my phone to make it update. Nothing. No messages.

At least I had made the first move for once, by kissing

him. I was quite proud of myself for that. I sighed again. Nick. I couldn't believe how good-looking he was. Why had I not noticed this before? Something to do with those rose-tinted glasses that hadn't let me see past Marc's testosterone-packed torso, I guessed.

I thought of those haunting grey eyes that betrayed his every emotion, his dark hair that was just begging me to run my hands through it and that firm body, which had pressed so fleetingly against mine. I shivered just thinking about it.

I had a quick look round to check no one was looking and typed 'Nick Cromwell' into Google. I selected 'images' and indulged my new guilty pleasure. I was ashamed to admit it but I spent quite a lot of time doing this at the moment. There was a whole page of pictures to choose from: Nick at Grand Designs Live; the profile picture from his own website; Nick at the opening of some restaurant in Manchester; he had even been featured in *The Herald* a couple of years ago, talking about his architectural vision for the city.

I'd confided in Emma and Jess on New Year's Day that I had a crush on him and they'd exchanged smug looks and congratulated me for admitting it.

'Not that it will do me any good,' I'd said with a sigh.

'Duh!' said Emma, rolling her eyes. 'And it's obvious he's got the hots for you.'

I'd tutted at that but Jess reckoned I should just ring him and tell him I how I felt.

'No way!' I'd replied, horrified at the idea. 'I might have been brave enough, or stupid enough, depending on how you view it, to give him a Christmas kiss, but he's still my architect. What if he said he didn't feel the same? I'd never be able to look him in the eye again.'

Nick would be submitting my planning application this week. Now Christmas was out of the way, I was feeling quite excited about my little house. Plus I had a new deadline; that baby was going to need a bedroom! And once the build was under way, I would have an excuse to speak to Nick every day. Hurrah and Happy New Year to me!

Since New Year, life had more or less resumed as before. Mum had packed herself back off to Spain and Dad had gone back to the States.

I was quite surprised how much I missed him. He wasn't a hero or a millionaire or a rocket scientist, just a nice, ordinary guy, but I really liked him and I was so glad I had given him a second chance. It was a good feeling knowing that I could call him for a chat or a bit of fatherly advice. That was a new experience for me; the nearest I had come to it before was Mr Whelan, my great-aunt's solicitor.

Only last week before he'd left, Dad and I went out for Sunday dinner and found out we both ate ketchup with everything and that our favourite pudding was treacle tart and even little things like that had been a joy to discover and had made us feel closer.

'Busy, Sophie?' Donna's minty breath with undertones of nicotine blew softly onto my neck.

How does she manage to creep up on people like that? Anyone would think she was on wheels instead of stilettos!

I tapped viciously at the computer to bring it back to life.

'Yes, Donna, I'm brainstorming my ideas for the Valentine's Day Wedding Proposal promotion,' I said brightly.

Donna ran an impatient hand over her platinum bob, which as usual was lacquered to within an inch of its life.

'On my own. Just in my head,' I added as the boss eyed up my blank computer screen.

'Hmm,' she said, losing interest and turning her beady eye onto me. 'Sorted out your plus one?'

'Er.'

I knew I had to be very careful here. She was referring to our table at the Property Awards. This glittering affair was to be held on February the fourteenth in Nottingham's most prestigious hotel and was attended by everyone who was anyone in the property industry. *The Herald* was the main sponsor and not only had Donna commanded that Jason, Maureen and I had to be there, we had to bring a 'useful' guest with us. If I didn't come up with a name soon, Donna would choose one for me.

'That's my very next job,' I said, pulling a scruffy stack of business cards towards me. I flashed her a confident smile and she swished over to Jason and jabbed a finger at him.

'And you. You've got two hours to bring me the names of your guests or I'll do it for you both.'

Jason dropped his head onto his desk. His shirt had come untucked and I could see at least a third of his underpants. Spending Valentine's Day at a work event had not gone down too well with his new girlfriend.

Who was I going to take? I couldn't invite Emma or Jess even if they'd been suitable guests: the National Silverware Awards were on the fifteenth of February, in London. Emma was taking Jess with her as it was the school half-term holiday and they were travelling down the night before. I was really proud of Emma; she had intended to invite her dad as he had been her main motivation for entering in the first place, but she had decided that a party was just what Jess needed to cheer her up. Besides, with me already out for the evening, I don't think Emma wanted to leave a jilted and pregnant woman on her own, especially not on the most romantic night of the year.

Not that I would be having a romantic time of it, I thought as I discarded card after card. Finally I came to Nick's business card and my stomach fluttered. I wondered what he would be doing on Valentine's Day? He would be my ideal 'plus one'. A leading young architect could easily be classed as 'useful', not to mention being sophisticated, well-informed and very passionate about property. Donna would love him.

I was pretty keen too.

I puffed my cheeks out. Jess had been coming up with convoluted excuses for me to get back in touch with him for weeks. But this was perfect. My heart raced as my hand hovered over the phone.

Don't over-think it, Sophie, just do it.

I dialled Nick's office and Poppi answered immediately. I couldn't decide whether this was good or bad.

'Poppi, hi! How was the New Year's Eve party? Sorry I couldn't make it,' I said.

'The best!' said Poppi. 'The police didn't come till five in the morning, by which time the vodka jelly in the bath had gone, the fireworks had finished and the fire brigade had put the flames out in next door's shed, so we called it a night. You missed a good party!'

'Sounds like fun!' I shuddered, reminding myself never to attend a student party, no matter how tempting the invitation. And not that I knew him very well, but somehow I couldn't imagine Nick enjoying that sort of thing either. I'd sat at home with my parents drinking Baileys, watching TV and thinking about him.

'Nick didn't come,' said Poppi, echoing my thoughts. 'He went home to his mum's. The wimp.'

'Is Nick there?'

'No.'

Silence. Poppi's dedication to customer service knew no bounds.

I sighed. 'Do you know if he's free on the evening of February the fourteenth?'

'Valentine's Day? Ah, that's so cute! I'll just check his diary.'

'It's not cute, Poppi, it's business: the annual Property Awards,' I corrected. Even so, that didn't stop my cheeks blazing like her next door neighbour's shed.

'Course it is,' she chirped in a tone that managed to convey that she was only humouring me because I was a client. 'Here we are. He's got a photo shoot early evening, you know, for the dogs. But he'd love to come.'

A photo shoot for the dogs? The mind boggled. Images of dogs posing on velvet cushions, with Nick urging them to 'Work it, baby' sprang into my head. My heart sank; whatever it meant it looked as if he was busy anyway.

'Oh! He's here now,' said Poppi. 'You can ask him yourself.'

I caught snatches of a whispered conversation as Poppi failed to put the call on hold while she filled Nick in. I turned over a new page in my notebook and wrote 'To Do List' at the top.

'Hello, Sophie, Happy New Year!'

My insides went all gooey at the sound of his voice.

'Thank you. You too.' I smiled down the phone.

'And thank you for paying my invoice,' he said. 'I'll be sending your planning application in for Lilac Lane on

Friday, so it arrives with them on Monday.'

'Great.' I sighed quietly, disappointed that he hadn't asked me about my Christmas. It was as if those precious moments in the coffee shop had never existed. Maybe this wasn't such a good idea? Maybe I should leave him with his dogs on Valentine's Day?

'Poppi said something about the Property Awards?' said Nick.

Was I imagining it, or did he sound interested? I perked up a bit and fidgeted in my seat.

'*The Herald* has a table and I'd like to invite you as my guest. Are you free?'

There was a moment's silence on the other end of the line. I held my breath and kept everything crossed.

'I'm free,' he said finally, 'thank you. I'd be honoured.'

Nick in a tuxedo, me in a posh frock, a candlelit dinner . . . Perhaps it would be a romantic occasion after all? Perhaps this was our chance?

'It would be a great networking opportunity for me,' he gushed.

'Oh, good,' I replied flatly. 'I'll add you to the guest list then.'

I promised to introduce him to the business editor, the property editor and some big cheese at the property industry association and then rang off, somewhat deflated.

I looked down at my to-do list. Plus one was sorted. Only new dress, new shoes, a manicure, haircut and lose half a stone left to tick off and I was good to go.

Chapter 33

A month later and the night had finally arrived. I couldn't take my eyes off the girl in front of me: elegant and demure and just a teeny bit sexy. I smiled and she smiled back, her eyes shining with delight at her own reflection. She was me. I was looking pretty damn fine, if I did say so myself.

I angled my tiny compact mirror to inspect the back of my head. My hairdresser had earned himself a fat tip and two fat kisses for his handiwork. It looked effortless. Only he and I knew that approximately two hundred and fifty hairgrips had been required. It would take me ages to take them all out. I might even have to sleep with my head hanging over the bed if I came home too late to deal with it.

My hands were trembling as I put in my earrings and my legs weren't doing a very good job of holding me steady either. I felt like a princess about to go to the ball to meet her Prince Charming.

I shuddered, remembering that that was what Marc used to call me. And to think that this time last year, on Valentine's Day, I had wanted nothing more than to be swept off my feet by Marc Felton! I wouldn't touch him with a barge pole these days.

I had grown up a lot in the past twelve months and I

felt quite proud of the person I had become. My next boy-friend would have to do more than call me 'princess', he would have to treat me like one too, respect my wishes, and love me unconditionally. It wasn't that I wanted to wear the trousers in my next relationship; I simply wanted to share them now and again.

I was highly unlikely to be sharing any trousers with Nick Cromwell, I thought, tucking the tickets into my bag, but all the same, I hoped he would be suitably impressed with my appearance tonight. He wasn't interested in me in the slightest, I could see that now. I'd been building up that conversation we had in Starbucks at Christmas into something it wasn't. He'd probably just been swept along by the festive spirit when he asked me to Poppi's party. Either that or I was a last resort. All I'd had from him recently was an email to check the timings for tonight's event. I had to face it: when all was said and done, I was a client. Nothing more.

I slipped my heels on and I was ready. But just as I was about to leave my bedroom my phone beeped. I looked at the screen, heart in my mouth in case it was Nick, sending his apologies. I breathed a sigh of relief at the sight of a text message from Dad.

Happy Valentine's Day, Sophie, have a fantastic evening. I bet you look lovely tonight. Send me a picture if you get chance. Love Dad x

Oh, bless him. I took a quick selfie, sent it off to him, dropped my phone in my bag and went in search of more compliments. Emma and Jess were packing for London and Jess bounded on the spot when she saw me.

'Babes!' she squealed, holding a hand protectively over her tummy. 'You are looking hot tonight!'

Emma appeared in the doorway and wolf-whistled. 'Nicky-boy won't be able to keep his hands off!'

I shook my head, cursing the two red spots on my cheeks.

'I'm sure he'll manage to control himself,' I laughed. 'But if he doesn't, I won't be batting him off.'

'Good,' she said. 'Make sure you enjoy yourself and we want all the details when we get back.'

I gave them a twirl, loving the sensation of the silk swishing against my skin. I'd shunned black – too boring – and red – too obvious – and picked a knee-length, sleeve-less green dress with a plunging neckline and a black silk bow at the waist. The half stone I had wanted to lose would be tagging along for the evening – no surprises there. Even so, my dress fitted me in all the right places and very kindly skimmed over the not-so-right ones.

I hoped Nick would approve.

'Text me as soon as you get off the train and again when you get to the hotel,' I said, hugging Emma tightly.

'Get off, you soppy git,' she said. 'You'll crease your dress.'

'Take care, Jess. Don't overdo it.' I kissed Jess's cheek and patted her stomach. 'Bye, baby, be good.'

The door buzzer announced the arrival of my taxi and I hurried to the door. 'On my way,' I called into the inter-com.

I ran down the stairs. It felt strange to be all dressed up and on my way out at six o'clock. Why was it that these dinners always started so early in the evening? Oh yeah – it was so they had time for all the boring speeches before everyone dropped off to sleep.

I flung open the front door and ran slap bang into a huge bouquet of flowers on legs.

'Oh, I'm so sorry!' I yelped. The apology died on my lips as Marc's face appeared from behind the cellophane.

'Hello, princess, Happy Valentine's Day!'

So it hadn't been my taxi.

For a moment I stared at him, totally stunned. Why now? After all these months, why tonight? Life was already complicated enough, thank you very much! Not to mention the fact that I was now in the freezing cold with nothing but a pashmina between me and the outside world and no taxi in sight.

'Marc!' I gasped.

He traced a finger along my collarbone, nodding appreciatively. 'You look stunning, Sophie.'

He stepped forward, taking liberties with my personal space.

I flapped at him and took a step back.

'Thank you,' I replied briskly.

I would have been lying if I didn't admit to getting a buzz from seeing his eyes pop out on stalks, I was only human, after all. What girl wouldn't be secretly pleased to bump into her ex when she was looking her best? What I really needed now was for the taxi to pull up to the pavement and for me to climb in, offer him nothing but a withering smile and glide off without a backward glance.

I peered over his shoulder hopefully. Not a sausage.

I took a deep breath and prayed he couldn't see that my knees were knocking.

'What are you doing here?' I said, giving my blasé look an airing.

'I came to bring you these,' he said, tweaking the crushed

cellophane and shoving the bouquet towards me. 'Let's give it another go, eh, Sophie?'

He twisted his mouth in a lazy smile and did that twinkly thing with his eyes that used to make my spine go all bendy. I felt a tide of anger rise through me as I stared at him. It was his confidence that really grated. How dare he turn up as if nothing had happened? As if a bunch of flowers was enough to set everything straight between us? Where was the sorry, the declaration of love? Even the 'I've missed you' was missing.

A diesel engine rattled to a halt beside us and a battered old taxi tooted its horn. I waved to the driver. It didn't quite fit my image of a glamorous carriage, but then this wasn't Hollywood.

I looked at Marc. And he wasn't my hero. Not any more. I looked at the flowers. Twelve months too late.

'Are you completely mad? I will never, ever go out with you again,' I said, turning to leave.

'Come on!' He grinned and grabbed hold of my arm. 'What does a man have to do to get a second chance round here?'

I shrugged him off.

'For starters,' I said, making a show of counting on my fingers, 'treat me with respect and not as a convenient B & B with laundry service. Then there's the small matter of listening to my opinions every once in a while; ooh, and of course not sneak around behind my back or trespass on my property.'

Marc blinked at me, looking confused and I rolled my eyes. Seriously – what did he expect? Me to welcome him back with open arms?

'I can change,' he said in a how-can-you-resist-me voice.

If I didn't know him so well I'd be flattered. But he had more chance of winning Miss World than becoming the sort of man I wanted. And the man I wanted was probably waiting on his own in the hotel bar. But I *had* changed and I wasn't prepared to put up with the likes of Marc Felton any more.

'It's a lovely offer, but I've moved on,' I replied, looking him squarely in the eye.

'I see,' he said, thrusting his jaw forward, 'that's why you're all tarted up. Who is he?'

I hadn't meant that, I meant that I'd changed, moved on from him but I answered him anyway.

'My architect.' I pulled the pashmina round my shoulders, avoiding his eyes.

Marc gave a laugh of contempt. 'That idiot? I bet I know things about him that you don't.'

I shook my head at him sadly as the taxi driver popped his head out of the window and shouted that the meter was running.

'Don't be ridiculous, Marc. Anyway, I'm late,' I said, stepping towards the taxi.

He dropped the flowers, jumped in between me and the car and snatched hold of my wrists. The confident smile had gone.

'But, Sophie, you can't do this! I've got to . . . I need you to . . . I *need* you!'

Stepping over the flowers, I peeled his hands off me and opened the door.

'We can stay friends if you like?' I offered.

'Business partners, then!' he said, bending down to talk to me through the gap as I slammed the door. 'Think about it!'

Chapter 34

Fifteen minutes later, the taxi pulled up outside the hotel and I hurried inside. The hotel bar was heaving with people and a string quartet was doing its best to be heard over the noise. I pushed my way through the crowds, looking for Nick, still feeling jittery after my contretemps with Marc.

A bubble of excitement fizzed through me when I spotted him. He was on the far side of the room near the double doors, a solitary figure with his hands in his pockets rocking on the balls of his feet in front of the table plan. I accepted a glass of champagne from a passing waiter and skipped over.

'Hi,' I said, tapping him on the shoulder.

I prepared myself to accept his compliments. I had a coy smile all ready to go and 'What, this old thing?' hovering on my tongue. I had my cheek lifted and ready for him to place a chaste kiss on it. Nick turned at the sound of my voice and for a second – no, make that a millisecond – his eyes lit up but then his face clouded over so spectacularly that at first I thought he didn't recognize me.

'Hello,' he replied.

He was stunned, that was all. So bowled over by my appearance that he was lost for words.

I launched the smile anyway.

'What do you think?' I smoothed down my dress and twinkled my eyes at him.

'Very nice.'

'Thank you,' I said, biting back my disappointment.

Not an auspicious start, I thought, sipping at my champagne. My nerves were already frazzled after the encounter with Marc. I'd hoped Nick's presence would be soothing, but it was more like wading naked through stinging nettles. What on earth was wrong with him?

He was staring at me oddly, as though he was waiting for me to speak. I twirled the stem of glass around and stared back. Black-tie suited him. I wanted to tell him how smart he looked, but something in those moody grey eyes of his held me back. There was a funny silence between us and it made me uneasy.

His next words took my breath away. And not in a good way.

'I nearly didn't bother coming tonight,' he said curtly.

'Why not, did your posing pooches misbehave?' I nudged him playfully with my elbow.

Nick exhaled heavily and pressed his lips into a thin line. 'Please don't make jokes about my charity work, Sophie.'

'You've lost me.' A tray of drinks floated past and I grabbed us both new ones. He nodded his thanks.

'The photographs are for the dog sanctuary website. I try to capture their personalities with my pictures. They are not "posing pooches", they are abandoned animals and if they don't get adopted, they get put down.'

'Sorry.' I swallowed, feeling small. 'I bet you're good at that. I remember you saying you could read dogs better than people.'

He swigged at his drink and shot me a sideways glance. 'You certainly had me fooled.'

I blinked at him. 'Nick, call me paranoid, but have I done something to upset you?'

He shook his head and mumbled something that could have been 'Unbelievable'.

My heart started to thump. 'You're scaring me now, Nick. What is it?' I asked shakily.

'I had a call from the planning office today about Lilac Lane.' He looked at me, letting the words sink in.

'Go on,' I rasped, my throat dry. It must have been bad news to have upset him this much. It occurred to me fleetingly that if he was so concerned about my building project, he must care for me a teensy bit.

'They've received an alternative scheme for the plot and wanted to know whether Cromwell Associates wished to withdraw their planning application.' He drained his glass and folded his arms.

'For number eight?' I gasped. 'That's terrible. We don't want to withdraw!'

Nick tutted. 'Of course for number eight. Apparently, you and Strong Developments are hoping to build three townhouses on it.'

'Oh, Nick!' I laughed out loud. He had obviously made a mistake. Or the planners had. Perhaps there was another Lilac Lane somewhere else. I had no idea, but at least I knew I was in the clear. And if that was all that was upsetting him, well, that was easily sorted out.

Nick glared at me. His usual calm features were all fierce and shouty.

'It's all a game to you, isn't it?' he said in a low growly voice. 'You've been stringing me along, using me to cherry-pick ideas for this shoddy development. You'll ruin a perfectly good piece of land, not to mention ruin my reputation by being associated with it. How do you think it makes me look? You know how I feel about over-developing. I can't believe I didn't pick up the signs when you asked me about it before.'

'Nick, I—'

He held a hand up to silence me. 'What makes it worse is that I trusted you and I . . . oh, never mind.'

Tears pricked at my eyes. 'Hold on a minute! I don't know anything about this.'

He stared at me for ages. The contempt on his face cut me to the bone.

'You expect me to believe that?'

'Thanks for the vote of confidence. Yes, I do, actually.' I would have folded my arms but for my glass being in the way.

He jabbed at finger at the table plan. 'The cosy little seating arrangement tells me otherwise. Excuse me.'

He strode off and left me to find my name on the plan.

Our department had been put on a circular table of eight. I groaned as I read who Jason was next to – Frannie Cooper from Fringe Benefits! What was she doing here? She wasn't in the least bit useful. Nick was sitting on the other side of her. Maureen was bringing a property lawyer she had known since the eighties. Come to think of it, he was about eighty. If he was still awake for coffee and mints it would be a miracle. And sandwiched between Donna and me was Mr Philip Strong from Strong Developments. He must be Donna's guest.

Phil Strong. It was all coming back to me now. The sharp suit, the smug smile, the black car parked outside my bungalow. I had to admit, it did look bad. No wonder Nick found it hard to believe me.

Marc was behind this mess. I was sure of it. There hadn't been a mistake at the planning office; he had submitted a second application without my knowledge. It looked as if he was determined to do a deal with this Strong fellow whether he had my say-so or not.

That explained the flowers. He'd had it all figured out: turn up at my house with a humungous bunch of flowers, watch as I fell to my knees in pitiful gratitude and then have another bash at changing my mind.

It was a terrible thing to do and I was determined to get to the bottom of it, but what hurt me even more than Marc's betrayal was the fact that Nick could believe I had anything to do with it and hadn't given me chance to explain.

All of a sudden, the room started to spin. What was it with me and Valentine's Day? Next year I was staying in on my own and getting drunk. But right now I needed to escape from public view and collect my thoughts.

I made my way to the Ladies and locked myself into the only free cubicle. I lowered the lid on the loo and sat down. What was I going to do? My first thought was to just go home, but I really wanted to sort things out with Nick. Besides, my boss would kill me.

I rolled up some toilet paper and pressed it under my eyes in readiness for the tears. But no tears came. Perhaps I wasn't sad at all? Perhaps I was very, very angry? With Nick for instantly jumping to the wrong conclusion and with Marc for, well, for everything else.

I was debating whether I should go and hunt Nick down and give him a piece of my mind when I caught the sound of quiet crying coming from the cubicle beside me. And was that a faint smell of cigarette smoke?

Poor thing whoever it was. Not even seven o'clock and locked in the loo in tears. At least I hadn't actually cried.

I bent my head down towards the gap between the cubicles.

'Are you OK in there?' I hissed.

'Can you pass me some paper, please?' came back the halting reply.

'Sure.' If only my problems were so easily solved. There was a pile of new loo rolls balanced on the cistern. I selected one and held it to the gap.

A hand with long fingers, a huge emerald ring and raised veins snaked towards mine and hooked the toilet paper back to her own cubicle.

My breath caught in my throat; I'd recognize that bony claw anywhere, I'd felt it land on my shoulder like a hawk descending on its prey often enough.

'Donna?'

I heard a muffled F-word. Definitely Donna. She blew her nose, sniffed a few times and then the quiet heaving continued.

I unlocked the door, washed my hands and waited until the woman reapplying lipstick at the mirror left.

'Donna, it's me, Sophie.' I knocked softly on the door of the cubicle. I pressed my face close to the door. 'Let me in.'

I expected her to tell me to go away and leave her alone but the bolt clunked across, changing her status from engaged to vacant. I steeled myself and pushed the door open.

The crying might have been quiet but the damage to my boss's face screamed 'war zone'. Her eyes were so puffed up that it looked like she had had an allergic reaction to her own tears. She had a wet nose and black tracks down to her chin. On top of that she was blowing cigarette smoke into a toilet roll tube stuffed with paper.

'Come in and shut the door then,' she sniffed.

Reluctantly I did as I was told. I locked the door from the inside and pressed myself against it.

I offered her a caring smile. Bad move. Her shoulders started to shake again.

'My life has turned to a bag of shit,' she squeezed out between sobs. I swallowed hard and tried to ignore the fact that she was perched on the loo.

She lifted a dripping chin up to me.

'I know you all think I'm a cow, don't you?'

Think, Sophie, think!

'Don't you?'

'No, no, of course we don't. Not all of us, anyway.' I patted her stockinged knee.

'Look what I'm reduced to,' she croaked, waving her cigarette at me. She took a long drag until it withered down to its gingery end and blew the smoke through her home-made loo roll filter.

'Smoking in the toilets like a fugitive.' She lifted a cheek and dropped the nub down the toilet.

'I mean, what's actually so bad about smoking?' She frowned up at me with a face as craggy as an Ethiopian riverbed.

I gave her a 'beats me' look and shrugged my shoulders. This was not the time to state the obvious. Anyway, her current emotional state hadn't been brought about by smoking, I was sure. And I couldn't believe it was because she'd only recently noticed how unpopular she was at *The Herald*. There had to be something else.

'Is there a problem at home, Donna?' I had never envisaged myself in the role of counsellor to my boss, of all people, but sometimes life threw you a curve ball and as I didn't yet know how to sort out my own problems, I might as well catch hers.

She clamped her lips together for a long time and stared at me. I could see she was weighing up whether or not to confide in me. None of us knew anything about her personal life. It was the thing I liked most about her.

She put a hand up to her hair and patted it. It moved as one. The tears were still leaking out of her swollen eyes and I handed her some more paper.

'My father called me a tuppenny whore tonight.'

I regarded her outfit: sequinned black knee-length dress, rather a lot of cleavage on display for a woman of her years, but she certainly didn't deserve that.

'Rubbish, Donna,' I said. 'You look lovely!'

She shook her head and dabbed her eyes. I glanced at my watch surreptitiously. We were due to go in for dinner in ten minutes and I didn't fancy her chances at repairing her face.

'Dad has Alzheimer's. He lives with us. I'm at my wits' end and my husband is threatening to move out. And I'm so tired. I barely get any sleep. Last night Dad left the house, walked three miles to the railway station in his pyjamas and tried to catch a train to London. The police brought him back. Most of the time he doesn't know who he is, let alone who I am.'

She stared at me with vacant eyes and shrugged. 'So now you know. That's why I am how I am. The only way I can hold it together is by being tough at work. The slightest thing can set me off and I end up in floods of tears. It's so difficult to cope with; he was always such a good dad. He is still my father but most of the time he's not there, he's off somewhere else inside his own head.'

I crouched down and took hold of her hands. I was out of my depth here. I wanted to help, to say something to make her feel better, to let her know she was doing a great job. What did I know about father–daughter relationships? Words from my own dad filtered back to me from nowhere.

'Look, I'm probably the worst person to be doling out advice. I've only had a dad myself for a few months. But I can promise you one thing. Wherever he is and whoever he might think you are, he will always carry you in his heart. That's what good dads do.'

Donna plucked at the hem of her dress and started to nod her head.

'You're doing your best for him and I'm sure deep down he knows that and he loves you for it,' I said.

'Thanks,' she muttered. 'I needed to hear that.'

I cleared my throat and eyed her tear-stained face. 'Aren't you presenting an award?'

She nodded.

'You might want to . . . powder your nose,' I said, standing up.

I left her in front of the mirror tipping out more cosmetics than I even owned and went in search of Nick. I was not prepared to let Marc ruin another Valentine's Day for me.

Chapter 35

The bar was eerily deserted except for the string quartet people slumped disconsolately over three violins and a cello. I followed the hum of people enjoying themselves through open double doors into the dining room and wished I was enjoying myself too.

Wavering at the doorway, I contemplated spinning around and getting a taxi home. I rejected taking the easy way out; this whole Lilac Lane fiasco needed to be sorted out sooner rather than later. I took a deep breath and scanned the room for our table. The organizers hadn't looked far for their theme: red heart-shaped helium balloons bobbed above arrangements of red roses on each table. The lighting was romantic too: hundreds of tiny spotlights twinkled from the ceiling like a clear night sky.

I weaved my way through the crowds and breathed a sigh of relief when I saw that Nick was still here and I took my seat between him and Phil Strong.

'Evening, everyone,' I said cheerily.

In stark contrast to the rest of the room, our table was sitting in silence. Maureen was fingering her pearls, her guest the elderly lawyer – whose name I'd forgotten – was snoring, Jason sat bleary-eyed behind a row of three empty pint glasses, staring at his lap, Frannie was alternating between eyeing up a petrified Nick and filing her nails, and Phil Strong was looking at his phone.

'Red or white?' I said, picking up a bottle in each hand in an attempt to break the ice.

'Red please,' said Phil Strong, holding up an empty glass.

I looked from Phil to Nick sharply. Somehow I needed to show Nick that I was on his side, that the three-house development on Lilac Lane was simply a figment of my ex-boyfriend's imagination.

'Phil,' I said, filling his glass and fixing him with an icy glare. 'Sophie Stone. We've met before. In Woodby.'

Nick looked up from folding his napkin into a pirate's hat. He mumbled something under his breath but I didn't catch it.

'Of course, I thought I recognized the name!' said Phil, setting his glass down and holding his hand towards me.

I shook his hand as briefly as I could.

'This is Nick Cromwell, the architect.' I leaned back, allowing Phil to pump Nick's hand. Nick glowered at him from beneath furrowed eyebrows.

'Are you up for an award tonight, mate?' asked Phil.

Nick breathed heavily through his nostrils before answering. 'No.'

How he managed to imbue one syllable with such contempt, I would never know.

'Phil is, aren't you?' said Donna, slipping into her seat just as the broccoli soup was served. She bestowed a kiss on his cheek and murmured an apology for keeping him waiting. Her repair job was amazing. I smiled at her encouragingly but she seemed not to notice.

'Oh,' said Nick coldly.

'Yes,' said Phil, slipping his phone into his pocket. 'We've been nominated for our waterside development. A casino, restaurant and—'

'Two hundred rabbit hutches,' I said.

'Apartments, Sophie,' corrected Phil with a glint in his eye.

'Well, watch this space at next year's awards,' said Frannie with a tinkly laugh. 'My husband and I are making a foray into property this year.'

Oh right. I did wonder what she was doing here.

'I'm thinking an award-winning, purpose-built hair and beauty palace. Like a spa, but without all the exercise and swimming pools. Luxury. That's what this area is crying out for,' she said, eyeballing me as if daring me to challenge her concept.

Odd. What I thought the area needed was affordable housing, more jobs and less crime. But what did I know?

Somebody agreed with me, though, because as if an invisible alarm clock had gone off, Maureen's lawyer suddenly sat up, opened his eyes and threw his bread roll, which bounced off Frannie's Botox.

'For such a vacuous young woman, you have a lot to say,' he proclaimed.

Frannie gasped and in the time it took Jason and me to exchange sniggering looks, there was an eye-watering thud of bone on wood and a vacant chair where the lawyer had been sitting.

'Saints alive!' screamed Maureen. 'Edward's collapsed!'

Edward, of course! That was his name.

We all dashed to Edward's side of the table. He was slumped on his knees with his head wedged between the chair and the leg of the table.

'Someone call an ambulance!' yelled Donna, who had been sitting next to him before he disappeared.

Phil had his phone out in a flash. The guests at other tables started popping their heads up and down like meerkats and a couple of waiters stood and gawped.

'Don't panic. It's on its way,' said Phil, inclining his head and pressing his lips together like he'd restored world peace.

'Well, that's that then, nothing more that we can do,' said Frannie, picking up her cigarettes. 'Just popping to the Ladies.'

Phil made a show of having an empty glass and wandered off to the bar.

Nick took hold of Edward's shoulders and Maureen tugged the chair out of the way. Between them they laid him out flat on the swirly carpet. Jason was taking sneaky pictures of the poor man on his iPad.

'Give us some room, please,' I shouted, elbowing Jason out of the way. 'The man needs air.'

I'd always wanted to say that. I quite fancied myself as a nurse, as long as I didn't have to deal with any bodily fluids.

A man in uniform and a badge that said 'Hotel Manager' on it pushed his way through the crowds. He had his arm in a sling. 'I'm the duty first aider.' He knelt down by Edward's limp body.

'He's not breathing,' said Nick, frowning at the manager's bandaged arm. 'He needs emergency CPR.' He quickly removed his jacket and pushed up his shirt sleeves.

'It's to the tune of the Bee Gees' "Staying Alive",' said Maureen, brightening up. She started singing the chorus and wagging her finger in time with the beat.

'Excuse me, sir,' said the manager to Nick. 'Are you qualified to carry out this procedure?'

'More qualified than you at the moment,' Nick muttered. He began pumping up and down on Edward's chest with his hands. I watched the muscles ripple in his forearms and a line of perspiration appear on his lip and my heart swelled with pride for him.

'No, Maureen,' argued Donna, 'it's Queen. "Another One Bites the Dust". Duh-duh-duh another one bites the dust. See?' She pounded on the table in time with Nick's pushes.

The two of them engaged in a sing-off until they realized that both tunes had the same beat.

I gazed goofily at Nick in action.

'OK, that's enough compressions, now you need to breathe into his mouth,' ordered the manager.

'You can do that bit,' said Nick, sitting back on his heels.

The manager went pale, but evidently couldn't find a reason to contradict him.

He stuck a finger into Edward's mouth and removed his false teeth. They were flecked with green bits.

'That'll be the broccoli,' said Maureen.

The manager retched and was just puckering up over Edward's lips when the paramedics arrived.

'Here you go, lads,' said the manager, sighing with relief. 'He's all yours.' He stood up and handed the dentures over.

The paramedics quickly lifted Edward onto a stretcher and wheeled him out to the waiting ambulance.

'OK, nothing to see here,' I told anyone who'd listen. 'Show's over.'

Yep, I'd always wanted to say that too.

'You were fantastic,' I said shyly to Nick.

He shrugged off the compliment, but I could see he was pleased. Within seconds, the babble of conversation

316

resumed, Frannie and Phil reappeared and everyone took their seats.

'Sophie, you've brought your camera, haven't you?' said Donna. 'Make sure you take pictures of me presenting the award for our Facebook page.'

'Sure,' I nodded. 'I haven't brought my camera, but I've got my phone.'

I took it out of my bag, snapped a few general ones of the flowers, the stage and a sneaky one of Nick. The one with the roses was quite good. I opened up *The Herald*'s Facebook page, posted the picture and wished all our Facebook followers a Happy Valentine's Day.

'Are you all right, Maureen?' I said.

She had gone a peculiar shade of grey and her lips were all blue.

'Shock,' said Donna, tutting at Maureen as if the poor woman was doing it deliberately to annoy her. 'Get her a brandy, Sophie.'

I didn't mind getting Maureen a drink at all, what did rub me up the wrong way was being ordered about. Take photos, Sophie, get the drinks, Sophie . . .

'I'll give you a hand,' said Jason, jumping to his feet.

I smiled my thanks but as soon as we got to the bar he pulled his phone out of his pocket and sent someone a message.

'Sorry, Sophie, but I'm doing a runner. Can you tell the boss I'm going?'

I opened my mouth to reply but he'd already turned away. Jeez, the men on our table were dropping like flies.

'Drink this, Maureen,' I said, setting a double in front of her.

I took my place at the table and found Donna discussing

the property world with Phil. Yawn, yawn. I glanced at my watch. Only nine o'clock! We had hours to go yet. Tonight had to be the longest night of my life.

'We operate mainly in the leisure industry. Especially in our northern region. Converting banks into pubs. Ware-houses into nightclubs.'

Something about Phil's monologue rang a bell and I seized my chance to bring Nick into the conversation.

'Nick used to do that sort of thing, didn't you? In Manchester.'

'What?' He looked up from making pellets out of the in-side of his bread roll.

'You used to design pubs and restaurants?' I repeated.

'Er, I worked for a commercial outfit, yes.'

Phil sneered at Nick. 'I've heard. Your reputation pre-cedes you.'

Nick stared back at him. 'I don't like your tone.' He took a sip from his glass, maintaining eye contact with Phil.

I didn't understand the subtext but the body language was clear enough. 'Some of my favourite bars used to be banks,' I said brightly.

Phil ignored me and carried on staring at Nick. 'My brother, whose girlfriend is Joanna Quinn,' he paused to let his words sink in and Nick's glass halted mid-air, 'has told me all about you.'

'Well,' Nick shot me such an icy look that the hairs on my neck formed their own Mohican, 'this is all very cosy.'

'What have I got to do with it?' I protested.

I understood the double planning application scenario and why he thought I was behind it. I could understand his anger. But this new thing was way over my head. I was losing track of what I was supposed to be guilty of.

'You're a piece of work, Sophie. You really are.' He pushed his chair back from the table and stood up.

'Wait! Please,' I cried.

Nick looked at me with disgust. But at least he waited. He sat down reluctantly and began pleating his napkin again.

I turned my back on Phil and addressed Nick directly.

'Nick, am I right in thinking that you don't have to own land to apply for planning permission?'

Nick didn't answer straight away. He took his glasses off and gave them a polish on his napkin, which by now was in the shape of a boat. His forehead creased in concentration and he pursed his lips.

I wished I could see what was going on inside that brain of his. I wanted to shake him. Couldn't he see where this was going? What I was trying to tell him?

Finally, he eyeballed me for the briefest of moments and spoke.

'Correct. As long as you have the landowner's approval.'

Ha.

I turned and smiled triumphantly at Phil. He shifted in his seat and buried his face in his wine glass.

'Looks like you've wasted your time and money, then,' I said.

'Sophie,' warned Donna, 'Phil is our guest.'

I waved a hand at her; I'd had enough of doing as I was told.

'You've put in an application on my land without my permission and presumably with a forged signature,' I continued.

At this point, I expected Phil to snatch up his napkin, throw it down on the table in a fury and leave.

He shook his head and laughed.

In. My. Face.

I picked up my knife and turned it over in my hands.

'Pshh! You girls change your minds like your shoes. Your fiancé said he would get you to see sense eventually,' said Phil.

'I didn't know you were engaged,' Nick frowned.

Fiancé? Fiancé? Fi-an-cé?

I stabbed the table with my knife. Phil flinched and Nick looked startled.

'For your information, I'm single. Very much single.'

Slowly I looked round at Nick and waited for the penny to drop.

'If Sophie knew nothing about this,' said Nick, leaning forward to pierce the property developer with his stormy-grey eyes, 'then the application is fraudulent. Invalid. It will have to be withdrawn.'

Hallelujah!

'I knew nothing,' I confirmed quietly. 'Nor about Joanna What's-her-face.'

'Somebody's going to pay for this,' said Phil, jabbing an angry finger in the air. 'Nobody takes Strong Developments for a ride.'

'What is going on?' demanded Donna.

I blanked her. Nick looked deep into my eyes, it was intensely hypnotic. His pupils pulled me in towards him like a magnet. My chest rose and fell as if he was doing his cardiac arrest thing on me. Everything around me slipped out of focus and all I could see was him and his big sorry eyes.

I could have played hard to get, made him work for my forgiveness. His assumption that I was in collusion with Phil Strong had stung. But my hormones were playing havoc with my nerve endings. All I really wanted to do was clear the room, sweep the stuff off the table cloth and jump onto his lap.

He smiled. The dimple. Yay! The dimple was back. I was so happy that I could have punched the air. I decided to save the punch for Marc.

Nick reached a hand out to touch mine. 'Sophie—'

'Toast!' cried Maureen.

Christ, what had happened to her? One minute she was ashen, the next she was red and sweaty. And where had all her brandy gone? She lurched to her feet and filled her brandy glass with red wine.

'To Shophie,' said Maureen, spilling red wine from her glass all up her arm. One eye fixed itself on me and the other rolled back in her head.

'And to all shingle gals everywhere. We wish we were young again, don't we, Donna?'

Donna took exception to this remark and gasped just as her own glass touched her lips. She inhaled a lungful of wine and started to heave and splutter. Within seconds her face had turned an ugly shade of puce. Maureen fell back down and grinned at everyone. The two of them were like matching Ribena berries.

Donna's coughing was so loud that at first I didn't notice the compère take to the stage.

'Now we welcome to the podium, to present our first award, from our sponsors, *The Herald,* it's Donna Parker!'

The audience obliged with a round of applause and the sound of Emeli Sandé' singing 'Read All About It' blasted out of the PA system.

'Donna, you're on!' I hissed.

'Donna Parker!' repeated the compère, shading his eyes

with his hand and looking from left to right. 'Donna, are you out there?'

'Can't speak,' wheezed Donna. 'You. Go!' She wafted her hands at me.

'Me?'

Donna stuffed a napkin in her mouth and dashed out, still coughing her guts up.

Nick shrugged and I huffed with frustration.

'Good luck,' he whispered.

With trembling legs I stood and wobbled over to the stage.

'About time!' hissed the compère, as I finally made my way up the stairs and onto the stage. 'Hey, you're not Donna.'

'Change of plan,' I muttered, snatching the gold envelope off him.

I stepped up to the microphone and ripped it open. The eyes of everyone in the room were on me as I fumbled to get the card out.

Act like you've done this a million times.

'And the award for best commercial property goes to . . .' My heart sank as I read the name on the card.

'To Strong Developments for their waterside project.'

The audience clapped, Kelly Clarkson belted out 'Stronger' and there were one or two whistles of approval. I watched as Phil sprang onto the stage with his hand outstretched.

The compère handed me an engraved perspex block. I was tempted to drop it on Phil's toe.

'Here,' I said, thrusting the award into Phil's hands and faking a smile for the photographer. 'Seems like you got what you came for.'

'Tell monkey-boy he'll be hearing from my solicitor.'

'If you mean Marc, you can tell him yourself.'

Phil pushed past me, off the stage and straight out of the door. Three men down at our table. Only Nick remained.

I made my way back to the table. It was deserted all except for Maureen, who seemed to be asleep in a plate of after-dinner mints.

Where was Nick? I scanned the room but he was nowhere to be seen. I picked up my bag and went out into the bar to find him, anxious to have a moment to ourselves. I rounded the corner into the corridor towards the toilets. There he was, squaring up to Phil outside the ladies' loos.

'You have the morals of a sewer rat,' said Nick, his hands on his slender hips, chest puffed out. 'You must have known all along that Sophie's signature was forged.'

Yay, go Nick!

Phil gave a disgusted laugh. 'Don't play the moral card with me, pal. We all know you're no saint.'

'You know nothing about me,' replied Nick harshly.

I pressed myself against the wall out of sight.

'Joanna has told my brother all about the two of you. Yes, that's wiped the supercilious smile off your face, hasn't it? The way you treated her when she was pregnant stinks. No decent man behaves like that. You're not fit to be a father.'

My hand flew to my mouth. I held my breath as my pulse thumped in my ears.

Nick had a child?

Chapter 36

I stood completely frozen to the spot and let this awful new knowledge sink in. Nick had got a woman pregnant and left her in the lurch. How could he? I racked my brains to recall all the photographs in his office. Definitely none of any children. He obviously had no contact with the child at all.

My hands were shaking. I was devastated and so disappointed in him; I'd thought better of him than that. And after how he'd reacted when I told him about Spike and Jess! And the comments he'd made about my own father wanting to stay in touch . . . Didn't he understand how important it was for a child to have a father?

I covered my face with my hands as giant teardrops began to fall. I was glad we hadn't managed to talk privately before now. In fact, Phil Strong had done me a favour. Nick obviously wasn't the man I thought he was at all.

Suddenly, Nick spotted me. 'Sophie!' he called, shoving Phil out of the way and darting towards me.

But I wasn't in the mood to hear his excuses. I wiped away my tears and started walking towards the exit. 'I'm leaving, Nick. I've heard enough.'

'Sophie, come back!'

I shook my head and picked up pace towards the hotel lobby.

'We need to talk!' he shouted as I ran outside and flagged down a taxi. 'At least let me apologize.'

'It's not me you need to apologize to,' I shouted back.

I climbed into a black cab and caught sight of him, hands on his hips, shaking his head as the taxi pulled out of the hotel car park.

Giving the taxi driver my address, I pulled my pashmina around my shoulders and tried to slow my breathing. I couldn't wait to get back to the flat, get these heels off and go to bed and more than anything, put tonight behind me.

Emma and Jess would be in London by now and the flat would be empty. I checked my phone to see if they'd sent me a message. Not a thing. They were clearly enjoying themselves too much to spare a thought for little old me. I wouldn't spoil their night for them; I'd keep my broken heart to myself for now.

God, what a disaster tonight had turned out to be. I wished I'd never invited Nick. There was something to be said for that never-mix-business-with-pleasure rule of his. And I was never attending the Property Awards again. Next year I would make sure I was out of the country.

I opened up Facebook on my phone and stabbed out a quick status update.

Worst night of entire life. Appears I am allergic to Valentine's Day. Property Awards suck. Hate men. Hate clients. #IHateMyJob.

In the split second that I pressed send, I was distracted by a call coming through from a blocked number. It occurred to me that it might be someone off the TV to say that I'd been pranked and the whole night was one big joke.

I braced myself and said hello. But it wasn't a joke, it was Emma. She and Jess hadn't made it to London and Jess had been rushed to hospital. Emma was in floods of tears.

Shivering with fear, I batted the glass screen open between me and the taxi driver.

'Change of plan, I'm afraid. Queen's Medical Centre please, as quick as you can.'

I ran as fast as my heels would let me and spied Emma in the foyer of the hospital. It would have been hard to miss her: she was banging the side of a drinks machine and swearing at it.

'Emma,' I shouted as soon as I was within earshot.

The face that turned to me was creased and pale under the hospital's harsh lights.

'Sophie! Thank God,' said Emma, collapsing into my arms. 'It's been a nightmare.'

'What's happened?' I asked. 'Where's Jess?'

My heart was thudding in my chest as I stared at her; taking in her tear-stained cheeks.

'She's lost the baby,' said Emma gruffly. 'They've taken her down to surgery.'

'Oh no, that's awful. Poor Jess!' I gasped.

Emma nodded and bowed her head. I closed my eyes and held onto Emma with one arm, the other hand pressed to my mouth. Her hot tears soaked into my neck.

'And it's all my fault,' sobbed Emma.

'Oh Em,' I soothed, leading her to a row of plastic seats. 'I'm sure that can't be true.'

'It is,' she choked. 'If I hadn't tried to drag her to London with me, this might not have happened.'

Through her tears, Emma managed to explain that almost as soon as the taxi dropped the pair of them off at the railway station Jess had complained of pains in her stomach. Emma had carried her bag and they made it down onto the platform. But the pain just got worse and worse and by the time the train arrived there was no way she'd been fit to travel. So they went back home and it was then Jess realized that she was bleeding.

'So I called for an ambulance and we made it here about an hour ago.' Emma retrieved some tissue paper from the back pocket of her jeans, tore it in half and shared it with me. We both dabbed our tears.

'Then what?' I asked, taking her hand. It was limp and cold and I covered it with my other hand to try to impart some warmth.

'They strapped her up to machines but there was no foetal heartbeat,' said Emma, shrugging helplessly. 'We were too late and now she's having an operation to remove . . .' She swallowed and shook her head.

'Is she going to be all right, though?' I asked.

'Eventually. Right now she's devastated and in shock,' Emma blinked at me.

'I can't believe it,' I whispered. 'Even though the baby wasn't planned, she wanted it so much.'

Emma's eyes narrowed. 'Thank goodness one of its parents did. If I ever get my hands on Spike, I'll kill him.'

'She's not alone though, is she? You've been here for her every second,' I reminded her.

'And now she's got you. And I've phoned my parents,' she said. 'Mum's on holiday with a friend and will get back as soon as she can, but Dad's on his way.'

We smiled at each other sadly and then I fetched some drinks from the machine. We sat huddled together waiting for news and half an hour later a nurse approached us.

'Jessica Piper's family?'

We jumped to our feet. 'Yes,' we replied.

She pointed to where we could find Jess. 'Mobile phones off, please. And no more than a few minutes, she's very tired.'

Jess was alone in a side room off the gynaecological ward hooked up to various monitors with tubes and wires. Emma and I exchanged glances as we knocked and entered. The main light in the room was off and a reading lamp above her bed cast ghostly shadows across her face. She was almost unrecognizable; her eyes were glazed, her skin devoid of colour and her body limp. My heart ached for her.

I waited for Emma to hug her first and then I leaned across the bed and placed a gentle kiss on Jess's cheek.

'You OK?' I whispered.

Jess nodded and smiled weakly. 'The doctor said I might have lost the baby a while ago,' she said turning to Emma. 'There's no specific reason for it, it just happens sometimes. And it's nobody's fault. OK?'

Emma reached for her sister's hand and nodded silently, tears coursing down her cheeks.

I sat down in a low chair at the side of the bed and reached for Jess's other hand.

'I'm so sorry, lovey,' I said.

She managed a wobbly smile. 'It hasn't really sunk in yet. I never realized how much I wanted to be a mum until I got pregnant. But I will be. One day. Now that I know what's important to me, I'll make sure it happens.'

'Of course you will,' I said, squeezing her hand. I was paralysed with hurt for her, she was being so brave.

'And in the meantime you've got family who love you,' Emma sniffed.

There was a box of tissues next to the bed and I passed one across to her. 'And me too.'

'Exactly. And a job I love. And the rest will follow, I'm sure. Although I'm definitely off men for a while.' Suddenly she widened her eyes. 'Oh Sophie, I hope I didn't ruin your night?'

I exhaled and was about to fill them both in on my catastrophic evening when the door opened. We all looked round and I half expected it to be the nurse coming to shoo us off but it was Jess and Emma's dad.

'Jess, my darling,' he said, gathering her up in his arms. 'How are you feeling?'

'Empty and hurting,' she whispered.

I withdrew from the bed towards the edge of the room to give the family some space while Jess and Emma told their dad the whole story.

'Emma, will you do something for me?' Jess asked, rubbing at her tears. Her eyes looked swollen and red in her pale face and I felt my own tears begin to surface again.

'Sure,' said Emma. 'Name it.'

'Promise me you'll get on a train in the morning. Promise me you'll still go to the awards ceremony.'

Emma shook her head. 'No way. Absolutely no way. I'm not leaving you.'

'Dad will go with you to London, won't you, Dad?' Jess urged.

Mr Piper looked nervously from one daughter to the other. 'Well, I . . .'

'I'm not going to the crappy awards without you and that's final,' proclaimed Emma. 'I never expected to get this far, so as far as I'm concerned, I've already won.' She folded her arms. 'And there's always next year.'

Mr Piper slipped an arm around Emma's shoulders. 'I'm proud of you, Emma. You're a winner, all right. I don't know what I've done to deserve two such talented daughters. I love you both so much.'

I grabbed another tissue from the box and wiped away my tears, deeply affected by their family bond. Perhaps Dad and I would be like that one day, if we worked at it?

Emma decided to stay for the night but I had to get up for work in the morning, so I kissed them all goodnight and made my way back through the hospital and out into the February night to find another taxi.

It was midnight by the time the taxi dropped me off outside the flat.

Once in my pyjamas, I heated some milk and sat down at the kitchen table. I blew on the top of it and took a tentative sip, hoping it would help me to relax. Not a chance.

My head was spinning after all the drama of the night. But more than anything I was struck by Jess's bravery, by her spirit and her optimism that she would get what she wanted out of life. She was going to be a mum eventually, even if she was off men at the moment.

I was with her on that one. I would be steering clear of all men for the foreseeable future. From now on I would be concentrating on me.

I lifted my feet up onto the chair opposite to get myself comfortable.

First on the list was my own home. Converting the

bungalow into my dream house would be a huge challenge, but I was determined to do it. With or without Nick's help.

My stomach churned at the thought of him. How could I have got him so wrong?

I sighed deeply . . . Enough of him, I was supposed to be focusing on myself for once.

Where was I? Oh yes. While I was at it, it was about time I started chasing my dream job, too. No more settling for second best. I was only in my early thirties, I had plenty of time to retrain and change careers. I only had to look to my mum for proof; she never let anything stand in the way of her dreams.

I should have pushed ahead with my plans to be an interior stylist years ago, but I hadn't. And that taster day at the London College of Interior Design which I'd had for my birthday from the girls had made me realize how much I'd love a career in interiors. And now, with some savings behind me and no man to tell me what to do, there was nothing and nobody to stand in my way.

Suddenly I knew exactly what I was going to do and this time, I wasn't going to give myself a chance to back out. Even though it was nearly one o'clock in the morning, I ran back to my bedroom and fetched my laptop before I changed my mind. I opened up a new document and began to type.

It was time to do things my way.

Chapter 37

The next morning, even though my stomach felt hollow with fear and I had had barely any sleep, I made it through *The Herald*'s revolving doors as the clock struck nine.

There was an unwritten rule for attending work events: you could dance on tables, drink yourself into a coma, even stay out all night if you so desired, as long as you weren't late for work the next morning. Today of all days I had no desire to get into Donna's bad books.

I wished the receptionist a good morning as usual but unlike every other morning, she looked up from her magazine and smirked at me. I wiped my mouth in case I still had toast crumbs on my face and carried on walking.

'Morning, Sophie,' chorused two women from Human Resources. They collapsed into giggles as soon as they passed by.

I checked I didn't have my skirt tucked into my knickers and pressed the button for the lift.

The lift doors sprang open and someone from Accounts jumped into the lift with me as the doors closed.

'I hate my job,' he muttered under his breath, shaking his head.

I wasn't sure if he was talking to himself so I pretended

not to hear. Poor thing. What he needed to do was to find his passion, chase his dream . . . like me.

The lift doors opened at my floor and I gave him a smile of sympathy as I stepped out into my own department. The doors shut again and I thought I heard a whimper from inside and I shook my head sadly.

Remembering what I had in my bag, I snaked my hand inside and curled my fingers round the envelope. My stomach lurched. Best get it over with. I would go and see Donna straight away to deliver my news and then I would phone the hospital and check on Jess.

I paused to get myself a cup of grey sludge from the machine and yelped as the scalding liquid burned my fingers, as it did every day.

Such was my concentration, trying not to spill my tea, that it took me a while to notice the tension in the air. I looked over at my desk. A semicircle of people from other departments were gathered around it and they stared back at me. Which was odd. Maureen was at her desk, her eyebrows practically plaited together. Jason was already there too, barely concealing a smile.

This wasn't normal. Not normal at all.

I wet my lips.

'Have you heard how Edward is?' I said, ignoring the crowd.

Maureen nodded her head vigorously. 'Fine,' she said in a trembling voice. 'Flat battery in his pacemaker, that was all.'

'Miss Stone. A word.'

That didn't sound good.

The loiterers around my desk stepped closer together and gave a collective gasp.

A tremor of fear ran down my spine. I glanced over at Donna's office. She was standing in the doorway, arms crossed, eyeballs dangerously wild. I could feel the static electricity fizzing off her from twenty paces away.

This had to be something to do with last night. Had somebody complained about me? Phil? Frannie? Donna couldn't be mad because I'd left without saying goodbye, surely?

I swallowed. 'Of course, Donna.'

I took the envelope out of my bag, strode to the boss's office trying to disguise my shaky legs and closed the door behind me. To my surprise, Donna directed me to her own chair. I sat down while she perched on the corner of her desk, looming over me.

The phone rang. She lifted the receiver slightly and slammed it back down again without breaking eye contact.

The hairs on the back of my neck began to prickle as I caught sight of the screen on Donna's laptop. I blinked and swallowed again as *The Herald*'s Facebook page came into focus.

The latest post was by me. Me *personally*. My body slumped as I read what I'd posted: *Worst night of entire life. Appears I am allergic to Valentine's Day. Property Awards suck. Hate men. Hate clients. #IHATEMYJOB!*

'Oh shit,' I breathed.

I'd posted my late-night whinge to the company's Facebook page instead of my own personal page. In the dim light of the taxi, I hadn't noticed my error.

'Oh shit doesn't begin to cover it,' growled Donna.

I rested my elbows on the desk, covered my face and groaned.

'I'm so, so sorry, Donna. It was a momentary lapse of concentration. It will never happen again.'

'You can bet on it,' she snorted.

My heart was racing. Abuse of the company's social media sites, whether intentional or not, was a sackable offence. I should know; I wrote the bloomin' policy.

'Have you any idea of the damage you've caused with this little stunt?'

I assumed it was a rhetorical question and kept quiet.

'The editor has already had *The Times* on the phone asking for a comment for their feature on the worst UK employers.'

'It was a heat-of-the-moment thing,' I pleaded. 'I didn't mean it.'

Donna folded her arms. 'And the Property Awards have threated to sue. Several major advertisers are threatening to pull their campaigns and there are more people viewing our Facebook page now, in our darkest hour, than since *you* set it up last year.'

It occurred to me that the 'all publicity is good publicity' mantra that I'd heard Donna use in difficult times must only apply to our clients and not to *The Herald*.

I shuddered as something else struck me. Our Facebook comments were linked directly to Twitter. I risked a glance at her. She had an ugly rash all over her neck and her lips were wrinkled and prune-like.

'What about Twitter?'

'Sixty-five retweets and that hash thing—'

'Hashtag.'

'Whatever,' spat Donna. 'Hashtag-I-hate-my-job is trending on Twitter!'

My hashtag was trending on Twitter. For all the wrong reasons. I gulped and stared at her, searching for something to say to make things better.

Donna leaned forward and whispered fiercely into my face. 'Meanwhile you – the employee handpicked by the board and the only one with the BLOODY password – drop the company in the shit and then promptly turn off your phone. I tried to call you last night but couldn't get through.'

My heart sank. I should have turned my phone back on after visiting Jess in hospital, but I'd been so preoccupied that it had slipped my mind.

'I'm sorry,' I repeated in a small voice.

Donna shoved the laptop closer to me. 'Remove all the comments and write your password down. The IT department will do the rest.'

It only took me a few seconds to remove the Facebook post, all the comments and the original tweet. But the damage was done.

'And that's the last thing you'll do for this newspaper,' said Donna fiercely. 'Because you're—'

'Wait,' I cried. I held my envelope out to her. 'Don't fire me yet.'

She tore it open and her eyes scanned the contents.

'I would like to offer my resignation.'

Donna narrowed her eyes and chewed the inside of her cheek. She looked at me for a long time. I held her gaze, willing her to remembering the moment we had shared in the ladies' loo last night and hoping she would take pity on me.

'Please, Donna. I'm planning on re-training. A resignation would look so much better on my CV than a dismissal. And last night, well, there was a lot going on, let's say. Not that that's an excuse. Well, it is . . .'

Donna held up her hand. I clamped my mouth shut and she gave me a curt nod.

'I accept your resignation. Out.'

Wonders will never cease. I sighed with relief. 'Thank you so much, Donna, I'm really—'

She cut me off with a flick of her head and I jumped out of her seat and ran for the door.

Chapter 38

By eleven o'clock I was back in the flat. I dumped my bags on the floor and stared at myself in the hall mirror.

I'd done it. Not quite as triumphantly as I'd planned, but nevertheless, I'd managed to extricate myself from *The Herald* if not with my dignity entirely intact, then at least without my CV being irreparably damaged. And if I was the subject of gossip for a while, then so be it. It would all die down soon enough when some other poor soul cocked something up.

'I'm unemployed,' I informed my reflection. 'Actually, I'll rephrase that. I'm free. Free to do whatever I want.'

I was just thinking that what I wanted right now was a long soak in the bath when my mobile phone rang. I rummaged through my bag to find it, my heart in my mouth in case it was Nick. Or in case it wasn't Nick, to be more precise. But it was Emma.

'Hey, Soph, sorry to phone you at work but I—'

'I'm not at work,' I said, giving my reflection a look of approval. 'I quit.'

'Oh my God, Sophie. Congrats! That's amazing. I'm so proud of you. Wait till I tell Jess, that will cheer her up no end.'

'Thanks.' I smiled down the phone. 'Feels a bit scary, though.'

'Pah, if you're not scared from time to time, you're not living,' declared Emma. 'This is that architect's doing. He's been a good influence on you.'

'Ah. Actually . . .' I hesitated; it could wait. Beside which, I was pretty sure Emma was phoning from hospital. 'Never mind. I'll tell you all about it later. How's Jess?'

Jess had been discharged and her dad was collecting both the sisters and driving them back to the family home. I sent her my love and agreed to drive over later with a bag of her things and ended the call.

Emma's words of encouragement had given me the motivation I needed to tackle my daunting list of jobs. I set myself up on the kitchen table with some milky tea, a stack of biscuits, notepad, pen and laptop and Googled 'Interior Design courses'.

My plan was still sketchy, but last night I had realized without a shadow of a doubt that life was too short to spend even one more day doing something that didn't inspire me. What *did* inspire me was interior design.

I had derived so much pleasure from working on the layout for my own house and doing that little job for Nick on the cowshed and of course my taster day at college. I hadn't felt so alive, so passionate about anything since I was a raw recruit at *The Herald* all those years ago when I'd had my future all mapped out. It was scary, letting go of the security of a monthly salary, a steady career and the knowledge that I could do the job blindfolded. But I owed it to myself to walk on the wild side for once.

I filled in a few forms online, requested several brochures from colleges and felt pleased with my progress.

When I'd exhausted that avenue I turned my attention to Lilac Lane. The situation with the double planning applications was a complete mess and I needed to sort it out once and for all so that everyone, especially me, knew where they stood. There was only one man for the job: I dialled the solicitor's office and asked to be put through.

'Hello, Mr Whelan, this is Sophie Stone,' I said glancing at the notes I'd made.

'Sophie, what can I do for you?'

My lips twitched. 'Can you write me a really angry letter?'

He laughed. 'Certainly. They're my favourite sort. Tell me more.'

I brought him up to speed with recent events and my new employment status and hinted that I might need him to act as my solicitor if I decided to sell the bungalow. But in the first instance, I asked him to write to Marc Felton and Strong Developments with copies to go to the planning office and my ex-architect ordering them to retract their fraudulent property development plans.

'They sound delightful characters,' said Mr Whelan. 'I shall use my firmest words with those two. And I urge you not to be rash about selling the bungalow. Have you spoken to the financial advisor I sent you to?

'She's next on my list,' I grinned.

I rang off feeling mightily pleased with myself and called Max Fitzgerald immediately.

'Oh yes, Sophie.' I heard her tapping on a keyboard in the background. 'I've got your file here. How's the property development going?'

I winced. 'I've had a bit of a setback . . .'

Max confirmed my suspicions. Without a job, I wouldn't

get a mortgage and without a mortgage I couldn't build a house. She gasped in horror when I told her I was thinking of selling the bungalow and warned me about sluggish markets, return on investments and maximizing assets. By the time I got off the phone, my head was spinning with percentages and interest rates but together we'd concocted a brilliant plan: I would keep the bungalow and put it on the rental market. This would give me a monthly income and I would still have the option to build my dream home as soon as I joined the ranks of the workers again.

It was the perfect solution and I was thrilled.

There was just time to make one more call before I set off to see Jess. And as much as I was dreading this one, it had to be done.

I picked up my phone and turned it over in my hand, trying to ignore the pang of sadness I felt at what I was about to do. I couldn't afford to build a new house now and no house meant no Nick.

But then perhaps it was for the best? My insides turned to jelly just thinking about him and the business with his ex-girlfriend. Even though I'd heard it with my own ears, I couldn't believe it of him. Everything I knew about Nick seemed at odds with this new information and my poor brain was struggling to process it.

My thumb hovered over his number. I was poised to call him and confirm that yes, I did wish to withdraw the planning application but I felt sick at the thought that this was the end.

The end of what?

I was so confused about my feelings for Nick and even more confused about his feelings for me. I thought back over the last few months trying to make sense of all the things he'd said, the gestures, the smiles, that kiss he'd given me on my birthday.

Oh well, it had to be done. I forced myself to get on with it and pressed dial. I would be polite and businesslike. I would banish this lump that was forming in my throat before—

'Cromwell Associates,' panted Poppi. 'Sorry. Out of breath. Playing Frisbee with the dog in the garden. Because it's lunchtime. Not because I should be doing something else.'

'Hi, Poppi, it's Sophie Stone.' Despite myself I couldn't help grinning at the sound of her voice. 'Is Nick there, please?'

'Oh my God, Sophie! What happened last night?' she squealed. 'I thought it was supposed to be some boring old awards do. No offence.'

'Er, what do you mean?'

'Nick appeared this morning looking like he'd spent the night on a park bench and now he's buggered off – 'scuse my French – to Manchester.'

'Really?' I gulped.

I remembered my last words to him last night that he owed someone an apology. Maybe he had gone to Manchester to do just that? I hoped so. But I still couldn't help feeling a bit hurt that he hadn't called me today. Didn't I deserve an apology too?

I forced myself to harden my heart. It was absolutely nothing to do with me. Not any more.

'How did he seem – contrite, guilty, ashamed?' I probed.

'No,' said Poppi, sounding confused. 'More like really, really angry. Like when he found out about the other application you've made for Lilac Lane.'

'That wasn't me, Poppi.'

'I knew it!' she cried. 'I told him you'd never do that. I think he was only angry with you because he, you know . . .'

'What? Poppi?' I demanded, clutching the phone tightly.

'Um, shall I tell him you called?' she said nervously.

'Can you tell him . . .' I hesitated, words tangling themselves in my mouth.

I shook my head with frustration; I couldn't say it over the phone. I needed to see him face to face, to draw a line under our relationship. Not that a few secret smiles, two kisses and an aching heart constituted a relationship . . .

'Tell him I'd like to meet him. Soon as he can.'

Chapter 39

Two weeks later and things in our little household had moved on apace. Jess had gone back to school this morning, clutching a peanut butter sandwich made by me and a fruit salad containing superfoods to boost her immune system made by Emma. Apart from one wobble when I flicked the telly on to a reality TV show about childbirth by accident, she was doing really well.

Emma was this very minute winging her way to London to accept a runner-up prize for her silver teardrop jugs. Not only had she won a prize, but when the Chairman of the Silverware Association had heard why she hadn't turned up to the awards ceremony, he had invited her down for a tour of the academy and lunch at his private club. She was so excited that she'd even worn a dress!

I, on the other hand, was perpetually dressed in my scruffiest clothes and warmest jumpers. I had spent every day since leaving *The Herald* at the bungalow immersed in what I called 'Operation Spruce Up'. Today I was tackling the flowery wallpaper in the living room and once this room was done I'd make a start on the bedrooms. I covered the carpet with dust sheets and went to fetch my bag of tools from the car.

The letting agent who I'd recruited and I had hatched a plan to get the place on the rental market in time for the Easter rush. The rent he had suggested was huge! Village appeal, apparently. The money would easily cover my share of the rent on the flat and help towards my other expenses. which was just as well because I'd been accepted on to a six-month interior design course and life as a mature student was about to commence.

The disappointment of having to postpone building my own home was hard to swallow, but I still had the flat with the girls and what you've never had you can't miss, right? Besides, I knew without a doubt that one day I'd do it; it wasn't simply a dream, it was a plan. A long-term plan.

Dad had been brilliant since I'd handed in my notice. He thought that going back to college was an excellent idea and had taken to ringing me to give me little pep talks. And I'd emailed him loads of times asking for advice on Operation Spruce Up. Everyone had been brilliant, in fact; even Mum was pleased for me.

The one person who hadn't shown any interest was Nick.

He hadn't been in touch. At all.

I carried this round with me constantly, like a stone in my shoe that I just couldn't shake out.

He hadn't called or texted or emailed or anything. I'd thought about contacting him, giving him the benefit of the doubt. What if Poppi had forgotten to pass on my message? I had his number, of course, and Emma had nagged me to call him. But I chose not to. Because even if Poppi had forgotten, surely if I meant anything to him at all, he'd have called me anyway by now, wouldn't he?

345

Somehow, the 'what you've never had, you can't miss' principle didn't work where he was concerned; I thought about him all the time.

I unpacked my new steam wallpaper stripper and scanned the instruction leaflet. But instead of taking in how to use it I found myself grinning with nostalgia. I remembered the laughter in the park, Norman covering me in muddy paw prints, Nick mistakenly thinking I knew all about Mies van der Rohe (I did now, thanks to a quick search on Google), and me barefoot on the grass. That was the good thing about memories, you could just pick out the good bits, no need to drag up the blisters on the feet or the crack on the skull.

I turned the radio on to non-stop nineties music and positioned my stepladders in front of the fireplace. Perhaps he was too busy throwing himself into fatherhood to think about me? Or perhaps he had taken on a new project for another woman. One who didn't cry on him or subject him to complicated family stories and who didn't turn him down when he asked her out on a date?

Whatever he was doing, I thought with a sigh as I climbed up the ladders, it clearly didn't involve me and I needed to stop thinking about those deep grey eyes and that tufty black hair and move on.

I subjected the chimney breast to a vicious blast of steam and scraped the wallpaper off for all I was worth; it was very therapeutic.

A couple of hours later I stepped down from the ladders, delighted with my efforts. The floor was covered in tiny scraps of paper, the room was hotter than a Turkish steam room and I was down to my T-shirt and knickers. But I had stripped two whole walls. I was about to make myself decent and call round to Audrey's for my lunch when the phone rang.

I switched off the radio, unplugged the wallpaper stripper and then grabbed the phone.

To my absolute amazement the name flashing on the screen was Nick Cromwell. I was so startled that my entire body trembled and for a moment I forgot whether I was still angry with him or not.

'Hello,' I croaked, my voice rusty from not speaking to anyone for hours.

'Hello, Sophie, this is Nick,' he said, 'Nick Cromwell.'

My heartbeat thundered loudly in my ears. 'Hello,' I repeated.

'I'm sorry for the radio silence,' he said.

I bit back a smile. It was lovely to hear his voice and who else says 'radio silence'?

'It's been a bit, well, hectic,' he continued.

'Good hectic or bad?' I asked politely.

'Mixed,' he said darkly. 'Very mixed. But on the work front, I've had a rush project on and it's finished and, well, I'm delighted with it.'

So he *had* got a new client. A wave of sadness flooded through me and finished up as a red blotch on each cheek. I started to pull on my jeans. Not that he could see me, but it felt weird, talking to him only half-dressed.

'Congratulations,' I said, trying not to sound at all bothered. I sat down on the dust-sheet-covered carpet and began to tear wallpaper scraps into tiny pieces. 'What sort of project?'

I crossed my fingers tightly and hoped that it wasn't a luxury spa for Frannie Cooper.

'A top-secret one,' he chuckled. 'Look, can we meet?'

I took a deep breath. 'Nick, I left a message for you to call me two weeks ago. And you didn't. Isn't it a bit late now?'

'I know, I know and I apologize for that,' he said hastily. 'But there have been things I needed to sort out first. I would really like to see you.'

Why? I wondered. Did he have some more work for me or was there another reason? I was about to ask him but a feeling as gentle as warm honey ran through my body and I realized that I didn't care why he wanted to see me because I really wanted to see him too.

'OK,' I said, getting to my feet. 'But I'm very busy at the moment, so you'll have to meet me in—'

'In Lilac Lane,' Nick finished for me. 'No problemo.'

I giggled and shook my head at his turn of phrase and he laughed too.

'Can you do three days' time?' he asked.

I took a sharp breath and eyed up the living room, which was about as messy as it could possibly be. Great-aunt Jane would be having kittens. Still, having a deadline to work to would spur me on to work even harder.

'Sure,' I agreed. 'Oh, Nick, can you bring Norman with you?'

'I can indeed,' he replied straight away. 'Why?'

'I've missed him.' *And you.* I held my breath.

There was a pause down the line and when he replied there was a smile in his voice.

'He's missed you too.'

Three long days later and I'd completely finished decorating my first ever room. I'd cheated and bought easy-to-hang wallpaper. All I had had to do was slop wallpaper paste onto the walls, slap the paper on and snip it to the right length. A piece of cake.

Picking up snippets of paper from the floor, I straightened up and cast a proud eye round the room. I had picked out something neutral to suit the rental market. It wasn't the design statement I would have made if I was going to live here myself. But I wasn't – not yet, anyway. And as I was letting the bungalow unfurnished, it needed to be clean and fresh and have broad appeal.

There was nothing broad about the tiny galley kitchen, though, I noted as I went through to check my refreshment supplies. Nick was due any second and I had pushed the boat out: new kettle and a tin of posh coffee. Not a juice carton in sight. I unpacked the mugs I had brought with me from the flat and re-boiled the kettle.

Right on cue, there was a knock at the door and my breathing began to quicken.

He's here, he's here, he's here.

I dashed into the hall, tripping over boxes and bags in my haste. But then I stopped, raked a hand through my wayward curls and took a couple of calming breaths.

Nothing was going to happen between us, I accepted that now. Even so, my stomach fluttered at the sight of him.

I could see his silhouette through the glass panel of the front door and it took me straight back to the first time I met him a year ago. So much had changed in that time and yet, here we were again still meeting as almost strangers.

I flung the door open.

'Hi there, come in!' I cried, my heart thudding so loudly that I hardly heard my own words.

Chapter 40

Dad opened his arms wide and I stepped into them, grateful for the support.

'How lovely to see you!' I cried. 'I thought you'd gone back to America?'

'What, and miss this lovely weather!' he laughed, pressing his cold face against mine.

'Ooh, yes, sorry, come in,' I said, peering over his shoulder. The lane was empty. I swallowed my disappointment and pulled him inside.

'What a day!' he was saying, removing his wet anorak. He looked around for somewhere to put it and I took it from him and hung it on a door handle.

Dad rubbed his hands together and blew on them. 'Blimey, this takes me back,' he chuckled, stepping into the living room. 'I haven't been in this bungalow for decades.'

'What do you think of my DIY skills, then?' I grinned as he ran his fingers over my new wallpaper.

'I'm impressed,' he said with a nod.

'I've surprised myself, to be honest,' I laughed.

We went through to the kitchen and I made us both some tea.

'Bet you wonder why I'm here?' My dad slurped his tea

and gave a sigh of satisfaction. His eyes twinkled at me like he knew something I didn't. 'And why Nick isn't?'

'Nick?' I blinked at him. I leaned back against the cupboard and wrapped my hands around my own mug. What did Dad know about Nick?

'Your architect. Nice chap,' said Dad, sipping his tea and glancing at me out of the corner of his eye.

'Yeah,' I said, keeping my voice light, although I needn't have bothered, my blush told him everything I didn't want him to know. 'He is still coming, isn't he?'

He nodded. 'Yes, he's coming. I asked him to give me a few minutes with you on my own first. He and his dog are next door with Audrey. I haven't seen her for thirty-odd years. She's still as bossy.'

My cheeks glowed and my shoulders relaxed. I felt much happier knowing that Nick was definitely coming, if confused.

'I'm here because Nick phoned me.'

My jaw dropped open. 'Why . . . ? I mean, how . . . ? I . . . Dad, I don't understand?'

'He told me that you'd withdrawn your planning application for this place. Which I already knew, of course. He told me what a talented designer you were. In fact, he showed me some of your drawings. Of course, I knew that as well.' He smiled and wrapped an arm round my shoulders.

'Thanks,' I mumbled into my mug.

'But he also explained how much having a home of your own means to you.'

Dad and I stared at each other until our eyes filled with tears and we both looked away, embarrassed.

He put down his tea and took his wallet out of the back pocket of his trousers.

'I want to give you some money. Now now!' He held up a finger to my lips as I began to protest. 'To pay for the build. A lump sum so you don't need a mortgage.' He took a deep breath and held out a cheque. 'I want my girl to have her dream home.'

My girl. I lifted my gaze to his. My heart surged with love and gratitude. I'd come a long way since meeting him last August. We both had.

Putting down my tea, I wrapped my arms round his neck and hugged him tight.

'Thanks, Dad.' I kissed his rough cheek and caught a whiff of his spicy aftershave. 'It's a lovely offer and I don't want to seem ungrateful, but I can't accept it. I've already had some money from Great-aunt Jane and although it might take me a while longer to save up for it, I really want to get there by myself.'

'But I want to help. It would make me happy.'

I leaned back in his arms and looked up at him. 'And I appreciate it. But sometimes the more help you have, the more helpless you become and I want to do things my way.'

Dad's face twisted into a smile and he stuffed the cheque back into his wallet. 'We thought you might say something like that.'

We?

'Did you?'

Dad nodded. 'So we've got an alternative suggestion,' he began but he was interrupted by a sharp rap of five knocks on the door. Definitely a Nick knock.

'That'll be him,' I said, galloping to the door.

I was grinning at the thought of a Nick knock as I let him in.

Norman launched himself at me first, wagging his tail

353

and making excited little yelpy noises before running off towards the kitchen.

Nick stood on the doorstep bundled up in a thick coat, he was practically brimming with excitement and my heart swelled with happiness at the sight of him.

'This is all very mysterious,' I said, unable to keep the smile off my face.

A large drop of water dripped off the porch and landed on his head and made him jump. 'May I come in and all will be revealed,' he said, raising an eyebrow.

Stepping aside to let him in, I felt my skin tingle as he brushed past me. His hair was wet and I had to stop myself from reaching up and touching it.

He peeled off his wet coat and laid it on the floor. 'Good grief, Sophie!' he exclaimed, looking round the living room. 'What a transformation. Have you done this yourself?'

I nodded. 'All my own work.'

It was then I noticed that Nick had my sketchpad tucked under his arm.

He saw me stare but grinned and gripped it tighter.

'We're in the kitchen,' I said, leading the way. 'I think you've already met my dad?'

The two men exchanged furtive glances while I made us all another drink.

'I was just saying to Sophie, that between us we've come up with a suggestion,' said Dad, beaming first at Nick and then at me. 'Well, Nick has.'

Nick held his hands up. 'Sophie did all the hard work.'

Me? I choked on my tea. 'Will someone please explain what this is about?'

'After I got the letter from your solicitor that you no longer wished to replace the bungalow – thank you for clarifying the situation so professionally, by the way – I came across your sketchbook,' said Nick. 'I'd meant to post it back after finishing the cowshed proposal, but well . . .'

Our eyes met, he ran a finger round his collar and I felt my cheeks heat up. *But then our relationship went downhill from then on*, I finished for him silently.

'Anyway, right at the front, I found those early sketches you did.'

I racked my brains to remember which sketches and then all of a sudden it came to me. It was the ones I'd done after my first visit here with Emma last year. And more specifically, the sketch he had inadvertently seen after squirting blackcurrant juice all over my pad. The one entitled 'Bungalow Extension'.

I pulled my scarf up over my nose to hide my embarrassment. Those sketches weren't intended for public view and I'd forgotten they were still in there.

'The more I looked at your ideas, the more inspired I became, playing around with what's already here, working with what we've got.'

'Show her!' said Dad, rubbing his hands together.

Nick flicked to the back of my pad and held up a drawing of his own.

I stared at the page, bewildered.

It was a plan of my bungalow, but not as I knew it. Gone was the gloomy 1930s exterior. Instead it was a light and airy, open-plan modern home. With an upstairs. It even had an upstairs! A single-storey glass extension added masses of space to the ground floor and the front had been completely remodelled to include floor-to-ceiling glass windows.

'Oh my goodness!' I whispered.

'It looks like a lot of work,' said Dad, scanning my face for my reaction.

'But most of it is cosmetic,' Nick finished. 'Nowhere near the cost of building from scratch.'

'It's beautiful,' I said with a shaky laugh. 'Absolutely perfect.' So perfect that it was slipping out of focus due to all the big bulgy tears that had filled my eyes.

'I know you have some money from Aunt Jane,' said Dad, jumping back in. 'But if you need it, I'll lend you the rest. Loan!' he said quickly, as I started to protest. 'You can pay me back once you're working again.'

'Thank you but that might take a while,' I said in a husky voice. 'I'll be on student wages for the next six months at least.'

'That's settled, then,' said Dad, clapping his hands. 'I'm paying for Brodie's education and I'm paying for yours. No arguments. And I'd be insulted if you didn't let me do all your tiling.'

'I'll bet there's a practical element to the course?' Nick turned the pages of the sketchpad until he came to my original drawing and placed it in my hands.

I nodded.

'What better place to experiment than your own home?' he said. 'We can work on it together, if you'll let me?'

I cast my eyes down at the page. Could I do it? Although I loved what he had done for me, I wasn't sure if I could work with him any more. Being with him – but not *being with him* – might be too painful to bear when he obviously only saw me as a client.

'Sophie.' He reached out and placed a hand on my arm. In front of my dad.

My face was probably on fire.

'Yes?' I raised my head and peered at him over my scarf. 'What do you think?'

Dad coughed, deposited his empty mug in the sink noisily and informed us that he was going for a stroll round the village. Norman leapt to his paws and trotted after him.

'I don't understand,' I said quietly. 'Why have you gone to all this trouble? I'm not even officially a client any more.'

He turned himself to face me in the narrow galley kitchen and the look that he gave me made my insides quiver.

'Because I can't stop thinking about you, because I know I've been a total idiot, because I didn't know what else to do to prove to you . . .' He paused and reached out to stroke my face and my heart soared. In fact, we were so close that I wouldn't have been surprised if he heard it soar.

'Prove what?' I whispered.

He lifted his mouth into a smile. 'That my intentions towards you are not entirely professional.'

I burst out laughing. That was such a Nick way of putting it.

'I must inform you,' I said, with a grin, 'that I fully intend to take that as a compliment.'

Nick visibly sagged with relief and took hold of my hands.

'How did you get my dad roped into all this? And more to the point, why?'

He cleared his throat and looked sheepish. 'I Googled you. Found you on Facebook. Saw your brother on your friends' list. Brodie put me in touch with Terry.'

I twinkled my eyes at him. 'Ooh, a cyber-stalker! Very clever. It wouldn't even occur to me to do that.'

Nick leaned back against the worktop and looked up at

357

the ceiling before gazing at me with such intensity that I couldn't drag my eyes away from his.

'And why? Because you told me in Starbucks that you were back in touch with him. I knew that once he had been reacquainted with you, he would jump at the chance to help you. That's what dads do.'

Nick was a dad. Was this a guilty conscience talking? My heart pounded.

'Is that how it is for you?' I nibbled on my lip.

He frowned. 'Sorry?'

'Would you do anything for your child? Joanna's child?'

Nick turned pale and he shook his head. 'I wondered if you'd heard Phil's accusations. Joanna is the ex I told you about. The relationship that nearly ruined my career.'

I knew that. I'd Googled her, obviously. I nodded at him to go on.

'What I didn't tell you was that she broke my heart. We'd been together a year when she announced she was pregnant. I was delighted and asked her to marry me. It didn't occur to me that she wouldn't be delighted too. She asked for time to think about it and disappeared for forty-eight hours.'

He rubbed a hand over his face and his eyes met mine. 'When she came back, she'd had a termination. I had no say in the matter. I lost the chance to be a father.'

'Nick, I'm so sorry,' I said quietly, reaching up to touch his face. It all made sense now: the pain in his eyes when I told him about Jess and his interest in my own family saga.

'Apparently, she is now ready to be a mother,' he raised an eyebrow, 'but she's having problems conceiving. And in an attempt to lay the blame elsewhere, she decided to tell her new boyfriend that I'd persuaded her to get rid of our baby and that it had somehow damaged her health. Anyway,' he shook himself and exhaled, 'I've been to Manchester and had it out with her. It's sorted now.'

'I'm so relieved.' I threw my arms around his neck and pressed my cheek to his and he hugged me back.

'That's why I haven't been around,' he said, smiling at me. 'I've been busy with that and designing your new home.'

A feeling of euphoria and anticipation crept over me. It was that smile of his. A smile that lit up his face, and carved a dimple in his cheek. A smile that hinted at unprofessional intentions. I smiled back.

'I've got an overwhelming urge to kiss you,' he whispered. 'In fact, I've wanted to kiss you ever since we first met and you hit me with your wet umbrella.'

'First impressions are so important, I always think,' I giggled.

And then time seemed to slow right down and I was glad because I wanted this moment to go on for ever, the moment when he slid his arms around my waist and pulled me in close. Then his lips dipped down towards mine and my body melted into his.

The relief at being in his arms was so sweet, I could hardly breathe.

I looked up at him and grinned. 'What about your "hands-off-clients" rule?'

'I've changed my mind.' He unwound the scarf from my neck and dropped it to the floor. 'I can see definite advantages to this type of working relationship.'

He moved his lips to my neck and placed a row of hot kisses down to my collar bone. I shivered and felt my knees go wobbly.

'Good,' I said, pulling his face back to mine, 'because otherwise I'd have to sack you again.'

We kissed again, holding each other tightly as if we were afraid one of us would change our mind. The intensity of my feelings for him was almost scary. But at the same time, nothing, no one, had ever felt so right.

'So you like the extension idea, then?' he said finally, pulling away from me to look deep into my eyes.

I missed him already and reached out to touch his dimple. I nodded. 'I love it.'

'Sophie, I'm rubbish with words, as you've probably noticed. I say the wrong things at the wrong time or sometimes I don't say anything at all. But I'm a good architect and this was something I could do.'

He lifted my chin up so that our lips were almost touching. 'And a home is the most precious gift you can give someone.'

I inched towards him until our bodies fitted together perfectly and then I wound my fingers into his hair.

'Except your heart,' I said and I pressed my lips against his to show him exactly what I meant.

The Thank Yous

Enormous thanks to my husband, Tony, and daughters, Phoebe and Isabel, for living and breathing this book with me for soooo long and still managing to look interested. I will not re-write it again. I promise.

Thank you to my lovely agent, Hannah Ferguson, who has made it possible for this edition of the book to happen. It's a dream come true, it really is.

Thank you to my publishers, Transworld, for all the help and support and flag-waving you have done on my behalf, with a special mention to Laura Swainbank and Bella Bosworth. Ladies, you are stars. Harriet Bourton – huge sigh of gratitude – your amazingly wise and perceptive editing has brought *Conditional Love* to new heights and yes, you were right (as ever) about the haircut.

Some people have been incredibly supportive of my writing and if they hadn't said such nice things at just the right time, I probably wouldn't have got this far. They are: Linda Hanbury, Lisa Thompson, Bobsie Hallam, Jane Diver, Tracy Tyrrell, Joanne Phillips, Sheerie Franks and Debi Alper. Thank you all very much.

Last, but not least, thank you to the wonderful readers who have been in touch with me either via Twitter, Facebook or email to let me know how much you have enjoyed reading my books. It really does mean the world to me, so please keep doing it!

*Enjoy an extract from another charming modern love
story from Cathy Bramley*

Holly Swift has just landed the job of her dreams: events
co-ordinator at Wickham Hall, the beautiful manor home
that sits proudly at the heart of the village where she grew
up. Not only does she get to organize for a living and
work in stunning surroundings, but it will also put a bit of
distance between Holly and her problems at home.

As Holly falls in love with the busy world of Wickham
Hall – from family weddings to summer festivals, firework
displays and Christmas grottos – she also finds a place in
her heart for her friendly (if unusual) colleagues.

But life isn't as easily organized as an event at Wickham
Hall (and even those have their complications . . .). Can
Holly learn to let go and live in the moment?

After all, that's when the magic happens . . .

Read on for a sneak peek at the opening chapter!

Chapter 1

I puffed out my cheeks as I turned the corner into Mill Lane. My throat was dry, my lungs felt squashed and achy and one of my laces was beginning to come loose, but I was determined not to slow down.

'Come on, Holly,' I muttered under my breath as the finish line came into view. 'You can do this. Nearly there. One last push!'

I broke into a sprint for the last hundred metres. The early June sunshine was warm on my back and I felt hot and sweaty in my T-shirt and shorts, not to mention ready for a drink. There was no stopping me now, though; I was through the pain barrier, I was in the zone . . .

'Good grief!' cried Mrs Fisher, my elderly neighbour, stepping out of her gate, her shopping trolley trailing behind her. 'You nearly gave me a heart attack, charging along like that!'

'Sorry, Mrs Fisher,' I wheezed as I swerved round her. 'Lovely morning!'

'How's your mum?' Mrs Fisher shouted after me.

'Fine thanks,' I yelled over my shoulder. 'Sorry, can't stop!'

I ran on to our gate, arms raised triumphantly above my

head as though I was breaking through some imaginary ribbon. I'd made it all the way back without stopping for the first time ever. Go me! I leapt over the boxes of rubbish that had been left out for recycling and came to a breathless halt at the front door of Weaver's Cottage, the honey-coloured stone terrace I shared with my mum.

I checked my watch: five kilometres in twenty-seven minutes.

Result! A personal best and not bad at all for someone who, until recently, would rather grab a box of French Fancies (lemon ones, preferably) and the TV remote and settle down in front of *The Hotel Inspector* than exercise.

I pulled off my headphones and grinned to myself as the front garden filled with the tinny sound of Shakira singing 'Hips Don't Lie' from my iPod.

You are so right, Shakira, I thought, wiping a line of perspiration from my forehead. *These hips certainly don't lie.* A month spent eating cake whilst applying for jobs had done absolutely zero for my figure. Hopefully, thanks to my new fitness regime, the truth would soon hold no fear for my hips – I was definitely feeling fitter. And as for the job hunt . . . I thought I might have sorted out that little problem, too.

I stood for a moment, hands on hips, while I caught my breath. There were a few weeds poking up between the paving slabs and I bent to tweak them out. I would make an effort to do a few jobs today, I thought, make the most of my last few days of unemployment. Perhaps Mum might even be in the mood to help; we could start with the boxes I'd just jumped over? No harm in asking . . .

Five weeks ago, I'd been made redundant from the Esprit Spa Resort. Since then, despite keeping myself busy with job hunting, I'd found myself with quite a lot of time on my hands and Weaver's Cottage, with its low ceilings and cluttered rooms, had become a bit claustrophobic. And because Mum only worked part time, we'd been spending far too much time in each other's company and I was beginning to feel the strain.

Don't get me wrong, I love Mum to bits. Adore her. I'd do anything for her. In fact, I *have done* anything for her: I'd put up with her 'peculiarities' for as long as I can remember but I'm only human and living with her in such a confined space had tested my patience to the max.

Which was why I found it such a joy to stretch my legs outside. Running was my safety valve; the country lanes around my home village of Wickham gave me the space to let off steam and the time to think.

And I had lots to think about. Because I'd been offered a job. Hallelujah!!

I leaned up against the wall of the cottage and began to stretch out my calf muscles one at a time, taking deep breaths and feeling pretty damn proud of this morning's achievements. Five kilometres, a month of gainful employment and it was only eleven o'clock.

For as long as I could remember, I'd always wanted to work in the events industry, preferably at prestigious international events. *No harm in aiming high,* I'd thought. Sadly, it wasn't to be. By the end of my first year at uni, it had become clear that Mum wasn't coping well without me at home and I'd had to adjust my plans accordingly. After three years living in minimalist heaven in my halls of residence, I came home to Weaver's Cottage. But while that might have hampered my globe-trotting plans, it certainly didn't curtail my ambitions.

The picturesque village of Wickham is in the shadow of Stratford-upon-Avon, a jewel in England's tourist crown and home to numerous jobs in the hospitality industry. After taking on a variety of roles – including a stint as a hotel receptionist and a ticket seller at Anne Hathaway's cottage – I landed 'a proper job' with the Esprit Spa Resort. And I'd stayed there for three years, working my way up to assistant events organizer.

Sadly, the owners had got themselves into a financial mess and Esprit was no more, leaving me and the rest of the team unemployed. I'd been applying for jobs like a demon ever since. I was desperate to stay within the events industry and keen to move up the career ladder, too. But as a 'Plan B' I'd enrolled with a temp agency in Stratford yesterday and lo and behold I'd had a call first thing this morning with the offer of a temporary office job at the conference centre in town.

I'd responded enthusiastically, of course, saying how pleased I was and had promised to let the lady know by close of play today. She'd been a little put out that I didn't snap her hand off there and then, I think, but I had my reasons. At that point the postman still hadn't been and whilst deep down I knew it was unlikely at this late stage, I was still carrying a torch for one of the other jobs I'd applied for.

Cool-down stretch complete, I sat on the front step, picked up the bottle of water I'd left tucked behind the empty milk bottles and took a long drink.

Unbelievably, my absolute, one-in-a-million, what-are-the-chances *dream job* had arisen a mere stone's throw from home: Wickham Hall was looking for a new assistant events manager. I felt my heart thump a bit harder at the thought of the Elizabethan manor house on the far side of

Wickham. The stately home was still privately owned by the Fortescue family and was renowned for its calendar of successful events. *This is destiny, written in the stars*, I'd thought when I'd spotted the advertisement in the *Stratford Gazette* two weeks ago. The description read as though it had been written with me in mind: meticulous planner, attention to detail, excellent communications and organization skills and experience running events. The job couldn't have been more 'me' if it had tried!

Plus I knew Wickham Hall inside out; I'd been going there ever since I was a little girl. In fact, when I was small I used to pretend I lived there and dreamed about waking up in a four-poster bed with my own maid, a wardrobe of Disney Princess outfits and acres of space all to myself . . .

I stifled a sigh and shivered a little as my skin began to cool. I rubbed the shin that had been aching and circled my ankles. As usual, my run had allowed my crowded thoughts some room to manoeuvre and I had reached a decision.

The fact was that despite putting heart and soul into my application for the Wickham Hall job, I hadn't been invited for an interview. And I would have heard back by now: the interviews were being held this week and the postman had had nothing for me again today. It was – to put it mildly – a bit of a blow. On the other hand, if I accepted the temp job, I could be out of the house and back at work on Monday. Hall-e-flippin-lujah.

Put like that, what choice did I have?

I jumped to my feet, intent on making my acceptance call immediately. I put two hands on the front door, which usually needed some force to open it, and pushed.

'Ooh, hold on; let me move out of the way!' cried Mum. 'OK, come on in, love.'

I stuck my head round the door and was greeted by the sight of my mum kneeling at the bottom of the stairs amongst stacks of newspapers and bags full of old clothes, wearing one of her favourite Boden summery dresses, a bargain from the charity shop where she worked. Her ample bottom pointed towards me and I caught an eyeful of dimply thigh.

'Sorry about that,' I said, squeezing through the gap. I closed the door and closed my eyes to the mess, focusing on her instead.

Mum and I were the same height, i.e. not high at all. We were both blonde and both prone to gaining weight in the tum and bum department. Her eyes were blue like my grandparents and mine were brown, which I guessed made them the same as 'he who shall never be referred to'. But the greatest difference between us – and incidentally the greatest source of tension – was stuff. Mum had stuff everywhere. I did not.

Right now she was ferreting through said stuff.

'Have you lost something, Mum?' I was still hot and the hallway felt airless. I opened the door again and fanned myself with it.

'Not me, no. But you have,' she said, pushing her hair off her face and dislodging her reading glasses, which nested permanently in her blonde waves.

'Me?' I gave her a wan smile. That was one thing I was careful not to do in this house: put something down and you might never find it again. 'I don't think so, Mum. Anyway, I've come to a decision about that temp job. I'm going to take it.'

'Hmm? It must be here somewhere,' she muttered, ignoring me and sifting through a pile of envelopes.

'What must?'

She shook her head anxiously so I closed the door and lowered myself onto the bottom stair, catching a whiff of my own post-run aroma. Shower-time next, methinks, just as soon as I've made that call.

'Mum,' I said gently, resting a hand on her shoulder, 'let me take all that post. We don't need any of it, it's just junk mail. Please?'

She picked up another handful and flicked through them.

'You should have had a letter from Wickham Hall. A lady called Pippa has just called to see if you'd received it. I was trying to find it before you got back.'

She abandoned her search and sat back on her heels, staring at me guiltily. 'It's my fault, Holly. It must have got lost in amongst my muddle. I'm sorry.'

Mum looked so dejected that it took a moment for her words to sink in. My eyes widened and I swallowed, hardly daring to think what I thought I was thinking.

'Oh my life, Pippa is the events manager! What did she say?' I grabbed Mum's hands and forced her to look at me. 'Exactly?'

Mum blinked her cornflower-blue eyes at me. 'She said you hadn't replied to her letter and she wanted to know if you could still make the interview this afternoon.'

My heart swelled with happiness and hope and pure unadulterated pleasure. The temp agency could wait. The stuff on the front path could wait. I had my dream job to go for.

'Yes,' I squealed, planting a kiss on Mum's cheek. 'Yes, I can!'

*

At three o'clock that afternoon, I was ushered into a seat at the end of a long oak table by Pippa Hargreaves, events manager at Wickham Hall. There were butterflies in my stomach and I knew my face was a bit flushed, but I was here, where I was supposed to be, and that was the main thing.

'Thank you for coming at such short notice, Holly.' She smiled, taking a seat opposite me. 'I can't think what happened to your interview letter. I'm normally very organized.'

I watched Pippa as she poured us both some water from a heavy glass jug. She was about five years older than me – mid-thirties at a guess – with carelessly pinned-up hair, a floral summer dress and a welcoming smile. She had talked non-stop since meeting me in the reception area at the bottom of a flight of oak stairs and I already suspected that the two of us would get along brilliantly.

'I'm sure it's not your fault,' I said, accepting a glass from her. 'It probably got lost in the post. I'm just so overjoyed that you rang. I've been keeping everything crossed all week that I'd be successful in getting an interview.'

I felt a flash of guilt for blaming the poor postman. We had, in fact, found Pippa's letter in the end; it had come in a thick cream envelope with the Fortescue family crest on it. It had somehow slipped inside an old Christmas card catalogue along with an unopened electricity bill and a leaflet for Mo's Maids home cleaning service. But I could hardly admit that, could I?

'Right, with any luck, there should be a copy of your details in here.' Pippa gave me a bright smile and pulled a jumbled sheaf of papers towards her.

I itched to take the pile from her and tap its edges on the

table to neaten them up. Instead, I crossed my fingers under the table and tried to focus on being the best interview candidate Wickham Hall had ever seen.

'I've brought a spare copy?' I offered, as she flicked though the pile.

'No, it's OK, here we are: *Holly Swift*,' she declared, producing my application letter, which I'd toiled over so painstakingly. She whizzed through my résumé, speed-reading under her breath. 'University . . . degree in hospitality and management . . . work alone or as part of a team . . . excellent organizational skills . . . assistant events organizer at Esprit Hotel and Spa.'

'Esprit? Very posh.' She stopped reading and looked up briefly. 'I was planning on taking my husband there for our seventh anniversary this year. I was surprised when it closed down.'

'So was I,' I said, raising an eyebrow. 'I loved the serenity of Esprit, but unfortunately it turned out to only be skin deep. The financial accounts were in a mess, according to the liquidators.'

Pippa's brow furrowed as she shook her head and I was conscious that I needed to steer the conversation into more positive waters.

'Esprit was very modern and luxurious,' I went on, nodding. 'But I adore the Elizabethan beauty of Wickham Hall. It seems to breathe with history; it's like you can hear the stories from the past whispering in the background. That beats the glass and gloss of Esprit, as far as I'm concerned.'

Pippa smiled and dipped her head again and I glanced around me, committing every detail to memory so I could tell Mum about it later. This part of the hall wasn't open to the public but it was just as charming as the rooms I'd seen on my previous visits. The events department, where the interviews were taking place, was housed on the first floor of the east wing. Somewhere below me was Lord Fortescue's private office. My stomach churned at the thought. A real lord, I could be working with a real lord . . . That would give Mum something to talk about at the charity shop!

The long narrow room was entirely wood-panelled, with a high ornate ceiling and a beautiful wooden floor covered with a large oriental rug. It smelt of furniture polish and of the blowsy old-fashioned roses arranged in a priceless-looking porcelain vase on the table and, for me at least, it smelt of hope and the possibility of a new career.

My gaze drifted through the windows to the grounds of Wickham Hall beyond. I could see the formal gardens, ablaze with colourful flowers, bordered with wide stone paths and dotted with exquisitely trimmed topiary shapes. A ride-on tractor mower leaving wide green stripes in its wake chugged across the manicured lawns, and in the distance, a plume of spray from the fountains cascaded down towards the deer park. I felt a deep pull of longing in my stomach. It was too perfect for words.

'So, Holly, tell me why I should give you the job as my assistant?'

Pippa sat back, laced her fingers together and smiled. Behind her, bands of sunshine streamed in through the mullioned windows and past the faded elegance of the brocade curtains, illuminating the otherwise dark room and creating a goddess-like halo around her head.

I blinked at her. 'Well, I . . .'

For a moment my mind went totally blank. Usually I'd

research and plan and practise all the likely interview questions. But I'd had no time for that today.

Come on, Holly, this is your big chance, the challenge you've been waiting for.

I took a deep breath and leaned forward. 'Because this is my dream job and I guarantee no one wants this job as badly as I do.'

Pippa cocked her head to one side and smiled softly. 'Really?'

I looked directly into her eyes and nodded.

'I've been coming to Wickham Hall with my mum ever since I was a little girl, for the Summer Festival, the fireworks displays, the Christmas decorations . . . every event, actually.' I uncrossed my ankles, which had somehow plaited themselves uncomfortably around the barley twist legs of my chair, and edged forward in my seat, forearms resting on the table.

'I even come here by myself sometimes,' I confided, tucking my blonde bob behind my ears. 'Just to enjoy the peace, the symmetry of the hall and orderliness of the gardens and . . .'

To escape from the chaos of Weaver's Cottage, I added mentally.

'I can honestly say it's my favourite place in the world. And the thought of being part of the team that makes all these wonderful events happen fills me with such joy that I can hardly contain myself . . .'

My chest heaved and a lump appeared in my throat. Pippa's eyes widened and she pressed a hand to her throat. I decided to revert to a more formal answer before we both ended up in tears. I coughed and ticked off my attributes on my fingers: 'I'm efficient, extremely organized, I love a challenge and I'm sure I will learn a lot from working with you.'

And I want this job. So. Much.

I leaned back and exhaled shakily. Maybe I'd overdone it, but it was the truth and telling the truth had to be a good thing, right?

Pippa smiled. 'Thank you. That was very heartfelt, Holly, I must say. Your résumé is very impressive too and it's a bonus that you're already familiar with our events.'

We talked for another fifteen minutes: me telling her discreetly about my personal circumstances and her giving me an outline of the day-to-day role of the vacancy, plus a run-down of her own story (married, four gorgeous children under six including twins, daughter of a vicar, lives in an old stone rectory that reminds her of home). What a superwoman! I was in total awe and it was all I could do not to reach across the table, squeeze her tight and beg her to pick me.

'It's not glamorous you know, this job,' said Pippa, twinkling her eyes. 'It probably sounds it, but running events here at the hall can be physically exhausting. Not only will you have to walk miles getting from one end of the estate to the other and back again, but we often have to set out chairs and tables, carry heavy boxes full of leaflets, climb ladders to fix signage—'

'I'm fit and strong,' I said, possibly sounding a little over-eager.

'Good. And we're rarely acknowledged for our efforts; Lord and Lady Fortescue are the public faces of the hall. Nobody even notices us half the time,' she finished.

'That's absolutely fine by me!' I declared, holding up my hands. 'Honestly. I'm much more of a behind-the-scenes person; give me a clipboard and a to-do list and I'm a happy bunny. I'm really not one to crave the limelight!'

'That's all right then,' Pippa laughed, 'because this job really wouldn't suit a diva who isn't prepared to get her hands dirty.'

'I love dirt,' I said hastily.

She grinned and I smiled and blushed and thought what fun we would have working together.

As Pippa made scratchy notes with her pen in the margin of my CV, I started looking around me again. These four walls would have been privy to hundreds of conversations over the past five centuries, I mused: shared secrets, rowdy debates, idle gossip, and now, Holly Swift's interview for the position of assistant events manager would forever be part of the room's illustrious past. I shivered; I had to get this job, I just had to.

'Do you have any questions for me before you go?' Pippa enquired, pen poised.

'Oh, yes, I do,' I said, thinking on my feet. 'Will I have an induction programme?'

This sort of thing is very important to me. I like to know what I need to know, upfront. No surprises. Be prepared, that's my motto.

'Induction. Right,' said Pippa, tapping her cheek with her pen. 'I'm sure we can sort something out.'

'Good, because I'd like to familiarize myself with the organizational hierarchy, key personnel and working practices first before I leap into the fray.'

Pippa's eyes twinkled with amusement.

'Um. If I'm successful, of course,' I added.

'Of course.' She pressed her lips together and I suspected she was swallowing a smile. 'Any other questions?'

'Ooh, yes, one more,' I said, taking a deep breath. 'What are the opportunities for progression in this role?'

Pippa pulled a face. 'In this department? None, I'm afraid.' She snapped the lid back on her pen and shoved my application to the bottom of the pile. 'Unless I leave. And I'm not planning on going anywhere. We're a small team. Of two, to be precise. Sorry about that. Is that all?'

I swallowed, giving the pile of application forms an anxious glance and worrying that my last question might have been too cheeky. But I was ambitious, I thought, no harm in being honest.

She pushed back her chair and stood up so I did too.

'I'm very pleased to hear that,' I said.

Pippa's mouth lifted into a smile and she gestured towards the door. 'I'll show you out.'

Other books for you to enjoy by Cathy Bramley

Nina has always dreamed of being a star. Unfortunately her agent thinks she's more girl-next-door than leading lady and her acting career isn't going quite as planned. Then, after a series of very public blunders and to escape a gathering storm of paparazzi, Nina is forced to flee the city, leaving nothing but an empty bottle of hair dye and a tiny bedroom behind.

Her plan is to lay low with a friend in Devon, in beautiful Brightside Cove. But soon Nina learns that more drama can be found in a small village than on a hectic television set.

And when a gorgeous man (and his adorable dog) catches her eye, it's not long before London and showbiz start to lose their appeal.

Will Nina choose to return to the bright lights or has she met her match in Brightside Cove?

Available now

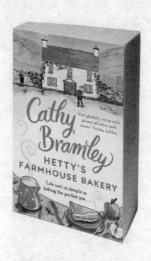

Thirty-two-year-old Hetty Greengrass is the star around which the rest of her family orbits. Marriage, motherhood and helping Dan run Sunnybank Farm have certainly kept her hands full for the last twelve years. But when her daughter Poppy has to choose her inspiration for a school project and picks her aunt, not her mum, Hetty is left full of self-doubt.

Hetty's always been generous with her time and, until now, her biggest talent – baking deliciously moreish shortcrust pastry pies – has been limited to charity work and the village fete. But taking part in a competition run by Cumbria's Finest to find the very best produce from the region might be just the thing to make her daughter proud . . . and reclaim something for herself.

Except that life isn't as simple as producing the perfect pie. Changing the status quo isn't easy – and with cracks appearing in her marriage and shocking secrets coming to light, Hetty must decide where her priorities really lie . . .

Available now

London has not been kind to Lottie Allbright. Realizing it's time to cut and run, she packs up and moves back home – but finds her family in disarray. In need of a new place to stay, Lottie takes up the offer of a live-in job managing a local vineyard. There's a lot to learn – she didn't even know grapes could grow so far north!

Butterworth Wines in the rolling Derbyshire hills has always been run on love and passion but a tragic death has left everyone at a loss. Widowed Betsy is trying to keep the place afloat but is harbouring a debilitating secret. Meanwhile her handsome but interfering grandson, Jensen, is trying to convince her to sell up and move into a home.

Lottie's determined to save Butterworth Wines, but with all this and an unpredictable English summer to deal with, it'll be a challenge.

And that's before she discovers something that will turn her summer – and her world – upside down . . .

Available now

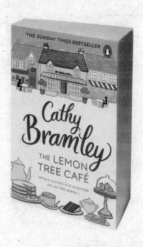

Rich espresso, delicious biscotti and juicy village gossip – will Rosie fall for this new way of life?

When Rosie Featherstone finds herself unexpectedly jobless, the offer to help her beloved Italian grandmother out at the Lemon Tree Cafe – a little slice of Italy nestled in the rolling hills of Derbyshire – feels like the perfect way to keep busy.

But Rosie is haunted by a terrible secret, one that even the appearance of a handsome new face can't quite help her move on from.

Then disaster looms and the cafe's fortunes are threatened . . . and Rosie discovers that her nonna has been hiding a dark past of her own. With surprises, betrayal and more than one secret brewing, can she find a way to save the Lemon Tree Cafe and help both herself and Nonna achieve the happy endings they deserve?

Available now

Cathy Bramley is the author of the best-selling romantic comedies *The Lemon Tree Café*, *Ivy Lane*, *Appleby Farm*, *Wickham Hall*, *The Plumberry School of Comfort Food*, *Hetty's Farmhouse Bakery*, *A Match Made in Devon* and *A Vintage Summer* as well as *Conditional Love*, *White Lies & Wishes*, *The Merry Christmas Project*, *My Kind of Happy* and *A Patchwork Family*. She lives in a Nottinghamshire village with her family and a dog.

Her recent career as a full-time writer of light-hearted romantic fiction has come as somewhat of a lovely surprise after spending the last eighteen years running her own marketing agency.

Cathy loves to hear from her readers. You can get in touch via her website: www.CathyBramley.co.uk,

Facebook page: Facebook.com/CathyBramleyAuthor or on

Twitter: twitter.com/CathyBramley